THE PERSIAN PRICE

EVELYN ANTHONY

The
Persian
price

Coward, McCann & Geoghegan, Inc. New York

To my dear friend
Shirley Chantler
with love

THE PERSIAN PRICE

Chapter 1

The little red post office van scurried around the corner into Eaton Square and came to a stop outside the tall white house with its elegant nineteenth-century portico and elaborate wrought-iron balconies. The telegraph boy rang the bell and a butler in the conventional dark coat and striped trousers opened the door.

"Mrs. Fields?"

"Yes," the butler said.

"Cable. Sign here please." The boy went off whistling. He had a glimpse of the splendid hallway, all white and gilt, with a massive arrangement of fresh flowers by the stairs, before the door closed. *How some people lived. . . .* The thought was without malice. Only the very rich lived in Eaton Square; he didn't envy them. Inside the house, the butler, a Portuguese who had been in the service of Logan Fields for over five years, knocked on the drawing room door. He liked his job, and respected his employer. Tycoons were not easy to please, but then so much depended upon the wife. Mrs. Fields was a lady, accustomed to having staff and knowing how to treat them. He came into the room, which was full of women drinking coffee, and gave Eileen Fields the cable.

"Thank you, Mario." She put it on one side and turned back to the middle-aged woman on her left. It was the aftermath of a luncheon she had given for the members of a charity committee of which she was the chairwoman. It wasn't a role she enjoyed, but Logan Fields insisted she play it in circumstances where Imperial Oil could project its image as a benevolent company eager to support good causes.

He made generous contributions to the better-known charities, and because she was so anxious to please him, Eileen submitted to the boredom and time wasting inherent in that kind of activity. The woman beside her was overdressed and wearing a lot of diamonds. She was the second wife of a textile millionaire who had recently been knighted. She disliked Eileen Fields because she was young, very attractive, and had an ancient name.

"Aren't you going to open your telegram?"

"Yes, I will," Eileen said. There were ten women in the beautiful green and gold drawing room. The atmosphere was heavy with expensive scents and warm because the afternoon sun was streaming in. She read the cable.

"My dear," the older woman said, "don't tell me Logan's been delayed *again*. . . . It's too dreadful the way these men of ours have to work. My husband is *always* away—"

"No," Eileen Fields said. "He wants me to go out and join him."

"How exciting. I've always wanted to go to Persia."

Eileen didn't answer. When the cable arrived she had expected a bald statement that his return was indefinitely delayed. The days when he sent long cables, with loving contents like a letter, were past. Everything he did concerning her was abrupt these days. The last thing in the world she expected was to be asked to go out to Teheran.

The lunch in the dining room had been long and rather formal. She disliked drinking at midday and her head was aching slightly. She wished passionately that her guests would go. She put the cable in the pocket of her dress. It was nearly three o'clock, and she had missed seeing Lucy go for her afternoon walk. Now she wouldn't see her child till teatime when she would be brought down for the statutory hour of playtime with her mother.

The newly titled lady on her left was watching her; she sipped at her coffee and criticized mentally. Eileen was too thin, and she seemed to be on edge. Pretty of course, but then she probably spent a fortune on clothes and beauty treatments. Nobody married to a firecracker like Logan Fields could afford to let themselves slip. He couldn't be an easy man to live with; she didn't really envy Eileen, in spite of having so much money and being ten years or more the younger. She didn't look a happy woman. It was a conclusion that comforted.

Eileen stood up abruptly. "If you'll excuse me," she said. "I've got to fly out to Teheran tomorrow. It's all very unexpected and I've got to get myself organized." She smiled and shook hands with the other women. Some were charming, intelligent, and congenial; if her mood had been less fundamentally uneasy, she would have enjoyed their company. But on the whole the trivial talk of clothes and servants and the spice of gossip about other people's marriages had depressed and riled her. She wasn't a woman who had ever enjoyed hearing about the humiliations or misfortunes of others or derived a vicarious thrill from their adulteries.

She saw them down to the front door, then ran upstairs to the drawing room. She opened the long windows to let some air into the room and chase the smell of cigarettes and scent away. It was a beautiful summer day and the house faced south over the square so that the rooms caught the full sun. She had decorated and furnished it herself, resisting the suggestion that the interior decorator who had done Logan's office suite should take charge of the arrangements. Logan had been delighted with the result; he had a natural eye for quality and her taste provided exactly what he wanted. Elegance and luxury but no touch of ostentation.

The drawing room was a fine example of Regency architecture with a molded ceiling picked out in gold leaf, furnished for formal entertaining with exquisite eighteenth-century English furniture. There was a Joshua Reynolds family group above the marble mantelpiece and a magnificent Irish Chippendale commode, her father's wedding present. It was the kind of generous, unrealistic gesture that Logan didn't appreciate, especially since James Fitzgerald was short of money. He would have preferred to buy his own furniture and not be milked for loans in later years that were never going to be repaid. Logan loved the drawing room and enjoyed impressing important guests by entertaining lavishly at home. He was aware without putting it into words that the effect was splendid without any suggestion that it was created by newly acquired wealth.

Eileen sat down and took the cable out. She read it again: NEGOTIATIONS CRUCIAL. IMPORTANT YOU COME OUT AND ACT AS HOSTESS DURING COMING WEEK. SUGGEST TOMORROW, TUESDAY. LOVE LOGAN. He had been away two weeks, part of which included a stop in Paris. There was no suggestion that she should go with him. When they were first married, he wanted her to travel everywhere he went. He had been very much in love with her in his possessive, masculine way, eager to show her off. If it was selfish, it was also touching, and she had never refused him. In the last year he seldom asked her, and the last two trips, one to the States and the other to Norway, when she hinted that she might come with him, he had been unenthusiastic. She had stayed behind. Now he wanted her; she might have made arrangements, like a dinner with friends and a play she particularly wanted to see, but nothing mattered except that her husband needed her. Some wives would have refused. They would have exacted a revenge for the times when they had been rejected, but Eileen was incapable of that kind of petty pride. She loved him, and for months now she had begun to suspect that he no longer loved her. She lit a cigarette and went out onto the sunny balcony. Below her the square gardens were a bright checkerboard of flowers and neat green lawns. Some of the older residents sat on garden benches, enjoying the July weather.

A small girl walked around the path on the perimeter with a joyously barking terrier on a lead. Eileen had suggested once to the nanny that instead of Lucy going for a walk she might play with her mother in the gardens instead. It was a futile move in the battle which she had lost long before. The offer was refused with firmness, as if she, and not Lucy, were the child.

It had taken her a long time to recover from Lucy's birth. Her health and spirits had been perilously low; without knowing it, she had suffered some degree of postnatal depression. Logan had been loving and solicitous. When they were told that she would never have another child, he had been comforting and tender. It wasn't until later that she realized how deeply he had felt the blow. He wanted a large family; her three earlier pregnancies had ended in miscarriage; the nine months before Lucy's birth were punctuated by alarms. She had spent much of the time in bed; when the baby was born she had nearly died. And there would never be the boy that Logan craved. He had never complained or reproached her even indirectly, but she knew that it was one of the greatest disappointments in his life. Logan was a fighter, a man who welcomed odds because they gave him an opportunity to do battle and to win. There was nothing he could do to turn this particular failure into a success, except lavish everything upon the one child. He had engaged the nanny himself when Eileen was ill. There was no suggestion that she would ever be competent enough to look after the baby; the initiative was taken from her while she was still too weak to protest. Lucy vanished into the nursery regions, surrounded by luxury and care, the charge of an experienced and determined woman who was adept at defeating mothers.

And Eileen had retreated, confused and hurt, finding that Logan was gently but firmly on the other side. And because she loved him, she devoted herself to the one aspect of his life which she knew to be the most important. More important than their marriage or his love for her, matched only by his possessive passion for Lucy—Imperial Oil. Naturally shy, she went out of her way to charm his friends, to play the role of the chairman's wife. She entertained lavishly for him, traveling between London and Paris to their splendid flat in the Rue St. Dominique, surrounding herself with people he liked and whom he considered important. She took an interest in every aspect of the oil company, and without realizing it, she established herself as a person in her own right among his business colleagues.

She was not only attractive, but charming, and in spite of her upper-class Irish background, unassuming and friendly to everyone. Logan had seemed to appreciate her efforts. They traveled as extensively together as when they were first married; he discussed his problems with her, and she believed that a new and deeper relationship had formed between them after Lucy's birth. The first indication that something was wrong came after a trip to the United States where he had gone alone. He was a man with powerful sexual impulses; she had been surprised and hurt when this side of their life, normally so dominant, began to diminish. It was some months before the suspicion crept in—suspicion that the reason for his indifference might be something more than tiredness and absorption in his business.

There had been a period, deeply humiliating to her, when she had watched her husband with their friends, wondering if there was a rival among them, if any one of the women she had seen trying to interest him in the past had finally succeeded. But there were no indications. Logan showed no special attentions to anyone. Once she checked up on him when he was said to be visiting one of the oil rigs in the North Sea, and found that he was exactly where he said he would be. The experience had made her guilty and ashamed. She had been eager to make amends to him for her suspicions. Her advances had been awkwardly rejected, and wounded as much by his tactlessness as by his refusal, Eileen had never tried again. As a result they hadn't slept together for months.

There was little time or opportunity for a discussion of their difficulties. Logan was not the kind of man to indulge in an analysis of their marriage. Either it was going well or it wasn't. She sensed the danger in bringing about a confrontation and they went on living a life filled with entertaining, his absences abroad and her artificial social life. And through it, like a pantomime fairy, the little girl whose birth had changed so much for both of them, flitted briefly into their days for what her nurse described as "mother's playtime."

Of all the aspects of her life, Eileen found this the most unnatural and frustrating. Only the parlous state of her relationship with Logan prevented her from wrecking the barriers he had built up around the child. His motives were good, but the methods were disastrous. Very soon, no matter how it affected them, Eileen would have to liberate Lucy.

Abruptly, distressed by the direction of her thoughts, she came back into the drawing room. She went to the telephone and dialed his office, asking for the travel department. She told them to get her a flight out to Teheran the next day, hung up, and lit a cigarette. She smoked too much; the habit had crept up on her the last year. She knew other women, married to similar men, who found escape in drink.

Perhaps this summons was a turning point. Perhaps he suddenly realized that he still needed her. It was possible he had been going through some private crisis during which he had felt it necessary to retreat from her and sort things out. Now, on the eve of the most important business deal of his career, he had sent for her to join him. The telephone rang and she answered it. It was the office, confirming her booking. The flight took six hours nonstop and arrived in Teheran at four in the afternoon, Persian time. Logan's secretary had sent a cable to the Teheran office informing Mr. Fields of her time of arrival. Eileen sat down to telephone and cancel all her engagements for the coming week.

Then she went upstairs to her bedroom. Bridget Hagan, who had been her maid since she married Logan, was putting some underclothes in the chest of drawers. The Hagans had worked for the Fitzgeralds for generations. Her father was head groom at Meath House and he had taught Eileen to ride. Bridget was a sturdy, independent girl of twenty-six, and although he didn't object to it, Logan had been puzzled by Eileen's relationship to her. There was a familiarity between them which had deep roots in feudalism. The Hagans had always worked for the Fitzgeralds and the Fitzgeralds had always protected the Hagans. Eileen didn't tell Logan that the reason she had brought Bridget to England as her personal maid was because the girl was three months pregnant and had to be taken away from her village to avoid disgrace. A month after Bridget came to Eaton Square she miscarried. Nobody had known about that either. Eileen nursed her and told the household she was in bed with flu. It was a secret shared between the two women and Eileen's kindness had bound Bridget to her for life.

"I've had a cable from Mr. Fields," Eileen said. "He wants me to fly out tomorrow. Can you help me get some clothes together, Biddy? I'm going to need everything cotton and silk—it's terribly hot out there at this time."

"Tomorrow?" Bridget stared at her. "He hasn't given you much time, ma'am. Couldn't you go at the end of the week?"

She had never criticized Logan Fields, but she resented the demands he made upon her mistress. She thought of him as a cold Englishman, somewhat jumped up, who'd made the bargain of his life when he married Eileen Fitzgerald. She had never forgiven him for what she considered his selfishness in making her pregnant again and again, when the poor soul wasn't strong enough for it. She had never said a word, but she watched over Eileen like a tigress with one cub.

"No." Eileen shook her head. "I have to get on a plane tomorrow. I've rung the office and asked them to book me on the earliest flight. Be a dear Biddy, and look out a couple of long dresses and some cotton skirts and shirts for me."

The cable had come as a complete surprise. She knew that the negotiations with the Iranian government were entering a crucial stage. Logan had told her that much, although he had become increasingly unwilling to discuss the details of his business in the last few months. It was as if he were closing one door after another and shutting her out of every aspect of his life. She helped Bridget sort through the clothes and chose some pieces of jewelry to take with her. She knew Logan would want her to impress the Iranians; meeting one or two of them she had learned very quickly that they weren't a people who appreciated the British love of understatement. She had never been to Iran, and all she knew about it was from a Book Club selection travel book, filled with descriptions of the ancient Persian city of Isphahan and the ruins at Persepolis, and the anecdotes, often unkind and very funny, told her by James Kelly, who was Logan's resident director in the capital city.

She had liked him the moment they met. He was younger than Logan, gentler and more cultured. They had a common background and a sense of the ridiculous. He was the first person connected with Imperial Oil that she had ever met who seemed able to treat it as a joke.

It would be nice to see him again. As she got ready her mood changed to one of optimism. The last months had been difficult and painful, charged with misunderstandings between her husband and herself. But she loved him, and it was just possible that the enormous burden of this negotiation for the Imshan oil fields was the real reason for the rift that had opened between them. Perhaps the pressures had been too great for him to share them with her; perhaps his withdrawal was some kind of husbanding of his resources against the strains and responsibilities to come. If this was so, then the cable was a call for help, the outstretched hand she had despaired of being offered. If she could go to him now, prepared to help him in whatever way he

wanted, then the love he had for her might reawaken. In spite of her
Irish ancestry, Eileen had no gift of foresight. She went to bed early
and was on the road to Heathrow airport by eight the next morning.
But as she boarded the plane she felt a profound and frightening pre-
monition that the journey to Iran would be a turning point in her life.

When James Kelly told people he worked in Teheran, they were
immediately interested. They found the idea of Persia fascinating;
especially women. He thought cynically that had he said he was an executive with Imperial Oil in Iran, few would have responded with enthusiasm. The same cynicism, which he preferred to call irony, had
chosen the Persian Room at the Teheran Hilton as a setting for a
reception in honor of the Shah's minister of the economy and his own
boss, the chairman of Imperial Oil, Logan Fields. He didn't expect
that the incongruity would penetrate the chairman's sense of the ridiculous. It was his own joke, to be enjoyed in private.

He didn't hate Logan Fields, although a number of people did. He
regarded him as a phenomenon, like an electric storm that suddenly
blew up, battering at everything in its path. He wasn't just a ruthless
tycoon, the caricature of the merciless, power-greedy businessman so
dear to the hearts of the left-wing progressives. He was a personable
man of superior intelligence and abnormal drive who happened to be
at the head of one of the world's fastest-growing corporations. Kelly
had met him at Mehrabad, the Teheran airport, ten days earlier, waiting in the broiling Iranian sunshine like an ambassador to receive his
king, flanked by equerries. The deputy resident director, the field
operations manager and his two assistants, with a junior official from
the Iranian Ministry of the Economy bearing the minister's welcome.

Kelly hadn't expected Logan Fields' wife to join him from London.
He had come to the Hilton early to supervise arrangements for the
party. Three years in Teheran had taught him not to rely upon Persian
efficiency or punctuality. The big room with its artificially domed ceiling and low lighting from reproduction brass lamps was heavily decorated with flowers. Jasmine and lilies overscented the air, but then
the Eastern taste in such things was flamboyant. Only in politics, business, and sex were the Persians a subtle people. Otherwise their pref-
erence was for the vulgar and emphatic. He checked with the head-
waiter that the champagne was cold and that there was a plentiful
supply of whiskey.

Kelly was a tall man, dark and thin, with hair that had overgrown his collar; he had authority and tact. He had demonstrated both in the last three years. As a result, Logan Fields was giving this reception for the most inaccessible and anti-Western of the Shah's ministers. No doubt that was why Eileen Fields had come at the last moment. The minister liked the company of women; he spoke impeccable English.

At five minutes to six the junior executives of the company and their wives began to arrive. James glanced at his watch and as he did so, Logan and Eileen Fields came through the doorway and he hurried to meet them.

On the way to the Hilton, Logan had turned to his wife. Kelly ran a Mercedes, but there was a two-tone blue Rolls-Royce, with a Mulliner special body which was reserved for the use of the chairman when he was in the city. Otherwise it stayed in the garage.

Although it was early evening, Teheran shimmered in a dry heat that made the streets dance in a haze. The car was air conditioned. Eileen Fields wore a silk dress and felt quite cold.

"Khorvan won't be there for hours," Logan said. "They make a point of keeping everyone waiting. They think it emphasizes their importance." He lit a cigarette and looked out the window. His eyes showed irritability. There were deep creases from his brow to his nose and his lower lip was sucked in.

"It doesn't matter," Eileen Fields said. "Our own people will be there; we can talk to them. I don't mind if he keeps me waiting."

"That's not the point," Logan said. "*I* mind, because it's an insult to you and it puts me at a disadvantage. We shouldn't have come before a quarter to seven."

"Then if by some chance the minister was early, we'd have insulted *him*. It's better this way round."

He should have appreciated her logic, but he couldn't. He hadn't wanted her to come, yet because of the Minister of the Economy he needed a wife to act as hostess. He didn't want her to talk about "our people" and identify herself with him and Imperial. He didn't want her to go in to the party and show what a perfect wife she was for a man like himself. People would tell each other how friendly she was, which was a way of saying that he was cold and unapproachable. He had always known this, and in the beginning he had been amused by the contrast, proud that she made such a good impression. But then she was to the manner born, as her father said, making a boast of it. Broken-down Irish gentry, living on their capacity to charm. He had been enchanted by it once, even a little awed, by the self-confidence of people like the Fitzgeralds. But that was long ago, seven years ago, when he had been so infatuated with Eileen that she seemed to be the only thing he wanted. He had already reached the top in Imperial Oil. The harshness of his thoughts made him feel guilty. He never wanted to be unkind to Eileen, even in his mind. It wasn't her fault that things were going wrong. He laid his hand on her knee.

"To hell with it," he said. "I'm just edgy tonight. Khorvan's been fighting us for eighteen months. It isn't going to be easy to trust him. They're the most difficult bloody people in the world."

"I know," she said. "I know it's going to be a strain on you. That's why I wanted to come." He took his hand off her knee. That kind of answer, loyal and innocent, only made him feel worse. There were moments when he longed for her to quarrel, or complain, to give him some excuse. . . .

Seated beside him, Eileen shivered in the artificial chill in the car. She wore a huge diamond brooch with a turquoise in the center. Her earrings and a bracelet matched. The jewelry felt cold and heavy; she had chosen it because the turquoises were Persian, bought as a present by Logan three years ago, after Lucy was born. Her reasons for wearing them were not a conscious reminder that he had been kind and loving then. She thought they were a compliment to the minister. For the last three years she had given that kind of attention to detail, to try to compensate Logan. She had always admired her husband; part of loving him had been her admiration for the qualities in him which were so alien to those possessed by all her family and friends. His ambition, his energy, his incisive thinking, his dynamic personality which didn't derive its force from inherited privilege or historical exploits performed by others. *"Une force de nature."* She remembered that phrase, culled from a book, though she had long forgotten the context. A force of nature. That truly described him, and she had loved him for it.

As they entered the Persian Room, she slipped her hand through his arm and together they walked toward James Kelly and the other guests.

As James shook hands with her, the silly shock went down his nerve endings; it had happened to him the first time they met, and he remembered his surprise. She looked pale, he thought, the beautiful blue Irish eyes accentuated by the dress and the well-chosen jewelry. He thought she had the warmest smile he had ever seen. What in Christ's name had a woman like her ever found to love in Logan Fields?

"Hello, Eileen. This is a unexpected treat. How are you?" He held her hand for just a second longer than he need have.

"I'm very well. It's so nice to see you, James. What an enormous party!"

"Well, we're all geared up and waiting. Let's hope the guest of honor decides to turn up!"

"Of course he'll come," Logan said irritably. Kelly's somewhat flippant attitude to matters of importance often annoyed him. It was unthinkable that Minister Khorvan should insult them by ignoring the reception arranged for him. There was a stir and a murmur near the door. Kelly turned around. "Don't worry," he said. "He's just coming in now."

Habib Ibrahimi moved through the crowd of Europeans and Iranians carrying a tray with champagne, whiskey, and soft drinks. He avoided anyone who tried to stop him and made his way to the small group standing a little apart. He came to Logan and stopped, offering the tray. The minister, Mahmoud Khorvan, was beside him. Habib had seen photographs of the minister, and he glanced up quickly to provide a firsthand image. This was the former Iranian patriot who had sold out to the Western capitalist oil company. His black eyes flickered over the minister's face. Light-skinned, black-browed, with hair receding from the base of his skull. He was a small man, immaculately dressed in a London-made suit. Heavy gold and diamond cufflinks gleamed as he waved his hands. He was talking to a European woman wearing fine turquoises, and looking as if he were enjoying himself. Habib Ibrahimi looked at her too, for a moment. He had seen her come in with Fields. She was the wife of the chairman of the oil company which was trying to wrap itself like an octopus around the throat of his country.

Habib was a humble man, but he knew his enemies. He served them with their alcoholic drinks, observing that the minister upheld his Moslem principles, at least in public, by drinking orange juice, and did what he had been told to do. He had been working at the Hilton for the last six months. When the reception was arranged, Habib suddenly became important; his friends had explained to him how he, the one who sat and listened at the feet of others, was to be of service to the common cause.

He gave a little bow to the minister and withdrew a few paces. He passed a tall Iranian in army officer's uniform and stopped at a word from him. He didn't look up. A hand, thin at the wrist, with long fingers and thick knuckles, lifted a glass of whiskey from his tray. Habib went on, his head down, not looking up. He knew Colonel Ardalan. Habib was a brave man, and dedicated, but he prayed with what superstition remained in his soul that he would never see the colonel any closer.

"It's going well," Logan spoke aside to James. "Do you think he's enjoying himself?"

"The hell of it is," James answered, "you only know when they're not. It's like trying to do something to please them. If you do it they're not grateful; if you don't they never forgive you. At a guess I'd say Khorvan was in a good mood. Largely thanks to your wife. She's marvelous with people."

"Yes," Logan said. Eileen was laughing at something the minister had said. Khorvan was grinning, his head slightly tilted back. Iranians didn't laugh loudly like Westerners. He touched her on the elbow. "He's enjoying himself," James said. "When he starts pawing it's a good sign."

"You've done a great job," Logan said quietly. "You've justified my judgment a hundred times over, and I'm always pleased about that! How does it feel to have rescued the economy of Europe?"

James shrugged. Logan in an expansive mood embarrassed him. He didn't need a layman's assurance that he had brought off a crucial political coup under the guise of a business negotiation. He had seen the opportunity present itself and his years of public service in the Foreign Office had enabled him to take advantage of it. He had to remind himself constantly not to be a snob. In his heart he despised industry and had little in common with Imperial Oil. He had met Logan Fields at a City lunch; he had no idea that he had registered with the oil man as anything more than a Foreign Office undersecretary, holding forth on the Middle East over the table. The offer of the job as resident director of Imperial Oil in Iran had come when he was disillusioned and rebellious. His path to a Grade I ambassadorship had been blocked, unfairly as it seemed, and a posting to Finland appeared to be a retrograde step. The prospect of Finland had daunted him for weeks. He had little private money and diplomats were notoriously underpaid. The massive salary offered by Logan Fields, with stock options, had made up his mind. He went to see Logan and accepted the offer after an excellent lunch at the Savoy.

There had been resentment among the senior executives of the company at the chairman giving such an important job to an outsider. That was why Fields referred to his judgment being vindicated. He had chosen a man who could deal with the Iranian government, and this in effect meant dealing with the Shah.

"It's bloody marvelous," Fields went on, speaking low. "The biggest oil field in fifty years—and the breakthrough on oil prices for Western Europe. Christ, James, we'll go down in history!"

"I'm not trying to be pessimistic, but I won't believe it till I see the minister actually sign the heads of agreement."

"With the Shah supporting it, he has no alternative," Fields said. "But I want him on our side, James. I want things to go ahead as smoothly as possible. And as fast. I know this party doesn't mean a damn, and tomorrow morning he'll start trying to squeeze our balls over the terms, but all the same, I'm feeling bloody confident."

James didn't answer. He sipped his whiskey and watched Eileen Fields. She was taking a great deal of trouble with the minister. He wondered if Logan realized how much she contributed. He was too fair-minded to criticize Logan Fields because he happened to be in love with his wife. He insisted that he admired Logan's dynamic qualities, and it couldn't be denied that when he wanted to, Logan could be charming. But he was a man motivated by things rather than people. He had a famous collection of Greek antiquities and when James admired it, he had told him frankly that it was better than money in the bank. It was typical of an attitude that irritated James intensely. Everything had to have a purpose; if it wasn't power then it had to be profit. He thought that Eileen Fields looked very pale.

"I'd like to give a private party for Khorvan," Logan was saying. "Something special. At your house—it's more intimate than a hotel."

"He's unlikely to come," James answered. "Ministers rarely accept private invitations, but we can try."

"Let's join them." Logan moved toward Khorvan. "You ask him." James was surprised when the minister accepted.

"I shall be delighted," he said. "I must have another opportunity of talking to this charming lady. She has been telling me all about you, Mr. Fields." For a moment there was a hostile gleam in his eyes. Logan saw it and responded with a friendly smile. "We shall certainly have a party, Minister. On condition that you are the guest of honor. I'll suggest a suitable date at our meeting in the morning."

The waiter was back with the tray. Logan took another whiskey. Habib waited, submissive and silent, while Khorvan ignored him.

"How long do you expect to stay in Teheran?" the minister asked Logan.

"For as long as it takes to conclude our business."

"And your charming wife?"

"She may go back ahead of me. We have a little daughter at home. She doesn't like to leave her for too long."

"Ah," said the minister, not understanding. Daughters were not important and he couldn't see what difference it made if they were left behind. He had little sympathy with Western sentimentality over children, but then he had little sympathy with the West. The chairman of Imperial Oil, trying so hard to ingratiate himself, had no idea what it had cost Khorvan to agree with the Shah that the British company should be admitted to partnership with the National Iranian Oil Company to develop Imshan. Nobody knew how he had writhed and twisted in his efforts to block their negotiations. He had used cogent arguments to defeat American interests; there was a big enough American military presence in Iran without permitting them another hold in what was expected to be the biggest oil field in the Middle East. The minister hated the United States and resented its influence in his country; he was able to say truthfully that the Soviet Union would be entitled to take offense if the Americans were admitted as partners. There were other contenders; a consortium of French and Germans, and the Russians had also sent a team. Until James Kelly obtained a private audience with the Shah, Khorvan had been gently steering Imshan in the direction of the Soviet delegation. He glanced at Kelly. His appointment to Teheran by Imperial Oil had been a very clever move. The Shah had been impressed by his diplomatic record, considering himself as more than the equal of any businessman, and, in general, he despised them. But with Kelly he could discuss the wider implications of the oil field. The first audience had been followed by private meetings during the next six months. Europe was facing bankruptcy because of the rise in oil prices. Khorvan viewed this prospect with indifference. His own political leanings were to the Left and he bitterly resented decades of exploitation by the West. The Shah's decision to start lowering the oil price without appearing to do so had been communicated to Khorvan after his last audience with James Kelly.

To Khorvan, the implications were disastrous. When he heard the decision, he had to pretend to agree with it. Disagreement with the Shah's policy was followed by dismissal. Only by seeming to acquiesce could he hope to sabotage the plan. He had agreed with the choice of Imperial Oil as the company which would develop the field. His unquestioning acceptance of the Shah's views left him in charge of the final negotiations.

He gave Eileen Fields a charming smile. The waiter was at his elbow again and he took another orange juice. Whatever the executives of Imperial Oil thought, visibly congratulating themselves and imagining that the attentions of a pretty woman made any difference to him, Logan Fields had not won yet.

"I shall be delighted to come to your house, Mr. Kelly," he said. "Now if you will excuse me, I must mix with some of your other guests." He walked away into the crowd.

"I'd better do the same," Logan said. "Look after Eileen, will you?" He had moved away before James could answer. Kelly turned eagerly to Eileen.

"You're looking marvelous, as usual. And you certainly made a hit with the minister."

"He likes women," Eileen said. "So do most Iranian men. I don't think it means anything. He was very easy to talk to and he has quite a sense of humor."

She had met James soon after he joined Imperial. He had been invited to dine at their house in Eaton Square, a privilege Logan reserved for his top executives. It was an evening he had never forgotten. He thought Logan's wife looked extremely frail; he learned afterward that she had been desperately ill after the birth of their only child and had not long been out of the hospital. There was an immediate rapport between them. They had many interests in common, and she seemed grateful for the effort James made at entertaining the other guests. She seemed to him the last woman in the world to have married a man like Logan Fields.

They met several times after that. Logan valued his qualities as a guest. Before he left for Teheran he was invited to a lunch given for one of the Arab sheikhs, and to a large company cocktail party, where he spent most of the time talking to Eileen in a corner. Once, on a reckless impulse, James had telephoned to ask her out when he was on leave in London, but she had been away in Paris, where Logan had a flat in the Rue St. Dominique. He liked entertaining there, and Eileen had mentioned casually that she had found the sudden instructions to fly over and get everything ready rather a strain since the baby's birth. That was his only attempt to develop the relationship independent of his association with Logan; it seemed that fate was giving him a hint, and he hadn't left a message or tried again. He watched her at that moment and wondered just how much she liked him, and whether behind the façade of friendship she felt anything more. He had no idea what made him ask the question, but he did.

"I'm surprised Janet isn't with you. I thought Logan was sure to bring her." Janet Armstrong was not Logan's secretary in the conventional sense. She had been a brilliant student at the London School of Economics and was his personal assistant. She had worked for Fields for the last two years. She was the most efficient and intelligent woman James had ever met, even in the exalted climate of the Foreign Office, where clever women floated by like leaves in autumn. Janet Armstrong had the mind of an exceptional man, with no visible feminine weaknesses like sentiment or emotion. He wouldn't admit that she was smart and attractive because he disliked the type so much.

"No. Logan left her behind this time," Eileen answered him. He had a thin, intellectual face with eyes that were alert and yet warm. She had liked him almost too much when she first met him. It was as if they had known each other for years. Suddenly she put her hand through the crook of his arm. There was no mistake about the way he closed it against him.

"Let's sit down for a minute," she said.

"There's a table over there." James steered a way through the crowd toward a little gilt table with empty chairs along one wall. He sat her down. "I'll go and get us both a drink," he said. "Don't let anyone come and drag you away."

"I won't," Eileen promised. She felt very tired and her head was aching slightly. She had tried hard to amuse the Iranian minister, hoping to please Logan. Perhaps it was her imagination, but the more she tried to contribute to his business and fill out her role as the chairman's wife, the more irritated he became. When they were first married she had been painfully shy and ill at ease with his circle of friends. Knowing how much he wanted her to impress them, she had summoned the good manners and natural courtesy which were part of her upbringing and consciously exerted the charm of her race to win his business colleagues and ingratiate herself with the denizens of his complicated industrial empire. She had succeeded, and he had been proud and delighted. Now he resented her efforts and ignored her success. James came back, carrying two glasses of champagne.

"Thank you, James. You're a darling." She took the glass and let their fingers touch.

"I wish you'd tell me what's the matter," he said quietly. "I know there's something. There's nothing wrong with Lucy, is there?"

Eileen shook her head.

"Oh, good Lord, no. She's fine. Growing sweeter and prettier every day. Logan absolutely worships her."

"I'm afraid I can't imagine him as the doting father, but I'll take your word for it. All right, if it's not Lucy, then what is it? You can tell me. You know that."

"I know I can," she said gently. "I feel I could go to you with anything, James, and you'd help if you could."

"That makes me very happy," he said. For a moment he covered her hand with his. Communication was passing between them. It was very disturbing. He looked at her, and she knew that if they'd been alone he would have kissed her.

"I can't talk about it. Not yet anyway. But I promise you if I talk to anyone it will be you. I think I see Logan making signs at us. We'd better go."

She got up and James pulled back her chair. He bent down to her a little way.

"Damn Logan," he said.

There were three people in the upstairs room in the apartment block on Torshab Road. The three-room flat had been rented two months previously by an American who described himself as a graduate student of archaeology and explained that he wanted a base in Teheran during his visits to the dig near Persepolis. He was often out of the city for a week or more, and when he brought visitors home, they were Iranians, and they were quiet and unobtrusive. The neighbors were middle-class families, and their curiosity became boredom when there were no parties, no women, and no brawls. After a time they forgot about the American, and the routine check on foreigners living in Teheran assured the secret police that he was what he claimed to be: an archaeology student who went to Persepolis and helped with the excavations.

He was twenty-eight, tall and squarely built, with blond hair cut unfashionably short and a Nordic face with blue eyes. The name on his passport was Peters. The last two names under which he had operated in Europe were Rauch and Glover, and in Guatemala he was known as King. The name which really belonged to him was well known and respected in Cleveland, Ohio, but he had ceased to think of himself in connection with it. He hadn't been back to the United States in five years. There was an FBI warrant for his arrest waiting if he returned.

Of his two companions, one was a girl, the other a slight, wiry Syrian. The girl was sitting beside Peters and she had one hand laid in a proprietary way on his knee. She had green eyes and her dark hair had been hennaed; her mother was German and her father Lebanese. She was twenty-five years old and she carried a French passport in the name of Madeleine Labouchère, with an address in Paris. She had met Peters in Dublin, where they had been attending a secret conference with some of the extreme left wing of the Provisional IRA. As a result she and the American had become lovers. To Madeleine, that was the most important thing that had ever happened to her since her political conversion. She had lived with many men, as any liberated woman should do, but never before had she been in love. She was sitting close to him now, waiting for the telephone to ring. It was past one o'clock in the morning; the room was gray with cigarette smoke, and there were empty coffee cups piled on the brass table. The Syrian, who was working in the Embassy as a commercial attaché, yawned and stretched his arms above his head.

"He should have called an hour ago."

Peters shrugged. "Maybe the party went on past midnight. They've got plenty to celebrate."

The girl leaned against his shoulder. She lit a cigarette. "They won't be celebrating for long," she said.

The Syrian grimaced. "The other plan appealed to me more."

"An attempt on the Shah would have been useless," Peters said. "It would just have brought Ardalan's butchers swarming all over Teheran. It was a stupid idea, my friend, and rightly vetoed by the committee." The Syrian shrugged; he didn't seem to mind the correction.

"I'm not complaining about the plan," he said. "It's very well worked out."

"I majored in political science," Peters said. "All the patterns are predictable because events repeat themselves. And this way, we'll come out of it without shedding blood."

"You're becoming squeamish," the girl said.

"Would you kill in this particular case?" He looked down at her.

She didn't hesitate. "If there was no other way—yes."

"Well, it won't arise," he said to the Syrian. "I'm in charge of this. I said there'll be no killing and no need to kill."

"You can't have a revolution without blood," Madeleine said. She didn't want to make him angry, but she had to disagree.

"I don't dispute that," Peters answered. "I've done my share. But this is going to be different. We'll come out with a moral victory."

"If the story gets out, you don't think public opinion will congratulate you for kidnapping—" Madeleine began, and then the telephone rang. It was the Syrian who answered. He only said, "Yes," and then listened.

Habib was in the kitchen of the Hilton. Most of the staff had gone home and the clearing up after the oil company's reception and dinner was finished. He was using the telephone in the chef's office.

"I am sorry to be late. I hadn't finished work. They were all here tonight and the wife is with him. He expects to stay for some time. She also, but will return before him. There are no immediate plans to go back." As he spoke he glanced behind him, afraid somebody might have heard a noise from the outside of the office and would then come to investigate.

"Good," the Syrian said. "You've done well."

The voice at the other end sank lower.

"The colonel was here."

"Don't worry, he would be. Why should he notice you? Be brave, my brother. Forget the colonel." He hung up.

"Well—" Peters was on his feet.

"He got close enough to hear that Fields has no immediate plans to return to England. Also, he's brought his wife with him. That's good. It'll make it easier still. But she's going back earlier, so we can't waste time. And he was very frightened because Ardalan was there."

"I'm not surprised," Peters said. "Anyone with sense is frightened of Ardalan. I heard you reassuring him. I don't suppose he did anything to draw attention to himself?" He asked the question calmly.

The Syrian looked at him for a moment before he answered. "If he did," he said, "the one thing he knows as a connection with us is this telephone number."

"Get him out of Teheran tomorrow. It's safer. Ardalan can smell fear at fifty yards."

"I shall see to it," the Syrian said. "So the date is set."

"We go the day after tomorrow," Madeleine answered. She got up and began collecting the dirty coffee cups. "Paris and then London. We split up in Paris and arrive in England separately."

"From there we will make the final preparations," Peters said. "Resnais will join Madeleine in Paris and they'll come in together."

"Good luck then," the Syrian said. He came and shook hands with Peters and the girl. He gave them a little bow as he stopped by the door. Then he quietly raised his fist in the clenched salute and went out.

Madeleine took the cups out to the kitchen. She was not a domesticated girl; at home in Beirut there were a dozen servants in her parents' house. She had reacted violently against a luxury she considered sinful and degenerate. At first she had worn shabby clothes and prided herself on being unkempt; even before she broke with her family at twenty, she had delighted in flouting her German mother's insistence on neatness. There was nothing striking about her to suggest that her father was a millionaire and that she was personally rich. But now that she had fallen in love with Peters, she indulged in pretty clothes and paid attention to her looks. She silenced the feeling of guilt by arguing with herself that she was supposed to be the conventional, middle-class Mlle Labouchère. But that didn't excuse the richly hennaed hair and the weekly manicure that went with it. She wanted to please Peters with all the passion of her quasi-Oriental upbringing, but above all she wanted him to say he loved her. She was too realistic to expect him to mean it. She left the dirty cups in the kitchen and followed him into the bedroom. He was stripped to his trousers and the sight of his finely muscled body aroused her. She came and stood close, pressing herself sensually against him, her arms twisted around his waist, stroking him with her hands.

She started murmuring to him in French; she found English a coarse unromantic language, as bad as German. He put his arms around her. Later she said to him, over and over before she drifted into a satisfied sleep, that he was wonderful and she adored him.

Peters didn't answer. She was a ferocious woman and he admired her courage and her dedication. He also understood her reasons, because they were much like his own. But he didn't love her, and he wished she wouldn't indulge in sentimentality. There was no room for emotional entanglements or for any other commitment outside their common cause. He had decided on that long ago, when he cast adrift from his background in the States. Paraphrasing the dictum of the revolutionary Christ, he had left mother, father, brothers and sisters, leaving all things to follow his ideal. If he was going to devote himself to the betterment of all men, he had nothing of himself to give to individuals. This didn't exclude sex, or even living with a woman, but it was more important to him to work together than to go to bed. He moved away from her in the narrow bed, and immediately he had forgotten she was there. His mind was alert and concentrating on the details of the plan ahead. It had been formulated at the conference held in Munich in May. It was easy for the members of the central committee to meet in Germany rather than attract attention by asking its European members to travel to Damascus, where Israeli intelligence would have been alerted. There was a large work force of Arabs in the Federal Republic, and it was simple for the Palestinian members to travel in as casual labor, while people like Peters arrived as tourists. The meeting had been held in the house of a German dental surgeon in a working-class district. Non-European patients came and went without causing comment. They had held their conference during his surgery hours. Peters had been a member of the commando group of the Palestine Liberation Front for the last two years. He had traveled to Egypt from Central America under the auspices of the Marxist cell with whom he had been operating in that area. He had been invited to Munich as a special observer. He had left the city with the committee's mandate to carry out the most vital mission against the forces of Western capitalism since Nasser had closed the Suez Canal.

James Kelly lived in a beautiful nineteenth-century house in Shemiran, a select suburb on the lower slopes of the Elburz mountains which lie behind Teheran. It was built of pink stone, domed and turreted, with exquisite stonework tracery and set in a large, secluded garden. He had rented it when he first came to Teheran, appalled at the prospect of living in one of the hideous modern houses the newly rich Iranians were putting up in the city. The house had been ramshackle and in poor repair, but there was no limit to the company's funds and he had restored it to its former beauty.

The car had brought Eileen and Logan back ahead of James. She got out and stood for a moment in the moonlight. It was a warm still night, and the scent of the jasmine from the garden was very strong. In the sky above, an enormous moon hung like a great pearl. The twentieth-century city, with its ugly buildings, its drab, traffic-clogged avenues, and its modern hotels, might have been a thousand miles away. The house and its fragrant garden, with the delicate sound of the fountains James had put in order, made sense of the magic that Westerners found in Persia. The ancient name was changed, the ancient rulers had vanished. The son of an army sergeant sat upon the Peacock Throne, and the Persian aristocracy, weakened and effete, were overridden by the brash and ambitious middle class, gorged with wealth from the great mineral resources they controlled. It was an ugly contrast in the country whose poetry and marvelous decorative arts were among the wonders of the world.

"I'm going in," Logan said. He had waited for his wife as she paused, and had seen her look upward and around her. It was a magnificent night and he, too, was aware of the jasmine and the interplay of shadows in the garden. Not so long ago he would have taken her arm and suggested they walk for a while before going to bed. But not now. "I'm dead tired," he said. And then he added quickly, "You must be, too. It's been one hell of a long day."

She followed him inside the house without saying anything. The room was simply furnished but in excellent taste. James had hung some fine rugs on the walls and displayed a collection of rare Luristan bronzes and Nishapur pots in a wide niche above the bed. It was comfortable and in some ways spectacular, but she thought how masculine it was. She wondered why he had never married, and because she was tired and on edge with Logan, she suddenly said so. "I wonder why James is still a bachelor?"

Logan was undressing in the bathroom with the door open. "I've no idea. There's nothing wrong with him—we checked all that."

"How do you mean—checked?" She couldn't undo her dress without his help. She unfastened the brooch and took off the earrings, holding them in her hand.

"Checked in what way?"

"We had him checked out." Logan sounded irritated. "It's always done. Cuts out trouble later. You know I won't have homosexuals in positions of responsibility."

"My God," Eileen said. She turned away and dropped the jewelry on the dressing table. "I think that's disgusting! I wonder what he'd say if he knew."

"I doubt if he'd be surprised. They've had enough trouble with pansies in the Foreign Office. You've got no right to criticize." He slammed the bathroom door.

For months she had held herself in control; ignoring his bad moods, excusing outbursts when he was rude. She had tried hard not to be hurt, deluding herself that it was the result of overwork and strain. She pulled the door open. "Don't you slam the door on me!" she said.

He was already in his pajamas. He looked first surprised, then furious.

"Don't bloody well shout at me!" he said. He came out, pushing past her.

"I'm not shouting," Eileen said. "I just won't put up with your bad manners. I think it's disgusting to pry into people's private lives and I said so!"

He turned and looked at her. The last months had been a strain on him too. His voice was lower, calmer, but it was more wounding than his rage. "I'll run my business as I think best. What you think doesn't interest me. If all I had to do was live in a bloody broken-down house in the Irish bogs and think about how to get money out of my son-in-law instead of doing a day's work, I might have time for your high principles. Unfortunately I haven't. So you can stuff them!"

"I'll give you the three hundred pounds! I'll pay you back the damned money you gave him! Then you won't have it to throw in my face." She sat on the bed and began to cry. He had given her father three hundred pounds toward a repair bill for fencing around their land at Meath House. She had written her father an angry letter, reproaching him for sponging on Logan yet again, and been fobbed off by a telephone call full of apologies and charm. Her father despised Logan Fields. He thought he was common and rumped up and that the life he lived was a waste of time. Logan did none of the things of which John Fitzgerald approved. He disliked horses and was bored by racing; he shot reasonably well but without much enjoyment. He was always traveling and chasing himself, and her family thought it was just as well he was so rich because everything else about him was ridiculous. They were not aware of the dynamic personality which had first attracted her. They merely considered him exhausting.

After a moment she felt him sit down on the bed beside her.

"I'm sorry, darling," he said. His arm came around her shoulder and pulled her against him. "I'd no right to say that. I was a rude shit. I'm sorry."

She couldn't answer immediately. Her emotions were confused; hurt and anger struggled against a feeling of deep despair.

When she raised her head he was staring at the ground, his free hand clenching on his knee. "I'm sorry," he said again, and she knew that he meant it.

It was not the moment for discussion, but she felt a lemming urge to hasten the process of disintegration.

"What's the matter, Logan? What's happening to us?"

"Nothing," he said. His arm slipped away from her. "We're just worn out. We need a good night's sleep. You probably need a holiday."

"I've never had a holiday without you," she said slowly. "I don't want one now." His head turned toward her and then away.

"It might be a good idea. Give us both a chance to think things out."

Eileen got up and searched for a cigarette in her bag. She found his lighter thrown on the bed.

"I've known we were drifting away from each other for some time. I thought it was just a phase, but it isn't, is it? Please, Logan. Look at me. Tell me the truth. Is there someone else?"

He glanced up; his expression unhappy. She knew by the set of his mouth that it would soon be resentful.

"Leave it alone, for Christ's sake, Eileen. Don't start all this tonight."

She started to cry again. "I can't. I can't live with the uncertainty. We haven't slept together for months. You're always too tired or you brush me aside. I know there's somebody else. There has to be!"

"All right." He got up and stood facing her. "All right, you want to force the issue. There *is* someone. I can't go on pretending either. Oh, Christ!" He picked up the lighter and hurled it across the room.

She didn't say anything. She had asked for the truth and he had told it. He was in love with another woman. Suspecting was not the same as knowing it. The certainty was not a relief. It was like a wound. The extremity of pain was yet to come.

At that moment, seeing her face, Logan Fields didn't know whom he hated more, himself or her. So long as he didn't have to hurt her, he could retain affection for her and even try to avoid a crisis. Nothing had been decided, certainly not in his own mind, so long as she didn't take the initiative. But she had made him admit he didn't love her, and from that moment it became a fact.

"Who is it?" She had stopped crying; she sounded calm. He had never seen her look so bloodless, the dreadful color accentuated by the blue dress. There was no going back now, and his distress was changing into anger. He was a man who welcomed decisions and hated any kind of vacuum, but this particular decision had been forced on him. It was her fault, and he was already blaming her so he could excuse himself. So long as she asked questions, she would get the answers.

"Janet," he said. "I want to marry her."

"I see," Eileen said quietly. "To have more children?"

"Not necessarily." Now he was retreating. This was a truth he couldn't face—the gnawing disappointment that his wife could never have another child. One girl, one beautiful precious little girl, to inherit all that he had created. . . . He couldn't admit that he wanted to remarry because he wanted a son to follow on. It sounded grandiose and ridiculous. But for three years he had been frustrated and guilty because it happened to be true. He saw Eileen put up a hand to the back of her dress.

"Here," he said. "I'll undo that for you."

She stepped away from him. "No. No thank you." She put both hands to the neck and ripped the back apart. The dress slid down and she stepped out of it. She had a beautiful figure, narrow-hipped—too narrow—with small breasts and the very pale skin that went with her coloring. He had desired her and loved her, and for the first four years in spite of her miscarriages and illness, they had known intense happiness. He had been so proud of her; proud of her charm and her good breeding, showing her off like a treasure. He had been tender, according to his moods; he had known that she loved him. And she had given him the child he loved more than anything in the world. Sexual desire did not awaken, seeing her; conscience made him step toward her.

"Eileen—"

"How could you?" Her voice was quiet but full of contempt. "That awful woman. . . . I'll go home tomorrow. It'll be less embarrassing for everyone. There's a sofa in the next room. I'd be glad if you'd sleep on it tonight." She went into the bathroom and locked the door.

Chapter 2

Janet Armstrong was asleep when the call came through from Teheran. She lived in a small flat in Chelsea, part of a conversion of a Georgian house in an elegant and expensive square. She had rented it for a year, and six months ago Logan Fields had bought her the lease. It was beautifully decorated in the best contemporary Italian style, and it was a faithful reproduction of her own personality. Crisp, clear, brilliant and positive. The bed was circular; Logan had thought it funny and refused to sleep in it when she first brought him there. He had soon admitted that it was more comfortable than the bed in the Dallas hotel room where they had first made love. It had happened by accident. Neither had anticipated that a late-night conference would end in his hotel suite with him taking off her clothes at three in the morning. Both of them had been drinking. Normally both were unaffected by alcohol; indeed Janet boasted of her capacity to hold her drink as well as any man. Logan was abstemious by choice, but that trip to the States had lasted three weeks and been particularly hectic. That night, when Logan called Janet into his suite to finish off the final draft for a press release, he had been tired and wound up. She gave him whiskey and drank with him. It began with a casual touch and ended in a sexual storm that left them both astonished.

Now, as she woke and reached for the telephone, registered the hour, 5:30 A.M. and the time change in Iran, she knew it was Logan. She pulled the telephone onto the bed; her blond hair was cut short and streaked with silver lights. He had asked her to let it grow, because he liked playing with long hair when he made love, but Janet had refused.

Long hair was untidy and a nuisance. Also it didn't suit her. She had
employed no feminine tricks to catch him; nobody could have accused
her of behaving like the secretary in every cliché-ridden situation,
angling to marry the boss. She had never thought of a closer relationship than working for him, until that night in Dallas. Then, added
to the intense interest they shared in the company, and the natural
fluency with which they worked together, had come the dimension of
perfectly matched sex.

"Logan?" she said.

His voice was clear. For once the line worked without atmos-
pherics. "Janet—it's me. How are you?"

"I'm fine. You woke me up. How's everything going?" It was typical that she mentioned the business first.

"So far, everything's fine," he said. "I have a meeting with the
minister this morning. Then I hope to see the Shah. I don't know how
long I'll have to wait for an audience, but if it's weeks, I'll come back
home and go out again. It looks all set though. We had a big party for
Khorvan and he was perfectly friendly. Kelly said not to be surprised
if he didn't turn up, and that would have been a bad sign. But it went
off very well. How's everything your end?"

"Going smoothly. There's a bit of a panic about the rig drilling on
Block 211/6. Apparently they keep losing drill bits down the hole and
they're worried about next month's long-range weather forecast.
Jenner's dealing with it. He's flying up to Lerwick today and out to the
rig tomorrow. There were items in all the financial columns about you
and Imshan. The same old photograph—you'll have to get a new one
taken, darling. I'll fix that up when you get back. The reaction on the
market has been very optimistic. There was a big article on the Shah in
the *Sunday Times* apropos of the oil field. Oh, and I hear the Saudi
ambassador has asked when you can see him. Nothing's been set till
you get home. Is that all right?"

Logan sounded gratified. "They're getting the wind up their asses.
Once we get Imshan into full production they won't be holding the
cards anymore. We can tell them to go stuff themselves." He had
always used what he thought of as "men's language" to Janet, without
any fear of offending her. He was only coarse in front of Eileen when
they quarreled.

"Listen, Eileen's coming home."

"Oh? Why? Nothing wrong with Lucy, I hope—" She sat up, tensing
slightly at the mention of his wife. She always asked about the child; it
was her only concession in the game, because she knew how much
Logan loved her. She had seen the girl several times when she came to

the house in Eaton Square, and thought her a lonely, overprotected child, in dire need of brothers and sisters. She had said so to Logan.

"No, Lucy's not the reason. I'm afraid things have come to a head."

"Oh, God," Janet said. "Jesus. Has she found out?"

"I told her," he said. There was a sharp crackle down the line, and she guessed he was having to shout. "I can't talk about it now. I want you to come out here. I'll need someone to act as hostess. Can you come out by the end of the week?"

"I don't know—" She was shouting back at him now; the connection had deteriorated. "I'll see what's on this morning and I'll ring you tonight. At James'—about seven—your time."

"All right. Seven o'clock. Take care of yourself."

"You too," Janet said. "I love you." She hung up and got out of bed. She wore a silk pajama jacket, and her legs were beautifully shaped. She went into the bathroom, all white carpet and glass, drank some water, and looked at herself in the mirror. A face that was pale without makeup—gray eyes that needed mascara, and a mass of curling silvered hair. She was thirty-one, with an early marriage which had ended in divorce after three years behind her, and the prospect of marrying Logan Fields suddenly ahead. She was healthy and she was still young. She could give him children, and she would. She would never be a wife like Eileen Fitzgerald, but then he hadn't been content with a graceful ornament. Logan wanted a partner and he wanted a big family. Looking in the mirror, Janet made up her mind that she was going to give him both.

He was a marvelous lover for her. Forceful, eager, extremely male. For a cool and independent woman, intellectually equal if not superior to most of the men she worked with, Janet had a slightly masochistic streak. She preferred to be dominated in bed, and Logan made love as he did business. He was the boss. None of the men she had lived with, for long or short periods since her divorce, had suited her as well as he did. Not one had ever measured up to him. She smiled, unaware that she did so. Happiness and excitement made her beautiful. She didn't often think about Eileen Fields. Janet was not without scruples, but she had never seen any reason to feel guilty about the other woman. She had married him and had the chance to make him happy. If she had failed, that wasn't anybody else's fault. Logan's marriage was over. She knew that more by what he'd left unsaid. Asking her to join him had been his way of letting her know.

She went back to the bathroom, showered, made up, and dressed quickly. She loved going to the giant Imperial building. She loved her smart office outside Logan's and the sense of excitement it gave her to get down to work. Power had always fascinated her. And Logan personified power. Her own secretary, a middle-aged spinster of superb efficiency who had been with Imperial for fifteen years, was surprised to hear the crisp, aloof Mrs. Armstrong humming under her breath as she read through her mail.

Eileen slept late. James' houseboy knocked on the bedroom door with coffee and orange juice, but since nobody answered he took the tray back to the kitchen. At seven o'clock, Logan had come into the bedroom to dress. He had glanced at her lying asleep, one arm above her head, and felt a pang of real regret. Last night had been an ugly incident that made him feel uneasy and ashamed in the chill of daylight. But there was no going back, even had he wanted to. He knew Eileen, and for all her natural gentleness there was an implacable Irish streak which had driven him out to the sofa next door. The moment when she turned on him, showing her contempt for the woman he had chosen, nagged at him and would continue to hurt for a long time. Rejected as she was, she had suddenly been able to despise him, and he hated the feeling. He had been able to despise her family while loving her—in his opinion they were useless parasites, contributing nothing but funny stories and racing anecdotes to any conversation, completely uninterested in world affairs, industry, or politics. They were arrogant too, under the charm, and he had never felt comfortable in the big shabby Georgian house on the estate where the family had lived for two hundred years. Eileen loved Meath House; she spoke of it with a nostalgia that he couldn't understand. The place was overrun with dogs of every shape and size; the servants consisted of an old couple who were lazy and untidy and treated their employers with unbecoming familiarity. But they made Logan feel he had left his fly undone whenever they looked at him. Her mother had died after their marriage; she was a tall horsey woman with a soft voice and her daughter's blue eyes. Logan tolerated her, but John Fitzgerald he actively disliked. A sponger, a snob—he had been sending money to the old humbug for years, knowing that he was never grateful. Now that was over too. There would be no more milking of the English son-in-law. He had packed his clothes and slipped out of the room. Downstairs he lit a cigarette, sent the houseboy who appeared from the kitchen to get him coffee, and put through the telephone call to Janet. He left the house before James Kelly came down to breakfast. He wanted to obliterate everything in work, and didn't intend to waste time on small talk. Talking to Janet had restored his spirits. He imagined her in bed, taking the call, and the pale image of his sleeping wife vanished from his mind. Janet was an extraordinary woman—a mind like a steel trap and a body that set him on fire. He was very lucky; no man could want a better combination than this blend of partner and bedmate. And she wanted children. That thought increased his sense of warmth and expectancy. A son, two sons; brothers for Lucy. Boys who would follow him into the company. He disappeared into the office block on Shah Reza Avenue, which was the headquarters of Imperial Oil.

In the Syrian Embassy, the commercial attaché who had spent the evening in the flat on Torshab Road was writing a report. The commando unit was ready to go on its mission. Peters and Madeleine Labouchère were booked out on a flight through to Paris and then on to London the next day. Resnais would join them independently. It should take about a week to perfect the final details of the operation and they expected to complete it within ten days at the latest. He added a personal commendation of Peters, whom he described as dedicated and reliable. Madeleine Labouchère needed no comment. Her part in the notorious Haifa massacre was too well known. He paused, hesitating over the only discordant note in last night's meeting. The American's insistence that they could carry out the operation without shedding blood bothered the Syrian. He knew the arguments were valid and he appreciated Peters' logic. But he was uneasy all the same. He preferred the uncompromising ferocity of the woman. If it became necessary to kill their victim she wouldn't hesitate.

Peters had told him to get the little waiter, Habib, out of Teheran. There was no reason in the world to suppose that Colonel Ardalan had noticed him among the crowd, or that he could ever be connected with what was to come. But Peters never took chances. Which was why he was just a series of aliases to Interpol, a faceless shadow with a deadly record of terrorism. The Syrian had to find Habib Ibrahimi and make sure that the million-to-one chance didn't happen.

Eileen spent the day in the garden. There was a group of chairs with shades set near the fountain. She took some of Kelly's magazines in a futile attempt to relax, but the antiques and articles on English country houses were a meaningless jumble seen through tears.

The tie with Logan had been cut; the world yawned ahead of her, and she realized how much she had depended on him. Now the support was withdrawn. From now on she would be alone. She and Lucy. She wondered whether her husband had realized he would lose his child. The idea that he might fight for her made Eileen feel physically sick. Lucy was an obsession with him. Once he had cast her mother out, she couldn't see him relinquishing the little girl. There would be arguments, legal action. She knew Logan too well to doubt his capacity for ruthless action when it was something he wanted. She put her hands over her eyes for a moment as if she could shut out the possibilities.

"My God," she said aloud. "If he takes Lucy. . . ." Then she saw James Kelly standing looking down at her.

"Hello," he said. He sat down in a chair beside her, reaching up to adjust the shade so that the sun didn't shine in his eyes.

"Hello, James."

"I thought I'd come back and have lunch with you," he said. "Logan's still working, and I didn't feel like spending the next two hours eating what they politely call French food in one of their ghastly smart restaurants. I thought we might have a quiet lunch together here."

She looked ill and tired. In the shadow of the shade, there was something suspicious about her eyes. He leaned forward and looked at her. He put his hand out and took hers very firmly.

"You've been crying," he said. "What the hell's the matter?" She didn't mean to tell him. She didn't mean to burst into tears and let him take her in his arms. James held her, soothing her gently, letting the story come out in her own time.

"What a bastard," James said quietly. "What an absolute bastard to do this to you. What are you going to do?"

"Go home," she said. "As soon as I can get a flight." He didn't want to offer the advice; he hated to see her suffer while his own happiness was growing. Selfish and unashamed happiness. Still, he paid lip-service to his sense of honor.

"Don't you think you should stay and try to work it out with him?"

"No," Eileen said, "I don't. It wouldn't be any use. And I don't want a man who doesn't want me. He can have Janet Armstrong. They can eat and sleep Imperial Oil for the rest of their lives."

He looked down and then directly at her. "I'm glad," he said. "I'm glad you feel like that. They'll make a bloody good pair. Hard as nails and worthy of each other. Don't worry, darling. It'll turn out for the best."

He raised her head and, bending forward, kissed her gently on the mouth. "I'll do anything for you," he said. "Anything in the world. Just ask me."

"He'll want to keep Lucy," she said. "I've been thinking about that and I'm certain he won't give her up to me. What am I to do?"

"The first thing you do is to see a good solicitor. Have you got one?"

"I've always dealt with the firm Logan uses."

"I'll find someone else. Don't worry about that. You must move out of Eaton Square and take Lucy with you. Possession is nine points of the law. If you really want me, I'll come back to England and see you through it."

"You can't do that," Eileen said. "You can't walk out on your job."

"I don't give a damn about the job," James said cheerfully. "I hate the bloody place and the oil business bores me stiff. Just say one word and I'll come back."

"James," she said. "Please—don't take on Logan. It isn't necessary; you'll only hurt your career and it's going so well. He thinks you're one of the best men he's got. Don't get emotional about me and damage your own future."

"As far as my future is concerned," James Kelly said, "it's never looked in better shape. I'm going to take you in and see that you eat lunch. Then we'll start telephoning the airlines."

Mahmoud Khorvan received Logan Fields, James Kelly, and the deputy resident director, John Phillipson, in his office at the Ministry. It was a large modern building, square and ugly like all the new buildings in the city. It was garishly furnished, with thick crimson carpets and gilt chandeliers; a huge Harrods reproduction desk and fake Chippendale chairs completed the effect of incongruity. A large colored photograph of the Shah with the Empress and the little Crown Prince hung on the wall behind Khorvan in a carved, gilded frame. A signed photograph stood by his right elbow. Coffee and orange juice had been brought in for his visitors. His secretary, a slim, beautiful girl, poured and passed the cups. The smell of Turkish cigarettes was strong; the minister smoked sixty a day. Although he never drank at public receptions, especially where foreigners were present, part of his bookcase housed a cocktail cabinet containing every kind of alcoholic drink except wine, which he disliked. His favorite was malt whiskey. He greeted Logan courteously, Kelly with amiability, and the subordinate hardly received an acknowledgment. Kelly had long since realized that they were not a gracious people. Khorvan offered cigarettes. All but Logan declined.

"Now, Mr. Fields . . ." he began. He spoke very good English, and understood even better than he spoke. He had spent three years in London studying economics, and it was during that period he had developed left-wing sympathies. "I have given very careful consideration to your offer. Very careful. I have reached an unfortunate conclusion." He made an arch with his fingers and looked at Logan. Logan didn't move—no change of expression, not a muscle twitch. The minister admired him for this. He might hate the man and try to wreck the negotiations, but at least he was going to enjoy himself.

James leaned forward a little, instinctively prepared to be the diplomat. "Not too unfortunate I hope, Minister."

"It depends on how serious you were when you submitted this offer," was the answer, directed at Logan.

"We have never entered negotiation except on a serious level, Minister," Logan spoke curtly. "Please explain why you find the offer unfortunate. I had been told it was acceptable."

"Acceptable to me, yes," Khorvan said pleasantly. "But to a higher authority—not."

"What's wrong with it?" Logan put out his cigarette in the visitors' ashtray. He wasn't in the least worried by Khorvan. Nobody with any experience of the Eastern methods of conducting business would have expected anything but a last-minute haggle over terms. He had come prepared to give something away.

"Let us consider the proposition as a whole," Khorvan said. "There were many contenders for the right to develop Imshan. Because of the size of the oil field, every one of them was prepared to offer as much or more than you, Mr. Fields. But his Imperial Majesty decided in favor of a British Company. Thanks to the persuasive powers of Mr. Kelly."

"It was more a political decision than an economic one," James interposed. "His Imperial Majesty is a very great man. He thinks in global terms."

"His decision to allow your company to export your share of the oil produced at Imshan at a discount on the OPEC price will not only have worldwide repercussions, but it will inevitably undermine the solidarity of the oil-producing countries, even though there will have to be some adjustments from time to time if inflation persists. It will also, if I am not mistaken, enormously enhance Imperial's position as a major oil company. You could become as important as Exxon." Khorvan looked at each of them in turn. "Yet in exchange for this, you propose to give no more than any of your competitors."

Logan leaned forward. "As I see it, Minister, our contribution to the joint venture with the National Iranian Oil Company is to develop the field at Imshan. The cost of this development alone will be in the region of three hundred million dollars to produce up to six hundred thousand barrels a day. There will also be a township, hospital, schools, full modern amenities in an area which is deserted at the moment, and a pipeline to the refinery at Abadan. Finally, there is the commitment to expand production up to a million barrels a day. If there's anything more the Shah wants us to do, I can't think what it is, but I'm naturally anxious to hear."

"His Imperial Majesty has made a gesture which will save the West from bankruptcy and revolution," Khorvan said coldly. "The price of oil is causing such massive inflation that a total breakdown is possible. Everyone knows that. The United States would like to declare war on the Arab States but she cannot because they are under Soviet protection. Governments are plotting and negotiating to try and save themselves; they cannot use the Israelis as a pawn because the Arab forces are equally well-equipped, as the last conflict proved. So his Imperial Majesty decides to save you. Once it is realized that Iran is letting some of its oil go at lower prices than are agreed between the OPEC countries, the others will have to reduce their prices in turn."

"Without any disrespect," Logan said, "this is not just a philanthropic gesture. The situation you describe is only too true, Minister. We are on the edge of disaster in the West. But if Europe suffers a complete economic breakdown, the result will be chaos followed by a Communist revolution. Iran could not hope to survive it unscathed. The Shah knows this. He is certainly saving us by breaking the price formula, but he's also protecting himself."

There was silence after he had spoken. Khorvan sipped his coffee. He didn't hide his resentment, and James tried to warn Logan not to say any more. But Logan ignored him. He leaned back in his chair and seemed perfectly relaxed.

"I take it you feel our investment is insufficient," he said. "What else do you suggest?"

"You talk of building a pipeline to Abadan," Khorvan said. "The distance from Imshan to the refinery is too far. For the quantity of oil that Imshan will produce, we want a separate refinery. Built by you in exchange for the discount on your oil price."

Logan looked at James. He turned back to Khorvan. "No mention of a separate refinery was made to Mr. Kelly."

"No," the minister agreed. "But it was to me. His Imperial Majesty is determined that a refinery should be built at Bandar Muqam, near Imshan on the coast. And that whoever goes into partnership with the

National Oil Company should finance it. He considers that is a fair contribution."

The suggestion had come from Khorvan himself. He knew the Shah's determination to squeeze the last dollar out of Western investors in Iran. The refinery investment would be a major step in the long-term industrialization of the country. If Imperial Oil wanted to develop Imshan and to break the oil price to save the West, then it was up to them to find the money.

Logan lit a cigarette.

"The cost of a refinery big enough to cope with even half of Imshan's eventual production would be in the region of another three hundred million," he said. "An investment of three hundred million, or possibly more because of inflation, would wipe out our profit margins for the next ten years."

Khorvan said nothing. He made another arch with his fingers and looked at the tips of them.

"I'm afraid it's not possible," Logan said. "No company in the world would agree to such a deal. My board wouldn't sanction it even if I recommended it. Surely you can appreciate that."

"I do," Khorvan said. "But unfortunately it is not my problem, Mr. Fields. I am not negotiating for our oil—*you* are. If you really cannot see your way to building the refinery, then the deal must be offered to someone else."

"That's perfectly fair," Logan said. "But exactly who is in a position to undertake it? Don't tell me Exxon, because I know as well as you do Iran doesn't want America having an interest in such a vital asset. You've got enough American soldiers and bases here already. You couldn't let them within a mile of Imshan without having Russia breathing down your neck."

Khorvan looked at him with dislike. He had turned rather a sallow color, a sure sign he was close to losing his temper. He wasn't accustomed to the tone used by Logan.

"There is a Franco-German consortium," he said.

"I know there is." Logan shrugged. "But they won't be able to make an investment on this scale, for no profit either."

James spoke to Logan. He could feel the tension in the atmosphere. "Perhaps we should go away and look at the figures."

"I know the figures," Logan answered. "So does the minister. If we build this refinery, we have no profit for ourselves. It's as simple as that." He offered his gold cigarette case to Khorvan.

"No," the minister said, forgetting his manners. "I only smoke Turkish."

"I used to like them," Logan said. "Now I use these things." He held up a mentholated filter-tip cigarette. "They're supposed to be safer. I don't suppose it makes any difference: *La Illah, Illalah wa huwa qadir alla kulli shayy.*"

James nearly fell off his chair. "There is no law above the will of Allah." He had no idea that Logan knew a word of Arabic or Farsi. Even Khorvan showed that he was impressed. Fields looked at him and the hard lines of his face creased into the smile which held such charm.

"And if Allah wills that we build you a refinery, Minister, then who knows? I'll take Mr. Kelly's advice. We'll go away and think about it. It would help if we could have another appointment with you before the end of the week."

Khorvan stood up. "Unfortunately I am going out of Teheran."

Logan didn't move. "Then when will you be back?"

"In ten days' time."

"I think we should have a meeting before then." Logan stood up. "I have an audience with the Shah and I can't go to the Palace with this question unresolved."

Khorvan hesitated. He had no knowledge of a date being fixed and he was unprepared. The last thing he wanted was for Fields to bring the question up before the Shah until he had successfully undermined the whole negotiation.

"How long will it take you to consider your figures, Mr. Fields?"

"When do you leave Teheran?"

"On Thursday. I don't like to travel on Friday." As a devout Moslem, Khorvan avoided working or moving about on the equivalent of the Christian Sabbath.

"Then it'll take us until Wednesday morning," Logan said. "Mr. Kelly will set the time with your secretary." He held out his hand and gripped the minister's hand until it hurt. "Good morning, Minister."

Khorvan sat down as they filed out. He had no intention of leaving Teheran, and as soon as Fields had gone, he put through a call to the Palace and asked to speak to the minister of the court. He learned that although the British ambassador had made a formal application for Logan Fields to see the Shah, no date had been given. Logan had scored a point off him that morning, but it was insignificant beside the battle Khorvan had just initiated with that impossible demand. They couldn't hope to comply, and he was confident he could make their refusal seem like intractable greed to the Shah. Once it became a matter of government policy, Iran had no choice but to force the terms on the Western company or suffer a loss of face. Either way, Imshan would not fall into the hands of Imperial Oil and Logan Fields, and the Russian technologists, with all due modesty, could re-present themselves.

Peters had finished packing. All that remained of his possessions were a toothbrush, shaving kit, and pajamas. Enough to see him through one night. He had been brought up surrounded by what he described as "things." His mother collected ornaments. The house in Cleveland was like an obstacle course, strewn with her expensive, maddening knickknacks. His father had cars, a workroom full of gadgets. For his eighteenth birthday they had given him an elaborate stereo system which he had never used. They were "thing" people, obsessed with what they owned or wanted to buy, and couldn't understand his contempt for material possessions. There were three children, an older sister and another boy, described by his mother as an afterthought. Peters thought this was the most humiliating thing he had ever heard—the fact that it was always said with an arch smile and a pat on the boy's head only made it seem worse. He had resented it, but his brother hadn't seemed to mind.

He was the odd one out, the silent, introverted child, the withdrawn hostile adolescent. His sister had gone through college and business school, married an ambitious young advertising man, and moved to San Francisco. Peters hadn't seen or heard of her since he left America. His younger brother was going through school when he took off; he seemed cast in the same plastic mold as his parents and sister.

Peters had never explained to them why he diverged. He had found it impossible to communicate, because their words didn't mean the same thing as his. When they talked of freedom, he saw it as conservative repression—his freedom was nothing but anarchy to them. Morals meant sexual behavior to them—to him they meant an ethical approach to humanity, not copulation. "Success" was a word they used like a weapon. He had to succeed. At school, with the neighbors' daughters. He had always to compete and be better. The effort not only repelled him, but with all his soul he rejected the prize. He didn't want to better his friends in order to win the approval of a generation he despised and whose standards he refused to accept. He had worked hard in school but not for any of his parents' reasons. He wanted to study life and history, to understand the riddle of the world he lived in without accepting ready-made answers. He never discussed anything with them or confided in them. They complained, sometimes to his face, that he was a stranger. Peters had long recognized this and adjusted to it. Birth was an accident; he had been left at the wrong doorstep.

He was not aware of being lonely until he went away to college. He didn't mix readily with the other students, although he found the atmosphere the most congenial he had experienced so far. There was a revolutionary spirit on the campus, a liberality of thought and a lack of convention that stimulated him. He made a few friends—discontented intellectuals from similar backgrounds—and formed the first deep relationship of his life. Andrew Barnes was his thesis adviser in political science. In many respects they were opposites. Barnes was slight and limped after an attack of polio as a boy; he was quiet and serious, with a sense of humor that usually worked at his own expense. By contrast, his favorite student was powerful, with a natural talent for athletics. Peters was reserved and silent, Andrew Barnes loved talking. He initiated Peters into the pleasures of debate. He taught him to think and to express his thoughts. He overcame the younger man's inclination to hold back from things and people that he disapproved of, and he preached the gospel of change through attack. Attack through education, debate, ideas. And as a last resort, through confrontation. Barnes was a Marxist; he would have rejected in horror the accusation that he lived a life of Christian unselfishness, wholly devoted to the welfare of others; he was a fearless champion of the less fortunate, determined to withstand injustice and to work for the improvement of society. To Barnes the world meant people. He lacked the cold intellectuality that sees humanity in terms of economics. To him, political science was about human beings, and his concern for them gave his own political beliefs a shining sincerity. He was the most attractive person Peters had ever met. His charisma gathered a devoted group of student disciples around him—but for Peters, the terms spent under Barnes' auspices was the step on the road to Damascus.

All his life Peters had felt rootless, an outsider condemned to a life of rejecting without an alternative choice. Listening to Barnes, he discovered that choice. All the resources of love that were in him found a double outlet. The frail, impassioned teacher took the place left vacant by his parents, and because he was light-years away from the limited, conventional father with whom Peters had no point of contact, he never mentioned Barnes or let his parents meet him. And Barnes' teaching gave his life a purpose. He adopted his mentor's political beliefs with the fervor of a man starving for a cause. He would have followed Andrew Barnes to hell and out again, and one bright morning on campus, shortly before Kent State, that was exactly what he did.

It began as a protest against the Vietnam war—a number of students had been called up for military service, a rally was organized, and Barnes was its leader. There had been other demonstrations; Peters had taken part and recognized the pattern. Speeches, slogans, an outbreak of stone-throwing against the police. The ugly baton charges, violence, injury, retreat, and regrouping. When the riot police were called out, he and Andrew Barnes were in the front ranks. He remembered afterward seeing the police begin to charge, and trying to get in front of Barnes. There was a second charge, more violent than the first. Some of the student ranks gave way, there was a horrible confusion when people seemed to be running in all directions and there were shrill screams from frightened girls. Peters heard Barnes shouting, telling them to hold on. Then the police surged forward, truncheons flailing savagely. Barnes' voice was cut off in mid-shout.

For years afterward, Peters woke from a recurring nightmare in which he was kneeling in the dirt, surrounded by fleeing, shrieking people, holding the dying man in his arms. His memories were confused. He had heard the groans of pain as Barnes bled from the mouth, and seen the head fall back suddenly as if he were holding a puppet and the string had broken. He was weeping when the police arrested him; it took four of them to drag him away and wrench the dead man out of his arms. He had been punched and kicked, fighting like a madman on his way to the police wagon. Inside, with his hands handcuffed behind him, he was punched in the kidneys and groin, and beaten up again in the station. His parents had come to bail him out, and there was a moment, when they saw their bruised and beaten son, that they reached out to him without conditions. But it was too late. Although they joined the outcry against police brutality, Peters didn't identify with them in any way. Their concern, their indignation meant nothing to him. The best human being he had ever met had been murdered by the society which they and their generation represented.

Peters said nothing. He spent ten days in the hospital and then returned to the campus. It was not the same and never would be. The limping figure, his head thrust a little forward as he tried to match the quicker walk of his students, was no longer part of Peters' life. There would be no more evenings spent debating, no suppers cooked by Barnes' pretty grad-student wife in their warm, colorful apartment, where the talk went on late into the night. When the press talked of Barnes' martyrdom it was a cliché which Peters dismissed with contempt. They hadn't known the man or loved him. Only Peters and the group which had been close to him knew the extent of the crime that capitalism had committed.

If Andrew Barnes had shown him the meaning of warmth and disinterested love for his fellows, the riot policeman who had struck him down had taught Peters what it meant to hate. And to hate with a singleminded, pitiless intensity that gravitated naturally to the ultimate extreme of which the gentle Barnes would never have approved. Only violence could hope to overcome the organized violence of modern society. Absolute ruthlessness and total dedication to the cause were the requisites of revolutionaries if they were to be effective in the struggle.

By the time Peters graduated he was a leading member of the extremist Marxist cell that existed within the student organization. He was arrested on suspicion of carrying explosives but the charge was dismissed for lack of evidence. The next time the police would provide the evidence. He was a marked agitator. Without saying good-bye to his parents, he took a plane to Mexico, and from there he sent them a postcard saying he intended to spend the next year or so doing social work and not to worry if he didn't communicate. After that he shut his mind to them completely. He never felt an exile. He lived and moved among people like himself, dedicated, efficient, perfecting themselves for the work in hand. He learned to kill, to use explosives, to travel long distances under rough conditions. He was sent to Chile where he did valuable work, organizing sabotage and leading a brief guerrilla expedition against an army camp. He stayed long enough to see Allende triumph, and he was in Germany when he heard that the brief Marxist reign was over and the oppressors had regained power. In Bonn he and Madeleine Labouchère hijacked a Lufthansa 707, killing a steward and injuring three of the passengers. As a result of negotiations, four Palestinian terrorists were released from jail and he and the girl were given a safe-conduct to Syria.

He stood by the apartment window for a moment; the sun was setting fire to the roofs of Teheran. There was no view but the streets and the blocks of buildings. An ugly city, built on a barren plain.

He had grown to love the real Iran, with its infinite variety—the lush northern slopes of the Elburz mountains leading down to the Caspian shore; the incredible carpet of spring flowers around Kerman that had inspired the carpet weavers for a thousand years. The aridity of the Zagros mountains, broken by little green valleys and clear streams—a contrast that had fired the poetic soul of ancient Persia and produced immortal verse. The brutal heat of the yellow deserts and the almost spiritual uplift occasioned by the beauty of the mosques at Isphahan; the marvels at Persepolis where he had helped with excavations. This was the land that drew pilgrims from the Western world, eager to sample the fruits of the ancient culture and exquisite visual arts of the great Aryan race that had been both conqueror and civilizing influence in the Eastern World. As a people they were proud, treacherous, cunning, and deeply hospitable; the inequality of life between the rich and the poor was as harsh as anything he had witnessed even in Central America. He had thought himself immune to misery and disease after seeing the plight of the Indians, but the gross display of wealth in Iran brought his rage to the surface.

He hated the rich, wherever they clustered, like sores on the body of the working masses. Overfed, artificial, swollen with profits, they lived in luxury and idleness while others slaved and hungered. Age hadn't mellowed Peters. He knew nothing but the reasoning of fanatics like himself. He made love to a woman who had knelt in the passenger lounge of an Israeli airport and sprayed women and children with machine-gun fire. There was no weakening of his resolve, no change in his opinions. But this time he didn't want to kill. He would have to be careful of Madeleine. In one way she was a bad choice. She had a light trigger-finger, and she wasn't influenced by age or sex. But a woman was essential to the operation, and he felt he could control her. Now that the time was so near, he wanted to start off. He wouldn't sleep that night, and he wouldn't want Madeleine, either. He wanted to be on the plane and coming down at Orly. . . .

She had been out and he heard the front door open. She came up and put her arms round his waist. He could smell the expensive scent she used and he frowned.

"What are you looking at?"

"Nothing. I was thinking."

"About tomorrow?"

"Yes."

"Don't worry," she said. "We've worked together before. I know what I have to do." She squeezed against him. "I feel excited," she said. "Like celebrating. Shall we celebrate tonight?"

He turned around slowly and looked at her.

"We celebrate when we've succeeded," he said. "I don't like that stuff you put on. The scent's too heavy. Go wash it off before we eat."

She was about to say it cost eighty-five dollars an ounce and then realized how disgusted he would be. She was surprised at herself for nearly making the mistake. It was conditioning, and she excused herself. In her home, women scented themselves to please their men—and above all she wanted to please this man.

"I put it here," she said, pointing to her breasts. "You could wash it away for me."

"For Christ's sake," Peters said, "I'm hungry."

The girl laughed at him suddenly. "You are a pig of an American," she said. "But I love you and I'll feed you. I'd forgotten you were like this before a mission."

She went into the dingy little kitchen and he heard her singing. She never suffered from nerves; danger excited her, like sex. He had never seen her blanch, whatever the risks. She was a remarkable specimen of the modern Arab woman, in spite of her German blood. Tough, determined, unscrupulous, and fierce; her nearest equivalent was her blood enemy, the female Israeli. She might set light to the bedsheets but it was impossible to love her in the conventional sense. For this reason alone, she was the perfect complement to him.

They drank a bottle of wine, ate an excellent kebab which she prepared, and made love until they were both exhausted. By nine the next morning she had left the flat and he was driving in a taxi down Eisenhower Road toward Mehrabad Airport.

"I hear you're going back tomorrow." Logan found Eileen reading in James' shady sitting room. The windows onto the garden were open and the evening promised to be cooler. Eileen looked up at him. It was a statement, not a question. There was little expression on his face.

"Yes," she said. "I told you last night. James managed to get me a seat tomorrow morning."

"I wanted to talk to you," Logan said. "But I've got to go out tonight and we're all working flat-out tomorrow. It'll have to wait till I get back."

"There's not much to say," Eileen answered. She let the book slip out of her hand—she hadn't been able to concentrate on it anyway. Now was the moment for him to retract, to make some move toward her, however slight. In spite of herself, of the hurt that was so real, it was like a physical pain, she still hoped. Whether it was because some love for him was left, or out of cowardice; she didn't know.

He shook his head. He seemed cool, even impatient, as if finding her and having to discuss it was an irritant. "There isn't, really. I've asked Janet to come. I explained I needed someone here to help with entertaining and she said she'd do it. We've run into trouble with that bastard Khorvan. I'll have my hands full out here for some time. Why don't you go to Ireland?"

It had never occurred to her to go home. Her father wouldn't be sympathetic. He'd thought she was a fool to marry Logan in the first place, and he'd say she was an even bigger fool to walk out on the money now.

"I could take Lucy," she said.

Immediately he frowned. "No," he said. "I don't like her being dragged around. She's all right where she is, in her own home." He lit a cigarette. "We'll sort things out when I get back to London. I'm sorry it's turned out like this. I'm sure you know that. But I can't give any time to it at the moment. I've got to get Imshan settled first."

She got up and went to the garden door.

"You certainly know your priorities," she said quietly. "And as far as my child is concerned, if I want to take her home with me, I will." She walked out into the garden without saying good-bye.

James Kelly drove her to the airport. He had given her the address of his solicitors. "They're a bit old-fashioned, not the kind of people to deal with Logan, but they'll know whom to recommend. Promise you'll go and see them."

They were waiting by the departure lounge. The flight had been called and she was just about to go through passport control. Two Iranian police were checking the passengers and their hand luggage with a detector. They were running it over the canvas grip carried by a man immediately in front of her. He was tall and blond and looked like an American junior professor.

"I will, I promise you," Eileen said. "I don't know what I would have done without you, James."

He smiled. His dark hair flopped over his forehead as he bent down to her. "You'd have been all right," he said. "You've got the guts of the Irish. Good-bye, Eileen. I'll ring you in a couple of days. Take care, and don't worry."

She reached up and kissed him; she felt his hand grip her shoulder. Then she turned, as the flight was called for the last time. She passed through the detector screen and was given back her handbag. She followed the blond man into the departure lounge and across to gate 7.

An Iranian woman, wearing the chador, her face covered to the eyes, walked a few steps between them. She carried a little boy with wistful black eyes, greedily eating his fist. There was no resemblance, but Eileen thought of Lucy. From the moment she came back from the fashionable nursing home, the child had been in the care of a nanny—the kind of nanny that Logan felt was competent to look after his precious baby. He had often talked of "my daughter," and at first Eileen had been hurt and vaguely jealous at being excluded. But she had accepted this, as another facet of his possessive, oversized personality. He worshipped the little girl, and there was no suggestion that

Eileen should take the responsibility for her. She had been too ill to protest at the annexation of the baby by the nanny, with Logan's full approval. She might be well enough to dress up and sit through the kind of business dinner which had introduced James Kelly, but she couldn't cope with the child. As she boarded the plane, she realized that for the first time since she was born, Lucy was going to belong to her mother.

She settled into a seat near the exit door, fastened her seat belt, and opened the novel she had tried to read the day before. She was not even aware that the American was beside her. They were each to remember, in very different circumstances, that their lives had joined for the first time when they shared that journey together.

Pierre Resnais passed the time at Orly waiting for Peters and Madeleine to arrive by watching the girls in the lounge. There was a pretty blonde who pleased him—a thin, sensual little girl with long hair and tiny breasts sticking through her shirt. He could have picked her up easily, and was sorry that he had no time. He was small and dark, with a sallow, intelligent face; his clothes were conservative and he carried a briefcase. He looked a prosperous businessman around thirty. His real age was nearer thirty-five and he was an expert rifle and revolver shot.

The plane for London was due to leave in an hour; he wandered over to the arrivals board and checked. Several women watched him. The plane from Teheran had landed. Madeleine should join him in the departure lounge. As far as he knew, Peters was taking a plane an hour later.

Resnais saw her walking through, carrying one light case. He went after her, went through passport control, and was stopped at the security point. Madeleine had gone through. The London flight was being called. A policeman ran his hands up and down him, while Resnais stood, with a slight grin on his face, as if it were all a joke, his arms lifted away from his sides.

The detector slid over his briefcase and pinged loudly. He shrugged, opened it and revealed a metal flask. It was full of brandy. They waved him on, and he boarded the plane. He didn't sit near Madeleine, or look at the other passengers. He settled into his seat as soon as the plane leveled off, tilted it back, and went to sleep. He didn't notice Eileen Fields because she was in the front of the plane in the first-class section.

When they arrived in London, he joined the taxi queue outside the number 1 building. Madeleine was beside him. He grinned at her, showing his white teeth. They had spent some time in Syria together on a training course and she had never liked him. When he smiled he reminded her of a dog that was preparing to bite.

"Where are you going?" he asked her.

"Victoria."

"So am I," Resnais said. "Why don't we share—these taxis are very expensive."

"You could have caught the bus," Madeleine answered.

"I have to get a train."

"All right, then, let's share the next one."

They climbed in and slammed the door. Madeleine gave the driver an address in Pimlico, behind the station. It was a third-class hotel, and not too particular about its clients. Couples had been known to take a room for an hour without arousing comment.

"Well," Resnais said. "Have a good flight?"

"Very smooth. Very boring. I hate flying."

"You're looking well," he remarked. He knew, as all the group did, that she was sleeping with the American. He also knew that she disliked him and he was amused by her attitude. He had never accepted women as equals; he had worked with them, but they had one primary function and it wasn't revolutionary. He had never loved anyone in his life, but he had a sentimental attachment for dogs which had almost got him killed.

He had adopted a starving mongrel during his stay in the Syrian outpost. When he took part in a dawn raid across into Israel the animal followed. It had run barking toward the kibbutz.

Even so he kept a half-bred Alsatian in his two-room flat in Paris. A friend was looking after it in his absence; he had explained that he had to go back to Marseilles to see his father, who was ill.

"Is everything going well?"

"Peters thinks so," she said. "And if he's satisfied it must be. He'll be meeting us tonight. We stay at this place in Pimlico for one night only and then move on."

"What about Peters?"

"He stays separately. We join up for the flight out."

Resnais laughed at her. "You won't like that much, will you?" Madeleine looked out of the window. Neat suburban houses, set in identical plots of garden, ran past the window. She thought irrelevantly that the English were a nation of individualists. Each garden was planted to be different; a few were bare and weed-ridden, but most showed the native passion for making things grow, however small the space.

"This is a job," she said, without looking at him. "Maybe the most important one we've ever done. It isn't time for making your stupid jokes."

He only laughed again. They booked into the hotel. The receptionist didn't even bother to look at the register. They signed as husband and wife under the name of Richards and gave an address in Kent. Peters had taken it from a magazine advertisement for a dressmaker. If their plan went wrong and there was a police check, nobody would associate a casual one-night registration with an English name and address, with what had happened. But public knowledge was not what Peters wanted. The essence of success was that nobody should know. Nobody except Logan Fields. When they were alone, Madeleine opened her suitcase and took out a nightdress. Resnais watched her.

"Ah," he said. "What a pity you don't like me, chérie. I suppose you expect me to sleep on the floor?"

"No." Madeleine glanced up at him briefly. "In the chair. We should stay here for about an hour. Then we can go out and get something to eat. Peters has told me where to go. He'll meet us there."

She took a French magazine out of her case, sat on the bed, and started reading. Resnais lounged in the scuffed armchair and wondered if his dog was missing him.

It was six thirty when Eileen arrived at Eaton Square. Kelly had sent a cable telling them to expect her. The Portuguese butler opened the front door, took her case, and said, "Welcome home, madame."

"Thank you, Mario. Everything all right?" It was not a serious question. The house was perfectly run by a large staff. Logan paid top wages but he required faultless service, and in spite of a shortage of domestic workers, it was typical that he got what he demanded. There were fresh flowers, boldly and beautifully arranged in every room, hothouse roses in her bedroom, and a maid waiting to take her coat and prepare a bath for her. For years Eileen had lived in this style and after the first reaction from her old, easygoing Irish life, she had taken it for granted. It was part of being married to a very rich, exacting man.

Eileen went upstairs to the top floor. There was a little white-painted gate, secured by a safety latch. Its purpose was to keep Lucy

Fields from toddling to the stairs and falling down them, but it always seemed to Eileen as if it were meant to keep her out.

She opened the nursery door and went in. It was a pink and white room, overdecorated and clinically neat. Toys were ranged along one wall, repeating the color scheme; pink and white fairies danced in frescoes around the room. The nanny was sitting down, sewing. When she saw Eileen she got up, smiling and distant, as if she were welcoming a visitor. "Oh, good evening, Mrs. Fields. Did you have a good journey? We weren't expecting you back so soon."

"No, it seemed pointless to stay on. I could have been there for ages. Where's Lucy—"

"She's asleep," the nanny said.

Eileen walked to the night nursery door and opened it. She didn't look at the older woman or say anything. She went inside. "Please, Mrs. Fields," she heard the voice behind her. "Don't wake the child. Surely in the morning—"

"She's not asleep," Eileen said. "Close the door please, nanny." She switched on the light and the little girl sitting up in the pink and white bed held out her arms.

Eileen was in her room unpacking when there was a knock on the door.

"Madame! There you are now. . . . I'm so sorry I was out." Bridget looked at her closely. "You're looking tired," she said. "Did you have a horrible journey? Let me do that, madame. I'll put everything away."

"It was tiring, Biddy. And I don't like flying anyway. Today's your day off, isn't it?"

"Sure and there's the Prince of Wales waiting to take me out tonight! I can go off anytime. Shall I get some tea for you—"

"No, thanks. Biddy, I'm going to need your help. I'm giving nanny notice tomorrow morning."

Bridget's face broke into a huge smile. "Thank God for that! Wait till Mario and Marianna hear about it! The old hag—won't she be mad!"

"Biddy, will you help me look after Lucy? I'm not going to get anyone like her again. I want the baby to myself."

"High time too, madame," the girl agreed. "What about Mr. Fields —what'll he say?"

Eileen hesitated. She decided to say nothing until a later stage. "He's very busy in Iran at the moment. I haven't bothered him about it."

"Don't you worry," Bridget said. "I'll do everything I can for Lucy.

I've always wanted to get me hands on her, and the old gorgon wouldn't even let me in the nursery!" She smiled at Eileen and started unpacking and hanging up clothes.

Eileen didn't feel hungry, but Bridget fussed over her and brought a tray into the library. It was a small, comfortable room, with the air of casual elegance that costs so much money to achieve. There were photographs of herself and Lucy, and a big portrait study of Logan which was often reproduced in the newspapers. Seven years of marriage to a man who had become a stranger. He had another woman now, a woman who could share his passion for business and stand on equal terms with him. Eileen had never been his equal or his partner. She had come low on his list of priorities and accepted it—she wasn't sure how high even Lucy rated when it came to Imperial Oil. He could never have said, like James, "If you need me I'll come back."

It would have been easy to cable, to call the lover in the wings onto the stage. Easy to follow the habit of seven years and leave the initiative to a man. But this time she wasn't going to do it.

Nothing shamed her more than the realization of what she had allowed Logan to do with their child. The fussy, elderly mother-substitute with her rigid routine, the spotless nursery and the regimented toys. The deliberate exclusion of the mother from real contact with her child.

All that was over. James had said she had guts, and she was glad to find that he was right.

She finished her coffee and went upstairs to the second-floor bedroom. Logan insisted on a king-size bed. He had given her a magnificent Poussin landscape two years before. She wondered whether he had given Janet Armstrong pictures or jewelry. More likely share options. She would appreciate them more. She got into bed and within minutes she fell asleep. It was just eleven o'clock. In a cheap Indian restaurant less than a mile away off Victoria Street Madeleine, Resnais, and Peters sat around a table, planning the kidnapping of Lucy Fields.

Chapter 3

For five years, Colonel Ali Ardalan had been the head of the Iranian Secret Police—*Sazemane Attalat Va Amniyate Keshvar*—the dreaded SAVAK. He had begun his military career in Army Intelligence, where he distinguished himself against the Kurdish tribesmen, who were fighting a guerrilla war for self-rule on the Iraqui border. His father had been in the same regiment as the Shah's father, the army sergeant who had deposed the last Qajar emperor and taken possession of the Peacock Throne. Ardalan belonged to one of what were known as the Thousand Families, the old Persian aristocracy. It had taken a generation before they felt comfortable serving the upstart Reza family. Ali had no such reservations. He admired the Shah for his courage, his fervent nationalism, and his ability to weld the people together in personal loyalty to him.

The colonel had spent some months in England on a course at the Military Academy. He had liked Sandhurst and admired the English. He was an openminded man, keenly intelligent, and ready to learn anything he felt could be used to Iran's advantage. He was a soldier and a patriot. He believed that the safety of his country and the personal safety of the Shah were above all other considerations. Since his appointment as head of SAVAK, he had perfected a system of espionage and counterterrorism which was the admiration of similar services throughout the East. His enemies described him as a monster of cruelty and repression; his torture chambers were places from which few suspects came out alive. He knew everything about everyone in public life—his shadow fell upon ministers and civil servants, on the armed forces, the diplomatic service, the universities. The intellectuals and the moderates shuddered when the name Ardalan was mentioned. He was a close friend and adviser of the Shah and the only man who could have access to him at any time, night or day. He was married, with a second wife and three young children. They lived together in a large, well-guarded house on the outskirts of Teheran.

In private life he was a quiet man, modest in his personal needs, and exceptional in that he had never beaten or ill-treated either of his wives. He had gathered together all the available information about Logan Fields. This was a routine precaution before anyone was allowed an audience with the Shah, and Ardalan insisted on it, regardless of who was involved. He knew that Fields' wife had gone back to England, because many of the foreign-owned houses were under supervision, and James' houseboy was in police pay. He also knew that Fields was having trouble with the minister, Khorvan. The colonel did not trust either of them. The Englishman was trying to exploit Iran's huge natural oil resources, and the minister was indulging his left-wing tendencies by impeding the negotiations. Ardalan knew all about the demand for a refinery because the Shah himself had told him. It would be interesting to see if Imperial Oil could be bullied into agreement. The Shah had no objection to Khorvan imposing the harshest terms on any European company. Ardalan had none either, so long as the motives behind the maneuvers were purely in the interests of Iran and the Shah. He was not sure that this applied to Khorvan, but he knew the Shah too well to say so at that moment.

If the minister succeeded, the Shah would be pleased. If he failed and the negotiations broke down, then it would be proper to question his motives. Ardalan didn't trust the minister and he didn't like him personally. He was having him very closely watched, but he hadn't told the Shah this either. The colonel was on his way to his office at Niavaran. He drove in a bulletproof army car and never used the same route in succession or left at the same time. On that morning he instructed his driver to take a way through one of the poorer districts of the city by way of diversion. From there they could proceed to his office. Since no one knew which way he was traveling, the colonel felt himself safe from ambush. It was not a prospect that worried him, although he took precautions. He was a brave man and unafraid of violent death.

They were driving through a narrow back street when their way was barred by a small crowd. A police motorcycle was parked against the wall. The driver jammed his hand on the horn and the people began to scatter. The colonel was in civilian clothes; he wore English suits and white shirts with a discreet tie. He leaned forward and told the driver to slow down. He always said that nine-tenths of an intelligence officer's equipment was a talent for doing jigsaw puzzles, and the tenth part was instinct. Instinct made him curious, and his curiosity made him stop the car to find out what had happened.

His driver called through the window to the crowd. A moment later the policeman came up. The colonel opened his window and asked what was going on.

"A man has been murdered," the policeman reported. "His body is inside."

"Ah," the colonel said. Teheran had a low murder rate; crimes of violence were rare, though the incidence of burglary was high. The colonel opened the door and got out. He said one word to the policeman—"SAVAK"—and the man cringed.

"Show me the body," he said. The inside of the house was dark. He heard the sound of a high, female wail of grief. In a little room at the back the policeman stopped and opened the door. Ardalan recognized the slaughterhouse smell. There was blood all over the floor and he stepped carefully to avoid staining his shoes. The dead man lay on his back. He was wearing only a greasy shirt. A woman crouched in the corner. Ardalan told her to be quiet, and the crying stopped. He bent over the body. Above the horribly gashed throat, the face was unmarked, the eyes open. The colonel looked for a full minute at the dead man.

"His name?"

"Habib Ibrahimi, sir."

"What have you discovered?"

The policeman stammered. "Nothing yet, sir. The woman is his wife. She couldn't tell us much. Nobody knows who did this."

"The woman is afraid," Ardalan said. "This is not the place to ask her questions. Send for a car. They are to bring her to Niavaran. I will talk to her. For the moment touch nothing. My men will come down and search the house. Are there any signs of robbery?"

"No, sir. He and his wife lived in this room. There are families in the other rooms. Nobody heard anything and nothing has been taken."

"Send the woman to me," the colonel said. "And tell her she has nothing to fear. I am sorry for what has happened and I want to give her money. Tell her that."

He went out into the street, and the crowd gave way for him. The policeman opened the door of the car for him and saluted. The colonel sat back, told the driver to go on, and sniffed at his pocket handkerchief. He used a strong cologne, and it drove the smell of sticky blood away as he breathed into the handkerchief.

The one-tenth instinct had not failed him. Nor would the other nine. A man called Habib Ibrahimi had been butchered in a mean little room in a poor quarter. The name was of no significance to the colonel, but he had instantly recognized the face. It was the waiter who had served him at the oil company's reception for Minister Khorvan. The same waiter he had seen hovering around the minister and Logan Fields.

It was not a coincidence. Ardalan knew that. It was a piece in a jigsaw puzzle. Half an hour later he was sitting in his office, talking very patiently and gently to Habib Ibrahimi's widow.

Peters had hired a Ford Cortina from a car rental firm at Victoria. He drove to Eaton Square a little after nine that morning, found a meter just past the Fields' house, and parked there. He slipped into the back seat beside Madeleine. It was a bright morning, and the gardens in the square were brilliant with flowers. He yawned, watching the front door of the house. He hadn't slept well, and he didn't feel like going out to eat breakfast. Nothing was provided in the boardinghouse where he had stayed the night. Madeleine looked rested and she was smartly dressed in a dark-blue suit with a colored scarf over her hair.

"They ought to come out soon," she said. "I don't think it's very warm. I wouldn't take a child walking in this wind."

Peters looked at her and for a moment he smiled.

"You're not English," he said. "They believe in fresh air." Time passed. A delivery van from an exclusive grocer came to the door and a box of goods was taken down the area steps to the entrance below.

Peters saw it was ten past ten on his watch. A traffic warden was patrolling the street, approaching them. She was checking the cars. "Put some money in the meter, quickly," he said to Madeleine. "It may have run out." She moved immediately—she never hesitated when he gave an order. Immediately she was back in the car. "There's time left," she said. "That woman was looking at me." Peters' hand grabbed her knee. His fingers bit into her leg so hard that it gave no pleasure.

"Look!"

The door of Logan Fields' house was open. A man wearing a white jacket backed down the short steps, carrying the top half of a pram. Holding it by the handle and taking the minimum of weight was a middle-aged woman in a brown coat and hat. The pram was gently set down on the pavement; the manservant went back into the house. The woman went around and straightened the covers. A small girl, wearing a pink beret and coat, sat upright, a cover over her legs. She was holding a white teddy bear.

"That's her," Peters said quietly. Madeleine didn't answer. She saw the woman, the pram, and the little girl. He went around and got into the driver's seat. The pram was moving down the street toward them in the direction of Belgrave Place. Peters started the engine and sped past them.

At the top of the road he went into reverse, driving carefully now. "We'll follow," he said. "I guess they'll go to the park. Then you can start the operation."

The nanny moved at a brisk pace. It relieved her feelings to walk quickly, steering the pram. She crossed the busy road to the rear of Buckingham Palace and headed for St. James's Park. It was her favorite walk. This morning, though, the crowds of tourists irritated her, gawping at the scarlet-uniformed sentries, staring mindlessly at the palace windows, although the Royal Standard was not flying and any fool knew the Queen was not in residence. The child was very sensitive to her moods; she knew when to ask questions and when it would provoke an angry command to keep quiet. There was a little plastic bag full of crumbs in the bottom of the pram. For twenty years the nanny had been bringing other women's children to the lake in St. James's Park and showing them how to feed the birds.

She found a vacant seat and sat down. Her back ached and she had tired herself walking so fast.

"Nanny," Lucy Fields ventured. "Get out?"

"In a minute," she said. "Just wait a minute, like a good girl." She couldn't believe what had happened. She had gone down to see Mrs. Fields, prepared to make her position plain and expecting unconditional surrender. She really *couldn't* have her mothers walking in and waking up the children at any hour, and she really felt Mrs. Fields should have shown more consideration. She hadn't been given the opportunity to say anything. She was given a month's money and told very politely that Mrs. Fields was taking the child away and she could leave in the morning. She was thinking back on the scene, reliving every word, wishing she had come out of it better.

The little girl sat mutely in the pram, waiting to be lifted out.

"What a beautiful child," a woman's voice said. The nanny looked around, startled. She hadn't even noticed that someone had sat down beside her. Normally she enjoyed talking to people, and it pleased her when Lucy was admired. The woman was young and spoke with a foreign accent. She was well dressed and she smiled at her.

"So pretty," she said. "Do you look after her?"

"Yes," the nanny said. Resentment was boiling up in her. To be turned out of the house. . . . In twenty years no other mother had ever dared. . . .

"She's a credit to you. How old is she?"

"Three," the nanny said. "I've been with her since she was born. Here, come to nanny, dear. You can have a little run but don't go near the water."

She lifted the child out and brushed her pink coat. "Play just here, dear, where I can see you. Show Teddy to the lady."

Madeleine Labouchère held the toy for a moment. She smiled encouragingly at the little girl, who smiled back. She was rather a small child for her age—pale and slight by comparison with the fat, spoiled children of the Lebanese rich. She seemed subdued.

"She's a dear little thing," the nanny said, and her eyes pricked. She was going to miss Lucy. And the splendid house, the easy life with servants to wait on her—she was going to miss it all. She brought a handkerchief out and blew her nose.

"I don't know how she'll manage without me. I've been the only mother she's ever known. Poor little mite."

"Oh, dear," Madeleine said. "Are you leaving, then?"

"Yes." The nanny sniffed and blew her nose again. She wanted sympathy. "I've been given notice. Just like that! The mother's decided to look after her herself! Huh. . . . I wonder how long *that'll* last."

The hands clasped around Madeleine's bag were gripping tight.

"How awful for you," she said. "When are you leaving?"

"Tomorrow," the nanny said. "I told her this morning, I'm not going to be treated like that after all I've done for that child. I'm going first thing tomorrow, I said. She didn't like that, I can tell you!" It was so easy to turn the truth around—she had almost convinced herself that this was how it had happened. "She wouldn't have dared do it if Mr. Fields had been there! He trusted me completely."

For one panic-ridden moment Madeleine thought that Logan had suddenly come back too. She opened her hands and there were sweat marks on the leather purse.

"I expect she'll get another nanny," she said. "But it's very hard on you."

"Oh dear, no." The sarcasm was heavy. "Says she's taking Lucy to Ireland! *That* dreadful place, I ask you—going to look after her all by herself. I hate the Irish. We ought to let them get on and murder each other, that's what I say. *She's* Irish. Now, Lucy, don't wipe your hands on your coat!"

Madeleine got up. The little girl stared at her; she had large blue eyes, with a hesitant look. Ireland. . . . Unconsciously she used Peters' rare expletive: *Jesus Christ on wheels. Ireland.* The mother was in London, the nurse was leaving. The child was going to Ireland. The whole operation was falling apart.

"I must be going," she said. There was a gun in her handbag. It had come in Pierre's brandy flask, wrapped in plastic. For one wild moment she contemplated shooting the old woman and grabbing the child. Their part of the lake was deserted. Peters was waiting, parked down a side road near the army barracks in Birdcage Walk. *What a silly name, what a fucking silly English name.* . . . They were both looking back at her.

"Wave good-bye, dear," the nanny said, and obediently the child waved to her. Now a couple were walking toward them; they had rounded a bend in the path without Madeleine seeing them. Even if they hadn't come, she couldn't have given way to the impulse. It hadn't a chance. Peters would kill her if she wrecked everything. He had the brains, He would know what to do. She waved back to them and walked away. When she was some distance up the path she began to run to where he was waiting with the car.

"We found this," Colonel Ardalan's assistant said. It was a strip of paper about two inches long, torn from a larger piece. It seemed to be the top of a newspaper. There were six figures written on it in pencil. They were faint and the paper was very crumpled.

"It was in the trouser pocket," the policeman said. Ardalan smoothed the paper down with two fingers and looked at it.

"And that was all?"

"Yes, Colonel. There were a few household things, another suit of clothes, and the wife's possessions. Nothing much. They were just ordinary poor people. He was employed by the Hilton as a waiter and I asked the personnel manager about him. He said as far as he knew the man did his work and that was all."

Ardalan was smoking a thin cigar. He looked at the end of it, then rubbed it out in the onyx ashtray.

"His wife said he was a clever man," the colonel remarked. It had taken a long time to get the woman to talk beyond a frightened mumble. When she offered this information about her husband, Ardalan had been impressed. Clever in what way? He knew about politics, she said. He had tried to talk to her, but he said she was too stupid and couldn't understand. She had dropped her head in shame. These things were not for women, but he had been very angry. He went to the cafés and talked with other clever men. Three nights before he died, he had come home and waked her up. He was excited and she thought he was going to beat her. But he only said bad things about the minister, Khorvan.

"What kind of things?" Ardalan prompted very gently.

Her husband had called the minister a traitor. The colonel had given her an encouraging smile. She was a pretty girl in her mid-twenties; the hand holding the black chador near her mouth was trembling.

She owed her life to Habib's appropriation of the bed. He made her sleep on the floor, so the murderer hadn't seen her when he crept into the room. She had crouched in the darkness, too terrified to cry out, while her husband struggled and fell out of bed. She hadn't seen them cut his throat; she heard a horrible gurgling noise and then the killer slipped away.

Ardalan gave her a sum of money and sent her back in a police car to her family who lived on the other side of Teheran. He looked at the piece of paper and the jumbled figures. Six, all running into each other.

He lifted his telephone, pressed for an outside line, and slowly dialed the figures. He heard the number ringing. It went on for some time until he hung up. He copied the figures on a memo sheet and handed it to his assistant. "Get someone to find the address for this. I believe Habib Ibrahimi was involved in some kind of subversion. There is to be a full investigation. Start at once."

Peters left the boardinghouse that midday. He checked into a respectable middle-class hotel in Cromwell Road, said he was staying for one night en route to New York, and booked a table in the restaurant for two friends for dinner. He spent the afternoon in his room, thinking. He had listened to Madeleine, not asking a question till she had told him everything. She had mentioned her idea of making the grab on the spur of the moment, and he had frowned. "Thank Christ you didn't do anything like that!" he said.

She hadn't wanted to go back to Resnais. She wanted to stay with Peters.

"What was the kid like?"

"Oh . . . rather a miserable little thing. Typical upper-class child. Listen—if we don't act immediately, we'll lose the chance!"

"We're going to do just that," he said. "But not till we've worked out how." He had sent her away and gone off alone to his hotel to think of a new plan. Madeleine was right. If they delayed, the child would be gone to Ireland. And there was no provision made for their escape from there. Whereas the organization had fixed the route out of England. All he had to do was pick up the telephone when they were ready.

At seven o'clock they met in the hotel lounge. He shook hands with Resnais and kissed Madeleine on the cheek. He was dressed in a suit and silk turtleneck sweater. He looked like a typical American in transit. Entertaining two foreign guests. They had a drink each and talked about nothing; three other couples were using the lounge. By twenty past seven they took their seats in the restaurant. At that hour it was almost empty. Four diners were scattered around at distances from one another. Peters ordered the set menu and a bottle of wine. Resnais leaned across to him.

"What are we going to do? Nothing will be as easy as our original plan."

"Taking a child is never easy," Peters said. "Madeleine mightn't have been able to get away with it."

"I could have," she interrupted. "That old woman didn't want to be bothered with the child. She would have let me take her."

It had been such a simple plan—the less complicated the maneuver the better. Peters had always used the shortest route to any target.

Madeleine was to make an acquaintance with the Fields' nanny. A way of becoming familiar to the child. A request to take the little girl out of sight for a moment—just to walk with her, show her something.

Peters and the car would have been waiting. The message would have been planted in the pram. "Lucy Fields is safe. If you want to get her back unharmed *do not go to the police.* Go home. We will contact you." It was so simple it was disarming. There would be no struggle with a frightened little girl being hustled into a car by strangers. She would know Madeleine and go with her happily. And by the time the frantic nurse returned to Eaton Square, a further message would be telephoned, repeating the warning not to go to the police but to contact her employer, Logan Fields, and do exactly what he said. It was unthinkable that a responsible employee, faced with a threat to the child's life, would have done otherwise than she was told by the kidnappers.

"*Merde,*" Resnais said, repeating it angrily. "*Merde de merde!* Everything has to be changed. What are we going to do? Cancel it?"

Peters looked at him. He hesitated while the waiter set the first of three uninteresting courses down before them. A halved grapefruit with a sticky cherry in the center.

"We're going to take her tomorrow," he said. "I'll tell you how. . . ."

Chapter 4

The telephone line between Teheran and London was clearer than usual. When James Kelly got through to Eileen he could hear faintly but distinctly. It was five o'clock his time, and he had booked the call at eight that morning. He had spent a long day at the company's office, going through the figures with Logan, the chief mining engineer, and the accountant who had come out from England.

Money bored Kelly, who had not been trained in its business application. He had no flair for complicated calculations and cash flow remained a mystery which he had to pretend to understand. He dealt in people and situations; there was a residue of Foreign Office snobbery in his approach to balance sheets. Logan had a brain like a calculator; he not only understood figures but he enjoyed them. His attempts to manipulate the figures so as to justify the additional investment were fascinating, if obscure, to James.

He didn't share Logan's belief that Khorvan was serious. He was sure this was a piece of Iranian face-saving, an exercise in mischief—a gamble even—anything but a proposal which had to be met or lose Imshan.

Logan had brushed his reassurances aside.

"The bastard is out to get us," he said that morning. "I felt it in his office and I haven't changed my view. He thinks the cost of the refinery will smash the deal. It's my guess *he* suggested it. I've got to think of some bloody way round it before we go to the Shah." Kelly had felt superfluous at the meeting, which went on all that morning and into the late afternoon. He had managed to excuse himself, without Logan really noticing, so he could get home in time for the call to London. Hearing Eileen's voice made him happy.

"How are you? How was the flight?" Banal questions which had to be asked, part of the ritual of communicating through the telephone, when what he really wanted was to say how much he missed her. And how much in love he was. He could imagine her while they talked. He had a poor visual memory, but Eileen's face was perfectly clear in his mind.

"I think I'll go over and stay with my father. He hasn't seen Lucy for ages. Biddy can come with us."

"You go over to Meath," he said. "Get the ball rolling first with the solicitors, then go home. It'll do you both good. You're sure you don't need me to come back?"

"No." Her voice was grateful. "No, James. It's sweet of you, but I can manage perfectly well. I've made up my mind and it's not as bad as I thought."

James hesitated. "Can I say something?"

"Of course. Anything."

"I love you," he said. "I'm not trying to rush you, but I just want you to know. Good-bye darling, and God bless you. Will you ring me when you get to Meath?"

"I will." He could hear that her voice was unsteady. "I promise I'll call as soon as I can."

But in spite of talking to James, and having her father's instant support, Eileen couldn't sleep that night. There were moments when old habits asserted themselves and she argued that what she was doing was unnecessary. There was no real need to uproot Lucy from her home. She didn't have to wage war on Logan. She had been his wife for seven years. There must be understanding and flexibility left after all they had been to each other. He wasn't a cruel or vindictive man. Just because he had fallen in love with someone else wasn't a reason for believing him incapable of decent feelings.

And then her instincts shouted down the logic. When it came to his child, Logan had excluded her ruthlessly. He had shown no sensitivity; he regarded his daughter as his property. His obsessive love for her had condemned the little girl to a stultifying regime and denied her a full relationship with her parents. He would never let Lucy go, and no arguments or appeals would persuade him. Much of his protective love for Eileen had been diverted to the baby, she realized that too. There was no virtue now in being weak or sentimental. Logan was incapable of either.

She gave up the attempt to sleep, switched on her light, and read for most of the night. At eight the next morning she was wakened by Bridget with coffee and the newspapers. She felt worse after the few hours of uneasy rest, but at least her mind was made up.

"I have some business to do today," she told the maid. "Then I'm going back home with Lucy for a few weeks. I'd like you to come with me."

"That'd be grand, madame." Bridget looked delighted. She had left under a cloud of family disapproval. She didn't mind going back as Miss Eileen's personal maid. "I'd love to go home. When will we be going?"

"Tomorrow," Eileen said. "I'll get our tickets through Mr. Fields' office. They can send them over." At the bedroom door Bridget hesitated. She looked at Eileen sitting up in the overlarge bed. There wasn't a trace of envy in the girl's nature where Eileen was concerned. She didn't notice the handmade nightdress, the beautifully appointed room with all its overtones of luxury, the tray she had brought up from three floors down. All she saw was how pale and unhappy poor Mrs. Fields looked, with great dark rings under her eyes as if she hadn't been to sleep at all.

"There's nothing wrong, is there, ma'am?" She lapsed into the familiar Irish.

"I'll tell you about it when we get to Meath," Eileen answered. She managed to smile at her. "Don't worry, Biddy. It'll be all right."

The nanny left at midday. Peters and Madeleine were stationed in the rented car at a place in the road where they could see the front door of the house. They saw the taxi come up and the old woman go down the steps with a manservant carrying two large suitcases. Lucy Fields had not come out for a walk that morning, nor had anybody else left the house. Peters lit a cigarette while he waited for the taxi to move off.

"In a way it's worked out better," he said. "We had to gamble on the nurse not going to the police. Sure as hell the mother won't. She'll have Logan Fields back here on the next flight."

"The risks are greater," Madeleine Labouchère said. "That house is full of people."

"You're not nervous, are you?" He looked at her briefly. She shrugged. "A little. If anyone interferes we're going to have to shoot them. So long as you realize that."

"As a last resort," he said. "Resnais will do his part and we'll walk out without any trouble. Don't go anticipating it. This isn't a commando raid."

"I wish it were," she said. "I'd feel a lot easier."

Peters looked at his watch. It was ten minutes past twelve. "Okay," he said. "We've got three hours to get to the field. Resnais just walked around the corner. Let's go."

It seemed as if the butler had been waiting by the front door for them to ring. Madeleine had scarcely stepped back from pressing the bell when the door opened. Mario saw a well-dressed woman and a tall American.

"Yes?"

"Is Mrs. Fields in?" Madeleine smiled and stepped forward. She had a natural authority with servants, having been brought up with them. Mario gave way and they walked into the hall.

"Yes, madame. Who shall I say?"

"Mr. and Mrs. Lyons, from San Francisco."

"If you'll wait in the drawing room, please, I'll call Mrs. Fields. I think she's upstairs in the nursery."

"Oh, then, we'll go on up." Madeleine hooked her arm through Peters'. "I haven't seen Lucy for so long—I'm sure she's grown." She gave a dazzling smile at the butler and started up the stairs. He heard her laugh and say to her husband, "My dear—what a lot of stairs! No *wonder* Eileen keeps her figure." He had a feeling they should have been shown into the drawing room, but he didn't see how he could have prevented the lady when she was so determined and seemed to know Mrs. Fields so well. An English butler wouldn't have hesitated. Mario didn't have the tradition of that intimidating breed behind him. He decided there was nothing to worry about and went downstairs to the basement. He wanted to gloat over the hated nanny's departure with his wife and Bridget Hagan.

Eileen had Lucy by the hand. The child missed her morning walk. She pulled gently at her mother. "Park," she said.

"I'll take you this afternoon, darling," Eileen said. "You're coming down to lunch with me—that'll be fun, won't it? We'll have a lovely lunch together in the dining room." She opened the door of the day nursery and moved onto the landing. The little white gate stood open. She heard the voices first.

They were low and they came from the floor below.

"It's at the top of the house. All the better." That was a man speaking, a man with an American accent, talking very low. "We'll just take the kid and walk out."

Eileen stood very still. She felt a pull on her hand and looked at

Lucy. The child was trying to drag her forward out of the doorway. *Take the kid. . . .* Panic rushed up in her, blind and horrified. *Take Lucy. . . .* Logan had sent someone to take her child. There was no time for reason, panic won. She swung Lucy into her arms and ran back into the day nursery.

"Mummy—" the little girl began to wail, sensing terror in her mother. Eileen rushed through to the night nursery: her instinct was to put Lucy somewhere safe, to interpose solid wood between her and whomever Logan had sent to take her. She put her daughter on her bed.

"Lucy . . . darling, stay there. Stay quietly there, like a good girl. I'll be back in a minute. Here, take Teddy. . . ."

There was a key in the outside of the door. She had never noticed it before. She slammed the door and locked it. When she turned around, Peters and Madeleine Labouchère were in the room. She didn't say anything or even cry out. She stood flattened against the door behind which she had locked the child. Peters brought his right hand out of his coat and pointed Resnais' smuggled pistol at her. He spoke very quietly. Madeleine had shut the door behind them. They were enclosed in the pink and white room with all the fluffy toys standing at attention.

"Mrs. Fields? Don't make any noise, please. Just stay quite still and listen. Then you won't get hurt."

"What do you want?" Her voice came out in a whisper. "Who are you?"

"Get away from that door," Madeleine ordered. Her tone was sharper than Peters'. She saw the frightened woman guarding her child as an enemy, nothing more.

"No," Eileen said, and suddenly she heard herself loud and clear, "No. You're not going to get my child!"

Peters took a step toward her. She saw the muzzle of the gun coming closer, and she felt nothing but panic for Lucy. The nursery windows were wide open, protected by iron bars painted white so that the little girl couldn't climb up and fall out. The key bit into her palm.

She moved so quickly that neither of them realized what she had done. The key flew through the window and vanished into the street below.

Peters grabbed her by the shoulder and pulled her away from the door. She gave a wild cry and started to struggle. He jammed the gun into her neck. Madeleine wrenched at the nursery door. She swore furiously in Arabic.

"It's locked! The key—" She swung on Eileen. "Where's the key?"

"She threw it out the window," Peters said. He had his hand over Eileen's mouth.

"Shoot her," Madeleine said. "Shoot her and we can break that door down!"

"No," Peters said. "We can't get the child. If we kill her the whole operation falls to pieces. It's a full murder and kidnapping. We've got to change the plan." He spoke in Arabic. He handed the gun to Madeleine.

"Do exactly what I tell you. We're going to take the wife instead."

He spoke to Eileen, holding her tightly around the waist, pinning her arms to her sides. "Listen, Mrs. Fields. It's quite likely your child is on the other side of that door listening to us trying to get in. I'm going to take my hand away. If you cry out or make any noise at all, my friend will start shooting through that door. Do you understand?" He waited a moment, then released her. She stared at him and then the girl, aiming her gun at the nursery door. There was a sound from the other side of it. "Mummy . . . mummy!" Eileen gave a cry that was a moan of fear and anguish that only they could hear.

"Don't . . . don't, for God's sake."

"We don't want to hurt her," Peters said. "Or you, unless we have to. You've got to come with me, Mrs. Fields. You've got to do exactly as I tell you or my friend will go on firing through the door until she kills your child. Or seriously injures her."

Eileen swayed for a second. Peters caught her by the elbow. "We're going to walk out of here. We're going downstairs and into the street. My friend will wait here for exactly three minutes, and if there is no disturbance, she'll follow us. No harm will come to your child. Just so long as you cooperate."

"Logan didn't send you," Eileen whispered. "He wouldn't do this. . . . Who are you?"

"You're in the hands of the Palestine Liberation Front," Peters said. "We're taking you as a hostage." He spoke to Madeleine. "I'll leave the door open. Listen carefully. If you hear anything unusual, open fire. Give us three minutes by your watch. Then if everything has gone quietly, come down. Now," he said to Eileen, "are you ready?"

She pulled away from him. The moment of panic had passed. She felt numb and cold with terror. All she could see was the woman pointing the gun at the door. "Lucy?" She heard the woman call out softly. "Come here, come to the door. . . ." Eileen grabbed wildly at Peters. "No, no, no! I'll come with you. I'll do anything—"

He guided her out to the landing, gave her a push when she hesitated, and turned back. "You won't," she begged. "Please, you won't do it. . . ." The girl gave her a look of cold contempt. "You'd better cooperate. I have another clip of cartridges in my pocket. I'll use them all."

She went downstairs ahead of Peters. He had no gun, no means of forcing her to go with him. Upstairs, her child was a foot away from mutilation or death. On the first landing, she met Bridget coming up. The girl stood back for her, and Eileen passed without a word.

Mario was in the basement, engaged at the area door by Resnais, who was asking for directions to an address in Eaton Place. He had kept the Portuguese talking for several minutes. There was nobody in the hall. Peters moved beside her and opened the front door. Eileen stopped. "Please," she whispered. "Please call her down. I beg of you. . . ." He opened the door and they stepped out into the sunshine. Resnais was coming up the area steps. Peters took Eileen by the arm.

"Just keep calm," he said. "Nothing will happen to the child so long as you do what I tell you. Over here." There was a Ford Cortina parked on the opposite side of the road. Peters opened the back door and told her to get in. Resnais came around the other side and got into the driver's seat. Peters sat watching the front door of the Fields' house. It opened and Madeleine Labouchère came out. She went over to the car.

Peters spoke to her in Arabic. "Everything all right?"

"Yes," she said. "The child was crying. I shut the nursery door. Nobody will hear from downstairs."

"Good," he said. "Telephone and tell them to meet us at Orval instead, then go straight to Heathrow and get on a plane. Get rid of that gun. We'll meet at the rendezvous."

Resnais put the car into gear and it moved off.

"My friend is going to wait around," Peters said to Eileen. "I've told her to go back into the house and kill your child unless you do what we tell you. She won't hesitate." He saw her lean forward for a moment, covering her face with her hands. "Sit still," he said. He was paying little attention to her. There was nothing she could do. And with Madeleine left behind, nothing she would attempt.

The child was locked in her nursery. Her mother, watched by a maid, had gone out. Something had to be done, but he wasn't sure what. The servants had to be reassured that the locked door was an accident, and the only person who could do that was Eileen Fields. They shouldn't delay for long. It was twelve twenty-five. Resnais was driving in the direction of Baker Street. Peters saw a telephone box. He told the Frenchman to stop. "Mrs. Fields. . . ." He looked dispassionately into the haggard face. "Nobody must know you've been taken. I want to impress this on you. The safety of your child depends on it. And your own safety."

"I don't care what happens to me," Eileen said. "I don't care what you do to me. Just leave Lucy alone." Tears were spilling down her face.

"You'll have to telephone home," Peters said. "Make up some story that'll satisfy your staff. Say the door was locked accidentally and put someone in charge of your child. Tell them you're going to be away for a while. I'll be right beside you so don't try anything funny. Wipe your face." He gave her his handkerchief. "Okay. Now get out."

They were side by side in the telephone box. Eileen dialed her own number and he put in a coin. "Watch it," he said. "Don't try anything."

"I won't." She turned to him, holding the receiver. "All I want is for Lucy to be safe."

She asked to speak to Bridget. Terror cleared her mind. She thought quickly and with desperate cunning. Ireland. The safety of Meath House.

"Biddy? Listen, I've got to be away for a few days. Yes, it's that business I told you about. Don't worry, I'll get it sorted out. Lucy's locked herself into the nursery. No, no—don't panic, it's quite all right. She slammed the door and the lock jammed. Just get a locksmith right away. Of course I'm sure—everything's fine. But I want you to take her to Meath. The tickets are being sent over this afternoon. Let my father know you're coming and I'll be following in a day or so when I've cleared all this up. Yes, Biddy dear, it *is* about Mr. Fields. I'll explain it all when I come over. Tell Mario I've gone out of London for a few days and I'll be going direct to Ireland. There's nothing to worry about and I'll see you both soon. Look after Lucy for me."

She hung up and began to sob helplessly. Peters gave her a moment to recover. "Okay," he said. "You did okay. Come on." People were passing in the street outside. He put his arm around the weeping woman and guided her back to the car. Resnais watched them. He noticed that their prisoner had beautiful legs. He hadn't had time to examine her properly.

"Right," Peters said to him. "Drive for the field. And go steady. We don't want to be stopped for speeding."

He lit a cigarette. Eileen was leaning back beside him, with her eyes closed. Looking at her, he remembered the woman who had been on the airplane from Teheran. From the moment he had walked into the nursery that morning, he'd had a sense that he had seen her before.

Janet Armstrong was booked into a suite at the Hilton. Logan had met her at the airport and driven her to the hotel. He thought she looked sleek and elegant, wearing a white suit, with her silvered hair glinting in the late sun. He had ordered flowers for her, and she noticed them with pleasure.

"This looks like a florist's—Logan, you *are* wonderful." She came and kissed him on the mouth. He held her greedily. Even a touch and they went off like a rocket together. She pulled back from him and laughed. "Who's been suffering from night starvation? Give me a moment, darling. I'd like a drink first."

There was no fuss about her; she was as direct as a man. It was an attitude that profoundly excited him. "I've ordered champagne," he said. "After all, we've got something to celebrate."

She sat down while he opened the bottle. She slipped off her shoes and pulled her legs under her. Logan gave her a glass and she raised it to him. "To you," she said.

"To us." He sat beside her, one hand resting on her ankle. She knew that he wasn't going to waste too much time on talking. He wanted sex and this was not the moment to say she was tired. She realized with surprise that this was the first time she hadn't been completely natural.

She had refused him on other occasions if she didn't feel like going to bed, but not now. He was determined to force the issue for both of them. She understood him so well that she sensed the self-defiance in his attitude. He wanted her to celebrate with him, to show that she was as untouched by conscience as he insisted that he was himself.

She wriggled her foot and he gripped her ankle and began to massage it.

"You look tired," Janet said. He did. There were deep lines either side of his mouth, and his eyes were tired. "What's happened with Khorvan?"

Logan put his glass down. "I don't want to talk business now. I want to talk about you and me. I'm going to get a divorce."

She sipped her champagne. "Are you sure, Logan? I love you, but I don't want you to do anything you'll regret."

"It couldn't go on," he said. "Eileen faced me with it and I told her. Things have been going from bad to bloody worse for months. I'd had enough of it anyway." He poured into his glass and it frothed over.

"That's lucky," Janet said.

"I want you to marry me," Logan said.

Janet looked at him calmly. It was the most important moment of her life and she felt the frozen calm of the great gambler as the ball drops into the numbered slot that means a fortune.

"Only if you're sure you love me," she said.

"For Christ's sake," he said angrily. "You know bloody well I do. Come here."

An hour later, Logan woke. She was already up, dressed in a long jersey dress that showed her superb figure. She stood by the bedside and smiled down at him.

"You're a marvelous man, Logan. The most marvelous lover a woman ever had. I'll marry you, darling. Just don't try and get away from me!"

"It's after seven," he said. "I've asked Kelly to have dinner with us —and bring Paterson. I told them to come here."

"That'll be a gay little gathering," Janet said. She sat on the edge of the bed and held his hand. "Kelly can't stand me; he doesn't like women with minds of their own, and Paterson bores for finance."

She brought his hand up and kissed it. "They'll sit there looking stuffy and disapproving. I thought we'd spend the evening alone."

"They're good men," Logan said. He wasn't offended. If Eileen had criticized any member of the company he would have been irritated. As far as Janet was concerned, they were all part of the family.

"Kelly's done a fantastic job out here. And I need Paterson more than anyone else in Imp. at this moment. Go and run a bath for me, darling. Then I'll tell you all about it." He got out of bed and stood naked, stretching. Janet watched him, openly admiring. He had a good body, well-muscled and without surplus fat. He looked a middle-aged man at the peak of fitness and virility. Only his face showed that something fundamental had happened to him since he had left England. He looked every year of his age. Janet saw this too. She came and embraced him from behind, leaning against his shoulder. It was a moment of rare tenderness between them.

"I'm going to have a lot of children with you," she said. "I'll go and run your bath now."

Apsley Field was normally used by racegoers. It was a small privately owned airstrip within five miles of Newmarket, and during the morning a dozen light aircraft had taken off with passengers for York, where a major race meeting was being held that afternoon. The pilot of the chartered Piper Aztec was not one of the charter firm's own men. He had motored down at nine o'clock, checked in with the office, and satisfied them of his flying credentials. He was waiting in the small outer office, drinking coffee and chatting to the girl typist who sat outside. The director of the charter firm hadn't been pleased to see him. He objected to an outside pilot being brought in, but the fee for hiring the plane had been increased by a third on condition that it was flown by a pilot known to the passengers. Times were getting tighter in the charter business—the number of owners and trainers rich enough to fly themselves around England to the races was decreasing.

The pilot explained that he always flew his clients. The wife was shit scared of flying, as he put it, and she wouldn't go up with anyone else. They were rich enough to pay him whatever he asked, and he flew them and their friends to racecourses all over England and France.

"Why don't they have their own bloody plane, then?" the director said. The young man shrugged. "They have, but it's in the middle of its bloody C of A. I'll just check the ship and see if she's ready, then I'll hang around. They didn't give me an exact time. Just told me to be ready. Typical."

He settled into the outer office with the typist and passed the time smoking and making a series of easygoing passes at her. He seemed a nice, relaxed type—couldn't care less about anything. She was beginning to fancy him when one of the ground staff came up and called him.

"Your load has turned up."

"Right. Bye, sweetheart. Next time I'm round this way I'll buy you dinner. Okay?"

"You've missed most of this afternoon's meeting," she said.

"They're staying overnight. Their nag's running there tomorrow. Bye!"

"Take these," Peters said to Eileen. "Just walk alongside me, and don't do anything to attract attention. We're going on a trip. So watch yourself." He hung a pair of binoculars on her shoulder. She stared at him, holding onto the leather straps with hands that shook.

"Where are you taking me—what are these for?"

"Never mind." He had hold of her arm and was walking her briskly across the airfield. A small Cessna took off a hundred yards away from them and buzzed into the sky like a red bee. He saw their pilot coming toward them. The man waved.

"Mr. Harris? She's over here, sir. We're all ready." Resnais was behind them; she heard him whistling. During the journey from London she hadn't heard him speak once. Peters knew the pilot. He was a free lance and the organization had used him several times to ferry people and guns. He didn't belong to any political party. His only concern was money, and provided he was paid enough he would undertake anything. The original passenger schedule was for two men, one woman, and a child. Now the child was missing. He looked briefly at the woman. She looked gray with fear. The reason didn't concern him. He led them to the small six-seater plane; an airport mechanic was waiting for them. Eileen saw him watching her. For a second she was tempted to tear herself free of Peters and scream for help. As if he read her thoughts, he hurried her to the steps. The mechanic had moved away. The few seconds' hesitation had cost her the chance.

She climbed up ahead of Peters and went inside the plane. He pushed her roughly to a seat and sat beside her.

"Fasten your belt," he said. She didn't move. It was too late now. Too late to save herself. He leaned over and pulled the webbing safety belt around her, buckling it tightly. The Frenchman sat behind them.

Eileen held tightly to the seat arms as the engines revved and caught and the plane began to taxi to the runway. As they took off she hid her face in her hands. Peters watched her, anticipating hysteria or collapse. He had seen that look exchanged with the mechanic and guessed that she was a hairline away from calling for help. But shock had slowed her reactions, paralyzing the will to resist. It wouldn't have lasted at their original destination, the airport at Nice, with Customs and Immigration, and people surrounding them. She would never have gone through without raising the alarm, whatever he threatened. His organization had been geared to carrying a child of three who had been added to Madeleine's false passport. Now the details had been changed. Ostensibly the plane was bound for York, where it would stay overnight and return the following day. There was no radio at Apsley Field, so that once airborne the plane's movements would be unnoticed. Twenty-five miles at the back of Nice, in a small valley at Orval, there was a field where the British had landed agents and supplies in the latter stages of the war. Peters had simply changed instructions to the pilot and Madeleine would have phoned through to alter the arrangements for meeting them on landing. The car that should have taken him, Madeleine, Resnais, and Lucy Fields away from Nice airport would now be diverted to the secret landing field and a supply of petrol brought to refuel the plane for its return journey. He turned to Resnais.

"Come and sit here for a minute." They exchanged places. Resnais eased himself into the seat beside Eileen. He buckled the safety belt and turning around, deliberately looked at her. She seemed sick and frightened, but she was still attractive. It amused him to frighten her even more. Eileen saw the appraising look and the slight smile on his mouth. She edged against the wall of the plane to avoid touching him.

"I am Resnais," he said. "I shall be looking after you."

Peters came back. For a moment Eileen thought he would leave the Frenchman where he was and take the seat behind them. She didn't realize it, but she gave the American a look of agonized appeal.

"Thanks," he said. He stood over Resnais and the Frenchman got up and resumed his former seat. Peters didn't look at Eileen Fields. Resnais had been upsetting her, and he was irritated. It wouldn't help to have a hysterical outburst during the flight. He spoke over his shoulder to Pierre. "Did you bring that flask with you?"

"Yes. It's here."

"Give it to me."

He unscrewed the top and passed it to Eileen. "It's brandy. Drink some."

"I don't want it." She shook her head and turned away.

"It isn't drugged," Peters said. "It'll steady you. Do as you're told. Drink it."

She sipped and then swallowed. He took the flask and put it to his mouth.

"Where are we going?" she asked him.

"France," Peters said. "That's all you're going to know, so don't ask any more questions. And the pilot's working for us, so you needn't try anything there. You can just relax, Mrs. Fields. Make the best of it. So long as you're sensible, nobody will hurt you."

He spoke calmly. The brandy had helped her; she wasn't so sickly white. He didn't know whether she believed him and he didn't care. In a way he admired her quickness in saving the child. It was just unfortunate for her that she had been so brave.

Chapter 5

Colonel Ardalan read through the report a second time. It was brief; it informed him that the telephone number found in the murdered Ibrahimi's trouser pocket had been traced to an apartment block on Torshab Road. The apartment had been rented by an American archaeological student named Peters. He had been living there with a woman and had left the previous week, paying his rent up to date. So far as the landlord was concerned the American had been an ideal tenant. The neighbors told the investigator that he had entertained few visitors, most of them seemed to be Iranians. But one woman remembered seeing a car with diplomatic plates. There were no noisy parties, nothing during his tenancy that had aroused suspicion. It was all very neat and tidy. Too neat and too tidy. It looked as if this unknown American had gone out of his way to avoid attention. Ardalan blew smoke rings and played with the sheets of typed paper. Peters' only visitors were Iranians. Except for the car with CD plates. He rang for his assistant and ordered his car brought around. Half an hour later they were sitting in the flat of the neighbor who had seen the CD car.

She was a woman in her mid-thirties, already too fat, with four children shouting in the background. Ardalan was patient and polite. He could see she was frightened and could easily be persuaded to say anything.

He asked her when she had seen the car. Her answer was vague—sometime in the last two weeks, maybe less. It hadn't stopped by her flat; she was looking out of the window—her flat was on the ground floor, and she had seen it draw up far down on the opposite side of the road and a man get out. She was surprised when he crossed over and came into the flat.

"Naturally," the colonel said, "you were curious. How do you know he went to Peters' flat?"

"Because I opened my front door and saw him go upstairs. I heard the American's voice. He said, 'Hello, Homsi. Come in.'"

"Homsi," the colonel repeated. "Thank you. That's very helpful. Do you remember if this man Homsi ever came again—or had been before? Did you recognize him?"

"No," the woman said. "I'd know him again if I saw him. He only came that one time. So far as I can tell." She glanced nervously at Ardalan, who smiled at her. He had a way of reassuring people. He stood up. "You've done well," he said. "Very well. Now understand one thing: You mustn't speak about this to anyone. You may tell your husband that we have been here, but what you told us is to be kept secret. Otherwise you will both be in great trouble. You understand that?"

She nodded, too frightened to speak.

"Great trouble," Ardalan repeated. "But if you are silent, and do what I tell you, you will be rewarded. Tell your husband so. We are going now, but I shall come again."

In the car on the way back to his office he turned to his assistant. His name was Sabet, and he had graduated from civilian police work to Ardalan's special political branch.

"Homsi," the colonel murmured. "What nationality does that suggest to you?" He paused in thought. "It could be Syrian, though—a man from Homs."

"Any Arab country really."

"Syrian. Yes, I think it could be Syrian. They are always involved with terrorism. How stupid to use a car with CD plates."

"People get careless. He didn't think anyone would notice."

"The woman said he only came once. I think it was more recent than she remembers. Otherwise she wouldn't have such a clear picture in her mind."

"She says she can identify him," Sabet said.

Ardalan smiled. "We will go through our list of members of the Syrian Embassy. We will see if we can find this Homsi."

* * *

Logan and James Kelly were on their way to the Ministry of Economics. Their appointment with Minister Khorvan was at ten thirty. To Kelly's relief, Janet Armstrong was not with them. The chief accountant, Ian Paterson, was sitting in front with the driver. The pale-blue Rolls-Royce slid through the traffic down Shah Reza Avenue. It was baking with heat at that hour. The air conditioning was full on inside the sealed car.

"Half the cost," Logan said. "We can start with that."

Kelly saw Paterson's face in the driver's mirror. It looked grim and disapproving. "He'll turn it down," James said. He felt gloomy himself, and irritable. He had put in a call to London early that morning and been told that Eileen had gone to Ireland. He didn't know the number and had no way of finding out. He could only hope she would contact him. He was prepared to quarrel with the minister because he couldn't vent his feelings on Logan. Or that bloody woman, stuck up under all their noses. He really hated Janet Armstrong, and he hadn't been trying to hide it. Whenever he saw her asserting herself in the meetings, which Logan insisted she attend, James' temper began to seethe. She was so sure of herself, so competent. He couldn't fault her opinions either, and this angered him more. Logan spent every evening out of the house. He hadn't suggested bringing Janet there, and James was thankful for that much tact. But he came back in the small hours, and twice he didn't return at all. He looked tired, and taut with nervous tension. By comparison the woman looked triumphant and serene.

"He'll turn it down," he repeated. Logan looked at him, frowning. "So you've just said. All right, he turns it down. This is a bloody poker game. He wants to get the top out of us and we know we can't pay it. Not until we've had more time to work on the figures. So we play for that time."

"No amount of time will make that a viable proposition." Paterson, an outspoken Scot, turned around in the front seat.

"It can't be done," he said. "And no board would sanction it. We'd be paying them for the right to bring their oil to the surface, and getting nothing out of it ourselves."

Logan leaned forward a little. "You let me worry about the board. We're not going to lose this field. No matter how tough the deal."

"I was thinking," Kelly said, "that in view of the importance to Western economy, we might consider asking for joint American and English subsidies."

"We daren't bring in the Americans," Logan said, "or we'd risk losing the deal to Exxon. As for getting anything out of our present government—you must be joking! When have they ever supported business interests? The bloody Civil Service thinks profit is a dirty word; wouldn't be any better if we had the other lot in power either. I'd go to Japan before I started farting round Whitehall." He hunched himself back into the upholstery. His expression was truculent. Kelly decided to let his condemnation of the Civil Service pass unchallenged. He knew Logan in this kind of mood, and nothing was going to get him out of it until he saw Khorvan. "In fact," Logan said suddenly, "that might not be a bad idea. Japan is starving for oil. They are literally dependent on oil and haven't got a barrel—and they've got plenty of money. They might be the people to enter into agreement with us over Imshan."

Kelly didn't want to admire him but he couldn't help it. Logan had this genius for throwing off ideas, for seeing a solution which was so simple it was ridiculous that someone else hadn't thought of it first. But they never did. It needed Logan's unique combination of ruthless logic and dashing inspiration. Ian Paterson had twisted around in his seat again and was looking at his chairman, his mouth pursed. He could hardly be described as a man given to quick enthusiasms.

"Japan might be a possibility," he conceded. Logan ignored him. He was furious with Paterson for emphasizing the difficulties that he already knew. The reference to his dependence on the London board would rankle for a long time. Democratic processes like voting at board meetings didn't appeal to him. His authority and his methods usually assured him of getting his own way. Kelly had seen him once chairing an annual meeting, which happened to coincide with the second Arab-Israeli war, and been mesmerized by his approach to opposition. The rare smile, the genial wit, and above all the overbearing sense that he knew what was best, had silenced critics from the floor and given him a complete mandate to meet the crisis as he thought fit. It was a different man from the brusque, autocratic chairman of the giant oil company, or the husband of Eileen who was not quite a gentleman at home in Eaton Square. There were so many facets to him— none of them appealing to Kelly—and yet he was fascinated. He could afford to be, without that unpleasant feeling of being patronized. He was going to marry Logan's wife. He didn't know how long it would take; he was just certain that it was going to happen. The car drew up outside the Ministry and they got out.

In his first-floor office, Khorvan told his secretary to keep them waiting. He had a cup of Turkish coffee he wanted to finish, also he was hoping to irritate Logan Fields by the discourtesy. He wondered what solution, if any, they had thought of to his impossible proposal.

A refinery costing another three hundred million dollars. Khorvan smiled as he drained the tiny silver cup. Actually, he thought it was a better idea than the high standard of township and amenities which were already in the terms. His people didn't need swimming pools and recreational centers. They wouldn't appreciate luxuries that were unrelated to their experience of life. Food, money, and a woman. That was the basic requirement of the Iranian worker. Add a corner of land to till, no matter how dry and backbreaking, and you had satisfied the peasant. It would take years of reeducation to change the attitudes of his people, and Khorvan despised the instant methods practiced by the West. All that resulted was waste and corruption. America had poured out billions in foreign aid after the last war, and only intensified the envy and contempt of those they imagined they were indoctrinating. Khorvan believed that the slow process of Marxist socialism provided the only solution to the underdeveloped peoples of the world.

He had sent a message to the trade secretary of the Soviet Union, telling him to delay the departure of the Russian technical team which had been hanging around Teheran for weeks, hoping negotiations between the government and Imperial Oil would come to grief. When his demands were not met, and he knew that Logan Fields was capable of bluffing till the last moment, he could gently reintroduce the Russians. He hoped profoundly that Fields could be induced to offer him a bribe. That would establish the purity of his motives when he exposed the offer to the Shah. He intended to hint that a gift might influence him. He pressed the buzzer for his secretary. The same beautiful girl came in. She was not Khorvan's mistress, although the idea occurred to him when he wasn't too busy. He admired her elegant dress and saw the expectant gleam in her eyes.

"Send in the gentlemen from Imperial Oil," he said. He lit a cigarette and stood up, holding out his hand to Logan Fields. Chairs were disposed for them, and Logan took the one nearest Khorvan's desk. Kelly sat next to him, with Ian Paterson on his left. Khorvan smiled politely at Logan. "My apologies for keeping you," he said. "I was very occupied. Tell me, how is your beautiful wife?"

"I'm afraid she had to go back to England," Logan said. "Our daughter wasn't well."

"Oh?" The minister looked annoyed. He had accepted an invitation to the party James was giving for him and he expected to find Eileen there. Her absence was quite irrelevant, but it gave him an opportunity to be offended. James felt his muscles stiffen in anticipation. Logan shouldn't have mentioned it. He hadn't thought to warn him.

He heard Logan say smoothly, "Of course, she's coming back to be at your party, Minister. She wouldn't miss the chance to entertain you."

"I look forward to meeting her again." Khorvan bowed his head politely.

"And now," Logan said, "my colleagues and I have been examining your proposals. Ian, have you got the folder? I'd like you to keep this, Minister, and after our meeting this morning, perhaps you'd find the time to study the financial breakdown in terms of the investment as a whole. I must say now that we haven't been able to meet your demand for the total cost of the refinery."

Khorvan leaned back. It was as if a shutter had closed on them.

"Equally," the strong voice went on, "we've come up with an idea for cost sharing between the Iranian government and ourselves. Ian, I leave this part of it to you."

Kelly watched Logan. He lit a cigarette, leaving his massive gold case on the minister's desk. He had never appeared more relaxed. His retrieval of the mistake about Eileen had been instant and faultless. Kelly had spent a lot of time over the last three years trying to understand Logan Fields. He had seen his bad temper, his intolerance and arrogance, his gift for coping with difficulties. But until now he hadn't appreciated how Logan glittered in adversity. He was like a great actor seizing and subduing an unplayable part. Combined with his ability to assume a role was the cold-blooded nerve of the born gambler.

Imshan was in jeopardy. The greatest coup of Logan's career was menaced by the hostility and greed of the minister. That was Logan's view, and the more he observed the minister's tactics, the more Kelly was unhappily inclined to agree. But Logan was neither worried nor discouraged. What Kelly saw that morning, during the slow, frustrating negotiation which all knew was already doomed to fail, was a man enjoying every moment of the game. It might well be that Khorvan had met his match.

"There are three Homsi or Al Homsis in the Embassy," the colonel said.

Sabet nodded.

"A trade attaché, a passport officer, and one of the military staff. I went back to see the woman again and she described the man she saw as being very thin with a full head of hair. The military attaché is short and fat; the passport officer is bald."

"So it looks like trade, then," Ardalan remarked. "We mustn't make a mistake. We have photographs of all three in our files. Show them to the woman and see if she can identify any one of them. The name Homsi might not be genuine, we have to consider that. But we have an interesting situation, don't you agree?"

"Very interesting," Sabet said.

Ardalan passed him a cigarette. "A man is murdered for no motive, and that means the only motive was to shut his mouth. He is some kind of political activist, and he happens to be passing drinks at a reception given for the minister of economics and the chairman of Imperial Oil. He carries the telephone number of an American archaeological student living in Teheran. This archaeologist blends so well into the background that he is unlike any American I've ever known. His friends are Iranian. And one Syrian from the Embassy. Go and take those photographs over to Torshab Road. I want an answer today."

Sabet went out, and Ardalan finished his cigarette. It was a jigsaw puzzle without pieces. His difficulty was to find the pieces before he could attempt to solve the puzzle. It might well be that the visitor to the apartment that night was not a Syrian. That left him with the American, Peters, and the girl who was living with him. Police records cleared them both. Neither had any suspect connections. Peters came from France via West Germany. West Germany. Ardalan didn't know why this worried him, but it did. He called the aliens section and asked for the report on Peters to be sent up. There would be nothing in it; he had already read the single sheet through. A graduate student of archaeology, intending to help with the dig at Persepolis. There were dozens of foreigners participating.

The paper was laid in front of him. Everything was in order. Peters had left Munich on March 28. *Munich.* That was what had set off the alarm bells in his mind. There had been reports of a top-level Palestinian terrorist meeting in the city. Interpol had been alerted. The watch on airports and Israeli embassies had been increased for some weeks in expectation of bomb attacks. March 28. It was the right time. The colonel sent for the details on Madeleine Labouchère. Age twenty-five, French citizen domiciled in Paris. Nothing suspicious there. Only her relationship with the American. The colonel was frowning, tapping each finger in turn against his thumb. He wondered how long Sabet would be. At a quarter to four the assistant knocked and came into the office. He placed a blown-up photograph, obviously the work of a hidden photographer, in front of the colonel.

"Saiid Homsi, trade attaché. She identified him at once."

For a moment Ardalan said nothing. He looked up at his assistant and down again at the photograph. "There was no doubt? No doubt at all?"

"None," Sabet said. "I showed her all three photographs and asked her to point to anyone she recognized. She chose Homsi without looking at the others. 'That's the man who came here.' That was what she said."

"Trade attaché," Ardalan murmured. "The head of espionage in an embassy usually hides in the passport section. Very well. We will have to talk to this Saiid Homsi."

"How?" the assistant asked. "How, without causing an incident?"

Ardalan leaned back and rubbed his forehead with one thin hand. Black hairs grew profusely on the back of it and crept under his sleeve.

"There is only one way," he said. "And I have to satisfy myself that it is justified. Then I will get the authorization. Until then we will set a nonstop watch on Homsi."

The villa was built on a rock. It was poised above the sea, surrounded by a two-acre garden, ringed on the shore side by a ten-foot wire fence. It was a long, low building, dazzling white, shaded by palm trees and giant pines. A huge purple bougainvillea sprawled over the front wall. They had locked Eileen in a room on the first floor overlooking the sea.

The landing at the field in the country had been a nightmare. The little plane bumped and shuddered and she was thrown violently forward; the seat belt saved her from being flung out of the seat. She had given a scream of terror, and felt the American grab her. She was dragged out of the plane, trembling and dazed, hustled by Peters across the grass at a run which brought her stumbling down, her high-heeled shoe turning under her. He had been extremely rough in his handling of her; he almost threw her into the back of the car. The Frenchman jumped in on the other side. A man was in the driver's seat and they swung off onto the road. The American leaned over and took something from the driver. She heard them speaking in a language she couldn't understand. He sat back and pointed a gun at her side. There was no expression on his face.

"If you make any attempt to attract attention, or do anything stupid, I'll kill you. Just sit perfectly quiet. You understand?"

"Yes," Eileen whispered. She had tried to identify the coast when they left the country roads and started on the road by the shore. It was very warm, and the sea was the bright Mediterranean blue; there were palm trees. They came into a big resort. Beach umbrellas and sunbathers, people sitting on the terraces of smart hotels. Several times they stopped at traffic lights and, as the car halted, the gun was rammed into her side. She recognized a magnificent hotel on the left —it was the Negresco. She and Logan had stayed there twice soon after they were married. They were driving through Nice.

They arrived at the villa some twenty minutes later. The tall gates swung open, and they drove up a palm-lined drive. When the car stopped, the Frenchman got out first. He stretched in the sunshine and yawned. Peters nudged her. "Outside." He had put the gun away. When she stood in the drive she felt as if she were going to faint. She clung to the car door for support and the Frenchman put an arm around her waist.

"Come inside," he said pleasantly. Peters came up beside them.

"Leave her alone," he said. He took Eileen by the arm. The villa was cool and spacious. The ground floor was open plan and luxuriously furnished, and an expensive modern abstract covered the far wall. The American walked her up a marble staircase and along a corridor. The room was simply furnished, with a bed and a chest and single armchair. There was wire mesh over the window. He came inside with her and let go of her arm.

"You'll stay here," he said. "There's a bathroom through there. Make no trouble and nobody will hurt you."

"Wait—" Eileen turned to him. "Wait—please. What are you going to do? Why have you taken me—"

Peters closed the door. He searched through his pockets and brought out a flattened pack of cigarettes. He lit one. "You look beat," he said. "Sit down."

She sat on the bed, watching him. "What do you hope to gain?" Eileen said. "I don't understand. I've never even been to Palestine."

"We haven't got anything against you," Peters said. "We were going to take your child. She wouldn't have come to any harm. We're reasonable people." He drew on his cigarette. He didn't offer one to her.

"Reasonable? You call kidnapping a little child reasonable? You'd have shot me in that car if I'd made a sound, wouldn't you?"

"Yes," he answered. "We have a job to do, and nothing must interfere with it. As far as you're concerned, Mrs. Fields, it was your bad luck to be there and get taken instead. We're not interested in you, but we can use you. Alive or dead won't make any difference, so don't get clever. I'll bring you something to eat."

He went out and she heard the door being locked. She got off the bed and stood looking around her. She went to the window first. It opened inward, secured by a catch on the wall. The wire mesh covering it outside was rigid and showed a view of blue sea with a curve of coastline bending from the right. It was impossible to see below. Eileen went into the bathroom leading off the bedroom and found another window, also protected. This showed the same line of coast continuing around. The house overlooked a bay, and the right-hand promontory connected with the mainland. There was no skylight in the bathroom, which was small and plainly equipped. From the glimpse she had caught of the interior, the room chosen for her was in the servants' quarters. She paused by the bathroom mirror, shocked by her appearance. She looked haggard and disheveled. There was a streak of dirt on her face, smudged by tears. She washed in cold water. There was no soap and no towel. She dried herself on the bedcover. The room was very hot and airless and she lay on the bed exhausted. She was almost asleep when she heard the door open. The American came in, carrying a tray. He put it down on the dressing table.

"You'll get three meals a day," he said. "And if you need anything, you can ask Madeleine. She'll come up and take this away."

Eileen sat up. "If that's the woman who threatened to murder my child, don't send her near me. I wouldn't ask her for anything!"

Peters shrugged. "Suit yourself. Resnais can come up to you."

Alarm flared in her. She didn't know why, but she didn't want the Frenchman coming into the room alone. "No! No, not him. You're in charge of this. I hold you responsible."

Peters had no intention of wasting time with her. To him she was dehumanized—an object rather than a person. He meant to put the tray down and go out. The use of that one word stopped him. Responsible. He looked at her.

"I'm not responsible for anything about you, Mrs. Fields, except seeing that you don't escape. And you're in no position to dictate who comes up here and who doesn't."

She got off the bed and faced him. "You've kidnapped me," she said. "You've dragged me here by force and you're holding me for some purpose that I know nothing about. By the grace of God, it's not my little girl that's locked up here. How exactly would you have treated her?"

"As fairly as we'll treat you," Peters said. "So long as you behave yourself."

She turned away from him. The eyes were so cold. For a moment she had been angry enough to challenge him, but there had been no response. It was like confronting a machine. She began to cry. "There's no soap," she said. "And no towels. I had to dry with the counterpane. I've no clothes, not even a comb! I don't want your food —I won't eat anything!"

"Suit yourself." He went out and locked the door.

She cried for some time, until she had worn herself out. There was a carafe of water on the tray and she was very thirsty. She drank most of it, leaving the food untouched. The outburst had relieved her; she felt clear-headed, and personal fear was minimized by the immense relief that she had saved Lucy. Logan wouldn't have expected her to act so quickly. Throwing the key out the window had been an instant reflex. Everything she had done since they confronted her in the nursery was dictated by the need to protect her child. She had gone out of the house, driven through the streets, entered the plane. When the American mentioned Madeleine, she had instinctively connected the name with the woman who had threatened to empty her pistol through that nursery door. His admission that it was the same person hadn't sunk in for a time. But now she knew it meant that there was no more danger to Lucy. They were all together in the villa. She had no one to fear for now but herself.

Eileen went back to the tray. Her stomach knotted against the idea of eating. There was cold meat, butter and bread, piled on one plate. Probably there was no one besides the three kidnappers in the villa. Then she remembered the driver. The Palestine Liberation Front. That was what he had said. Arab terrorists. The driver had been very dark-skinned, certainly not European. She forced herself to eat the bread and butter. She had a vague idea of conserving her strength without knowing why. She believed herself to be quite calm, and in one sense she was. In another, her whole body was quivering with shock, and in spite of the heat she felt clammy and cold. She went to the window again and hooked her fingers through the mesh. It was fixed to the outside wall and didn't yield when she tried to pull it. They had made their preparations very carefully. Which meant that Lucy's kidnapping had been planned some time ahead. But why Lucy? Why her? Facing the bright-blue sea through the steel mesh, Eileen understood that the reason lay in her connection with Logan Fields. And through Logan, Imperial Oil. But why? The question hammered at her, making her head ache. What had Logan or the company done—or what could the terrorists hope to gain by holding her? Their original target had been Lucy. That was a clue. A child held as hostage. But against what? It must be money. A large sum from the oil company. . . . She heard the door open again and swung around. The woman stood inside. She was casually dressed in a white shirt and dark-blue slacks. She looked like a smart holidaymaker.

"Have you finished?" Madeleine was a French name, but she wasn't French. The eyes were green, but there was a dark tinge to the skin that was stronger than sunburn. Eileen remembered her at Lucy's door, calling the little girl to come into range.

"I told him not to send you up here," she said. "Get out! Take your filthy food and get out!"

The girl laughed. "You won't be so full of fight in a few days. Think yourself lucky you're not shut up in the cellars. That's where I'd have put you!"

Eileen looked at her. The sneer was fading on the girl's face as she met the contempt and disgust of the older woman.

"You'd have murdered a child," she said slowly. "You'd be capable of anything. You're not even a woman." She turned back to the window. Without knowing it, she had said the one thing to which Madeleine was vulnerable. She had denied her identity as a female.

She didn't see the blaze of hate directed at her as the girl took the tray and went out. To be less than a woman was the ultimate insult to a Lebanese, however liberated and equal with men she thought herself to be. Peters had told her to bring the prisoner soap and a towel. An impulse of feminine spite had made her ignore this. It irritated her that he should pay the woman's needs any attention. Let her do without the amenities. There weren't any luxuries in the refugee camps. She went back downstairs, dumped the tray in the kitchen, and found only Resnais in the lounge. He looked up at her and grinned.

"How is our charming guest?"

"Insolent! And arrogant. . . ." Madeleine settled into one of the white sofas. The owner of the villa was an Algerian millionaire with strong terrorist connections. He had a passion for white.

"I'll deal with her if she gives any trouble," the girl said. Her expression was vicious and sulky. Resnais watched with amusement. Women never surprised him when they displayed cruelty. The idea that because they bore children they were more compassionate and squeamish than men was a myth. Women were capable of absolute savagery, provided the motive was strong enough. There was a thread of female dislike between Madeleine and the hostage which had nothing to do with politics.

"Where's Peters?"

"Out on the terrace."

"I don't think that room is safe enough," she said. "I think we should put her down in the cellars."

The Frenchman lit a cigarette. "She must have really made you angry," he said. "I wonder what she said?"

Madeleine swore at him and jumped up. He watched her go out in search of Peters and his laughter followed her.

James Kelly's solicitors had never heard from Eileen. That was the first result of a series of telephone calls he undertook after days went by and he had heard nothing from her. This in itself worried him badly. She had promised to protect herself and Lucy. All he knew from their London staff was that she was away, staying in Ireland. A second call to Eaton Square elicited the telephone number of Meath House, and began the incredible frustrations of attempting to link one erratic line of communication with another equally unpredictable.

James' anxiety was based on his fear that she might have decided to try for a reconciliation. He had no reason for supposing that Logan would agree, or that the influence of Janet Armstrong was not stronger every time they met. It was just a nagging fear that his hopes were going to be disappointed, and because of the distance between him and Eileen, there was nothing he could do. Ireland and its telephone system defeated him for a full twenty-four hours. He had agreed to take the call at any time. If Logan was in the house it couldn't be helped. James doubted if he would have noticed or cared. All his energies and concentration were bent on the problem of reaching a solution that would safeguard their concession at Imshan. Paterson, the finance director, had already been dispatched to Tokyo to sound out the Japanese oil importers. A favorable response would bring Logan himself flying out.

Time was not on their side. As Logan pointed out in one explosive meeting, there was a board meeting scheduled for two weeks' time in London. Something had to be presented to them which would pass; if the present situation became known, there would be opposition that might defeat even Logan's persuasive powers. They had to have some indication of solid financial support from the Japanese before a whisper of the outrageous demand for the refinery reached London.

Equally, the Iranian government had to be assured that Imperial Oil was working on the problem and was optimistic about an acceptable solution. Added to which the British Embassy in Teheran had informed James privately, through the unofficial channel open to an ex-Foreign Office member, that the Russian technicians were still in the city, and were remaining on advice from Khorvan himself.

That night the party in honor of the minister was taking place at

James' house. He had left the office after lunch to supervise the arrangements, and was asking Logan what explanation could be given for Eileen's absence when Logan took a call from Tokyo, and there was no question of interrupting him. James had a flair for giving parties. He had learned the art in embassies abroad, when his help had been enlisted by various official wives. He had an instinct for entertaining people which caused a lot of envy among his bachelor colleagues. It was often said that James didn't need a wife to make a party go. He had decided to hold the reception in the garden. A lot of extra plants and potted shrubs had been brought in; there were two big tables set under the trees, crates of whiskey, gin, and champagne, and quantities of fresh fruit juice for the teetotalers among their Iranian guests. As a compliment to the guest of honor, the floral arrangements were in the Iranian national colors of green, red, and white. As a bonus, and again through the good offices of the British Embassy, James had organized a display of fireworks to climax the evening. He had checked everything and decided there was time to have a leisurely bath and change even before Logan returned, when the houseboy told him there was a telephone call.

Hoping it might be the call to Ireland, James raced back to the house. It was an unfamiliar voice, heavily accented.

"Mr. Kelly? Good evening. My name is Saiid Homsi. I am from the Syrian Embassy."

James scowled. He had no contact with the Syrians and no wish to establish one. He had really thought it might be Ireland. . . .

"Yes." His tone was not encouraging. "What can I do for you?"

"I think there is something I can do for *you,*" the caller said. "I have some very important information for your Mr. Fields."

"In that case," James said, "I suggest you speak directly to him."

"Unfortunately I cannot do that. It might be dangerous. I need your help, Mr. Kelly."

James hesitated. *Dangerous.* He didn't like that word. "I don't understand," he said. "Can you explain, please. Do you want me to pass a message to Mr. Fields?"

"No," the man said. "No, I have to speak to him myself. Believe me, it is very important. I have something to tell Mr. Fields and the matter is personal. Very delicate. Would it be possible to meet him at your reception this evening?"

"Mr. Homsi, I don't believe we've met. What is your position in the Embassy? And why can't you make an appointment with Mr. Fields in his office?" James was listening carefully. He spoke calmly, trying to decide what to do. Orientals loved intrigue, but this was extreme.

"I am a poor attaché here, Mr. Kelly. I am not an important person. But my message for Mr. Fields *is*. I cannot be seen to approach him; all of us are watched here by Colonel Ardalan's men. What I have to tell Mr. Fields can only be whispered in his ear in a public place like your party. May I present myself tonight?"

"Yes," James said. For a moment he had hesitated. "Yes, please come. Introduce yourself to me and I will bring you to Mr. Fields." He heard a murmured "thank you" and then the line buzzed clear.

By the time he was ready to receive his guests he had thought of a dozen possibilities for the extraordinary call and rejected them all. He wished profoundly that it had no connection with the Syrians. They were the least-welcome embassy in Teheran, and the object of suspicion to the secret police as a headquarters for subversives.

He was surprised to learn from the servants that Logan had not returned to change. The explanation was obvious, but it infuriated him. He had gone to bring Janet to the party. Entertaining her—seeing her in Eileen's place—was going to tax his good manners very hard. When Logan's car swept up to the front door twenty minutes before the party was due to begin, he deliberately went to the bar and got himself a drink. When he turned around, Janet Armstrong was advancing on him. She looked very cool and smart, wearing a long dress of pale green. He saw a handsome emerald and diamond brooch on her shoulder and guessed it came from Logan. Logan was behind her.

"Congratulations," she said. "It all looks marvelous. Doesn't it, Logan? You certainly manage well without a wife!"

James gave her a look of plain dislike. "What will you have to drink? Logan?"

"Scotch," was the answer. "Soda and plenty of ice." Janet came back and hooked her arm through Logan's. "I'll have the same," she said. James gave the houseboy the order, and a waiter came forward with the glasses on a tray. A silence hung over the three of them. James made no attempt to break it. To hell with his diplomatic training. He hated the woman and he despised Logan for flaunting their relationship. Logan either didn't notice or couldn't be bothered to make conversation.

Janet faced James and smiled. She knew he disliked her, although she had no idea it was more than male antipathy toward a successful woman. His opinion didn't interest her. He was extremely clever and Logan thought highly of him but he wasn't her type. He was too much a gentleman. She liked a little roughness around the edges. She hugged Logan tightly for a moment and then let him go. They had been to bed before coming, and she felt very close to him.

"It's a lovely evening," she said. "I'm sure the party will be a great success." Logan would expect her to carry the situation, and she was too self-confident to be outfaced by James. "I expect it'll be a bit of a drinking marathon, so I'd better eat some of those delicious things over there." She walked over to the table and began to pick among the canapés.

James went over to Logan. He had decided to tell him about the telephone call and give him the choice of meeting the man or not. Logan listened, sipping his whiskey.

"What the hell can it be? We've never touched the Syrians with a ten-foot pole. Have you any idea, James?"

"None," James said. "But if you're going to talk to him you'd better be very careful. This might be some game thought up by Khorvan; something they could use with the Shah to discredit us."

"Trafficking with subversives. . . . Could be. But if I don't talk to him I might be making a mistake. And he doesn't seem anxious to compromise himself, either. Otherwise he'd have come to the office. I'd better talk to him and find out what it's all about."

"All right," James said. He could see Janet walking back to them. "But I think you ought to safeguard yourself. I've asked Ardalan tonight. He loves parties; he came to the other one. I'll mention this to him. That way no one can accuse you of going behind the government's back."

"Right. Do that. If this is some trick of Khorvan's it'll blow up in his face." Janet came and stood beside him.

James saw the first car coming into the main drive.

"Have you heard from Eileen?" he said.

"No," Logan answered. "And I don't expect to. Janet will look after Khorvan. But the news from Tokyo is very encouraging."

"Oh." James showed no enthusiasm.

"Paterson called this afternoon—you were there, weren't you?—anyway he said he's had strong support from the importers. He's seeing the deputy prime minister the day after tomorrow. If he gives his blessing I'll fly out and see the prime minister next week. I'm bloody hopeful, James. I think we're going to pull it off!"

"You will if anyone can," Janet said. They stood together to receive the guests. It seemed to James as though Eileen Fields had never existed. He decided quite calmly, while talking to a director of the Bank of Iran, that he really hated Logan.

Soon after seven he saw Colonel Ardalan in the crowd. He had brought his pretty wife with him although Iranians tended to leave their women at home when attending European parties. James went up to him and the two men shook hands. They had met on many occasions, and James found the colonel an attractive personality. It was difficult to believe the stories about his savage methods.

"A charming party, Mr. Kelly," Ardalan said. His wife nodded and smiled. She didn't speak good English and was shy of exposing it.

"Thank you," James said. "Could we have a word in private—just over here?" They stood together under a plane tree which Iranians call the chenar. There was no one near them.

"Something rather unusual has come up," James explained. "My chairman felt you ought to know about it. He's very anxious not to do anything contrary to the wishes of the government."

"Naturally," the colonel said. "Please let me help in any way I can. What is this unusual occurrence?"

"I received a telephone call. From a man calling himself Saiid Homsi. Says he's an attaché at the Syrian Embassy."

"I've heard of him," Ardalan said mildly. "What did he want?"

"To come here and speak to Mr. Fields. Privately. He said he had something to tell him. Mr. Fields felt he'd better see the man and find out what it's all about, but we wanted you to know."

"I appreciate that," the colonel said. "I wish more of our European expatriates showed such good sense. And goodwill." He smiled at James. "My function is to protect the state, Mr. Kelly. I am also happy to protect our friends, whoever they may be. Syrians are dangerous people. Let Mr. Fields see this man and then if you will tell me what he wanted, that would be the wisest way."

"We'll do that," James said.

Colonel Ardalan laid a hand on his shoulder for a moment. "I hear rumors," he said, "that your negotiations for Imshan are not proceeding smoothly. I hope you won't be discouraged. His Imperial Majesty wants a British firm to develop the oil field."

"I'm very happy to hear that," James answered. "Minister Khorvan drives a hard bargain. We are trying to meet his terms."

"I hope you succeed," Ardalan said. "I see him over there. Talking to the lady in the green dress."

"Yes," James said. "She's the chairman's assistant."

"I don't see Mrs. Fields," the colonel said.

"She's in England." James moved away, the colonel following.

"As soon as this man Homsi makes himself known, I'll take him over to Mr. Fields. I'll let you know what happens."

"I will be obliged," the colonel said. He went back to join his wife.

The party was going under its own impetus. The garden was

crowded and there was a roar of conversation. People were eating the canapés, and waiters with trays of drinks slipped in and out. James stood aside and listened. It was a success. Logan had Khorvan in a group composed of Janet Armstrong and the deputy resident director —the minister was laughing. The first hour was the most important. If they were bored, the Iranians left early. If they stayed on for the buffet supper, then it meant they had enjoyed the party and might stay until the early hours. There were a number of women, and some of the senior Iranian officials had brought their wives. There were couture dresses and lavish jewels; the new rich among them adored making a display of wealth and the wives glittered like Christmas trees. It pained James to see some of the British Embassy ladies looking dowdy; he thought how Eileen would have redeemed them all, had she been there. The steely elegance of Janet Armstrong didn't count with him. There was no grace about her, no natural style. He felt a little tug on his left sleeve.

"Mr. Kelly? Good evening." It was a slight man, very swarthy, with bright black eyes. "I am Saiid Homsi."

James had planned the manner of Fields' meeting with the Syrian. It couldn't take place in the open with dozens of highly placed Iranians as witnesses. He didn't waste any time.

"Come with me, please," he said. He went into the house with the Syrian following. The drawing room opened onto the garden. James turned to the man. "Wait in here. I'll tell Mr. Fields. He'll come in a moment."

He gave Logan the message in a quick aside. He saw Khorvan watching him, and he eased himself into Logan's place.

"Minister? I haven't had time to do more than welcome you. I hope you have everything you want."

"Everything, thank you," Khorvan said. He was enjoying himself; the food was excellent. He loved the rich, spiced tidbits which were a feature of Iranian parties, and the beautiful setting had put him into a genial mood. He disliked Logan Fields, but found him stimulating. They had spent some time in semifriendly sparring. Khorvan was very sensitive where his own feelings were concerned; the slightest condescension or tactlessness would never be forgiven. But Logan had trod with feline delicacy over this thin crust of self-esteem. Khorvan would never like him, because he was almost a symbolic enemy, but he enjoyed his company. "Everything," he repeated to James. "Except that I miss my hostess. I am very disappointed not to see her."

James hoped that Janet had heard. A fractional change in her expression satisfied him that she had. "Mr. Fields said their daughter was ill, and she couldn't leave England. I am sorry to hear it." Khorvan was needling him a little and James knew it. The absence of Eileen Fields was only important in that it gave him an excuse to carp at his host and put him on the defensive.

"We all miss her," James said loudly, hoping that this too went to its target. His attention was claimed by a beautifully dressed, exotic Iranian girl, married to one of the few Persian aristocrats still in public life, and herself the heiress to a vast fortune. Her father owned one of the largest mines in Iran. Substantial gifts of "A" shares to influential ministers and a part holding to the Pahlevi Foundation had saved the mine from being nationalized. She was vivacious and attractive; she spoke French and German fluently and perfect English. She was bored with her husband and had often indicated to James that she found him attractive. If it hadn't been for Eileen he would have taken up the challenge. While he flirted with her, he wondered what was happening with Logan and Saiid Homsi in the house.

Chapter 6

"I've brought you towels. And some soap." Peters put them on the bed. Eileen was sitting in the chair; the bedside lamp was on. It was dark outside. The room was stiflingly hot.

"Thank you," she said. "At least I can wash properly." He took something out of his pocket and dropped it onto the heap of towels. It was a man's pocket comb. "You can have this," he said.

"I'm so terribly hot." Eileen got up slowly. She moved as if she were exhausted.

Peters didn't mean to, but he balanced on the edge of the bed. He didn't intend to stay and talk.

"Do you have to have that steel mesh over the window? It looks high enough and I promise you I'm not going to jump out. It stops the air from circulating; I feel suffocated in here."

"The mesh was put there for the child," Peters said. "To stop her from falling out."

"Would you have really kept her locked up in here?"

"No." He took out a cigarette and lit it. "She would have slept here. Madeleine would have looked after her; she'd have had the run of the garden. We meant to treat her properly."

It was all so logical, and at the same time so inhuman. She didn't argue with him, and the split-second impulse to spit her condemnation in his face was quickly mastered. She felt as if she were groping in total darkness whenever she talked to him. It wasn't so much a dialogue, however brief, as an exploration of a species quite unknown to her. And unlike the woman, he showed her no personal hostility.

"Could I have one?" He looked surprised for a moment. Then he got up and offered her the cigarettes. He gave her a light.

"Would you tell me something?" Eileen asked him. Peters waited.

"Why have you kidnapped me?"

"I can't tell you that. It's nothing personal against you."

"It must be something to do with my husband. Why can't you tell me?"

Peters looked at her and drew on the last of his cigarette.

Madeleine had said she was arrogant. She had spent a long time with him on the terrace, arguing that they should imprison the woman in the cellars and insisting that she was the type to give trouble. Peters hadn't agreed with her then and he saw no sign of it now. There was nothing about Eileen Fields that antagonized him personally. She had saved her child at her own expense and he gave her credit for courage. She wasn't being truculent with him, whatever Madeleine said. "It *is* to do with your husband. That's all I can tell you."

She picked up the comb and used it. One tooth was broken. It was his own comb. He noticed that she had pretty hair, which waved naturally around her face. She looked at him and shook her head.

"And if he refuses the ransom—whatever it is—"

"He won't. But the little girl would have been better."

"That's a filthy thing to say," Eileen said slowly. "Don't you have *any* feelings? Don't you see that to use a little child for a purpose, ransom or anything else, is the lowest, most despicable thing anyone could do? I'm not trying to argue with you, because thank God you didn't get her. I simply can't understand how you could *say* a thing like that!"

"We have a different set of values." He wondered whether she could be brought to understand them if he did explain. It was a Liberation Front axiom that no opportunity to put their case should be neglected. There were cases where prisoners had become converted and asked to join in the struggle. She was intelligent and courageous; she didn't remind him of the mindless rich women he had known in the States, creatures of such superficiality that they wouldn't have survived Eileen Fields' experience with enough wit to ask a question. She hadn't whined or groveled. And the room was like an oven. His own clothes were sticking to him.

"You see a little girl," he said slowly. "I see a whole people. Thousands of children, not one child. Children without food or shelter, or hope for the future. I see their families, living with disease and dirt in

hovels made of packing cases. To do something about that, I would
have snatched your child, Mrs. Fields, and I don't see anything wrong
in it. So long as she came to no harm."

"If she did come to harm—if she got ill or had an accident—you'd
still be able to justify it?"

"The end would justify it."

"That old lie about the Jesuits," Eileen answered. "It's been made
the excuse for every crime under the sun. Tell me, what happens to me
if my husband refuses to accept your terms? Supposing he won't give
you the money—what will you do with me?"

Peters got up. "I'll leave you these," he said. He put the cigarettes
and a box of matches on the bed.

"I shouldn't have asked that," Eileen said. "You don't have to answer. I can imagine. Please, couldn't you take that wire off the
window?"

He went over and tested it, as she had done earlier. He knew that
the drop below was fifty feet to the rocks, and that the sea boiled
around them there in a strong undercurrent. There were no pipes or
ledges on the outside walls. Nothing but a suicidal drop.

"Okay, I'll have it taken out tomorrow."

"Thank you. Would you tell me your name?"

"Peters. Do you want anything else?"

"Something to read."

"I'll see what there is."

When he had gone, Eileen ran to the window. She pulled at the wire
mesh. Once that was down, at least there was a possible way out. She
could see the sea below and guessed that there must be a sheer drop or
he wouldn't have agreed to take the mesh away. The encounter had
left her taut with nervous tension. He had been neutral, giving the few
necessities without making her beg for them. There was a disturbing
lack of personal animosity toward her; she would have found it easier
to fight him if there had been. He wasn't going to treat her cruelly or
indulge in petty persecutions. But if the order came through he would
take her out of the room and shoot her. She knew that without any
doubt. As a young girl her experience of men had been limited to the
jolly young Irishmen with whom she had grown up—friends in the
hunting field, partners at the rowdy Horse Show parties and the lavish
balls where throwing bread rolls and squirting siphons of soda were a
ritual part of the entertainment. Men had been in love with her, and
she had flirted happily with many of them. If Logan Fields hadn't
come to Ireland to look at a property owned by their neighbor, she
would have married one of the gay young men who slid down the

banisters at parties and known nothing different. There was no one in her experience comparable with the man who had kidnapped her.

She had traveled widely with Logan just after they married; a month in the United States had brought her into contact with Americans from many different groups. They had been friendly, hospitable, and easy to like. She could even recognize Peters as a physical type. Tall, showing traces of Scandinavian ancestry, physically very strong; he had the loose, easy way of moving that was typically American. She remembered saying to Logan that they made Englishmen look jerky by comparison.

He didn't waste words; he had cold eyes, very blue, and when he looked at her there was no expression in them. No antagonism, no suspicion—nothing. She had felt instinctively that to be aggressive would gain her nothing. It hadn't been easy to master the impulse to fly at him with her nails when he talked about what they had planned to do with her child. She had stayed calm, and by doing so, she had wrung a major concession from him. The wire was coming off the window. She wondered how high above the sea it was. If it was possible to climb down even part of the way and then drop . . . she was a strong swimmer. The bed sheets and the counterpane. The towels he had brought her. It might be possible to make a rope. She went into the bathroom and splashed her face with cold water. The heat was sticky and close, stifling. She had never resorted to cunning in her life; it had never been necessary to wheedle and maneuver with a man to get something out of him. It was strange how quickly adversity instructed.

She lit one of the cigarettes Peters had left her. He needn't have done that. They weren't a necessity. She paused, struck by the thought. Logan wouldn't have left her the cigarettes if he had been Peters. He certainly wouldn't have taken the wire off the window. Not because he was inhuman or enjoyed being harsh. But because he was a total realist. Prisoners lived with bars and didn't smoke. She turned the cigarette over in her fingers.

The cold eyes, the impersonal approach to her. She remembered how rough he had been when they landed, the gun pressing hard into her side through the drive to the villa. She didn't know why, but she shivered. She mustn't antagonize him. She must be quiet and dignified, because it seemed to have the best effect on him. She must thank him when he brought her food, and appear to be quiescent, waiting for news of her release.

And that release would come. It must. Thinking how best to outwit Peters had brought only critical thoughts of Logan to her mind. She felt ashamed and petty. Jealous still of his choice of another woman, of the dismissal of all their years together and the happiness that both of them had known. She finished the cigarette and took her dress off. She lay down in her slip on top of the bed, propped up on the pillow. It was too hot to sleep. She remembered their first meeting, and closed her eyes, willing herself out of the stuffy room with its implications of nightmare, back to Clonagh Castle, nearly eight years before.

The son of the house had wanted to marry her. The family were their neighbors and her father's oldest friends. Their name was Louth and the title went back to the twelfth century. They had a magnificent house with an original Norman keep, and a bank manager in Dublin whose patience was coming to an end. Clonagh was up for sale, and the Fitzgeralds had been invited to meet the prospective buyer, a very rich Englishman whom they hoped to persuade.

Eileen was twenty; her dress was made by the dressmaker in Meath, and was five years out of fashion. She had no idea how beautiful she looked the night she met Logan Fields. She only knew that he dominated the room. Beside him, her own father, even Lord Louth, who was a considerable personage in the county, and certainly his son, her suitor, seemed like a group of out-of-date ghosts, with their insular jokes and their endless talk of horses and neighbors. The Englishman had shamed them by his knowledge, his range of interests, and his authority. She had felt him as a physical presence, and when they were separated at the dinner table, she had seen him looking toward her.

Logan hadn't bought Clonagh Castle. He didn't like Ireland or the Irish, only she didn't discover that till after she was married. He had met her and made up his mind. Within a month they were engaged, and within three they were on their honeymoon.

She was back in the room again, with the ugly bedside light burning and a mosquito whining overhead. They had been deeply in love. She had been shy and untutored; he had been patient and tender until she understood his passion and could meet it. It couldn't go for nothing. Love might die but there were always traces left. If he were in danger at that moment—if positions were reversed—she would have given anything, done anything, to rescue him. He was a strong man, a powerful force, excited by obstacles. She had been part of his life, even if not the major part. Thoughtless and ambitious above all, but in his way he had loved her very much. With hindsight, she admitted that she had forced the issue of their marriage into the open. Had she stayed quiet, there might have been no crisis, no breakdown. Logan would get her out. She didn't doubt it for a moment. She fell asleep, and started a long incoherent dream about climbing out the bedroom window on a rope that had no end toward a sea that came no nearer.

And suddenly it stopped and she was falling. She woke from the throes of finding herself struggling violently in Peters' arms and being borne down onto the rocks.

"I don't believe you," Logan Fields said. He had taken a step toward the Syrian, but Homsi didn't retreat. He shrugged, both his palms turned upward.

"I am only a messenger, Mr. Fields," he said. "A go-between. I can assure you, these people seized your wife three days ago. And they mean what they say." He shook his head a little.

"Naturally this is a great shock to you. I do sympathize."

"I don't believe it," Logan repeated. "My wife's in England. If anything had happened to her, I'd have been told at once!"

"Apparently it was done in such a way that nobody knows she is missing," the Syrian said. "The terrorists want this kept completely secret. That is one of their conditions. You must tell nobody. I advise you to do as they say. They are a very dangerous, extremist group."

"I'll find her," Logan said. "I'll get every police force in the world on to it. . . ."

"The moment you go to the police or say anything, she will be killed," Saiid Homsi said quietly. "Make inquiries by all means, Mr. Fields, but if you want your wife alive, you must be very, very discreet."

He watched the Englishman. The man had lost color, and his hands were clenching and opening. For a moment Saiid had feared he might be punched to the ground when he first gave Fields the news.

Logan turned to him. "You're hand in glove with them," he said. "Syria supports these bastards, everyone knows that. You're no bloody innocent! You tell me where she is, and I'll see you get more money than you've ever dreamed of—cooperate with me and get my wife out of danger, and I'll pay you any price you ask!"

"Unfortunately," Saiid said gently, "I can't be any help. I don't know where Mrs. Fields is being held and I couldn't assist in a rescue. It isn't a question of money, Mr. Fields. This is a problem even you can't solve by signing a check. These people aren't interested in ransom."

"What *do* they want then? What's the deal?"

"They haven't told me that. All I know is that Mrs. Fields is in their hands. They want you to know this and to be ready to hear their terms for releasing her. They will tell me more in the next twenty-four hours. That's all I know."

"Jesus Christ," Logan muttered. "I still can't believe it."

"I think you will find," the Syrian murmured, "that it is unfortunately true. I will go now, Mr. Fields. If you will contact me the day after tomorrow, I will have more news for you. That gives you time to verify their information. If you find Mrs. Fields is safe and well at home, nobody will be more pleased than myself." He opened the door to the garden and walked into the crowd.

Logan didn't move for a moment. Then he went to the table where James kept a tray of drinks and poured himself a whiskey. He drank it straight down, then picked up the telephone. At that hour there was no delay in putting a call through to London. He sat by the phone waiting for the operator to ring back. He didn't have another drink, and slowly the shock was wearing off.

At one moment he had almost attacked the Syrian. There was something so hypocritical in the dark face, so maddening in the precise polite English that Fields wanted to punch and pummel him into a bloody mess. When the phone rang he seized it and shouted down the crackling line.

"Mario? Mr. Fields here. Is my wife there? What? When? Oh, for Christ's sake—speak up, the line's impossible. . . . When did she go? And Lucy? Bridget took her. . . . Have you heard from her—from Mrs. Fields? I see. All right. No, never mind." He dropped the receiver. She'd left the house on Wednesday. They understood she was going to Ireland. Lucy had been sent in advance with the maid. They'd heard nothing from her since. That was three days ago. Three days. The Syrian had said she was taken three days ago. . . . He heard a noise and looked up. James had come into the room.

"Logan?" He was sitting in the semidarkness. "I saw Homsi come out. What happened?"

James switched on the lights and saw Logan's face.

"My God," he said. "What's wrong?"

"Get me a drink, would you?" Logan said. "Not too big, I've already helped myself."

"What's happened?" James put the glass down in front of him. "What did he tell you?"

Logan rubbed both hands over his face—they were greasy with sweat. "He said he'd been approached by an Arab terrorist organization." He spoke quietly but it sounded as if he were only just keeping control. "They had a message for me, and he was acting as the go-between. It seems they've kidnapped Eileen. Anyway, that's what they claim."

He wasn't looking at James Kelly. "I've just called London. She's not there. They say she's gone to Ireland. If this kidnap threat is true, that's just the place they'd grab her. I'll have to go back and make sure."

"You won't need to," James Kelly said. "I've booked a call to Ireland. It should come through any time. Then we'll know. Who are the people who say they've got her?"

"Homsi didn't give a name. He just said they were very dangerous extremists. Black September by the sound of it. Do you believe it, James? Do you believe they've got her?"

"Syrians don't play games," James said. He felt physically sick. "What do they want? What's the ransom?"

"Not money. The bastard told me that much. They've given me twenty-four hours to establish that she's missing. Then they'll tell me their terms. If I go to the police or let anyone know she's gone, they'll kill her." He looked up at Kelly. "I still can't believe it," he said. "I can't take it in." The noise of the party outside came through the garden doors as a pleasant murmur. Logan finished his drink. "Why were you telephoning Ireland?"

Kelly ignored the question. "When do you contact Homsi again?"

"Tomorrow. James—what am I going to do? I tried bribing him, but he'd have no part of it. In Christ's name, what *do* they want, if they don't want money?"

"They wouldn't single you out for that," Kelly said slowly. "You're not that rich. It's something else. Don't try buying Homsi again. He might be tempted to take money from you and that could wreck the whole chance of negotiating with these people. I know the type. One move that looks as if you're trying to pull something and they'll murder her. They're not criminals. They're fanatics. Go to Homsi tomorrow and for Christ's sake do exactly what he says. I've got to dream up some reason to satisfy Ardalan. I promised to let him know what Homsi wanted."

"Make some excuse, invent something," Logan said. "You don't think if we contacted Interpol and explained—"

"No," James said. "No. Say nothing and do nothing. It's too dangerous. I'll tell Ardalan some story."

"Why doesn't that bloody Irish call come through? I'll get on to them. . . ." Logan reached for the telephone. Kelly stood by while he shouted at the international operator.

"It's no good, Logan," he said. "You stay here and wait for it. I'll go and see Ardalan."

"No." Logan stood up. "I've got to rejoin the party. We don't want to upset the minister."

"Of course. I'd forgotten about business for a moment. I must get my priorities right."

On the way to the garden door Logan turned back. "Coming apart at the seams isn't going to help Eileen," he said. "Talk to Ardalan and then wait for the call. Let me know the moment it comes through. She may be perfectly safe, staying with her father." Kelly watched him push his way through the crowd, moving toward Khorvan. Janet Armstrong's green dress looked white in the fading light. The garden was illuminated with lights discreetly placed among the trees and shrubs. As soon as it was dark the fireworks display would begin. Logan had left the doors open and there was a steady flow of talk and laughter; glass tinkled as something was broken. He could see Khorvan talking to Logan—Logan seemed to be laughing.

Kelly sat down. He looked for a cigarette and couldn't find one. It was a reflex, and he made no further effort, although there was a box on the desk. A dangerous extremist group. Logan was clinging to a secret hope that somehow Eileen was safe; he thought the telephone call might prove the Syrian wrong. Kelly could understand this. He wished he could have shared that hope. But he knew that it was vain. Eileen Fields was not at Meath House. The men who had sent Homsi to her husband didn't make mistakes. They would demand impossible terms for her release—he couldn't even guess their nature. There would be days of negotiation, perhaps weeks. He knew the pattern. Until the last moment they would preserve the hostage alive. They had a code, brutal and pitiless but predictable. If they got what they wanted, they wouldn't sacrifice the human pawn. But one infringement of the rules by Logan, one suspicion that he was trying to hold something back, and Eileen would be murdered. Executed, in their terminology. He remembered the horror of a photograph of a German diplomat, ritually shot through the head after a similar kidnapping had failed to gain its object.

For a moment he felt sick and overcome. An ugly thought came to him. Logan was distressed and shaken. But supposing the price they asked was something that he didn't want to pay? He stepped out into the garden to find Colonel Ardalan. He had already thought of an ex-

planation for Homsi's visit. Nobody must suspect that anything was
wrong. His talk with the colonel was interrupted by a message that his
Irish telephone call was coming through.

Colonel Ardalan had enjoyed the party. He was a gregarious man
who liked meeting people. The fireworks display had been a great success. He drove home with his wife, and sat on his terrace, smoking and
sipping whiskey after she had gone to bed. He didn't believe a word of
James Kelly's explanation. It was all very glib—the Syrian had had
some rare Coptic manuscripts which he thought Logan Fields might
be interested in buying. He had understood, correctly, that Fields was
a collector of antiquities, and Logan got the impression that the items
were prohibited for export. He had no intention of involving himself
with a dubious purchase and had told Homsi to look for another cus-
tomer. It was a very plausible explanation, and in different circumstances the colonel would have believed it. There was a flourishing il-
licit trade in rare antiquities for which no export license was available
in certain countries, notably Greece. Anything of exceptional quality
commanded a high price. Ardalan had listened politely and thanked
Kelly for telling him. He even added a mild caution that the Syrian
might offer something really tempting at a later date. He had noted the
absence of both men after Homsi's interview. When Logan Fields
rejoined the party he didn't look as if someone had offered him a
smuggled manuscript. And James Kelly's hand was trembling when he
shook it as they said good-bye. Ardalan never failed to detect fear,
and that was what he saw in the eyes of both Logan and Kelly. He
finished his whiskey. The pieces of the puzzle were assembling. One
key piece was the Syrian. The second, and equally important in its
solution, was Logan Fields.

"Darling," Janet said, "aren't you going to come in?" Logan had
driven back to the hotel; he had gone as far as the lift with her and she
was taken by surprise when he kissed her briefly on the cheek. He
hadn't seemed in very good spirits for the last half of the evening.
Knowing him so well, she detected a forced note in the friendly sparring with the minister.
"Not tonight," he said. "I'm tired out."
The lift was coming down, the red eye winking on the indicator.

"There's nothing wrong, is there? You don't seem yourself." She put one hand on his sleeve.

"No, of course not," Logan said. "I'll ring you tomorrow before we go to the office."

The lift doors slid back and she stepped inside. He had turned and was walking away before they closed.

Eileen had never arrived at Meath House. Her father had been curt and uncommunicative on the telephone. Logan had mastered the impulse to shout at the old sponger that his daughter was missing and in great danger. He didn't seem worried by her absence. Logan suspected furiously that the old man was too busy spoiling his granddaughter to think of anything else. He had hung up. He didn't look at Kelly. The hope had been a flimsy one, but until he followed James in to speak to his father-in-law, he hadn't admitted how much he had clung to it.

"She's not there," James had said and handed him the telephone.

Logan drove back through the empty Teheran streets. The last half of the party reminded him of the classic nightmare in which the dreamer is isolated from contact with everyone surrounding him. The evening had begun with making love to Janet; he had come to the party in a mood of high optimism. His personal life was exciting, and the difficulties of securing Imshan might well be surmounted by a deal with the Japanese. He had never felt more in command of the future than when he arrived at Kelly's house.

He had closed his eyes during the drive to the hotel, and all he could see was Eileen. It couldn't be true. She couldn't be shut up in some blacked-out room, at the mercy of fanatics who would kill her without hesitation. Her face floated free in the darkness, the face he had thought so beautiful that he had commissioned Merton to paint her. She couldn't be helpless and afraid, perhaps even ill-treated. He sat up with a jolt, unable to bear his imagination's choice of possibilities. What did they want in return for her? What was the price they would ask through Saiid Homsi? Twenty-four hours. A full day and a night before he would know. If it wasn't money it was going to be something political. Something advantageous to the cause of Arab fanaticism, with which, next to outright Communism, he had the least sympathy of all. The lights were on when he went into Kelly's house. The moonlit garden and the jasmine scent reminded him of the evening he had told his wife he wanted someone else. There was no evidence of the party—everything had been cleared away. James came out of the sitting room as he went to the stairs.

"Do you want a whiskey? It might help if we talked about it."

"No, thanks," Logan said. "We know what the score is now. That little bastard told the truth. They have got her. All I can do now is wait to hear the terms."

James stood in the doorway. He had been drinking since the party ended.

"Whatever it is, you'll pay?"

"Don't be a bloody fool," Logan said. He went upstairs and Kelly heard the bedroom door shut. He stayed in the hall for a few minutes, finishing his drink. Money would have been easy. He knew Logan wouldn't hesitate to pay whatever they asked. He could have given them money. Imperial Oil would subsidize if it went beyond his personal capacity. James had been drinking, but his mind was clear. Only the pain was dulled. Logan was ready to do anything to save his wife. James had been telling himself that in the hope he could still a growing sense of doubt. Logan wouldn't sacrifice her, no matter what he had to do. It was irrelevant that they were breaking up, that he was in love with someone else. He might be a ruthless bastard, whom James disliked as a person, but he wouldn't hesitate.

James went back into the room and poured another whiskey. He didn't think of going to bed. He had to get drunk before he fell asleep in the chair.

The window mesh was taken down by the Algerian who had driven them from the airfield. He didn't look at her and he didn't speak. He pried the wire away from its battens on the wall, picked up his tools, spat as he passed Eileen, and went out, locking the door. She ran to the window. Now she was able to lean out and to see the distance to the sea below. She could have wept with disappointment. The villa was built on a rocky protuberance.

Below her was a sheer wall of rock, and then a jagged outcrop, around which the sea foamed and battered. She waited, trying to judge the exact footage to the ground. It was obviously beyond knotted bedsheets and a jump into the sea. Peters had known what he was doing when he had the protective mesh taken down. She pulled herself up and leaned farther out, looking for anything that might serve as a hold if she tried to climb down. She didn't hear him come up behind her. He caught her by the waist and dragged her back into the room. She twisted around, struggling, and he pinned her arms behind her. For a brief moment they faced each other, and Eileen felt the impact of his body.

"What the hell were you doing?" Peters said. He moved her away from the window. She was breathless, and he was holding her tighter than was necessary. He let her go suddenly. "What were you doing leaning out like that?"

Eileen faced him defiantly. "Looking down," she said.

"You won't get out that way. There's no toehold and it's fifty feet, so forget it. Otherwise I'll have the wire back on."

"How do you know I won't jump out?" she said. Peters looked at her.

"I don't. That's up to you. All you have to do is wait."

She turned away from him. "I'm going mad shut up in here. Isn't there any way I could have some exercise?"

"No," he said. He pointed to the bed. "I brought you some books. Try reading." There were three books, the biggest she recognized as a best seller, written by one of the popular purveyors of sex and sensation.

"It's been ten days," Eileen said. "And you've told me nothing. Hasn't my husband been contacted?"

He lit a cigarette. "I guess so."

"But you've no news? Or you just won't tell me!" He saw her turn quickly away and realized that she was crying. She had lost a lot of weight; he noticed that when he held her. She had felt very slight. She looked as if she were sleeping badly, and often the trays came back with most of the food untouched. He had said so to Madeleine, who disgusted him by suggesting that she be left to starve for a few days as a hint not to sulk. When he came in and saw her at the window, he had thought for a second that she was going to jump. He remembered the times he had been in jail. Ten days could be a long time when you were a prisoner.

Eileen turned and faced him. She wiped her eyes. "Has he said anything? I can't believe there's no news."

"So far as I know," Peters said. "He's negotiating."

"Negotiating?" Eileen got up slowly. "I don't understand. What have you asked him for? Why couldn't he just say yes?"

"Why don't you take a look at those books," Peters said. "You'll know when there's any news. And don't go hanging out that window again."

She picked up the second book and the third. A travelogue about an expedition to Katmandu and a novel by someone whose name she didn't know.

"Do you want anything?" Peters asked.

"I haven't a change of clothes. I feel filthy dirty. I haven't even a toothbrush."

"Madeleine will get some things for you. I'll tell her." She didn't look up at him.

"Thank you for the books."

"There wasn't anything else in English. Except some pornographic magazines. I didn't think you'd want those." He left, and she heard the door lock.

Negotiating. It was a word she had heard Logan use so often. Dealing, bargaining, pulling something off. Negotiating with the terrorists. She had a vision of him sitting in his office off Cheapside behind the tycoon-sized desk with its batteries of telephones and intercoms, negotiating for her life. Giving a little, holding something back; going through the business routine while she waited in the stuffy little room, with people who were under orders to kill her if he didn't give way to their demands. It was an unfortunate word for Peters to use. It explained the ten days without a decision. She couldn't believe it. Logan must know that she was in mortal danger—he had no way of knowing that she was not being ill-treated, kept in some hole underground. But, she reminded herself, her reaction was hysterical. In all cases of kidnapping and hijacking and all the other modern means of extortion by terror, negotiations had to take place. As to how the money was paid—in what denomination. How the hostage would be released. It always took time. A little time. But not ten days, for the love of God. She remembered Logan in moments of crisis. They had been in Paris, in the apartment on the Rue St. Dominique when the Arab sheikhdoms stopped their oil exports to the West. She had seen Logan with his back to the wall then. They had been entertaining when he got the news of the sheikhs' action. It was in the middle of a cocktail party in their elegant drawing room, with the Austrian ambassador and his wife as guests of honor, and some of the most influential people in French political and industrial life as their guests. Logan had been called to the telephone. When he came back, he walked over to her, smiled, and suggested they select a few friends to dine at Maxim's afterward. It was not until they came home at one in the morning, after a successful dinner party and a brief visit to Regine's fashionable nightclub, that Logan told her what had happened.

"They've shut off the oil," he said. "The bastards have got us by the short hairs."

"What can you do?"

"Negotiate," was his answer. "Deal with them, give as little as possible, and hope to Christ they back off." He had gone to bed with her that night, made love, and fallen instantly asleep. She wondered whether he had taken the news of her abduction with the same ruthless calm. She picked up the sex novel and it fell open as always at a well-handled page full of graphic sexual details. She didn't mean to read it. It brought Peters to her mind. There had been a moment while he was pulling her away from the window when there was something sexual in the way he held her. She had felt it instinctively and fought against him. He had let her go so quickly that it was an indication he too was aware of it and had been taken by surprise. She tried to close the memory out of her mind. It frightened and disturbed her—it added a dimension of danger to the already terrifying situation of her captivity. He reminded her of a powerful animal; he moved very quietly and he gave the impression of tremendous force, ready to be let loose. She had seen the ugly, merciless side of him when she was kidnapped. It was unrealistic to forget that, just because he had shown her a little humanity and brought her a few books. Whatever had flared up between them because of the rough physical contact, it had to be forgotten, buried. She had to think of Logan, rely on him to rescue her. He wouldn't gamble with her life—he wouldn't wheel and deal with organized terror. It had been wrong to doubt him and lose faith. She picked up the book on mountaineering and began to read. The Algerian brought her food that evening and she didn't see Peters again for two days. When he did come, he brought Madeleine with him.

He hadn't told her the reason; it didn't seem necessary to explain. He unlocked the door and Madeleine walked in. Eileen was sitting in the upright chair. She alternated between the bed and the chair, trying to read, sometimes just dozing in the heat. When it was cool, in the early morning, she walked up and down the narrow space between the walls, trying to exercise. When she saw the Lebanese girl she got up.

"Well," Madeleine said. "She looks all right to me." She turned to Peters. Her manner was aggressive. "All this about her not eating—I don't see anything wrong with her." She looked at Eileen with open hatred. She had expected to find her cowed and disheveled. Instead she was in full control of herself, and her look of contempt was stinging.

"Why have you come here?" Eileen asked. "Keep out. I'll have nothing to do with you!"

"You shut your mouth!" Madeleine shouted at her. She swung around to Peters. "Are you going to let her talk to me like that?"

He looked angry. The spectacle of Madeleine bristling like a cat annoyed him. He wasn't going to tolerate a scene between two hostile women. He had expected Madeleine to show more self-control.

"Shut up, both of you," he said,

Eileen looked at him.

"That creature would have murdered my child. I'm going into the bathroom until she gets out of my room." It was Madeleine who moved, blocking the way. "You do as you're told, *trainée,* or by Allah I'll deal with you!" Eileen stood still. The other girl's fists were opening and closing—she was coiled like a spring, waiting to lash out at her. She turned and walked back to the chair. She spoke to Peters. "What do you want?"

"You said you wanted clothes. Madeleine—for Christ's sake stop behaving as if you were in a bazaar brawl!"

"How *dare* you say that to me?" she blazed at him in Arabic. "Didn't you hear her insult me?" She turned to Eileen. "As for you, remember one thing. Your husband isn't in any hurry to redeem you. Maybe he doesn't *want* you back. And when we know for certain, madame, I shall be the first to come and watch Resnais do his job. And you can guess what *that* is, can't you?" She put her head back and laughed. "We'll see how high and mighty you are then!"

Peters came up to her. He gripped her arm and it hurt.

"Go downstairs," he said. "Go on. Get out! I'll talk to you later." He hurried her to the door and pushed her outside. She slammed it after her. He put a slip of paper and a pencil down on the chest of drawers. "Make a list of what you want," he said. "Just the necessities. I'll see she gets them for you. And don't pay any attention to what she said."

"He hasn't answered, has he?" Eileen said. "It's two weeks now, and I'm still here."

"I told you not to listen to her," Peters said angrily. "She hates you and she'd say anything."

She looked up at him. "Is that Frenchman the executioner?"

"Get on and make the list!" he almost shouted at her. He went over to the window and looked out while she wrote. He was furious with Madeleine. She reminded him of a wild animal when she spat the threat at Eileen and taunted her with Logan Fields' delay. It had been cruel and spiteful, and these were qualities that repelled him in a woman. Of the two women, it was their prisoner who had come out the better in the exchange. He wished above all that Madeleine hadn't told her about Resnais. . . . Eileen came up behind him.

"Here it is," she said. He brushed against her as he turned. She stepped back quickly.

"Don't let her come up here again," she said quietly. "Please." He went out without answering. He found Madeleine waiting on the terrace. She had a drink in her hand and she was sullen, the explosive temper only just under control. He gave her the piece of paper.

"Go into Nice tomorrow and buy those," he said. She took it from him, looked at it for a moment, and then threw it in a crumpled ball onto the terrace floor.

"Clothes! Toothbrushes and soap and all the little luxuries? Have you gone mad? I'll see her damned in hell before I get her any of them!"

"I am responsible for her. You'll buy them," Peters said. "And that's an order."

"Oh, no it's not!" Madeleine shouted. "You've gone soft! Madame has everything brought up on trays—you come telling me she isn't eating—what does it matter if the bitch starves? She has to have a change of clothes—where is she, in a luxury hotel? What do you think happens to our women in Israeli prisons? What's got into you, Peters? You stood there and let her insult me, instead of smashing her face in to teach her some manners! Do you fancy her for yourself, is that what it is?"

He slapped her sharply across the face. She didn't flinch and no tears came into her eyes. She called him a name in Arabic.

"I won't do it," she said. "And you can't make me. Get them yourself!"

That night he moved out of her room. She hadn't believed it at first when she came upstairs and found he had left her. She loved him and she was wild with jealousy because her instincts detected that he was losing interest in her, and that however much she exerted herself to please him in bed, her hold on him had weakened. Now it had gone altogether. She looked at the empty bed, and though the physical blow hadn't made her cry, she did so then. She was too proud to go after him, although she padded down the passageway until she saw a light under one of the unused bedroom doors, and knew he had moved in there. He had left her, and she knew it was because of their quarrel and her refusal to buy a few necessities for Eileen Fields. She saw his concern as weakness. While he talked about responsibility, Madeleine dismissed this as an attempt to delude her as well as himself. He had never felt responsible for any enemy before. He hadn't shown the same softness toward the stewardess in the airliner who had lain bleeding from a bullet wound in the back, or for the terrified passengers. Only for *this* woman, this hostage taken against a vicious capitalist plot to undermine the Arab strength . . . for a representative of the class he was supposed to hate and had sworn to annihilate. Smooth hands and skin, rich clothes, a house with servants and luxuries. Madeleine had burst out of similar circumstances, eager to prove herself by hard work and rough living—proud that she was as capable as any man. For a woman like Eileen Fields she reserved her most brutal contempt. Peters should have felt the same. He should have been repelled by a useless parasite whose only value was in her relationship to one of the capitalist tyrants they were dedicated to destroy. She couldn't understand or forgive his tolerance toward the prisoner. The only explanation for it was so painful that it throbbed like a wound. He was attracted by her. Perhaps he didn't realize it, or would not have admitted it, but Madeleine knew. Something about that woman had touched a responsive feeling in him. If it were purely sexual, it would have been tolerable. Rape wouldn't have worried Madeleine— she wouldn't have objected if her man had satisfied an urge to have the woman and then kill her. But it was more than that. She was a person to him. She had feelings, needs. Madeleine went back to her room and wondered how she could risk showing Peters that he was betraying himself and everything they both believed in. Even if she did, she couldn't be sure of getting him back. But at least she had to try.

They were eating lunch on the terrace. It was prepared by the surly Algerian who seldom spoke except to Madeleine. Resnais had spent the morning swimming. He was in a mischievous mood. The atmosphere between Peters and the girl was tense and this irritated him. The villa was beautiful, the food and wine very good, and the weather magnificent. His thoughts were not occupied by anything except occasional anxiety for his dog in Paris, and he intended telephoning to make sure it was all right. He decided to pass the time by goading the Lebanese girl. If she hadn't been so jealous of Peters and the hostage, she might have been pleasant to him. He knew Peters had left her room.

He had been days without a woman, and it would be a nuisance having to pick one up from outside. He knew Peters would forbid it if he found out.

"Why don't we go into the town this evening," he said to Madeleine. "If Peters will spare you for an hour."

"She can go," the American said. "I've no objection."

"Why don't we all go?" Madeleine said. "We've been shut up here too long. It's getting on our nerves." She glanced at her lover; it was a plea for reconciliation. She saw that he had completely ignored it—he didn't even look up at her. Anxiety made her persist. "We could go and have dinner somewhere. We don't have to sit here playing nursemaid. Ahmed can keep watch on her. Let's have a little fun tonight."

She leaned over and laid her hand on Peters' arm. She loved him so much it was torment and she wanted him more than ever before. "Please," she said, not caring that Resnais was watching them. "Let's go together."

"You go," Peters said coldly. He moved his arm and her hand slid off. "I'm not leaving her to some goon like Ahmed. We're here to do a job."

"He's right," Resnais said. "Just suppose Ahmed felt lonely and decided to pay the lady a visit. You come out with me, Madeleine. Peters can watch over her."

It was a cunning choice of words. Madeleine reacted as if she had trodden on a snake.

"Watch over is right," she snapped. She spoke to Resnais.

"You know the wire's been taken off her window? I saw it the day before yesterday. Isn't that crazy?"

"I didn't know that," Resnais said. He looked at Peters. "Why?" He asked the question softly. The situation was no longer amusing him. "Isn't that risky?"

"No," the American said. "There's a fifty-foot drop to the rocks. She was half suffocated in there."

"How do you know she won't throw herself out?" Resnais asked. "I think you should have consulted us about this. The wire should be put back."

"She shouldn't be up there at all," Madeleine broke in. "I've said from the beginning—"

"I know what you've said," Peters interrupted. "Just because it's a woman and you've got some spite against her. From now on, Madeleine, you keep your mouth shut about how she's to be treated. Otherwise I'll shut it for you." He turned to Resnais. "You're right about the wire. I should have told you. But I'm in charge of this operation and responsible for her safety. You can take my word she won't escape. Or try to jump out. She's not the type."

The Frenchman shrugged. "If you're satisfied." They separated for the afternoon. Madeleine, sullen and silent, went to the rocks to sunbathe, Peters called for the car and went out, and Resnais lounged in the shade in the garden. The situation was no longer funny. Now there was friction among the three of them, with himself and the Lebanese girl drawing together in opposition to the American. Resnais had never worked with Peters before but he knew his reputation. The girl was typical of the fanatic Arab female—so far as he was concerned she was wasted out of bed. He despised liberated women. A man like Peters was only effective because he was immune to human weakness.

And that included small humanities, like removing a safeguard because it was making their prisoner uncomfortable. He remembered the hijacking of the 707, the world headlines over the deliberate shooting of the steward and the photographs of the wounded stewardess and passengers being taken by stretcher from the aircraft. Peters and Madeleine had been responsible for that and there were stories about the American's activities in Chile which were chilling enough to be legends. Now he and the girl were falling out over Eileen Fields. Their relationship was disrupted and their common loyalty no longer bound them. He stretched in the lounge chair, raising his arms above his head. Up there, on the first floor, was the cause.

Peters hadn't let him go near her since they arrived. She had something, that was evident. He had felt it when he sat beside her in the plane and murmured that he was going to look after her. It had amused him to frighten her. She was the class of woman with whom he felt especially sadistic. He had a mistress in Marseilles who was refined and well-educated; it excited them both when he debased and abused her. He didn't share Madeleine's personal motives, but he wouldn't have objected in the least to keeping the wife of the chairman of Imperial Oil in an underground cellar haunted by rats. He had never felt that the rich deserved anything else. He couldn't see her window; it was hidden by the pine trees. He wondered what it was about her that was turning Peters into a human being. The American wouldn't like it, but he felt he should go and find out for himself.

The Telex came through from Paterson in Tokyo. Logan had been in the office for an hour when it arrived. Janet was with him; he phoned as he had promised, and she sensed the same tension. She didn't make the common feminine mistake of asking what was wrong a second time. She met him at the office, not as his mistress but as a colleague. Whatever was worrying him, he wasn't ready to tell her about it, and the worst thing she could have done was to press for answers. Janet thought of herself as a cool woman; even admitting that she loved Logan, she insisted on her individuality and freedom from dependence.

She was surprised at the extent to which his off-key attitude had shaken her. She hadn't slept, and it needed a real effort to assume her own executive personality. Surprise gave way to irritation—not with Logan but with herself. Loving a man was one thing, but to be tempted into an emotional scene was a weakness she couldn't excuse. If he had a problem, he would discuss it when he was ready. Equally, she could have reserved some crisis in her life from him. When the Telex arrived, Logan got up and came over to her.

"It looks as if the Japanese are ready to come in! Listen: DEPUTY PRIME MINISTER TOMO FUNASAKA REQUESTS YOUR PRESENCE AT CONFERENCE WITH PRIME MINISTER TO DISCUSS POSSIBLE FINANCING OF PROJECT. SIGNS EXTREMELY ENCOURAGING. IMPORTERS MEETING AGAIN TODAY. SUGGEST YOU ARRIVE TOKYO DAY AFTER TOMORROW. PATERSON. If that bloody Scot says anything's extremely encouraging it must be in the bag!"

He threw his arm around Janet, and suddenly the strain was gone. They were together; she understood the meaning of that Telex in terms of Imshan and he could feel the same excitement in her.

"Darling," he said, "isn't this great? I feel sure we're going to work something out now. Do you want to come with me?"

"Just try and leave me behind!" she said. "I wouldn't miss it for the world." Logan switched on the intercom. His Iranian secretary came through. "Send in Mr. Kelly and Mr. Phillipson right away." He turned back to Janet. Her response had been just right. She loved the game as much as he did. "If I can get them to agree to a government loan in return for a guaranteed supply of oil, we can make up the total cost of building their bloody refinery without cutting too deep into our own profit margins. I reckon we'll just be able to do it."

"Are you going to inform London?" Janet asked him.

"No," Logan said. "I'm not going to tell anyone, except Kelly, Phillipson, and you. And I don't want Khorvan getting a sniff of it either. Otherwise, he'll dream up something else by the time I get back. You make the reservations for us, darling. I don't trust the staff here. Ah, come in, James—Phillipson. Sit down. We've got some good news."

Kelly had a hangover. He ignored Janet and sat watching Logan. Confidence, authority, a controlled excitement. He had completely lost the look of drawn apprehension since last night. For a moment, disoriented by a blinding headache, Kelly imagined that the good news he was about to hear concerned Eileen.

"This is the Telex that's just come in from Ian Paterson." Logan passed it to James. He read it and without speaking handed it to Phillipson, the deputy resident director. He heard an exclamation of approval.

Logan was addressing them. "Tomo Funasaka is supposed to be the policymaker. If he supports something, the prime minister usually goes along. I'm going out immediately, and taking Janet with me. I believe this has to be kept as quiet as possible, so she's making the reservations outside the office, and I don't want anyone in the building to know where I've gone. As far as they're concerned I've simply taken off for a week."

"What about London, sir?" Phillipson asked.

"Say nothing," Logan said. "I'll Telex them from Tokyo when I've got some kind of deal going. It may take a few days."

James didn't contribute anything, and Logan didn't seem to notice. The discussion was brief, and he heard Janet making suggestions about revised cash flow projections. It was a concert of voices, coinciding with the hammers in his head. Phillipson, making the right noises, but not contributing too much. He knew how to handle men like Logan. There'd be a future for him with Imperial Oil. And the woman, with her masculine mind, playing the asexual role. Logan generating his own excitement at the prospect of turning Khorvan's attack on them into a triumph.

He was leaving Teheran immediately to conduct negotiations with the Japanese. On his own admission he could be away some days—a loose term which could encompass up to two weeks. Logan was dismissing them. James got up. "Could I see you for a minute—in private?"

"Yes. Janet—you don't mind, do you?"

She smiled at Logan and went out of the office. Kelly faced Logan, who genuinely didn't know why Kelly wanted to speak to him alone. It was incredible, but quite true. He had forgotten about his wife.

"You have an appointment with Homsi today," James said. "What happens to that? What happens to Eileen while you're in Japan?"

Logan didn't hesitate. His mind switched direction. James could see it happening. "I'll see Homsi as arranged. I'm going to contact him this morning and set up a meeting. If there's anything immediate to be done, then you can handle it for me. My guess is we'll have quite a negotiation on our hands."

"Would you mind telling me which negotiation you're referring to?" Kelly lit a cigarette. His headache seemed to be improving. Logan leaned back in his chair.

"Both, if you want me to spell it out. And I might as well spell out a few other things. I am going to do everything to get Eileen released. Whatever they want, I'll give them. You asked me a question last night. I thought you were pissed, so I let you get away with it. You asked if I'd pay the price, no matter what. I said yes, and I'm saying it now. Though why it's any of your bloody business, I'm not sure. I'm seeing Homsi today and then I'm going to Tokyo. Nobody else can go instead, it's got to be me. Everything depends on it. Without a Japanese deal we can pack up and go home, and leave Imshan to the Russians. While I'm away, you handle the ransom, whatever it is. I may be back in a few days. Is that clear?"

James got up; he put out his cigarette in the ashtray on Logan's desk.

"Crystal clear. You go off on business and leave me to bargain for Eileen's life. Most people wouldn't do it for you. But I will. I'll do anything and everything I can for her while you fart around Tokyo looking after fucking Imperial Oil. And you'll have my resignation this afternoon. If there's one thing I won't work for, it's a prize shit like you."

"You're in love with her," Logan said, "so you ought to be glad of the chance. Now get out of my office. I've got work to do."

When the door closed, it slammed. Logan swore, not so much at Kelly, but at the circumstances. He had realized the situation with Kelly when he heard about the call to Ireland. It hadn't disturbed him because, beside the issue of Eileen's disappearance, it was unimportant. But he had stood there, accusing him, and suddenly making Logan defend himself. To himself. A prize shit. That had stung—the contempt implicit in the term had stung him even more.

Kelly thought he should stay and negotiate with Homsi. But that was unrealistic—he had no doubt about it. He was going to hear the kidnappers' terms and set the deal in motion, leaving Kelly to tie it up. At the worst he was a Telex away and a plane flight if he was needed. But nobody else could sit around a table with the Japanese government and secure investment backing which would give Imperial Oil access to the richest oil field in the world. If it was a question of priorities, and this was the essence of Kelly's condemnation of him, then he insisted he had got them right. He wouldn't help Eileen by sitting in Teheran. If he delayed, the Japanese would take offense and the seriousness of their approach would be questioned. There was nothing else he could do but go. Nothing.

He told his secretary to get him the Syrian Embassy. A moment later he was speaking to Homsi. He arranged to meet him in the Bank of Iran, where the state treasures were on display. It was suggested by the Syrian as a place where they could meet without being conspicuous. There were always crowds of tourists looking at the Iranian crown jewels. He hung up before he could be asked a question. Logan called for coffee and settled down to work. He never found it difficult to close one problem out and concentrate on another. The Telex from his finance director had pushed Eileen out of his mind; she would have remained in the background until it was time to see Homsi, not because he was inhuman or unconcerned about her, but because for thirty years his business had always had first claim. It was as much a reflex as a decision that booked for Japan, regardless of other responsibilities. It had never occurred to him to do otherwise until James Kelly questioned it.

And now the question was in his mind and he was having to fight to answer it. He couldn't think clearly, and he pushed his work aside. He was going to Japan. That was an irreversible decision. He wouldn't permit Kelly to make him feel guilty to the extent of changing that. But until he had seen the Syrian he couldn't apply his full concentration to anything else. He had to know what they wanted. Then he could agree to it. Having agreed, he could go to Tokyo without scruples. James Kelly could set what was needed in motion. And he wouldn't take the resignation seriously. Kelly was in an emotional state. When he had something to do to help her, he would regain his perspective. The terms were sure to be political, and goddamn it, as Logan excused himself, Kelly was an ex-diplomat who was ideal as an intermediary until he got back. But it seemed a long morning till he was ready to take the car to the Bank on Ferdowsi Avenue.

Chapter 7

Peters had never bought clothes for a woman before. He hesitated
outside the little boutiques, which were all that Nice offered. The toilet
articles were easy. He had been pressured into buying a bottle of
cologne by the assistant in the druggist's shop. He had a hairbrush,
a comb, and a plastic bag with a toothbrush, paste, and a sponge. He
disliked strong scent, but the cologne, which he hadn't wanted to buy,
was fresh and clean. He remembered how hot that upstairs bedroom
was. Even without the mesh over the window, it caught the full afternoon sun. Perhaps the cologne was a good idea. Inside the boutique he
caused confusion by asking for a size 12 in a dressing gown. There was
a long caftan, which would be useful, and this was finally wrapped for
him when the French sizing was established. He found a blouse and
a light cotton dress which weren't too expensive, and went back to the
car. He had been disgusted by the prices, and the salesgirls irritated
him by their attempts to foist things upon him which were unsuitable.

He drove back feeling resentful and suspicious that in some way he
had made a fool of himself and that everything he had bought was too
expensive and wouldn't fit. He couldn't excuse Madeleine's attitude to
Eileen Fields—it showed her in a mean and spiteful guise which literally repulsed him. He didn't want to sleep with her again. He regretted
having done so in the first place. She had been a comrade in arms
then, an equal in the struggle against a capitalist world. He had admired her courage and relied on her in the hijacking enterprise. She
hadn't disappointed him. There was no reason why her exceptional

qualities should fall away on this mission, leaving a jealous, quarrelsome virago—except that women were generally unreliable and he had been a fool to think she wouldn't prove to be the same.

He was in charge of the mission, and he needed full cooperation from Resnais as well as from Madeleine. The Frenchman's apparent acceptance of his explanation for removing the mesh from Eileen Fields' window hadn't deceived Peters. Resnais didn't like it—he resented not being told, and Madeleine had put a suspicion into his mind that Peters was being soft. He eased the accelerator back and the car slid to the side of the road. He stopped, found a cigarette, and lit it. He was the leader, and it was his job to unite the other two behind him. Resnais could be mollified, and if Madeleine could divorce herself from her personal relationship with him, he believed she would stop making trouble. Otherwise she would have to be recalled. Finishing his cigarette, Peters decided this might prove the proper course, but he had to give her a chance. To be fair to her, too. Because of her real courage during the hijacking. He started the car and drove back to the villa.

Madeleine found Resnais in the hall. She had come in from the rocks, her body gleaming with sun oil and sweat and tanned a deep brown. The bikini showed big breasts, a little waist, and stocky thighs.

"It's nearly as hot as home," she said. The Frenchman had one hand on the stair rail and a foot on the lowest step.

"Where are you going?"

Resnais' foot came back to the level.

"I've been thinking about that window. People have been known to climb down bed sheets. I thought I'd go upstairs and look."

"I'll come with you," she said.

"I think you should wait here. I want to have a look around. It would be better if he didn't come and find us both in with her. You stay and keep a watch for him."

Madeleine looked at him. "You don't trust him?"

"Do you? Isn't that why you're fighting all the time—because you don't like his attitude to the lady?"

"I'm not jealous!" Madeleine raised her voice. "I wouldn't be jealous of that miserable, stupid—"

"Don't shout," Resnais said quietly. "You *are* jealous, my dear Madeleine, and I respect your instincts. She has changed your man toward you, and I don't blame you for being suspicious. So I am going

up to take a look at the window. And at her. If there is something between them, maybe I will find out."

"How?" Madeleine asked him. He stepped on the stair again.

"I may decide to ask her," he said. "You stay here and keep Peters
away till I come down."

"She'll tell him," the girl said. "Don't cross him, Resnais. He's not
safe to cross."

"She'll do what she's told," Resnais said. He began to walk up the
staircase. "I have a way with ladies. She won't say a word."

Eileen had fallen asleep. The novel lay on the bed, turned downward. The sun was flooding the room and the heat was at the high
peak of the afternoon. When Resnais unlocked the door he did so very
quietly. It didn't wake her. She was stretched out on the bed, wearing
a thin silk petticoat, one hand laid across the cover of the book. He
transferred the key to the inside, closed the door, and locked it. Then
he walked very softly over to the bed. The petticoat was damp with
sweat and it clung to her, showing the nakedness underneath. Madeleine's brown, voluptuous body, almost nude in the flimsy bikini,
hadn't aroused him. The pale skin, the slender line of arm and thigh,
sheathed in pure silk, with handmade lace framing both breasts,
turned him suddenly hot. He lowered himself onto the bed beside her,
and as she woke he closed his hand over her mouth.

"Good afternoon, madame," he said. "We're going to have a little
talk."

"I know," Homsi said, "how much this means to your company.
But after all—it is your wife's life at stake." Logan Fields had his back
to the huge display case. He had made many trips to Teheran, and
never thought of visiting the crown jewels. He had never been interested in sightseeing. His collection of antiquities was purely for investment.

"I can't do it," Logan said. "By Christ, I *won't* do it!"

There was a subdued glitter in the low electric lights around them, a
reflection of millions of diamonds and precious stones. Showcases
aflame with crowns, tiaras, necklaces, were ranged through the exhibition rooms, deep in the bowels of the Bank of Iran. The men who had
kidnapped Eileen Fields might just as well have demanded the contents of the treasure vault in hard cash.

"Mr. Fields," Saiid said, "I know this seems impossible. But don't
give me your answer now. Think what it will mean to your wife if you
refuse."

Directly in front of Logan, protected by bulletproof glass, was a case containing a huge solid gold globe of the world, completely encrusted with diamonds, rubies, and emeralds. There were no sapphires to denote the seas; the stones were considered unlucky by the Persians. Why couldn't it have been money? Every penny, every share, everything he possessed. . . . Why hadn't they asked for these? . . . But not Imshan. Not to give up one of the richest oil fields in the world.

"I can't talk here," he said suddenly. "I've got to have time to think."

"How much time?" the Syrian asked. "These people are impatient. They want your promise. And they want proof that you are keeping it. Otherwise. . . ."

"You're asking the impossible," Logan said. He moved away, pushing past a crowd gaping at the Shah's imperial crown. Its value was said to be a million pounds sterling. The Syrian threaded his way after him. Logan had moved to the exit when he caught up. He tugged at his sleeve.

"Give me an answer tomorrow," he said. "We can meet here again. In the same place."

"I'll give it to you now," Logan said. "I can't do it. I can't pull my company out of the oil field."

The Syrian stood still. There was a grim look on the Englishman's face that worried him. He had expected protests, abuse, even threats, but it sounded as if Fields had given a final answer. Saiid was blocking his way out.

"Mr. Fields," he said, and his voice dropped very low, "there is something else I have to tell you. I hoped it would not be necessary. Unless you give me a favorable answer by tomorrow, your wife will suffer the loss of a finger. It pains me very much to tell you this. Please reconsider. Every succeeding day that you delay, she will be mutilated further. I don't think you would be happy to receive the evidence. Believe me, it's not an idle threat. I will telephone you in the morning."

As Logan lunged toward him, he slipped to the side and hurried through the exit. The man whom Colonel Ardalan had detailed to follow him broke from the covering crowd and vanished after him.

People were staring at Logan Fields. His attempt to grab the Syrian had been seen, and one of the security police on guard in the vaults was on his way toward him. He leaned against the wall for a moment. Then he turned and began the climb up into the street. Outside, in the hot, dusty air, he felt an urge to be sick. It was so strong that he

grabbed for his handkerchief. The blue company Rolls was waiting by
a corner and it began to glide toward him through the traffic. He got
inside. He was due back in the office; there was a meeting with the
chief consulting engineer and geologist. He was still feeling sick. For
the first few minutes he didn't know where to go. Kelly's house was the
first choice. Somewhere he could be alone—where he could vomit if he
wanted to, and then somehow face the reality of what had happened in
the bank vault.

*Give up Imshan. Pull out of the negotiations with the Iranian gov-
ernment and go home. Recall his team and close down the exploration. Otherwise they would cut off Eileen's fingers one by one and send
them to him.*

He leaned toward the chauffeur. The partition was down. "Go to
the Hilton. Then go back to the office and get Mrs. Armstrong. Tell
her I'm not feeling well. I must have eaten something."

He had always made his decisions alone. He had decided, im-
promptu in the vault, when he told the Syrian that he couldn't do what
they had asked. At that moment, his mind had been made up, again by
a reflex as natural to him as breathing. He couldn't deliberately sabotage Imperial Oil's interests; he couldn't wreck the chance of breaking
the world oil price and saving Europe's economy, whatever the consequences. He had said it and meant it. But he had no defense against
that last threat. He had stood alone all his life, neither wanting nor
welcoming help. But now he needed it. And Janet, who loved him, was
the only person who would do. He went up in the lift to her suite, and
as soon as he could reach the bathroom, he was sick. Then he poured
himself a whiskey and sat down to wait for her.

Saiid Homsi drove back to the Syrian Embassy. He was feeling optimistic. Just for a moment, he had nearly lost the gamble. His intuitive sense, that most valuable asset to a man in his position, warned
him that Logan Fields was going to hold out. Threatening to mutilate
the wife had been Saiid's idea, and it had been employed at the crucial
moment. Europeans had a horror of physical cruelty. To a people long
accustomed to mutilation as a means of punishment, it meant nothing.
In many sheikhdoms thieves lost a right hand, traitors were castrated
and blinded. But to the European it was unthinkable. He had been
very clever to threaten Logan Fields with that. It had probably done
more to persuade him than any threat of death. Although no such arrangement had been made, Saiid felt the threat might have to be carried out. He had never favored the plan to pressure Logan Fields by
kidnapping his child—he had favored the outcome even less. He
believed that kidnapping and negotiation were too complicated a

method of avoiding the threat implicit in Imshan to the power of the Arab world.

He had not been present at the high-level meeting in Munich, but he knew that his government had proposed an assassination attempt against the Shah as the surest way of stopping a European company getting their hands on the oil field. As soon as Khorvan reported to his Russian contact that the Shah was having talks with James Kelly, the organization had made its plans and set its spies to work. KGB intelligence had been a considerable help in finding out details of Logan Fields' family life; his deep attachment to his child was well known. The preparations were made, Peters and his team were briefed, and the operation set in motion.

Syria had been obliged to agree; it was too dangerous to rely on assassination. There had been several attempts in the past, some masterminded by the Russians when the Communist Party was outlawed in Iran, but because of the efficiency of Ardalan none had come anywhere near success. The Shah was encircled by one of the most effective security services in the world. The only vulnerable target was the oil company.

Saiid ordered Turkish coffee and began composing his report to Damascus. He emphasized Fields' initial resistance, but his own view was optimistic. He felt that Fields would collapse under the threat of his wife's mutilation. And if he were really hesitating, it might be necessary to show that they meant what they said. . . .

By five o'clock that afternoon, Colonel Ardalan was studying the surveillance report on Saiid Homsi and the companion report on Logan Fields. His dismissal of James Kelly's explanation was correct. The story was a lie, concocted out of panic. Whatever the attaché in the Syrian Embassy wanted with Logan Fields, it wasn't to sell him stolen manuscripts. The choice of the imperial treasure exhibition showed the true professional touch of Saiid Homsi. A crowded place, where nobody would notice a European and a Syrian in conversation. Ardalan's man had seen the incident when Fields apparently tried to strike Homsi. He must have said something unpleasant to provoke a public loss of self-control from somebody like Logan. Fields had left looking ill; he hadn't gone to Kelly's house where he was staying, but to his assistant's suite in the Hilton. She had been brought from the office, in the middle of a meeting, to join him there. Ardalan read through the reports and spent some time thinking quietly afterward.

He had switched his intercom to Off. Logan Fields was a very important man in the Western world. His chairmanship of the big oil company made him a target for intrigue. He was engaged in high-level negotiations in Iran at that time, and the outcome of these negotiations could have a vital effect on the political and economic future of the West.

Ardalan understood from the Shah that provided the terms were satisfactory, Imperial Oil would get the concession.

And yet the Russian technical team, with a spearhead of negotiators, was still in Teheran. Therefore they must believe the door was still open to them. And that pointed to Khorvan. None of this could be linked to Logan Fields' encounter with Saiid Homsi. Syria was not involved with Imperial Oil in any way. Its only record as far as the company was concerned was in organizing the destruction of sections of desert pipeline during the first Israeli war.

So why had the Syrian contacted Logan Fields? And why was the Syrian visiting an American archaeology student, whose telephone number was in the pocket of a murdered man? A humble man, a talker around the coffee shops, but a friend of dissidents—and by coincidence, hovering around Logan Fields at that reception for the minister. *If* it was coincidence. . . .

What had begun as a puzzle without pieces was taking on a shape. One thing was certain. Whatever the reason motivating the Syrian government, anything they undertook was never in the interest of Iran. If they had contacted Logan Fields, it must be for a purpose that was injurious to the Shah and the country in some way.

Ardalan sent for his assistant, Sabet. He offered him a cigarette and showed him the two reports. When Sabet had finished reading them, he asked the assistant his opinion. Sabet hesitated. He didn't want to make a mistake. The colonel wouldn't forget a hasty or ill-considered view.

"I think," he said, "that Logan Fields is being pressured by Homsi. Whether this is personal or through the oil company I don't know." Ardalan nodded. "I think so, too. But it's unlikely to be personal blackmail. Homsi is acting for his government. If he is putting pressure on Logan Fields, then Syrian policy is guiding him. We have to know why. In case it concerns us."

"And you think it does?"

"Yes." Ardalan nodded again. "Yes, I do. Homsi is involved with an American who is also somehow connected with that waiter at the Hilton who was murdered.

"The American worried me as much as Homsi. We've had him

checked by Interpol. Nobody knows anything about him. He came through Munich at a time when a terrorist conference was taking place there. There is no proof that he was connected with it in any way. He stayed at a hotel, went sight-seeing, left for Teheran, and went to work at Persepolis from time to time." He paused and looked at Sabet, his eyes narrowed.

"But I know he was in Munich for that conference. I feel it here." Ardalan tapped his chest above the heart.

"I can't say this, because it is only my instinct that tells me. I cannot say what I would like to say. Not yet. I have to add more pieces to my puzzle so that it makes some kind of picture. I have to be patient for a little longer and hope that something more comes to light. Another little piece here and there. Just enough." He got up from his desk and Sabet did the same. The colonel might treat his staff with informality, but he didn't expect it to be returned.

"You can't go to his Majesty then," Sabet said.

"No, I cannot go to his Majesty with nothing but this." He pointed to the reports. "There is not enough there to justify the action I want to take. We will have to wait and watch a little longer. I am sure that my friend Mr. Kelly knows exactly what is happening. But he will protect his chairman and the company. He will lie as he lied last night. However, I might talk to him." He stretched and yawned. "There is a reception at the French Embassy on Saturday. I will see him there."

Janet sat on the arm of Logan's chair, her hand resting on his shoulder. "My God," she said. "What are we going to do? It's like a nightmare."

"I don't know." He passed his hand over his head, sweeping the hair backward. He felt comforted by having her with him. She had taken the news calmly. He couldn't have borne a hysterical reaction. She had listened, sitting with her arm around him, got up and refilled the glass with whiskey, and waited until he had told her everything.

"There's no doubt about it?" That was her first question. "They have got her?"

"No doubt at all. I'll have to meet their terms, there's no other way. Do you know, I haven't been sick for years. . . ."

"I'm not surprised," Janet said gently. She leaned down and kissed him. "You've had a terrible shock. It'll take a little time to get over it. Drink your whiskey."

He had never associated her with tenderness—she wasn't a woman who wasted words or gestures. As a personality she had a diamond brightness—he didn't realize how much she had attracted him simply because she was the opposite of Eileen.

"I've got to work out what to do next," he said. "How to explain it to the board. Christ, I *can't* explain it! It's all got to be done secretly." He looked up at her. "How do I pull my company out of Iran without a reason? Ten million spent on exploration, six bloody months of work and negotiation—a deal coming to the boil in Tokyo—a major breakthrough in oil prices! I'm responsible to my board—and to the shareholders, leaving aside the wider issues!"

"You can refuse to meet Khorvan's terms," she reminded him. "Without Japan you couldn't go ahead with Imshan anyway."

"And let the bastard win," Logan said. "Let him pull the rug from under us. . . ."

"I know you don't want to give in," Janet said. She got up and took a drink for herself. She turned around and looked at him. "At the moment you don't see any alternative. If you don't do what these people say, they're going to cut off Eileen's fingers and send them to you, one by one. That's the real threat, isn't it?"

"Yes," Logan said. He lowered his head for a moment. "Yes. That finished me."

"It would finish me too," she said quietly. "Except that I don't believe they'd ever do it."

The room was very quiet, except for the faint buzz of the air conditioning. Logan looked at her. She was very pale, and the tinted silver hair emphasized this. She sipped her whiskey.

"The people who've kidnapped Eileen don't go in for that kind of thing," she said. "They're fanatics, they're absolutely ruthless, and they don't mind getting themselves killed. I won't argue for a moment that if you refuse to do what they want, they'll murder Eileen. But I don't believe they've ever mutilated any victim or ever will. Keeping the West out of the Imshan oil field is a massive political stratagem, masterminded from the top. This isn't some crackpot revolutionary movement leading a raid on a kibbutz. This is the Arab world, backed by the Russians. They can't afford to do anything like that to Eileen because of world opinion. Think if an atrocity like that were known. . . . It's a bluff, darling. Make up your mind what you're going to do, but don't take that into consideration. Homsi just said it to frighten you." She sat down.

"What are you advising me?" He asked the question slowly. She was being practical and thinking clearly. He should have expected her to take an impersonal view.

"I wouldn't dare advise you," she answered. "How could I? If I tell you to be tough, I might be thinking of myself. You'd never forgive me for it, I know that."

He didn't deny it, he waited. Perhaps she sensed that everything between them hung in the balance at that moment. "So? What are you saying, then?"

"Don't be angry with me," Janet said. "I'm trying to help you." To his amazement she turned to one side and began to cry. He came over to her.

"It's so horrible," she said. "So dreadful for you, facing this. . . ."

"I've got to give him an answer tomorrow," Logan said. "It'll have to be yes. It'll give me time to think it through." He got up and brought back two cigarettes for them. He leaned forward, smoking. He had never seen Janet cry; it relieved him. At that moment he felt able to discuss his wife without excessive guilt.

"You wouldn't risk going to the police—Interpol?" she asked. "Surely they could start looking for her without the story leaking."

"I suggested that to James," Logan answered. "He said it was too dangerous. He said I'd have to play it straight across the board with them if I wanted her released. You know he's in love with her?"

"Then you must bear that in mind when he gives you advice. He'll only be thinking of Eileen; not you or the company. Darling, there's one awful possibility I think you've got to face. Before you do anything drastic."

"That something's already happened to her?"

"No." Janet shook her head. "No, I'm sure she's alive now. And probably well cared for. What I'm afraid of is that if you give in to them and back out of Imshan, they won't keep their part of the bargain. They'll have got what they wanted, and there won't be any witness to stand up and say what happened. Or to identify them. That's what really frightens me." She leaned toward him. "I'd do anything to help Eileen," she said. "But I just don't see how they can ever let her go."

"What you're saying," Logan muttered, "is that I could throw Imshan away for nothing . . . that I could play into the hands of Arab extremism by sabotaging Europe's interests, betray my own company, and incidentally finish my career—and Eileen is murdered anyway. Is that what you really think?"

"Yes," she said. "I'm afraid it is. I'm afraid she's a lost cause, Logan. It's the most horrible thing I've ever had to say in my life, but I don't believe you'll ever see her again."

The telephone rang. She got up to answer it.

"Yes," she said. "Hello, James—yes, he's here." She covered the mouthpiece. "He wants to talk to you."

"Tell him to come up. He'd better know the position. He's got to deal with Homsi while I'm in Japan."

She held on to the telephone. "You're still going, then?"

"Yes."

She spoke to James Kelly: "Come to the hotel. Logan wants to see you."

Then she said, "What are you going to tell him?"

"The truth. That Imshan is the price. And he's to hold them off while I'm away. This can't be a snap decision. There's too much at stake. Apart from Eileen."

"You're going to be nice to me," Resnais whispered. "Like you are to the American. . . ."

The woman underneath him was so terrified that he misjudged her. He took his hand off her mouth and ripped the flimsy petticoat away.

Madeleine had come to meet Peters as he got out of the car. He had been irritated, but suppressed it. He saw her looking at the box with the boutique label on it, but she didn't comment. She put her hand on his arm to detain him, and he decided not to shake her off. He had promised to be fair.

"Don't be angry with me," she said. "I'm sorry about last night. And today. I don't want to quarrel with you. Come to our room—let me make it up to you." They had walked inside the house. It was cool and white after the outside glare.

"We've got to talk," Peters said. "Where's Resnais?"

"I don't know," she said. "Sleeping in the shade somewhere—"

The scream was faint but very clear. It rose for a few seconds, sharp with pure terror, and then stopped. Peters flung the girl aside and leaped up the stairs. One push established that Eileen's door was locked. He stepped back and threw his full weight against it. The lock burst. He saw Resnais getting up from the bed and reached him before the Frenchman was fully on his feet. Peters grabbed him with the left hand, the right smashed sideways into his face. Resnais fell backward, hitting a chair that shattered under him as he collapsed onto the floor. Peters pulled him upright. Resnais' mouth was split and pouring blood. He hit him again. Then he dragged him to the door and threw him into the passage. He shouted for Madeleine. She came running up the stairs; he saw the terror on her face and knew that she had been a party to the rape. She cringed physically as he came near her. "Get him downstairs before I kill him," Peters said. Then he kicked the broken door shut and went over to the bed.

No one had ever hurt Eileen; she had no experience of violence. It was unthinkable that a man should have held her down and inflicted agonizing pain on her. She had been stripped, assaulted. If Peters hadn't burst into the room, the Frenchman would have raped her. The shock was tremendous. Her vision swam as Peters bent over her; she was shivering violently and she reacted from pure instinct. She caught him around the neck and held onto him with all her strength, weeping hysterically. He lifted her and carried her into the room he used for himself. He put her into the bed and sat down, waiting for the hysteria to wear itself out. He could feel the trembling in her body.

"Easy now," he said. "It's all over."

"Oh God," Eileen whispered. "Don't leave me . . . please. Don't leave me. . . ."

"I won't," Peters said. "Tell me what happened."

"I was asleep," she said. "I woke up and he was sitting on the bed. He had his hand over my mouth. He asked me if you were sleeping with me."

She closed her eyes for a moment and then opened them wide as if she were seeing Resnais and not him. "I wouldn't say yes," she whispered. "He wanted me to . . . he hurt me. He went on and on hurting me . . . on my breasts. I couldn't scream. . . ."

Peters pulled down the bedsheet. She had small breasts, beautifully shaped. They were beginning to purple with bruises. The pain must have been agonizing. "I didn't say it," Eileen said. "I wouldn't. Then he said if I told you he'd kill me. He was going to rape me. . . ."

"Did Madeleine come with him?" Peters asked the question. "Or Ahmed?" She shook her head. "No. Just him. I can't stop shaking."

"You'll be all right now," he said. She looked terribly pale—she was badly shocked, and the rigor that was part of it was making the bed shake.

Resnais had tortured her to implicate him. He could imagine what he had done to her breasts while he held her mouth closed. He drew the sheet up and covered them.

"Why didn't you say what he wanted?"

"Because it wasn't true. We haven't—"

"No," he said. "We haven't. I'm going to get you a brandy and put some ice on your breasts. That'll help the pain." He went to the door and yelled for Ahmed. She heard him giving orders in Arabic. The man came up quickly with a glass of brandy and some ice cubes packed into a towel. Peters uncovered her; she made no effort to stop him. She lay and watched him while he wrapped the towel over her breasts; he lifted her while she sipped the brandy. He had held the only real friend he'd ever had, Andrew Barnes, in his arms in the dirt and dust, while the crowd stood appalled and the smell of terror was in the air. There was no comparison between the dead teacher and Eileen Fields—they had nothing in common except a brand of steadfast courage and the role of victim. What he was feeling for her at that moment was a disaster and he knew it. From the moment he brought her to the villa, he had been trying not to see her as a person. Above all, as a woman. If Resnais hadn't attacked her as a woman, he might have succeeded.

"Stay quiet, Eileen," he said. "I'm going downstairs to deal with that bastard." It was the first time he had used her name.

Everything Logan said made sense. James couldn't fault the logic; he sat in the suite at the Hilton, drinking whiskey and listening to Logan explaining the full implications of the terms demanded for Eileen's release. Janet Armstrong didn't contribute, but as she heard the arguments, he detected her brand of frigid detachment. An easy attitude to take when it was Eileen's life at stake. But she had been tactful enough to stay a spectator in the background.

The company's withdrawal from Imshan was not a decision Logan could make from personal motives. However strong. The consequences on all levels had to be considered. James had just sat there, waiting. Logan looked gray and appreciably older. James hoped he felt as ill as he looked.

Imshan was not just vitally important to Imperial Oil. The reduction in oil price would contain the Arab stranglehold on oil for the Western world until oil started to flow from the North Sea and American technology developed new sources of energy. The political factors went far beyond the company's acquisition of rights in a massive oil field, or his own personal commitment to it. These considerations wouldn't have weighed against the threat to Eileen. James watched him when he said it, and didn't believe him. He was being less than honest because he was making a case.

James put his whiskey down. If Imshan was developed by the Russians, then it would be a major political defeat for the West. "There's no guarantee the French and Germans wouldn't get it. The Shah doesn't want the Russians either. So it's only Imperial Oil that's the loser. That's what you really mean, isn't it, Logan?"

"Please, James, be reasonable." Janet spoke for the first time.

"Logan isn't going to abandon Eileen. He'd never do that. He's just trying to find some kind of compromise. He has other responsibilities too. We all have."

"Speak for yourself," he said. "You know there's no compromise with these terrorists. You're just trying to justify letting them murder Eileen. I don't give a damn about Imperial Oil or the economic situation or anything else." He turned to Logan Fields. "I promise you one thing," he said. "If you let Eileen die, I'll make sure the truth gets out. I don't think there'll be many doors open to you after that. Either of you." He was on his way out when Logan stepped in front of him.

"Just wait a minute," he said. "All right, I give in to their demands. I pull out of Imshan. Never mind the consequences. Europe doesn't matter, the company doesn't matter, nothing matters but getting Eileen back alive—right?"

"Right," James said bitterly.

"And then they kill her anyway. Have you thought of that?"

"They won't," James said. "They keep their bargains."

"Not on this level," Janet said behind him. "They can't let her go and have the story come out. That's why they've insisted on secrecy! The world mustn't know how the West was blackmailed out of its oil. They'll promise and the minute the negotiations are wrecked beyond recall, they'll get rid of the star witness. My belief is they'll fix up some accident. Then nobody will believe Logan, even if he *did* try to tell the story. And let's face it, there wouldn't be much point. With Imshan gone and Eileen dead, he'd just ruin his own reputation for nothing. People would think he was covering for having lost the deal."

"Christ Almighty," James said slowly. "You've got a lovely mind."

"I'm thinking straight," she said. "Because believe it or not I'm not emotionally involved. You and Logan are. In my view the only hope you've got of saving her is to go to the police. And in the meantime play along with Homsi. That's my advice to Logan."

"I'm going to Japan tomorrow," Logan said.

"To negotiate the loan," James said. "To go ahead no matter what. . . ."

"To keep my bloody options open!" Logan suddenly shouted at him. "And to make it look good. If I have to screw up the deal I'll do it when I come back. And that's where you stop calling me and Janet names and take your own bloody finger out. You see Homsi tomorrow morning. Tell him I'm going to scuttle the talks with the Japanese government. In the meantime, he keeps contact with you. And you reassure him all along the line that we're pulling out. Convince him. Try to get a date set for her release. Keep talking. . . ."

"And the police," James said. "If you bring them in she's finished. Mind you, your reputation's safe then. You can stand up as the hero, trying to save his wife from the kidnappers, knowing the first word that leaks out pulls the trigger on her. Bloody clever, Janet. I hadn't thought of that!"

Logan opened the door. "Get out," he said. When James Kelly had gone, she came up to him. "I didn't mean it like that," she said. "You must believe me."

"I know. You're trying to do the best you can. Jesus, I've never felt so tired in my life!"

"You go to bed," Janet said. "It's a long flight tomorrow and you've got to have a clear head. I think I should stay here and keep an eye on James. I wonder how long the affair's been going on?"

"What affair? What the hell do you mean? Eileen's never been to bed with anyone behind my back!"

"If you say so." Janet shrugged. They were in the bedroom and he was pulling off his tie. "But I don't see why you should mind if she had."

Logan didn't answer. He kicked off his shoes and rolled onto the bed to try to sleep. An affair with James Kelly. . . . Janet was right. There was no reason why he should mind if it were true. But he did. It took him a long time to go to sleep.

Resnais had loaded his revolver and was waiting for Peters. Madeleine was with him. She had stopped the bleeding, helped him to clean up, and given him a brandy. He was sitting in the lounge facing the door, and she was standing beside him.

He had refused to take her advice and go off in the car, leaving her to talk to Peters. It was a brave offer, and she rose in his estimation because he knew she was shaking with fear of what the American would do to her. She had pulled on a shirt over the bikini, as if she felt that seeing her seminude would only incense him more against her.

"If he comes down and starts anything," Resnais said, "I'll shoot him. So keep out of the way!"

"Listen." She knelt beside him quickly, all her feminine instincts of survival to the fore. "Listen—we can't afford to fight this out. You made a fool of yourself—all right, he beat you up! Ever since that bitch came here she's come between us. It's got to stop now. We have a job to do, Resnais, and instead we're falling out among ourselves. Peters won't attack you again."

"He'd better not try," the Frenchman said. His mouth was stiff and swollen. It hurt him to talk. He gripped the gun, hiding it down the side of the cushion. He waited, quivering and vicious like a wounded cat. As a boy his father had beaten him for laziness and stealing. Being small, and growing up in a tough district, he was a natural target for bullies. By the time he was twelve he had learned to use a knife, and his threshold of provocation was very low. His graduation from petty crime to full-scale terrorism was not so much a political choice but a natural orbiting to the center of violence.

"I'll kill him," he repeated, and he was hoping for the excuse. They heard Peters coming down the stairs, shouting for the Algerian. They heard him tell the man to go upstairs and keep watch outside the prisoner's room. Then he came through the doorway. He expected the Frenchman to be armed. He knew from his position in the chair, his right hand tucked into his side, that he was hiding a gun.

Peters looked at him for a moment, and then at Madeleine. He went to a side table, found a cigarette in one of the alabaster boxes, and lit it. He spoke directly to Resnais.

"I'm sending you both back to Damascus," he said. "I'll give you a break you don't deserve. I won't say why. I'll send the message through tonight. If either of you goes near her again, Ahmed'll put a bullet into you."

"You can't send us back," Madeleine said. "They'll want to know the reason. We'll come under suspicion!"

"Too bad," Peters said.

"You bastard," Resnais said. "You have her for yourself, eh? Nobody around to see? *You* are the one who should be taken off the mission!"

Madeleine looked at each of them. One was her lover, the other her comrade. Now far more than personal issues were at stake.

"Resnais was wrong," she said. "But it was your fault, too. You took the wire off her window without consulting either of us—your comrades. Resnais didn't like it and I agreed with him. He went up to see if it was safe. What happened afterward was probably her fault."

Peters looked at her—now it was she who had no identity. "He tortured her," he said. "Trying to cook something up against me. Our orders were to keep her safe until we were told otherwise. She wasn't to be hurt. She told me you threatened to kill her, too. What would have happened to our mission then?"

"Let him explain," Madeleine said. "Please—we've worked and fought together. He's your brother-in-arms. He has a right to be heard."

"Okay," Peters said. "Explain. But first take your hand off that gun."

Resnais didn't move. The Lebanese girl was right and he knew it. Her pleas for a truce touched no chord in him, but instinct urged him to comply. He didn't want to be sent back and to have to explain why. He might be believed, but there was no guarantee.

"I went to see for myself if that window was safe," he said. "She woke up and started making a scene. I got rough with her, but she asked for it. To you she's something precious. To me she's the wife of a capitalist pig, and I'm the one who'll shoot her if he doesn't do what he's told."

"For God's sake," Madeleine begged, "let's stop all this. Who *is* this woman—what makes her so special to you, Peters? I'm not asking for myself now—it's gone too far for that. At any moment we could get an order for Resnais to execute her. What will you say when *that* comes?"

"*If* it comes," the American corrected, "I will do it myself. As far as I'm concerned, she's in my care. I'm responsible for her and you come under my orders. Both of you. I have no personal interest in her one way or the other. But you're not to be trusted. That's why you've got to be replaced."

"You're making a mistake," the Frenchman said. He brought his right hand up and laid it in view on the arm of the chair. If Peters asked for a replacement, it would look very bad for him. His complaint against the American wouldn't be believed.

"I made one too," he said. "I admit it. I shouldn't have touched her. Wait till tomorrow before you do anything."

Peters finished his cigarette.

"I'm going to get us a drink," Madeleine said. She went out to the kitchen and came back with a bottle of wine. She gave Resnais a glass and handed one to Peters.

"We should be united," she said. "We've forgotten our common cause. Let's drink to it now!"

She had a sense of theater which was less Eastern than Germanic. She chose the role of catalyst, and with the toast she shamed Peters.

He drank, and the others did too. He didn't promise anything. He left them to sit on the terrace outside. Before he could decide what to do about them, he had first to examine himself.

It was a beautiful warm evening and the sky was rose and purple with the setting sun. He sat overlooking the sea; from far below there was a hiss and gurgle of waves breaking gently over the rocks. For years he had been committed to violence. The decision made after

Barnes' death during that campus riot had never been challenged. The world was a bloated capitalist corpse. There had to be a burial before the resurrection. He had conditioned himself to kill, just as he was unconcerned by dying.

He remembered his mother's reproach, made during one of the futile scenes when he was still at college. How could he claim to love humanity when he wasn't capable of loving another human being? They had known nothing of his devotion to his teacher and friend. They were referring, as always, to themselves. He was disturbed at recalling it now. He had given of himself in the fullest sense and for a higher purpose than a personal relationship. Suffering in the mass could move him to tears, and he had never indulged in personal brutality. That was the weapon of the capitalist enemy—the truncheon-swinging riot police, the sadists in uniform. The cigar-chewing generals and the faceless bullies of the CIA.

His adult life had been spent in revenging the murder of Andrew Barnes, in a crusade against injustice and oppression. From the day she was captured, he could have put a bullet in the back of Eileen Fields' head and felt no qualm of guilt, because the act was totally impersonal. But now the screen protecting him had crumbled. She was no longer an object in the class war. He would have beaten Resnais to death for what he had done to Eileen Fields. He sat in the darkness and tried to rationalize what had happened.

Her courage had impressed him—inevitably, then, her vulnerability had touched him. He had fallen into the trap of allowing a personal relationship to develop between them. Of talking to her instead of slamming down her food and walking out—of accepting the responsibility which she had thrust on him that first morning when she faced him in the little room. It was all clear and logical, and he had no excuse for letting it happen.

And now he wanted her as well. He wondered whether she knew it, whether she had sensed that even as he wrestled with her by the window, his body had turned traitor and wanted to make love to her instead.

Madeleine, with her sharp intuitive sense, had realized it long before he did. Resnais had gone up to the room to prove it. They had drawn together against him because they felt he could no longer be trusted. Now he didn't know if he could trust himself. The truce between them was a false one, but he dared not send them back to Damascus. The central committee might send out a new team to take charge of Eileen Fields. He couldn't risk that—she mustn't be handed over to anyone else. He could still protect her against Madeleine and

Resnais. He got up and went back inside the villa. They were waiting for him, drinking the last of the wine.

"You're right"—he spoke to Madeleine—"we've all got out of line. We have a job to do, but it's got to be done my way. I'm in charge of the prisoner and nobody else interferes with her. If that's understood we can forget what's happened today."

"You're the boss," the Frenchman said. Madeleine only nodded. Peters didn't stay. He went out and up the stairs.

The girl looked at Resnais. "Do you trust him?"

He shook his head. "No. He didn't send us back to Damascus because he didn't dare. He's gone soft on the woman. We'll have to watch him very carefully."

Madeleine stretched in the chair; she turned her empty wineglass over and over. She looked at Resnais.

"I hope the mission fails," she said. "I hope Logan Fields refuses the terms. I want to see you shoot her."

"If that's what you want, chérie, be prepared for one thing. I shall have to kill Peters first."

"I know that," she said slowly. "And if you don't, I will."

Eileen lay still. It hurt her so much to move that she couldn't raise her arms. The immediate trauma of shock was dulled by the brandy. She was still shivering slightly, and the ice-packed towel was a soggy mess which she had thrown off. The window was open and she could see a little balcony. It was dark and the sky was clear and bright with stars.

For a long time she had wept, after Peters left and she heard the door lock. She felt brutalized and degraded, and more than at any time since her abduction, she experienced the anguish of being abandoned by the outside world. The days had gone by, interminable, nerve-racking, and nothing happened. No word from Logan. No move to release her. Just Peters coming in, or the Algerian. Hour after hour of solitude, keeping her spirits high with hope. And then that explosion of violence—the outrage of pain and savage sexuality. If she closed her eyes all she saw was Resnais, bending over her. Logan. . . . She cried the name out loud and turned her face into the pillow. Why hadn't he helped her? Why was there not one word, one sign that he was trying to get her out?

James Kelly would have paid the ransom. If it had been James and not Logan she would have been freed long before. Then, in the despair that shock and isolation brings, she doubted him as well. Nobody knew what was happening to her, and their silence proved that they didn't care. They had given her up. In spite of the pain in her breasts, she dragged herself up and looked at the window. The room was on the same side of the house as the one where she had been imprisoned. It would be equally impossible to climb down. If Logan wouldn't save her she would have to escape. She would have to find some way of getting out of the villa. Peters wouldn't help her. She didn't even consider that. She didn't want him as an ally. She was shocked and ashamed of the way she had let him handle her body. She admitted in horror that after Resnais' attack she hadn't a resource left with which to fight Peters. And she had to fight him. She had to resist the temptation to give in and let herself depend on him and look to him for the protection that was not coming from outside. It was going to be difficult. She kept listening for his step outside the door. He was her only friend in a situation of dreadful danger. Without him Resnais would certainly have raped her. She mustn't think of Peters as a friend. He was a killer, a terrorist like the other two. She pulled the covers over herself and shivered in spite of the heat.

When she heard the door open, she shut her eyes and forced herself to pretend she was asleep.

Chapter 8

Logan left for Tokyo at four in the afternoon. It was a long flight with stops in Bangkok and Hong Kong. He had a case full of papers on Imshan to occupy him, and two sleeping pills Janet had pressed on him. He had no intention of taking them. He despised crutches of any kind, and had always been able to sleep when he traveled. She had driven to the airport with him, but stayed in the car. He didn't want to draw attention to his departure. He had been surprised and touched to see tears in her eyes when they said good-bye. They had drawn together in the crisis, and this was important to Logan. He hadn't much faith in fair-weather relationships. He valued her cool commonsense and he needed her sympathy. He leaned back in his seat on the plane and decided that he had never been so much in love with her as he was now.

Champagne was offered; he declined in favor of whiskey, opened his briefcase, and set out his papers. He had told James Kelly to contact Homsi and demand proof that Eileen was still alive. Janet said he had made the right decision, Kelly looked at him as if he were a murderer.

Whatever the outcome, James Kelly was finished as far as a career with Imperial Oil was concerned. Logan had no complaint against him as an employee. He had played a brilliant and vital part in the negotiations, and his personal impact on the Shah had tipped the balance in the company's favor. There would be a termination of contract and a substantial compensation. But he was personally unacceptable to

Logan. He had decided this, without allowing himself to trace that decision to Janet's remark about an affair with Eileen. He resented James' attitude and his lack of loyalty to Imperial's interests. When it was all over, he would be told to go.

All over. Logan had read the first paragraph of a memorandum twice without being able to concentrate on a word. There was a cold finality about the way he had expressed it to himself. Janet insisted that there was no way of saving Eileen. He didn't doubt her motives for a moment. She wasn't the kind of woman who would influence him out of anything but an honest opinion. She believed that his wife was going to die no matter what he did. Kelly, condemning him at every step, was sure that Logan had a choice.

In a flash of painful insight, he understood why Janet had been such a source of comfort to him. She denied him the choice, and relieved him of the responsibility. He didn't want to lose Imshan. It was hypocritical to pretend that he could throw away the greatest coup of his career, forsake the power and importance of operating the key oil field in the Western world. The very thought of giving it up caused him such mental agony that he writhed away from it, desperate for an alternative. There must be a way that wasn't the chilling deduction of Janet Armstrong. There must be a hope of saving Eileen and keeping Imshan. He wanted the oil field because he wanted the power and the success implicit in it. He wanted it for the company which he saw as an extension of himself and to which he was deeply committed.

But no decision could be made until he knew for sure that she was still alive. He settled back to his papers, forcing himself to concentrate. When the hostess came around with the cocktail canapés, he was completely absorbed in his work.

Six miles below and two hundred miles away from the plane as the crow flies, the brother of the waiter Habib Ibrahimi sat brooding in a coffee shop. He was a poor man who worked as a loader at the airport. He lifted heavy crates for ten hours a day for a miserable wage, his back was bowed and aching, and only the dream he shared with his brother brought light into a life dark with poverty. Equality for all, an end to misery and exploitation. He was not clever like his brother, he was content to listen and admire. The meaning of Habib's message was beautiful and clear. But Habib was dead, his wife taken away by the secret police. There was no doubt in the mind of Habib's brother who had commanded the killing. Habib had denounced his betrayal of the people often enough. "Khorvan, the traitor." These were the words of Habib, and his brother murmured them like a prayer from the Koran.

For some days after Resnais' attack Eileen had been ill. Her breasts swelled up and the pain kept her from sleeping. Shock made her lethargic; she cried copiously and without reason. Peters got her a sedative from the store of medical supplies in the villa. In common with many rich men, their wealthy sympathizer was a hypochondriac, and there were remedies for everything.

There was no suggestion of moving her back into the little room. As she suspected, the window looked over a sheer drop and she was equally secure where she was. But it was airy and comfortable. Psychologically the new surroundings helped her to recover. By the end of the week she was up and dressed, and her spirits had risen. Peters noticed it without realizing that the motive was her determination to escape. It had grown while she lay in bed, depending on him more and more, finding herself fretful when he didn't come. He sent wine in with her food, and the quality in those days when she was ill showed care in the selection. The signs were clear and there were times when she was overcome by panic at her own acceptance of his changing attitude toward her. At no point did she consider asking him to let her go. The locked door and the attention to security told her it would be useless. She didn't want to expose herself by such a move. And secretly she shrank from the rejection that must follow. If she put herself at his mercy, it would be at a price she wouldn't pay. The least part would be her self-respect. She had to do it alone. And since she had been sick, he might well be off his guard.

He came up that morning carrying a portable tape recorder.

"You look better," he said.

Eileen denied it. "I feel awful. I'm dying for fresh air."

He thought how pale, almost colorless she looked—he decided he might take her down and let her walk in the garden.

"I want you to send a message to your husband," he said.

"What kind of message? Have you heard from him? Oh, tell me, please!"

"He wants evidence that you're alive and well," Peters said. That message had been relayed through on the radio the night before.

"Of course," Eileen said. "How stupid of me not to think of that. He's a businessman. He never does anything without collateral."

"Sit here," he said, "and talk into this mike." She shrugged. He had never seen her show bitterness before.

"What am I supposed to say? Please pay them the money or they're going to kill me? He knows that already."

Peters bent over her. Last night's radio message had been less confident than the earlier reports. Logan Fields was not acting in a hurry. He had left the last part of the negotiations with Homsi to a subordinate. He wanted proof that his wife was alive before he would proceed any further.

"Look," he said. "You've got a chance to talk to him. Pull out all the stops. It's for your own sake."

She had sat down and clasped her hands in front of her. She looked up at him.

"I'm not going to beg," she said quietly. "And anyway it wouldn't do any good. He could have paid the ransom by now if he really cared what happened to me."

"You're wrong," Peters said. "It's not as simple as that. It can't be fixed in a few days."

"Then it's not money?"

He hesitated. He wanted her to send the message and to make it as poignant as she could. Whatever was holding that bastard of a husband back, a frightened plea from her might tip the balance.

"No, it isn't money."

He saw her glance down at her hands and then up at him.

"God help me if it's something to do with Imperial Oil," she said.

He slipped the tape into the machine. "Don't be a fool," he said. "Give him a chance. He'll get you back. Now talk into this. Give him your name and the date. Make it a personal message, something he'll know is genuine. And for Christ's sake don't be proud! You can't afford it."

She took the little microphone on its lead and held it near her mouth. He pressed the switch to Record.

She did as he had asked—gave her name and the date. She said she was alive and well and she asked him to get her released so she could go back to Lucy. "I wish you and Janet well."

Peters switched off the machine. "Why did you say that? Who's Janet—what does it mean?"

"You needn't be suspicious," Eileen said calmly. "It will just prove I sent the message, that's all."

"It's too cool," he said. He was irritated because she wouldn't help herself. "I'm going to erase it and you do it again. Tell him you're frightened. Tell him you're in danger."

She got up. "I told you," she said. "I'm not going to beg. If you rub that out I shan't say anything else. He knows perfectly well what can happen to me. It's just possible he won't care."

Peters picked up the machine. "Okay," he said. "Have it your way."

She came up to him as he reached the door and touched him on the arm. "I know you're trying to help me. I'm sorry. I think I've begun to give up hope. I've been very frightened these last few days."

"It's because of what happened," Peters said. He wasn't angry with her any more. She looked wan and miserable. "It shook you up. Don't give up on your husband. He's doing his best."

"It's being shut in here all the time," Eileen said. Her heart was beating very fast. "If I could just go outside for a few minutes. Sit in the sun. . . ."

"I was going to take you out in the garden," Peters said. "So long as you promise to behave yourself."

"I won't do anything," she said. "I promise."

They stayed at the back of the villa, away from the sea. They sat under the shade of a pergola, roofed with vines. She leaned back, looking at the pattern of the leaves over her head, the sunlight fragmented through them. He sat beside her. They hadn't spoken since they left her room.

"Thank you for this," Eileen said.

"You needed fresh air. So long as you're sensible you can come down every day."

"Have you ever been in prison?"

"Yes. Twice."

"It's a very strange experience. You feel completely cut off. As if nobody in the world knew or cared what happened to you. Did you feel like that?"

"No," Peters said. "I had friends. I knew they'd get me out." He was thinking of a filthy cell in Santiago, where he had been held on suspicion without trial. A bomb explosion had released him. That was the first time. The night of the campus riot when he was beaten up in the police station was in a special category. He knew what Eileen meant by feeling isolated but he had never experienced it in that sense. He had been isolated from society in the mass for many years.

"You have plenty of time to think," she said.

He was leaning back in the chair, his eyes half closed. He was close enough to grab her if she made a move. It was very warm and drowsy under the shade. A large yellow butterfly sped lazily past them, pirouetting on the way to a hibiscus bush. Eileen watched it. She could see the villa through the trees. From her memory of the front when they arrived in the car, there was a wall around it, and the gates to the road were down a short drive from the front door. She was wearing the caftan he had bought in Nice. Under the long skirts she slipped out of her high-heeled shoes. Coming down through the garden she had plotted the way around to the gate in her mind, while she walked beside Peters, his hand holding her arm. There was no specific plan in her mind, only an instinct that clamored for her to take this opportunity because there might not be another. In bare feet she could run fast. He wasn't carrying a gun—the casual dress of shorts and a sweatshirt told her that. If she could reach the gate and the road. . . . She was sure there was a villa not more than fifty yards away on the left.

"I'm sleepy," she said. He turned his head toward her.

"Go ahead," he said. "It's getting very hot."

She shut her eyes and let herself relax. Her arm was resting near to his; the lounge chairs were side by side. She let it slip onto her lap.

She stayed quite still, keeping her eyes closed. The effort was agonizing. She began to count under her breath, marking off the minutes.

After she had calculated a quarter of an hour, Eileen opened her eyes enough to glimpse him. He was lying back, his arms folded across his chest, his head turned away from her. She waited for some minutes, watching him.

He didn't move. She slid one leg to the side and followed it with the other. One foot was on the ground. Again she waited. She couldn't see his face but he seemed to be asleep. The chair didn't creak as she moved. She eased herself upright, watching him in terror in case his head suddenly turned and he should find her poised to run away. He stayed still. Very slowly and carefully she levered herself by her hands until she was half out of the chair with both feet on the ground. She felt as if she were suffocating, her heartbeat was so rapid. He seemed to be breathing heavily; his posture in the chair was completely relaxed. She was on the ground. She turned and fled to the right, toward the avenue of trees and the front of the villa.

Peters was not asleep. He thought that she was. He didn't hear her creep out of the chair; he was in the twilight when the mind is blank and the body relaxed. She had almost reached the gates when he turned around and saw that she had gone.

The driveway was gravel and sharp under her feet. The surface was also very hot; as she ran she felt the sting of burning. She was gasping for breath, fighting the weakness of confinement without exercise, seeing the gates in front of her. Twenty-five yards and she would reach them. Peters was superbly fit. He ran like a stag and he caught her as she was wrenching at the locked gates in despair, tears streaming down her face. She started to scream wildly as he pulled her back, holding onto the bars. He heard a car approaching down the road. He slammed his hand over her mouth and hurled her bodily into the bushes out of sight. He held her there, pinned to the ground until the car had passed them.

Then he pulled her onto her feet. She stood, disheveled and weeping. He pushed her around to the back and into the villa. They went upstairs, and he unlocked the door, still holding her.

"You fool," he said. "I trusted you." She turned in the room and faced him. The reproach was suddenly more than she could bear.

"I *had* to try!" she cried out. "Don't you see, he's never going to give you what you want? He doesn't want me back!"

"Shut up!" Peters shouted at her. He slammed the door behind him and advanced upon her. He was angry enough to hit her. "Shut up!"

"Tell me what you've asked for," Eileen said. "I have a right to know." The moment of collapse was past. She had never had a chance of getting out. He had known the gates were kept locked. "Oh, God," she said. "I wish you'd get it over with."

"You could have been killed out there," Peters said. "If Ahmed or Resnais had seen you, they'd have shot you dead."

"That's going to happen anyway," she said. "I know it. That's why I tried to get away."

"It isn't going to happen," Peters said. "You keep on saying that. I know he'll give it up. Nothing's going to happen to you."

"Give up what?" Eileen asked slowly. "What have you asked Logan in exchange for me?"

He didn't want to tell her; she should have been kept ignorant either way. But he was losing hope himself because of her despair.

"Imshan," he said. "He's got to pull out of the oil field. That's why it's taking time."

"I see." She turned away and sat on the edge of the bed. She pushed her hair back and there was a streak of dirt across her cheek from where she had clung to the gates.

"Now I understand why you wanted to kidnap Lucy. He might have done it for her. But you've asked the one thing in the world that my husband will never do for me."

"You're his wife," Peters said. "He won't let you die."

"He wants to marry someone else," she said, and her voice was flat and calm. "I came back from Teheran because he'd asked me for a divorce. You took the wrong person."

Outside, a distant airplane hummed like an angry bee. It was the only sound.

He stared at her. She was sitting very still. The caftan had been torn when they struggled by the gate.

Logan Fields wanted a divorce. They had kidnapped her instead of the child, and all the time she had no value as a hostage. Fields was going to discard her anyway. He couldn't believe it—he refused to accept what she said. There was a slow dejection about her that was unbearable to watch as she sat on the bed.

He came over and caught her by the shoulders. "You're not lying to me? You're telling the truth?"

"Janet Armstrong is his assistant," Eileen said. "That's whom he wants to marry. I mentioned her in the message."

"Oh, Christ," Peters said very low. "Oh, Christ, what a mess. . . ." He was holding her so tightly that it hurt.

"I wish you'd told me before," she said quietly. "I've gone on hoping, thinking it was money. He'd pay money for me, I know that. But never Imshan. It's the most important thing in his life. He'd never give it up for anything or anyone in the world. Except Lucy. Never for me."

Peters looked down at her. Her face was upturned, with the dirty smudge on the right cheek and the stains of tears around her eyes.

"How many people know about this?"

"Only the resident director in Teheran. I told him about it before I left."

Peters lifted her off the bed. He held her a little away from him.

"If it's not common knowledge, it doesn't matter," he insisted. "Fields may think better of it. He can't live with himself if he walks out on you now. We've got to keep hoping that he'll crack. So long as our people don't find out—" If Damascus discovered that she wasn't any use to them, he knew what the order would be. Execute her. He had been insisting to himself that if Fields accepted the terms, Eileen would be released, but he had begun to doubt that too. Now her life wasn't worth a spent match. He suddenly drew her close to him. He didn't kiss her, but for a moment his hand came around and stroked her hair.

"I can't let you go," he said slowly. "I can't do that. But I promise you, nobody's going to hurt you. Whatever the outcome, I'll see nothing happens to you. Will you trust me?"

Eileen leaned against him. She felt very tired, as if the will to resist had emptied itself in that attempt to escape. When she reached the gates and found them locked it was the end. Even before she knew that the price for her survival was the one Logan Fields would never pay. The man holding her cared, as her husband did not. He was promising her something that she knew meant his betrayal of his friends and his political beliefs. "Nobody's going to hurt you." For almost three weeks she had been holding out against the temptation of all prisoners to form an emotional attachment to a captor who was kind to them. She had lived with fear, uncertainty, and physical assault, and somehow kept her courage and her hope. Now all she could feel was his strength and the warmth of his body. He wanted her, and she could feel the tension growing in him as he held her. She had no friend in the world left but him. The mental and physical temptation to give in to him was the strongest feeling she could remember. Beyond him was the outside world. She had no contact with it, it had forgotten her. She had lived in the villa, preserved in her isolation and captivity like a fly in amber. Only Peters was real. Peters had saved her from Resnais. He was promising to save her again.

"I'll make it as easy as I can for you," he was saying. "You can't get away and you know it now. Do as I tell you, and we'll have to hope it turns out right."

Eileen lifted her head and looked up at him. The message was clear.

"I've got to go down," he said. "I've got to keep the others sweet. They mustn't suspect anything." He stepped away from her.

"Come back," Eileen said.

"Only if you want it," Peters answered. "You don't have to. It's not part of the deal."

"I never thought it was," she said. And she repeated it. "Come back."

The party at the French Embassy was to celebrate Bastille Day. There was a reception in the garden. James Kelly had arrived early, and was talking to a group of French Embassy officials. He had been posted in Paris for two years during his Foreign Office career and formed a deep attachment to France. His appreciation of French culture had made him many friends, and an introduction to the ambassador in Teheran had come from one of them as soon as his arrival in Teheran was known. He had come early because he couldn't stand being alone in the house. He had met Saiid Homsi that morning. The rendezvous was in the bazaar in South Teheran. He had faced Homsi in a dingy little office behind one of the shops selling brassware to the tourists. And he had delivered Logan's demand. Proof that Eileen was still alive or no deal on Imshan would be considered. The interview was brief and the Syrian was just as smooth and hypocritical as he had been with Logan. He had expressed alarm at Logan's trip to Tokyo, but James had reassured him it was only undertaken to block the negotiations begun by his subordinates. He had added a brief of his own. "Tell the PLF that I personally will ensure that Imshan comes to nothing, side by side with Mr. Fields." The Syrian had smiled a little, showing a gleam of gold teeth, as if he understood how personal James Kelly's motives were.

James had gone to the office and somehow got through the day. He didn't want to work; he wanted to call everyone together and tell them that the company wasn't going through with Imshan and they could start packing up to go home. He didn't trust Logan. He believed, quite wrongly, that Janet Armstrong was influencing him from personal motives, and that Logan was willing to be influenced.

He could sense the hesitation, the open-ended option in Logan's mind. He wanted the oil field; he had already rejected Eileen before there was a choice between them. Above all he was ruled by ruthless logic. Even his admirers described him as an archpragmatist, catfooted in his ability to leap from one position to another as a situation changed. Logan was trying to convince himself, not that he couldn't make the decision in Eileen's favor, but that it wouldn't help her if he did. James was not inclined to violent feelings. His nature was steadfast and deep in affection, reserved and disinterested in dislike. But for Logan he experienced visceral hate. He showered and changed, and fled from his house and the torment in his mind, to the relief of human company that was not connected with Imperial Oil.

The wife of the first secretary was chatting with him. She was a charming woman in her late thirties, endowed with the wit and chic which so attracted him, and she had managed to make him laugh and relax a little. He felt a touch on his elbow.

"Good evening, Mr. Kelly."

"Good evening, Colonel. Is Madame Ardalan with you?"

The colonel shook his head. "Unfortunately she has a fever. Some small thing. . . . She was looking forward to coming this evening." The garden was filling with people; the Frenchwoman excused herself, and James was alone with Ardalan.

"You look tired, Mr. Kelly," he said. "Have you been working hard?"

"Yes, fairly hard. Mr. Fields likes to keep things moving pretty fast."

The colonel offered him a cigarette. "And how are the negotiations going?" He glanced up for a fraction of a second from lighting his cigarette, and saw the change of expression on Kelly's face. It was only a glimpse, a sudden tensing of the facial muscles, but it told him that the answer wouldn't be the truth.

"Not too well," James said. "We're a bit worried about things at the moment."

"I'm sorry to hear that," Ardalan said. "Mr. Fields must be very anxious. I have heard that he is very enthusiastic about the field."

"Oh, yes." James' diplomatic training wasn't proof against his terror for Eileen. He abhorred discussing Imshan, and he couldn't hide his reluctance.

"Tell me," the colonel said, his black eyes very mild, "is Minister Khorvan responsible?" He hoped that Kelly wouldn't lie or take refuge in evasions. He knew Khorvan had tried to block Imperial Oil, and had only given way on a direct order from the Shah. If the negotiations were failing, as Kelly indicated, then Ardalan wanted to know if the minister was to blame.

"Well"—Kelly hesitated—"I don't think I should commit myself on that. Can I get us both a drink, Colonel?"

"That would be kind," the colonel said. He followed James in search of a waiter. They both stood sipping champagne.

Ardalan watched the Englishman for a few moments. He didn't look tired—that was an understatement. He looked as if he hadn't slept for days, and there was a drawn, haggard expression on his face when it was in repose. He radiated inner disquiet. Ardalan had seen a similar look on Logan Fields the night he saw the Syrian.

He didn't expect James to tell him anything. He just wanted his opinions confirmed.

"Apart from Imshan," he said, "is there anything else that might worry Mr. Fields?"

"No—not that I know of."

"I see." Ardalan sounded disappointed. "Tell me, has that Syrian approached him again? People like that can be very persistent."

"No. No, definitely not. Mr. Fields wouldn't touch anything illegal. He made that very clear. I see the minister has just arrived. Would you excuse me, Colonel? I ought to go and have a word with him."

"Of course. Mr. Kelly—"

"Yes?"

"If at any time you need my help—please let me know."

"Thank you," James said. "I'll remember that." Ardalan saw him edging his way through the crowd toward Khorvan. He watched for a moment, before turning to find someone else to talk to. His prediction to Sabet was correct. James Kelly hadn't revealed anything, except that he and Logan Fields had something very definite to hide.

The Embassy garden was filled with trees and ornamental shrubs. It was early evening and quite light, but the shrubbery was thick enough and dark enough to hide a man from view. Among the shadows along the wall, there was one that moved.

The minister was in a sour mood. He had felt unwell the previous day, and in common with many Iranians he was morbidly afraid of illness. A dozen alarming explanations for his feeling of malaise occurred to him, and the reassurances of his fashionable doctor hadn't satisfied him. He preferred to go to London for medical advice. He had an audience with the Shah the following day, and this was as much responsible for his symptoms as any germ he might have picked up. The Shah wanted a report on the negotiations with Imperial Oil. He was about to give the chairman an audience and he was expecting the minister to provide full details. The one gift his Imperial Majesty possessed above all others was the capacity to judge other people. Khorvan might feint and dodge effectively with James Kelly and Logan Fields, and his fellow Iranians. He had no hope of deceiving the Shah. The Shah wanted Imperial Oil to have the concession, albeit on the toughest terms. It was the test of Khorvan's skill to maneuver them into a position whereby the oil company couldn't comply with Iranian terms and the government couldn't back down on them without a loss of face. Walking this tightrope was difficult enough, but doing it with the resourceful Logan Fields tugging at the wire was sufficient reason for a stomachache. Khorvan sipped at the orange juice, when he craved a healing draught of Scotch whiskey, and made little effort with the other guests. He felt no obligation to be sociable, and when Kelly came up to speak to him, he pretended not to notice him. There were four people surrounding the minister, two of them French, an official from the trade department of the British Embassy, and Kelly. Immediately behind them, the tall bank of shrubs cast an impenetrable shadow. James had waited for some moments without being acknowledged and suddenly lost patience. In the service of Her Majesty's Government he had endured bad manners and boredom, but he owed Imperial Oil no such allegiance. As he prepared to turn his back on the minister, his thoughts were dwelling sourly on the vanished "gunboat diplomacy" of past decades, when one of the shadows took shape and left the protection of the shrubbery. It became a crouching form, one arm raised. Before Kelly realized what he was seeing, it lurched against the minister.

Khorvan was speaking when the knife struck him. His glass fell and shattered, spattering orange juice; he gave a grunting cry and toppled forward. It was Kelly who acted instinctively and grabbed the assailant as he ran for the shelter of the bushes. Kelly struggled briefly with a small, wiry man who kicked and clawed at him, spitting insults in Farsi. Someone in the crowd screamed. The momentary shock had paralyzed the onlookers, now the woman's cry released them.

Seconds later the attacker was seized by other hands and brought to the ground. Kelly knelt down beside the minister. Khorvan was lying on his back. One of the French officials had opened his jacket and pulled his tie loose.

His head lolled to one side. There was a hurried movement among the crowd standing around them, and Colonel Ardalan knelt beside James. He turned the minister's head toward them. The face was a ghastly color and the eyes were turned up. He laid a hand on Khorvan's chest, and then gently turned him on one side. A knife handle was sticking out of his back below the left shoulder blade. Ardalan looked around.

"The minister is dead," he said. He got up and went to where the assassin lay, pinned to the ground by two of the guests.

"Take him into the Embassy, please," he said. "My men will remove him. I must ask everyone who saw the murder to come with me. If the ambassador will permit me to make use of a room. . . ."

It was the ambassador himself who brought the colonel into the building and placed an office at his disposal. The party was ended, and those guests who couldn't assist the colonel went home. James was the first person to make a statement; there was no change in Ardalan's manner. He was soft-spoken and polite, but it was the head of the dreaded SAVAK who was asking the questions, wearing the face of the amiable colonel like a rubber mask. James described how the man had run out from the shrubbery, struck the blow, and how he had prevented him escaping.

"That was very brave of you," the colonel said. "The English always keep their heads in emergencies. His Imperial Majesty will be grateful that you caught the assassin."

"It's a shocking thing," James said. It was his first experience of violent death and it disgusted him. Equally repellent was his brief glimpse of the murderer being hauled by the hair into a police car. There was a grimace of agonized terror on the man's face that haunted him.

"Who was the man? Why did he do it?"

"We shall soon know," Ardalan said.

James drove back to his house, past a police guard that had been set

traitor who was giving Imshan oil fields to the capitalists. And so the minister had had Habib's throat cut.

Ardalan went back and sat down. The room was sour with physical smells and gray with cigarette smoke, writhing upward under the lights directed at the prisoner. At last the puzzle made a picture that was recognizable. A major piece had just been fitted into place.

Habib Ibrahimi had been told to spy on Khorvan. His direct connection with the American, Peters, led to Saiid Homsi. And from him to Logan Fields. And from the mouth of Khorvan's assassin had come the proof that linked them all together. Imshan oil fields. He got up and stretched to ease the tension in neck and shoulder muscles; he spoke to the group of officers standing in the background.

"Stop," he said. "And don't let him die. The Shah will want him executed." He went upstairs to his office. It was growing light. He had already reported to the Shah by telephone before leaving the French Embassy. Now he had all the information that he needed to take action. An international terrorist group, masterminded by Syria, was intervening in Iran's most valuable economic and political asset.

Oil. . . . One assassination had already taken place. It wouldn't be difficult to present the unimportant brother of Habib Ibrahimi as a politically motivated terrorist. A good policeman could judge when it was right to doctor the facts. At eight in the morning he set out for the Palace. His assistant, Sabet, went with him.

The moment Eileen woke she knew that he was in the room. It was an instant transition from sleep to full awareness, and she lay very still, waiting. She could see his outline in the semidarkness. There was a moon outside and the blinds were up. He was standing still, looking toward her. She sat up, and turned on the lamp beside her bed.

He didn't speak, he came and stood beside her. There was no expression on his face at all, and he was fully dressed. A sense of absolute fatality overcame her as she looked up at him, and with it a strange excitement and relief. The current was flowing between them, without words and without touch. It was the most powerful presexual experience of her life, those few seconds while she waited.

"If you've changed your mind," Peters said, "I'll go."

"Don't go," Eileen said.

He sat on the bed and slowly put his hands on her shoulders.

"I won't force you," he said. "I'm not Resnais." It was Eileen who caught his face with her hands and kissed him on the mouth.

It was an urgent, wordless lovemaking. Even so, its intensity was matched by tenderness from him. He made love to her, and afterward when they were quiet together, Eileen remembered the words of a friend who had also been a priest. Any fool can have intercourse—it takes a real man to make love. They lay close, their bodies dovetailed, loath to lose contact. For Peters it was a strange experience; sex and emotion had never mixed before. She was less accomplished as a lover than Madeleine, there were no acrobatics, but there was no comparison in either the satisfaction or the aftermath. He wanted to feel her near him, to touch and kiss. He remembered how other women's desire to cling had jarred on him. Now he held her possessively until the cycle began again. Passion, exploration, self-loss; Eileen met and matched him as the night passed. It was a different woman who woke in his arms before the dawn. Marriage and childbirth, love and loss, all the human experience of her life with Logan Fields was muted.

Peters was the reality, the fulfillment she had never imagined could exist. He had made her a part of himself. He woke soon after she did and she felt his hand claiming her breast. She laid her own on it.

"I'll have to go soon," he said. "Will you be all right?"

"Yes. You mustn't be seen."

"I'll be careful." He pulled himself upright; his fingers twined in her hair, curling it around.

"I'll come back as soon as I can. You go to sleep." He bent and kissed her. "You gave me a lot," he whispered.

"We gave each other," Eileen said quietly. "I wish you wouldn't go."

"Ahmed gets up early," Peters answered. "I don't want to take risks. Not now. You do as I say. Go to sleep. I'll come up later." She watched him dress and go to the door. He turned and in the pre-dawn light he made a gesture which she couldn't see. Then the door closed and she heard the lock turning. The room was very quiet, the atmosphere heavy and still. Slowly she ran her hands over her body, miming what he had done. Sleep. To make the voyage of self-discovery and then to sleep. It was impossible. Marriage to Logan for seven years. She had thought of herself as a woman, a wife and a mother, a mature human being. A woman whose life ran along a single well-defined track. Meath House and Eaton Square; the smart flat in the Rue St. Dominique. Trips abroad. Dinner parties and business entertaining. A little child, immaculately dressed in pink. Not a hair ruffled or a seam out of place. Mrs. Logan Fields. Whoever she was, Eileen didn't recognize her anymore. And never would know her again.

* * *

"It's taking too long," Madeleine complained. "We get messages saying Fields has capitulated but no proof! How do we even know it's true? He never lets us near the radio set."

She and Resnais were sitting in a café in the center of Nice. They spent a lot of time together now. On the surface the atmosphere between them and Peters was friendly, if reserved. None of the three was deceived by it. It was a truce, and waiting to be broken.

"So we only know what he tells us," Resnais said. "I'm going to make contact with Damascus myself."

"No," Madeleine said quickly. "Don't do that—it's too dangerous. If he finds out you've talked to HQ behind his back. . . ."

"He's keeping control of that radio link in case the husband backs away at the last minute. Then he'll be the only one to know. He won't carry out the sentence and he'll make sure that I don't." Resnais lit a cigarette.

"Ahmed says he hasn't slept in his own room for the last four nights. He takes her out in the garden, hidden around the back of the villa," Madeleine said. "He brings her wine, cigarettes, books to read. I admit to you, Resnais, when all this started I was jealous. I loved him and I didn't like him being soft with another woman. But it's more than that now." She lifted the glass of *orange pressée* and then put it down without drinking. "He's not just sleeping with her, he's corrupted," she said. "He's gone over to the enemy. I've been watching him and it's not the same man. It's not the man I lived with in Teheran and I promise you it's not the man who took that jet. . . . I know he means to let that woman go. Even if he has to wreck the whole mission."

"And sacrifice himself?" Resnais asked her. "He must know the consequences. Perhaps he plans to defect with her. Give himself up and trade information about the PLF. . . ." He lit a cigarette. "We'll have to stop him, chérie. And I don't think we should wait any longer. We've held that woman for three weeks. Very soon now there'll be a decision. Only we won't know it. He can tell us anything—any lie. They can escape together. The next thing we'll know will be when the police pick us up."

Madeleine swore viciously in Arabic. "He was one of the great ones," she said. For a moment her eyes filled with tears. "He gave up everything for the Cause. He was an inspiration to so many of us. And that woman destroys him. I promise you, Resnais, she's not going to get away with it."

"I don't quarrel with that," the Frenchman said. "After all, we are only anticipating events. First, we have to get rid of him. Then we hold her. And I won't interfere with you if you want to be unpleasant."

"What are we going to do? We can't try to take him unawares—he's very dangerous."

"I know that," Resnais said. "But so am I. We will arrange an accident and that way nobody will ask questions afterward. As far as the PLF is concerned, he will have died a hero. And you and I will carry out the mission." He put a ten-franc note in the bill and folded both under his empty glass. "We'll go back now," he said. "And we must be very friendly to him. Especially you. He must think he has nothing to fear from either of us."

Chapter 9

Resnais watched Madeleine with admiration. They were eating dinner on the terrace. She had brought out two bottles of wine, sat next to Peters, and linked her arm through his. She gave him a warm smile.

"I feel like a party tonight. We've been gloomy long enough. I drink to you. . . ." She passed him her glass and Peters had to drink from it. Resnais made his contribution.

"To the success of the mission. I feel very confident it will go our way."

"It's looking promising," Peters admitted. "I had a radio message this afternoon saying Fields had agreed to the demands in principle. It may take a week or two before they announce that Imperial's pulling out of Imshan. I think we've got it made."

"But that's wonderful!" Madeleine exclaimed. "What a triumph for the PLF—to shut off that oil supply to the West! It's such a pity no one will know."

"That's the whole point," Resnais said. "It's got to be kept secret. Otherwise the oil company would dispense with Logan Fields and go ahead. They wouldn't care *what* happened to his wife."

Peters had been waiting for them to bring Eileen into the discussion. He looked up at them both; he sounded quite disinterested.

"If the deal goes through," he said, "nothing *will* happen to her."

"I want to go to Nice tomorrow," Madeleine said. She spoke to Peters. "Will you drive in with me? Resnais doesn't want to come and

I'm bored on my own. Please, Ahmed can sit outside her door if you're still worried about that old business—not that you need to be. Resnais is all right now, aren't you? He's got himself a woman."

"More than one," the Frenchman said, grinning. "There's a very nice little brothel just behind the Place Gambetta. Pretty girls and not too much money. Not that you need it." He shrugged and leaned back, smiling at them both. The girl was very good. He wasn't surprised by her deceit—he had never trusted a woman in his life—but he admired her acting skill. There was no trace of bitterness or hostility; the violent rupture might never have taken place. She was behaving as if their old relationship would be resumed. And she was leading Peters in the direction he had told her.

"I've been Madame's chauffeur long enough," he said. "While you and she were sulking. Now it's your turn to run after her. I'm going off tomorrow to fish. There's a man on the beach who runs a motorboat and takes people out for the day. I'm fed up with sitting around here."

Peters hesitated. The atmosphere between them had been sour and suspicious, in spite of the superficial truce. He needed to keep them at least neutral. He disliked the feel of Madeleine's body pressed against him, and her scent—expensive gardenia mixed with female sweat—nauseated him. Everything animalistic which had once aroused him now chilled him with disgust. The oiled skin, the breasts bursting through the cotton shirt, its ultimate button deliberately left undone, the flashing smile and hot green eyes. He couldn't have touched her after holding Eileen Fields. But he needed to keep her quiet. If Resnais were out of the house, there was no danger in leaving Eileen in the Algerian's care. He knew better than to open that door and go inside. . . .

"Okay," he said. "We'll go into Nice. When do you want to go?"

"In the morning. We can swim and I can do some shopping. Maybe you'll take me to lunch?"

"Maybe. If you don't want to go to the Negresco."

"Don't be cruel, chéri," she said softly. "I haven't been near a place like that since I left home."

There was a moment, after they had finished dinner and Resnais had gone upstairs to bed, when Madeleine had made a genuine move toward him. She had suffered considerably when he left her bed. Pride and jealousy had corrupted her love for him into a fiery hate. She despised him for his weakness and raged against him for forsaking the political principles that had brought them together. But worst of all was the knowledge that the woman they had kidnapped—the epitome of the spoiled, useless female of the capitalist species—had roused feelings that Madeleine herself had been unable to touch. She had agreed with Resnais that he must be killed, and she had spent the evening maneuvering him into position for the Frenchman. But when the moment came she tried once more—the love which had not completely died in her was crying out for a reprieve.

"I miss you," she said. She caught his hand and brought it to her mouth. She bit his fingers and kissed the hard palm.

"Come back to me," she whispered. "Come to bed tonight." She had never begged in her life. She was an independent woman, mistress of herself, capable of withholding or giving her body as she felt inclined. She abdicated everything by slipping down by his knee and stroking it.

"I want you so much. I still love you."

It was an effort to touch her. An even greater effort not to move aside and escape the caresses that he did not want. He laid his hand on her head and tried to be kind. He knew as he did so that all she would understand was the rejection.

"I'd better not," he said. "It was starting to complicate things. And we can't afford that. We're friends and comrades now. We've got to be content with that."

She got up, and to her credit managed to shrug as if she didn't mind. He didn't understand the motive and he admired her self-possession.

"As you wish," she said. "I suppose a lot of women have made themselves look foolish over you. So I have joined the club. I'll go up then. But we're going to Nice tomorrow."

"I'll be ready at ten," Peters said. "Goodnight, Madeleine."

As soon as she had left the terrace he forgot her. She hadn't made a scene and he was grateful. It was eleven o'clock. Resnais must be asleep and he would have to give Madeleine time to go to bed. Then he could go upstairs and into Eileen's room. He felt in his pocket for the key. He had tried to analyze himself and her. Sexual desire was an easy explanation. He had wanted to go to bed with her, and this was the motive which had made him attack Resnais and reject Madeleine. Equally, she was frightened and lonely, and had conceived a masochistic hunger for the man who held her prisoner. It was all very glib and probable, but it wasn't the explanation. There was something much more fundamental than a physical bond or a twisted psychological urge. All the protectiveness in his nature, the singleminded championship of people in the mass, had suddenly narrowed and channeled toward one person. She wasn't the most attractive, and certainly not the most beautiful woman he had known. But she was the only human being for whom he felt personally responsible. Nothing must happen to her. That was as far as he had allowed himself to go. Nothing else had changed. His beliefs were the same. His loyalties were unchanged. He regretted nothing he had done in the name of his political creed and he would do it all again. But Eileen Fields was set apart from it. He took the key to her room out of his pocket. There was a mark in his palm. He had never loved anyone in his life since the death of Andrew Barnes. Not his parents, or a friend or a woman. Now he did. It was very simple, and he didn't argue with it. He put the key back and went inside. Upstairs, waiting by her bedroom door, Madeleine heard him cross the passage and walk on past his own door. She opened hers and saw him going into the room where Eileen Fields was kept.

At six that morning, Resnais went downstairs and into the kitchen. It was fitted with every modern convenience; it looked more like an operating room than a place where food was prepared. He passed the stove complex with its eye-level oven and gleaming hood and pressed a switch on the control panel. He then turned the knob counterclockwise, and pulled at the cupboard fitting on the left. It swung outward; behind it, in a space big enough to walk in, was a room stacked with guns and ammunition. He lingered for a few moments, examining the assorted rifles, revolvers, and a selection of the latest small arms, including the autoloading Armalite AR-15, a popular weapon in guerrilla attacks. Resnais loved guns—they were said to be a phallic symbol. He dismissed the idea as typical bourgeois claptrap. There was nothing wrong with his penis, and he still loved to use and handle guns. He chose a Russian M-1930 rifle with a telescopic sight and a box of ammunition. He went back into the kitchen, closed up the cupboard, reset the knob on the control panel, and packed the rifle and bullets into a long case he had brought with him. It came from a sports shop in Nice, and normally contained a fishing rod. He went out to the garage; there were three cars. A Renault which was usually used for going short distances, a big Rolls, gleaming white, which was the Algerian millionaire's favorite toy, and a long, low-built E-type Jaguar. He put the case into the trunk of the Jaguar, locked it, and pocketed the key. He didn't want Peters taking the fast car. Then he went to the terrace, pattered lightly down the fifty rock steps to the sea, and went for an early swim. He was eating rolls and drinking fresh coffee when Madeleine came down. He grinned at her and pulled out a chair with one hand, the other waved a buttered roll. He was in excellent spirits, laughing and joking, describing his swim. Madeleine didn't respond.

She didn't eat anything; she drank the strong coffee, tight-lipped and sullen. Her eyes were tired and she hadn't slept well. Jealousy was a bloody goad, applied by the memory of where the man she had loved had spent the night. There was no mercy, no trace of sentiment left in her now. She looked at Resnais.

"Is everything ready?"

"Everything," he said gently. "You do your part and I'll do mine. And smile, chérie. Make it a happy morning for him. He won't see another."

Peters woke very early. He left Eileen before the dawn broke, and it was the only sad note in their lovemaking that she so often woke up to find he had gone. The bedroom was no longer a comfortable prison, a cage in which she paced up and down dreaming of rescue or escape. It was a haven, a private place where she lived a new life with a man she loved. There was no other word to describe what she felt for him. From the first night when he made love to her and the metamorphosis began, her passionate need of him had only increased. Beyond the boundaries of sex, a range of feeling she had never suspected was developing. She had loved Logan, but she had never been an integral part of him. The unity between her and Peters was so fundamental that it was like being connected to his spinal cord. She understood the meaning of that metaphysical expression in the marriage service about the man and woman being one. She was one with him. When she touched him it was like an extension of herself. And if her commitment to him was complete, then it was mutual.

She talked about herself, about her life and her marriage, and it sounded like the recital of someone else's life. Flying from London to Paris to entertain for Logan; dressing in clothes that cost a poor man's yearly wages, dispensing fine food and exquisite wines like some character in a prewar play. Living a life where the values were prefixed by a dollar sign, making relationships with people where there was no common ground beyond expediency. It sounded degrading, and telling him made her ashamed. It was all far away and, having told him, she wanted to forget it. He hadn't confided in her about himself. He wasn't the kind of man who looked back. He was himself and she accepted it. And now she never thought about the future. She lived for the day. For their walks in the garden, where they sat in the sun and there were no more thoughts of running away from him. Of the nights when her door was unlocked and he came in to her. It was like a beautiful dream, filled with tender sensuality. That morning he brought up her breakfast tray. She insisted that he share it with her. Afterward they went to the window. She loved to look out. Peters had his arm around her.

"I have to take Madeleine into Nice," he said. "I don't like leaving you, but Resnais won't be here. I'll be back as quickly as I can this afternoon. I thought I might take you for a swim. Would you like that?"

Eileen leaned her head against him; below them the sea was blue and glittering in the sunshine.

"Aren't you afraid I might escape?"

"I can swim pretty fast," Peters said. He kissed her hair. For years he had never thought about another person subjectively. Now the quality that added luster to their relationship was the total generosity with which she gave herself to him. And asked for nothing. He couldn't imagine any woman in a similar position who wouldn't have tried to persuade him to let her go. She didn't ask because she trusted him and because the understanding between them was so deep that neither sought advantage.

She hadn't asked him for the final commitment, but he knew that he would have to make it. On balance, Damascus was confident her husband meant to carry out the terms for her release. Homsi believed in him. But neither of them knew that the bargaining card they held had never been a trump: a man like Logan Fields didn't throw away Imshan for a woman he no longer wanted.

"I shall miss you," Eileen said. "I can try to finish that dreadful sex book you gave me."

He turned her around and kissed her. It took a long time. When he went downstairs Madeleine had brought the Renault out of the garage.

"You drive," she said. "I'm sick of that coast road. Let's go along the Moyenne Corniche for a change. We'll see some wonderful views, it's so clear today."

Logan was having breakfast in his suite in the Okura Hotel when he got Janet's cable. KHORVAN MURDERED. NO CHANGE IN THE OTHER NEGOTIATION. PLEASE TELEX YOUR PROGRESS AS AM ANXIOUS FOR NEWS. JANET.

He had slept well, after a long and tedious dinner with a dozen senior Japanese oil men. He felt relaxed in mind and body. The Japanese importers and the government had agreed to a partnership, the terms of which would provide the extra money needed to finance the building and installation of the new refinery. The heads of agreement were being drawn up and he expected to sign them before leaving for

Teheran. He had kept the question mark at bay, ruthlessly excluding it
from his calculations. He went ahead as if there were no such man as
Saiid Homsi, and his wife were at home with their child in London. He
closed out everything, and brought the negotiations to a successful
conclusion. Then he slept, because he knew that in the morning the
truth would have to be admitted. He was gambling and he was doing
so deliberately, because he couldn't bring himself to back away and
lose without a fight. There had to be a way out—a way which would
save Eileen's life and still leave Imshan within grasp. When he read
Janet's cable he jumped to his feet with excitement. It couldn't have
been more fortuitous. Imperial's main enemy and opponent was gone.
It was incredible luck. He didn't think in human terms, and the minister's death was not even a shock. It was a bonus.

Without him, it might even now be possible to get the construction
of the refinery deferred until Imperial had got the bulk of its investment back. Already he was dealing with Khorvan's successor in his
mind. It was likely to be Amir Momtaz, former ambassador in Washington and known to sympathize with the West. The way was clearing
for Imshan; he could never have calculated on the removal of Khorvan. Nothing seemed to stand between him and the apex of his career
—the solution to the savage inflationary problem of Western countries
was within his personal grasp. He, Logan Fields, head of Imperial
Oil, was in a position to conclude a deal with the government of Iran
which would result in the breakup of Arab solidarity over oil prices,
something that the diplomacy of the West had signally failed to
achieve.

From far below, the sound of Tokyo's frenetic traffic was a muted
hum. His company would rank with the oil giants through the development of Imshan. Sitting in the tenth-floor suite in the luxurious Japanese hotel, Logan felt as if he were standing on the mountain peak,
looking down at the kingdoms beneath with the promise that all could
be his if he would only pay the price.

And the price was Eileen. Deliberately he tried to call her face to
mind, and nothing came. It was a blank, as if he were subconsciously
rejecting her memory. One life, balanced against the solution of a
global problem. He had said to James Kelly that if it were no more
than his own interests and those of the company, there would have
been no conflict, and in that moment of self-examination, he persuaded himself that it was true. Janet believed Eileen would be killed
whatever he did. He wasn't prepared to accept that view, but it raised
a terrible doubt. It could all be thrown away for nothing. There was a
reflection of himself in a mirror across the room; he looked up and

saw it, a man sitting hunched in his chair, fighting against two impossible alternatives.

To sentence his wife and his child's mother to an assassin's bullet, or to destroy his life's work—and then find that she was not to be returned alive. "I don't think you'll ever see her again." He remembered Janet saying that. He shuddered. Now her face was clear in his mind, the protecting screen dissolved, showing her to him in a dozen guises: Walking through the soggy Irish fields to show him some horse in which he had no interest, reaching out to him on their honeymoon, leaning over his shoulder as he opened a Christmas present she had given him. He could remember exactly what it was. A little sepia study of hands, by an unknown eighteenth-century French artist. It hung in his study in London. The man reflected in the mirror bent over, his head hidden in his hands.

He realized he had been thinking of her in the past tense.

Resnais had left the villa early. He checked that the fishing-rod case was in the trunk and drove off in the Jaguar. The coast road branched off toward the Corniche about five miles farther on, and he drove fast. At the junction leading to the mountain road he eased the car back and pulled into a lay-by. He changed his rope-soled sandals for strong shoes with rubber grips, and pulled a black sweater over his white sweatshirt. He swung back onto the road and took the route up the mountainside. It was a hot morning and he was oily with sweat; his watch said nine fifty-five. Madeleine would leave with Peters at ten o'clock. He calculated that it would take them just over twenty-five minutes to reach the spot on the road he had indicated to her when they drove back from Nice. They had done the journey in reverse and arrived at the villa exactly half an hour later. He drove on, climbing the twisted road; below him the mountainside fell away, carpeted with pine trees. There was a steep bend, with a blind corner, and he slowed down. Rounding it, he drove on for another hundred and fifty yards. The road widened here and there was sufficient room for a car to pull up against the rock verge without impeding traffic. Resnais stopped the car, pulled out the angler's case, and began to run back to the corner. It was ten fifteen exactly.

He climbed off the road, swinging himself up over the rocky overhang; there was a patch of scrub growing up just ahead of the blind corner. He had crouched there the day before, and it gave him a perfect view of the road and anything approaching on it, before the corner itself had to be rounded. The angle was very steep—no car could hope to take it at speed. On the right-hand side the drop down the mountainside was hundreds of feet into the valley. Resnais unpacked the rifle and clipped on the telescopic sight. He heard the sound of a car and flattened himself in the scrub, sighting along the barrel. He had a clear view of a red Peugeot as it came along the road below him, and plenty of time to identify it by the license plate. The Peugeot turned the corner, slowing as it approached, and then disappeared.

Resnais didn't move; he stayed in position, squinting through the tiny rangefinder on the rifle, waiting for the car driven by Peters to come into view.

Madeleine got into the front seat of the Renault beside Peters; she threw a raffia bag onto the back seat. She remarked on the heat, and he said something noncommittal; neither of them talked for the first part of the drive. She watched the road ahead through dark glasses, and as they swung onto the Corniche she glanced across him and down. The drop was increasing. He drove fast, but without being reckless.

The corner where she knew Resnais was waiting was about two hundred and fifty yards ahead of them.

"I have to get this mended," she said. She had taken her watch off and was looking at it. "It stopped last night."

"There's a place on the seafront," Peters said. She was putting the watch back on her wrist; her window was down and her arm was lying across the edge of the door.

"Oh, *merde!*"

Peters slowed at the exclamation. "What's the matter?"

"My watch has fallen off—you'll have to stop." He halted the car and Madeleine sprang out. The corner was just ahead of them and he could neither see anything coming around it nor be seen.

"Hurry up," he said. "I can't stop here!"

She had been searching along the ground; she straightened up and looked at him. "Go on," she said. "There's a lay-by just around the corner. Wait for me there. . . ." She heard him say something irritated under his breath, and stood still, watching as the car moved forward, gathering speed—a hundred yards to go. Resnais waiting above the road. She felt nothing but a calm detachment. As the car came into Resnais' view, he saw that Madeleine wasn't in it. He sighted on the nearside front wheel, and as Peters came into the straight stretch of road before the corner, he squeezed the trigger.

Peters knew the road and the corner; he didn't slow down as much as someone who was unfamiliar with the curve might have done. He saw, up above and without taking his attention off the road, a movement in the scrub bushes on the overhang. When the tire burst, there was a second or two when he tried to take avoiding action. He slammed on the brakes and wrenched the wheel to the right, hoping to take the corner. But the impetus of his own speed was too great. The rear wheels slewed around and the Renault nose-dived over the edge.

The sound of rending metal and shattering glass reverberated. There was a sickening distant crash, followed by the dull boom of an explosion as the gasoline tank caught fire. A plume of ugly black smoke drifted up over the lip of the road. Madeleine was running toward the place where the car had gone over. Resnais scrambled down and they stood together looking over the edge. There was a fire burning among the pine trees down the mountainside.

"Adieu, Peters," Resnais said. He slapped her on the back. "Come on, chérie. Get in the car."

She turned away too quickly for him to see that her eyes had filled with tears.

The accident was reported to the police within the hour, but by the time the rescue squad climbed down to the site of the fire, there were little outbreaks among the trees and a thick pall of black smoke hung in the air. There was nothing left of the car and anyone in it but a mass of twisted, red hot metal.

Eileen spent the morning lazily. She bathed and passed some time resting on the bed; she dozed for a few minutes, her thoughts full of Peters. She dressed in the cotton dress he had bought her. There were more clothes in the cupboard, an assortment of lipsticks and a box of expensive embroidered handkerchiefs which she hadn't the heart to tell him were less use to her than Kleenex.

She brushed her hair and made up her lips. She looked tanned from the hours spent in the sunshine, and the look of anxious strain had gone.

It was a different face that looked back from the mirror, with satisfied eyes and serenity in her smile. She was aware that she looked younger; she felt as excited as a child at the promise to take her swimming when he got back. She went on brushing her hair, and when she heard the key in the lock and the door opened she turned eagerly to meet him. Madeleine and Resnais were standing there. Resnais held a gun.

Eileen dropped the brush and gave a cry of alarm. The Frenchman smiled.

"You're looking very well, madame," he said. "Our friend has been taking good care of you." He walked toward her and she ran to the other side of the bed.

"Keep away from me! When he gets back he'll kill you if you touch me again!"

Madeleine moved closer. She was very pale and there was a something in her face that frightened Eileen more than the slow grin on the Frenchman's mouth.

"He won't *be* back," Madeleine said. "He's dead." Eileen stared at each of them. She shook her head. "I don't believe you. *I don't believe you.*"

"Put your hands on your head," Madeleine said. "Otherwise he'll shoot you in the legs. Hurry up!"

"It isn't true." Eileen was crying. "You're trying to frighten me. . . . He's coming back this afternoon. . . ."

"He's dead!" Madeleine shouted at her. She strode around to where Eileen stood, cowering by the bed with her back to the wall. She stepped up and hit her hard across the face with the back of her hand.

"Thanks to you," she said. "You corrupted a good man. You ruined him. Now you're going to pay for it. Resnais and I will see to that! Now put your hands on your head, you bitch, before I smash your stupid face!"

She had been trained in unarmed combat; she was fit and very strong. She caught Eileen and spun her around. She gave her a violent push toward the door. Resnais stood by, pointing the gun at her.

"Go on," he said. "I wouldn't provoke her, madame. You took her man away. I don't think she liked that." Eileen heard him laugh. She saw the Lebanese girl give him a venomous look. She raised her arms, placed her hands on her head, and walked ahead of them out of the room. She passed Ahmed in the hall as they crossed from the stairs. She gave him a look of appeal, but he turned away. They went through into the kitchen and out into a passage where Resnais opened a door and down a flight of stairs. She found it difficult to walk down them and she lowered her arms. There was a door at the end. In front of it she stopped. She looked at the Frenchman.

"I don't care if you *do* kill me," she said. "If he's dead I don't care what happens to me."

"Shut up," Resnais said.

Madeleine unlocked the door at the foot of the steps. "Get inside," she said. It was pitch dark. Blinded by the contrast to the electric lights outside, Eileen could distinguish nothing as she walked into the room. Her hands lowered in expectation of the shot in the back of the head. She felt no fear. Her sole sensation was a grinding pain of grief. But there was no shot; the door slammed and she was left alone. She sank down on the ground and sobbed, not for herself but for the man she loved as she had never loved anything or anyone, not even her child. It was a long time before she got up; she was exhausted from crying. There was a dim light in the room, coming from an air vent high up in the wall. She could see the outline of racks filled with bottles, and knew she was in the wine cellar. She found the door and ran her hands over the walls, looking for a switch, but the lights were turned on from outside. There was a cold, musty smell. She went around the wine racks, and made a circle of the room. There was only the one door and the one little vent letting in the feeble light. There was no bed, no facilities, not even a bucket. She sank down on the floor again, and knew that this signified their intention to kill her. Her feelings were confused.

Shock had deadened fear—agony for Peters overrode the terror implicit in being at the mercy of the Frenchman and the woman. Now that fear mounted, and Eileen began to shiver in the cold and darkness. They hadn't killed her. She gave a moan of fear at the idea that they intended to punish her in some way. "Thanks to you," the girl had said before she hit her. They had murdered Peters. They had murdered him because they had discovered that he and she were lovers. And they had brought her down to this cellar—for what purpose? The Frenchman had tortured her and almost raped her; she could imagine what that woman with hate blazing in her eyes would do. . . .

Panic swept up on her, and she fought to keep control. Peters would want her to stay calm. She fixed his image in her mind, and the threat of hysteria receded. She remembered his kisses that morning, the comfort of being held in his arms. It had been a final leavetaking. She had that to strengthen her and give her courage. The end didn't matter. To face it with dignity was important. To keep him in her mind and to go to meet him. The idea gave her peace. She knelt for a time, her face covered by her hands and prayed for him and for herself. Then she settled down to wait.

"Mr. Kelly?" James went stiff at the sound of the voice over the telephone. He was sitting outside the drawing room, smoking and listening to the gentle nighttime chorus in the garden. A French diplomat and his wife had dined quietly with him that evening; most of the time was spent discussing Khorvan's murder. He had retreated into the garden for a last cigarette before going to bed. The British Embassy had obtained an audience with the Shah in three days' time. He picked up the phone and heard Homsi's voice.

"What is it?" James asked. "Is anything wrong?" Alarm made him abrupt. It was nearly midnight.

"That's for you to say," Homsi answered. "I've just had a disturbing piece of news, Mr. Kelly. I hear that Mr. Fields has signed an agreement with the Japanese government."

"Oh, Christ!" James groaned, covering the mouthpiece. "Where did you hear that? I'm sure it's not correct."

"From a private source," the Syrian said. "I am afraid this may have very serious consequences."

"Wait a minute!" Kelly almost shouted at him. "Listen to me. If it *is* true, I can explain what's happened. When can I see you?"

"Tomorrow," Homsi said. "I feel this is very urgent, Mr. Kelly. Unless you can give me a satisfactory explanation, I am very much afraid of what may happen."

"Where and what time?" Kelly asked. "As early as possible."

"I will wait down the road from your house," the Syrian said. "Pick me up in your car at seven thirty. We can go for a drive, and you can go on to your office. I think it is very foolish of Mr. Fields to go back on his word." Before James could deny it, the man had hung up. He stood and looked at the phone in his hand; the line was buzzing clear. He put it down and dialed the Hilton. There was a long pause and finally someone on the night switchboard answered. He told them to put him through to Mrs. Armstrong. She answered immediately, but he could tell by her voice that she had been asleep. He didn't waste time.

"I've had a call," he said. "Apparently Logan has signed with the Japanese. Have you heard anything?"

"Yes," he heard Janet say. "He cabled me this morning. The negotiation has been a complete success. They've agreed to finance the refinery. What do you mean you've had a call? Did he call you?"

"No," James said. "He bloody well didn't. Homsi phoned me. He says this could have serious consequences. They think he's gone back on his word. You realize what this may mean for Eileen?"

"How did they find out?" She sounded wide awake now. "Nobody knew, it was highly confidential."

"Listen," James said. "Listen to me. If you don't want her death on your conscience, you cable him to get back here. Send it tonight and tell him to take the next flight available. I'm seeing Homsi tomorrow and I can maybe hold him off till Logan gets here."

"All right. . . ." He heard Janet hesitate and called her a vile name under his breath. "I'll send it."

"He's made his choice, hasn't he," James said. "And you knew it. You knew when he signed with the Japs that he was going to rat on the terms. He's a murderer—a cold-blooded murderer. You'd better get him back here." He hung up.

At seven fifteen the next morning, Saiid Homsi took a car from his embassy and it left him at the end of the road leading to Kelly's driveway. It was overcast and hot, with a suggestion of a storm in the air. He walked slowly down the road; his own car had driven off. There was nobody about at that hour. Homsi heard the car coming up behind him, and he stopped, waiting for it to draw level. Before it came to a halt, the two rear doors were flung open and three men jumped out. Homsi didn't have time to turn around before they reached him. He was knocked unconscious and heaved into the back of the car in less than a minute. It drove off at speed toward the north of the city.

At seven thirty exactly, James Kelly came out of the driveway and pulled into the road. He waited until eight for the Syrian to appear, and in a mood of desperation gave up and went to Imperial Oil's offices on Shah Reza Avenue.

A call put through to the Syrian Embassy gave him no information. Homsi had not come into the building. He left a message asking him to contact him urgently, and when the morning passed and there was no call, he phoned the Syrian Embassy again. This time he was cut off abruptly without being told anything. By the middle of the afternoon, the Embassy itself had begun to make enquiries. The Teheran police were unable to assist them. They took details of the missing trade attaché, and Syrian security men visited his rooms. The driver of the car that had taken him to Shemiran that morning was questioned, but knew nothing which could explain the mystery.

By eight the following morning, Saiid Homsi had told Colonel Ardalan a number of things which enabled him to fit the vital pieces into his puzzle. The colonel went home for breakfast; he was very tired because it had been a long day and a long night. He had not permitted the prisoner an hour's respite. There was a SAVAK doctor in attendance who listened to the Syrian's heart and checked his blood pressure at intervals during the interrogation. The colonel didn't want the prisoner to collapse and die with any question left unanswered. Homsi proved to be wiry and tough. He sustained pain with fortitude, and held out until the unbearable threshold was reached and overtaken. Ardalan watched the transformation into a mindless animal, and in the later stages, put a knob of cotton wool into his ears. When he returned to his family and took breakfast, a habit he had picked up during his course at the Military Academy at Sandhurst, the doctor had advised him that the prisoner would not survive without a respite. He drank coffee and ate hot bread rolls, baked with honey and raisins, and played with his smallest child before it was taken to school. He now knew why Saiid Homsi had contacted Logan Fields. He made a report over the scrambled telephone to the Shah's private number at the Saadabad Palace. It was regrettable, but on medical advice, he had to defer further questioning until that evening. In the meantime the prisoner was being given injections to raise his blood pressure.

It was the worst day that James Kelly could remember. Contact with Homsi was his only link with the kidnappers. He had presented himself at the Syrian Embassy that evening and asked to see Homsi's superior. He was turned away without an interview, and the attitude of the staff was openly hostile. Nobody could tell him anything and nobody would see him. He returned defeated to his house at Shemiran to find Janet Armstrong waiting for him with the Telex announcing Logan's arrival from Tokyo the next day. He read it and threw it aside. He didn't ask her to sit down and when he poured himself a whiskey, he didn't offer one to her.

"He needn't bother," he said. "They cut off all contact with us. Homsi didn't turn up this morning and the Embassy is denying all knowledge of him." He looked at Janet. She was cool and smart as always but there were dark rings under her eyes and she seemed subdued. He hoped he was conveying his feelings toward her.

"What does it mean?" she asked.

"It means," James said slowly, "that they know Logan was double-dealing. Promising one thing and doing another. They don't stand for that kind of thing." He took a swallow of his whiskey. "My guess is, you don't have a problem anymore. I think by now Eileen is dead."

He was surprised to see her turn away.

"Don't say that. It wasn't Logan's fault."

Kelly didn't answer.

"They never meant to let her go," Janet said. "Whatever he did, she hadn't a chance."

"If you don't mind"—Kelly finished his drink—"I won't come out to the car with you."

"I suppose you blame me for saying so," she said.

Kelly shook his head. "I don't blame you. You had your eye on the main chance. She wasn't your responsibility. Common humanity might have counted with some people, but you don't have any. No, I don't blame you. I'm sure you won't blame yourself."

She started to say something and then suddenly she burst into tears.

"You bastard!" She ran out of the room and he heard the door slam. The house was very quiet. It had been better when she was there; he had been able to vent his feelings. The silence was unbearable. He wished he could have gone after her and made her stay. He poured a second whiskey and sat down with it. He had to find Homsi. If the Syrian was avoiding him, he still had to find him. To plead, beg, promise . . . do anything if there was *any* chance left. He put a call through to Colonel Ardalan. It was no good waiting for the Shah and presuming on a relationship which had its origins in political pragmatism. He needed help immediately.

Madeleine had been drinking. Resnais had never seen her drink as much wine as she did that night. They ate a good meal on the terrace, and she shouted at Ahmed to bring brandy. She leaned over the table toward Resnais.

"I wonder if that bitch is feeling hungry by now."

He shrugged. "If she's thirsty she can open a bottle." They both laughed. "You were very good today," he said.

"So were you." Madeleine raised the glass to him. "What did Damascus say?"

"All Arab patriots will mourn." Resnais imitated the high-pitched voice of their radio contact. "And so they should," he added. "He was a hero, killed accidentally. I said that you were lying down in a dark room." He looked at her and grinned. She was no longer laughing with him.

"He was corrupted," she said. "You didn't know him before. He was like a tiger. But she ruined him."

"Come on." Resnais shrugged. "He's paid for it. Be satisfied." Madeleine pushed back her chair. She was drunk but quite steady.

"I'm going down to pay her a visit," she said. Resnais leaned over and caught her wrist.

"No," he said.

She pulled at him furiously, trying to free herself. "You said you wouldn't interfere! You promised me!"

"I never said you could beat her to death. You're in a nasty mood, chérie. I'll make a bargain with you. When the time comes, you can shoot her. And I promise you that. But I'm not having any Arab games played with her."

She looked at him with hatred. "You want her for yourself! Now you've killed Peters you want the bitch yourself!"

She cried out as he twisted her wrist and jerked it downward.

"We both killed him," he said. He got up and pushed her back in the chair. "You were the decoy—you set him up. So never say *I* killed him. Never say that again!"

She slumped, rubbing her wrist. She called him a gross name in Arabic and he slapped her face.

"You behave," Resnais said. "I'm not Peters. You won't throw tantrums with me. I'm in command here now and you'll do exactly what you're told. Otherwise I'll take the hide off you. Understand?" He hadn't lost his temper; he was cool and calm. He had never liked her and they were only allies through necessity. Peters had never controlled her properly. And Peters was dead. He had no motive in protecting Eileen, except a dislike for women who asserted themselves. The sight of the Lebanese girl drunk had irritated him. Now that he had frightened her, he found her more attractive. He pulled her out of the chair.

"I don't want her," he said. "I feel like having you. Get upstairs!"

Ahmed, the servant, hid himself behind the door of the kitchen as they went. He had been told of the American's death and been surprised at what seemed to be a celebration. He saw the Frenchman and the woman going upstairs and into the man's bedroom. He had been told to leave the prisoner in the cellar without food or water and to ignore her if she called out. He guessed that the other two were responsible for the American's death. Europeans quarreling among themselves did not concern him; he hated them all. They could starve the woman in the cellar if they liked and it wouldn't disturb him. Like his counterpart Habib Ibrahimi in Teheran, he was a humble servant of the Arab cause. When Peters was in charge, he had obeyed him without question. The radio was never left unattended. Ahmed slept in the room where the transmitter was kept. His Algerian master had used it as an office. He had a bed in the corner, and his instructions were to wake Peters at any hour of the night if a call came through. The Frenchman had given him no instructions. They had both drunk a lot of wine; he had seen them quarrel and not come near to clear the table till they went away. He had respected the American, but he was afraid of Resnais. He was the *jallad,* the executioner. When the transmitter call came through at two in the morning, Ahmed woke and lay awake listening to it. He didn't go upstairs. When it stopped he went to sleep again.

"Why didn't you come to me?" Colonel Ardalan asked. "I told you I would always help if there was any difficulty. Now it may be too late."

James was walking beside him down the passage of SAVAK headquarters at Niavaran. His call to Ardalan had brought a car to the house. The colonel was occupied, but he asked Mr. Kelly to come to him.

They stopped at a lift, went inside, and it descended two floors. The colonel showed him the way down a yellow washed corridor with ugly fluorescent lighting overhead. There were several doors on the right and left, and he stopped at one of them. He turned to James.

"This isn't very pleasant," he said, "but I assure you it has been necessary." He opened the door and James went in. The first impression was the smell. It was acrid and bit into his nostrils. Urine, vomit, and a stench of human excreta. He covered his mouth with his handkerchief and was almost sick. The room was in darkness except for a single powerful light directed upon something sprawling in a chair, held there by webbing straps.

He didn't recognize Saiid Homsi. There were wires leading from the chair to a desk. The colonel sat behind it and offered James a chair. "We have asked him everything," he said. "His answers are taped; sometimes it's difficult to make out what he says. You have a question, Mr. Kelly. Ask it." The colonel's hand rested lightly upon a small switch in a portable electric control panel. James couldn't speak at first. He had never fainted in his life, but he came close to it in the first few minutes in the room.

"Ask him where they're holding Mrs. Fields."

Another voice asked the question; there were several SAVAK officers in the background. There was no answer. James saw Ardalan press the switch.

He turned away and choked into his handkerchief.

"We will repeat the question," the colonel said. "But we have to be careful. The doctor says he is near the end. We don't want him to die before he tells us. Why don't you have a cigarette?"

This time there was a mumble. James couldn't distinguish a word.

"Repeat it!" came the order. The switch was pressed once more.

James had had his back to the scene. But this time there was no sound.
He turned and saw a man bending over the figure in the chair.

The colonel shook his head. He seemed genuinely upset.

"My friend," he said, "I am very sorry. You came to me too late.
The man is dead."

Ardalan took him into his office; he gave him a glass of whiskey and
a cigarette. Even here, in the crisp modern decor, it seemed that the
smell of pain came with them. James sat with the glass in his hands; he
felt too sick and stunned to speak. "You came too late. . . ."

Nothing would have saved Saiid Homsi. A few hours earlier he
could have told them where to find Eileen. Now he was dead, and all
hope for her had died with him. Ardalan hadn't spared him.

"It must be known by now that we arrested him," he said. "Syria
has spies even in SAVAK. So they will realize that the whole plot is
discovered. I am afraid poor Mrs. Fields may already be dead."

"She hadn't a chance anyway," Kelly said slowly. "Logan went to
Tokyo to make a deal over Imshan with the Japanese government.
They found out he was going to sign an agreement with them. Homsi
told me." The colonel had been monitoring James' telephone ever
since the assassination of Khorvan; he was aware of all that had
passed between him and Homsi including the rendezvous his men had
intercepted. But he said nothing.

"Do you really think she's dead?"

"I would think so," the colonel said. "But even so, I have sent for
that last tape. We can play it back and see if it makes sense."

"I don't believe it will," James said. "It sounded gibberish to me."

"He was incoherent," Ardalan said. "Toward the end he was very
confused. We will play it over and see. I think you should drink your
whiskey, Mr. Kelly. You look unwell."

Chapter 10

It was a tree that saved Peters. It was a small pine growing out of the red rock, and the Renault had somersaulted twice before it hit the trunk. The impact threw Peters through the passenger door, which had burst open. He knew nothing about the escape; he was knocked out within seconds of the car diving over the edge. Being unconscious, his body offered less resistance, and therefore he escaped serious injury. He fell into the scrub about ten yards from the tree that sent the car bouncing and somersaulting down the mountainside. He lay there undiscovered by the police who came to investigate reports of a fire and an accident. When he came to, the sun was blazing fiercely down, and the rock was burning to the touch. For some time he had no idea where he was or what had happened.

He was bleeding from facial cuts and his hair was brown and matted with dried blood. Every part of him ached and throbbed, and a pain in his side made him jackknife as he pulled himself up. He knew he was concussed; the ferocity of his headache and a blurring in his vision told him that.

He crouched for some time, fighting the nausea and malaise, trying to bring his equilibrium under control. Something was driving him, something that wouldn't let him roll over and slide back into darkness. Something sharper than the ribs he sensed were broken and the chaotic pounding in his head. He had to get to his feet. He had been in an accident—there was a memory of a bang, and then a terrible crash of glass and metal. . . .

He dragged himself upright and the sky slid away from him. He began to crawl back up to the road on his hands and knees, forced on by the fear which couldn't be identified. A motorist found him staggering along the road. There was a blessed period when he faded out on the way to the hospital in Nice, and woke in time to get to the casualty department on his own feet. He gave his real name, and genuinely could not remember his address. Although the headache was intolerable, he protested violently but in vain when he was given a painkilling injection, and recovered consciousness to find himself in a side ward, with a gendarme sitting by the bed waiting to take a statement from him.

By this time it was dark, and he knew now what had driven him back up the mountainside and onto the road. Madeleine had left the car just before the tire burst. There was no question of coincidence. She had insisted on taking the Corniche road instead of the faster coastline route. She had set him up for Resnais. Seconds before the tire blew apart, he had seen a movement in the brush above the road. They had tried to kill him.

Eileen. He had to stop himself yelling at the policeman and leaping out of the bed. He had driven off in the morning; he had been unconscious and concussed for most of the day.

"You don't remember your address, monsieur?"

"No," Peters said. "Just my car going over the edge. But my memory is improving. After a night's sleep I will be able to tell you everything."

"You were very lucky," the man said, putting his notebook into his breast pocket. "That car of yours was completely burned out. Nobody even thought to look for you. I'll send in the nurse." He went out and Peters waited. He smiled at the nurse when she came in.

"You're feeling better? Very good. I've got some tablets here; you take these and have a good sleep. That *flic* will be back tomorrow."

Peters took the tablets and palmed them, pretending to swallow them with a little water. "Thanks," he said. "I'll sleep now. What time is it?"

"Past eight o'clock," she said. She went out, drawing a screen around the end of his bed. Eight o'clock. Ten hours. Ten hours in which they could have done anything to her. He thought of Resnais and flung the bedclothes back. His side was strapped up with adhesive and there was very little pain from the broken ribs. His head was the worst. There was a dressing on it. He crept on bare feet to the locker by the bed and opened it. His clothes hung inside. His shirt was torn and bloodstained, but his shoes and trousers were there. He pushed back the screen; it was a little room, leading directly into a bigger ward. The window was masked by a mosquito screen. He unhooked it and opened the window. The ward was on the first floor and a balcony with a fire escape stairs ran around each of the five tiers of the hospital building.

He pulled his pillows down into the bed, wrapped the cover over them, and thumped them into some kind of shape that might deceive a casual glance. Then he climbed out into the darkness and began to make his way down the iron steps into the grounds.

At ten o'clock that night one of the casualty officers came off duty and couldn't find his car. The police were not very sympathetic when he admitted that he had left his keys in it.

Peters drove slowly. He kept suffering periods of dizziness, and in the lights from oncoming cars his vision played tricks. Twice he almost veered across the road. There was a blare of horns from outraged drivers and he swung back to safety. The drive from the center of Nice took him an hour because he missed a turning and circled for twenty minutes. The pain in his head was getting worse. On the coast road he pulled into the side and rested. Nobody would expect a raid on the villa. They must think he was dead. He remembered that he carried keys to the gates and the front door and frantically searched for them in his trouser pockets. But they and his money had been lodged in the hospital for safekeeping. He would have to break in. He put the car into gear and drove on. He couldn't take it too near the villa because it would be reported stolen and the police might well call in to houses in its vicinity in case anyone had seen the thief. He parked down a side road and began to walk the three hundred yards to the villa. His watch had been taken, and he had no idea of the time.

When he approached, the house was in darkness. He could hear the sea breaking on the rocks at the back. The gates were closed. He had been taught to pick locks, but he had nothing, not even a pin. The only way he could get in was to go down to the beach and swim the distance to the rocks below the villa.

Fortunately the night was clear and bright. By the time he reached the shore, he was staggering like a drunken man. He had climbed a fence and stumbled down three hundred steep stone steps to the sandy beach which was the private preserve of a neighboring villa built up on the headland. It belonged to a German industrialist who had built a huge swimming pool and never used the sea. Peters fell onto the sand; he fought off the weakness that wanted to give up and fall asleep. The sea hissed and murmured in front of him.

He knew he had to rest before he attempted to swim around the rocks. There was no current there, but a rough sea would have proved too much for him. It was as smooth as black silk, with the moonlight painting a silver path out to the horizon. He leaned back against the rocks and closed his eyes for a moment. He had suffered injury before, but he was very strong and always fit. A bullet wound would have been easier than the waves of dizziness and weakness that were the legacy of concussion.

Peters had always believed in the power of the human will. He had seen men in the jungles of Brazil, fighting and surviving in conditions lethal to civilized people. Dedication, fanaticism—these had been the driving forces in his life. Now it was fear that sent the adrenalin pumping, a personal fear so acute that it transcended actual injury to the central nervous system, forcing him to get up when his hurt brain was clamoring for rest. He tied his shoes around his neck and waded slowly into the water. He had never prayed, even as a child. His family were agnostics who declined religious education for their children. He asked for no external help. He only knew he had to swim the distance and get to Eileen before the dawn came. He made the journey on his back for part of the way; his broken ribs made it impossible to swim effectively overarm or even breast stroke. His legs were powerful and they drove him around the promontory; the water was warm and buoyant. For the last few yards he stretched out and swam, grunting with pain, and stumbled onto the rocks below the villa, where Madeleine liked to sunbathe.

There were fifty steps up to the terrace. They looked as steep as a mountainside as he began to climb. The salt water had soaked through the dressing on his scalp and the wound was stinging. He didn't even notice it; the effort of getting up the steep, narrow stairway was taking all his concentration. When he reached the terrace he collapsed and blacked out. He lay sprawled in full view of the bedroom windows upstairs.

It was light when he recovered consciousness. The blackout had slid into a deep sleep that lasted through the rest of the night. He blinked and moved, confused by his surroundings. His wet clothes had dried on him. There was a rime of salt on his skin. He scrambled up and froze, listening. There was no sound from inside the villa; the sun was not yet risen and he guessed by the gray light that it must be near five. His head ached ferociously but he felt stronger. The doors to the terrace were locked, but it only needed his weight to push them open and he was inside.

He stepped into the hall through the big living room and listened. Ahmed slept lightly and would be up within an hour. He came to the stairs and looked up. Eileen wouldn't be there. If she were still alive he knew exactly where they would have put her. He had to find the Algerian first.

The door to the radio room opened silently. Peters couldn't see because the blinds were drawn, but after a moment he could hear movement and a grunt as Ahmed turned over on his cot. He edged through the door. Enough light came from outside to show him that the Algerian was huddled up asleep.

There was no question of asking him for help. Ahmed had no personal loyalty to him, any more than to Resnais and Madeleine. He belonged to the PLF. Any attempt to rescue Eileen would have him screaming for the others. Peters killed him with a single blow on the throat as he slept. Then he switched on the light and began to search for the keys to the gates which were in Ahmed's keeping. He hadn't found them when he heard the transmitter call sign. He hesitated. His vision blurred again and he swore, catching onto the table to steady himself. His head was churning and pounding like a cement mixer. He had to think clearly. Resnais would have reported his death in the car accident. Damascus would expect Resnais or Madeleine to answer. He put on the earphones and threw the switch to receive. He gave the call sign in French, and used Resnais' name. The message came through and was repeated twice. He knew the formula so well he could decode it in his head. "Our contact arrested in Teheran. The operation is blown. Execute the hostage immediately. Evacuate the villa and disperse." It was signed by the chief of staff of the Palestine Liberation Front.

Eileen was sobbing in his arms. She was awake when he opened the cellar door and switched on the light. She had slept lying in a huddle on the floor, and wakened stiff and cold. When she saw him in the doorway she cried out. He tried to hush her, but she flung herself on him weeping hysterically. He held her in his arms and begged her to be quiet.

"They said you were dead," she repeated. "Oh, God, they said you were dead. . . ."

He found it difficult to speak. She was alive and unhurt. It had taken all the effort of which he was capable to find her, and suddenly he had nothing left. She found herself supporting him.

"You're badly hurt," she said. "Oh, my darling. . . ." There was blood on her hands from the head wound which had opened and soaked through the dressing. She held him and wept. She was shivering with shock and chill. Peters made her look at him. He spoke gently but with firmness. It cost him a great effort.

"Listen to me," he said. "You've got to get away. I've killed Ahmed. The others are asleep. There's nobody around. Take the keys in my pocket. They open the gates. There's a car in the driveway—take it. Go on, now."

Eileen looked at him. He was a dreadful gray color, and quite suddenly his legs gave way and he sat on the ground. He put his hand to his head. She knelt beside him.

"I had an accident. I'm concussed to hell. I can't do any more. You take the car and get out of here."

"No." She shook her head. She wiped her eyes and face with the back of her hand. "No," she said. "I'm not going anywhere without you."

He turned on her fiercely. "For Christ's sake! I've just had the radio order to kill you! Get going!" He pushed her.

Eileen didn't move. "I'm not leaving you here. If I'm gone those two will kill you. I stay, my darling, or we go together."

He looked at her, and she saw the glaze in his eyes. "I can't make it," he said slowly. "I'm going to black out any minute. I love you. Will you for Christ's sake go now?"

She put her arms around him and drew his head onto her shoulder.

"I love you, too. And I'm not leaving you. We'll just have to wait till you've had a rest. It'll be all right. We'll get away together."

He tried to say something, but his eyes closed and he slid into the dark.

Eileen held him; she kissed him gently. The door was open, and she had only to reach into his pocket for the keys. She could be free in a few minutes, provided she did as he wanted and left him behind. There wasn't even a moment when she considered it. She held him close to her and soothed him, although he couldn't hear. She felt very little fear. That had been conquered during the long night. If they were going to die, and she felt instinctively that this must be the end, then they would be together.

Upstairs, in the bed she had shared with Resnais, Madeleine awoke. He was still sleeping, his mouth slightly open, one leg stuck out over the edge of the bed. She had hated everything he did; she hated herself for submitting to it, and the situation which bound her to him. There was a moment, as she looked at him, when she thought of killing him and setting herself free. But it wasn't a real possibility and she gave up the idea. He had taken control; he was a vicious and unpredictable man of whom she was justifiably afraid. Until the mission ended, there was no way she could escape him. She went into her own room and took a shower. To her shame, tears mingled with the water, and they were for Peters. Crying for him reminded her of the prisoner in the cellar. She was the one responsible for everything going wrong. It was Eileen Fields who was really to blame for Peters' death. She had soft hair which Madeleine imagined tearing out in handfuls. Resnais was not likely to wake up for some time. At least she could go down and see how Eileen had enjoyed being left without food and water for nearly twenty-four hours. She dressed and went downstairs. The light was on in the radio room. "Ahmed?" she called out. She looked around the door and saw him lying on the cot. Blood was running out his mouth. She had seen men killed like that before. She forgot about Eileen Fields, ran to the foot of the stairs, and yelled for Resnais.

Logan was met at the airport by a government car flying the Iranian flag. James Kelly came to meet him. There were no customs formalities, he was hurried through by airline officials and James didn't explain anything until they were in the car.

"The Shah has sent for you," he said. "The Minister of the Court telephoned this morning. Thank God the plane wasn't late."

"What the hell's happened?" Logan demanded. "Has anything gone wrong with Imshan?"

James could hardly bring himself to answer. "The whole thing has blown up in our faces," he said. "That's why the Shah wants to see you." He gestured toward the driver; there was no partition between them. "I don't think it's wise to discuss it." He spoke very quietly. "A lot of the Palace staff speak English. Anyway, we're there."

Saadabad Palace was a long two-story building built of dazzling white stone at Tajrish. It was just visible beyond the towering ornamental gates. The car stopped and both men got out. An army officer came forward and James gave their names, which the officer checked against a list. They walked through onto a wide road, flanked on one side by trees, which led directly to the Palace. It was a very hot, clear morning and the sky behind the white building was a dazzling blue. It was a modern conception, built with a strong Greek classical influence, with a steep flight of wide steps to the entrance and flanked by pillars down each side.

"What does he want?" Logan demanded. "For Christ's sake, what do you mean it's blown up in our faces?"

"Homsi's been arrested," James said. "He died under torture. Ardalan knows everything."

"Jesus." Logan groaned. They began the climb up the stairs to the palace entrance. A palace chamberlain, dressed in the magnificent blue, gold, and white uniform of the Shah's court officials, met them at the door. They crossed a vast white hall, with chandeliers and a few huge pieces of gilded furniture, and were shown into a waiting room. The chamberlain spoke to James, whom he knew well from previous visits.

"His Imperial Majesty will see you and Mr. Fields in a few moments." The doors closed behind him. It was the largest room Logan had ever seen, and he was not unused to palaces and presidents' official residences.

There was an impression of extreme luxury about the furniture, which Kelly's more practiced eye identified as French nineteenth century of the best quality, and there was a huge colorful Qum carpet and alongside it a magnificent Nain, also fresh from the looms. A life-sized portrait of the Empress Farah, dressed in ceremonial robes with the priceless Iranian emeralds on her brow, in her ears, and around her neck. The impression was one of overpowering wealth, newly acquired. The gleam of gilt and mirror and multicolored chandeliers was pristine. Age had not had time to mellow anything. It glittered and dazzled, like the incredible carpets. It was the showpiece of every self-made millionaire, with little taste and a contempt for the antique, except that its size alone overwhelmed criticism.

Logan didn't speak. He was marshaling his forces for the interview. He refused to allow the implications of what James had told him to penetrate beyond the immediate necessity of meeting the Shah. And of all the men in positions of power, Mahommed Reza Pahlevi was likely to be the most formidable. He remembered James' description of him. Cold, supremely intelligent, endowed with a quiet authority. Incapable of being fooled by bluff or intimidated by bluster. Absolute master of his country and his people; holding, by reason of his oil resources, the Western world in supplication at his gate. The chamberlain came back and held the doors open.

"His Imperial Majesty is ready to see you. Please come with me."

They recrossed the hall and were shown into a small room, pleasantly decorated in pale green, with a fine reproduction desk between tall windows overlooking the palace gardens, and a comfortable sofa with two armchairs, separated by a long marble-topped coffee table. The Shah of Iran came forward and shook hands with them. The Shadow of God, Shahanshah, King of Kings, Light of the Ayrians. He was of medium height. Logan was the taller by at least four inches, but it gave him no advantage. The face was deeply lined and thin; the hair gray and very curly. He wore slightly tinted glasses which made it difficult to see his eyes. His light-gray suit and dull-red tie were a contrast to the gorgeous uniforms of the court officials. He smiled at James.

"How are you, Mr. Kelly?"

"Very well, thank you, sir."

"Sit down, Mr. Fields." It was very informal; the Shah was relaxed and friendly. He reminded Logan of the head of a giant corporation more than a Middle Eastern autocrat.

"First," the Shah said, "let me say that I am sorry we meet in such painful circumstances for you, Mr. Fields. I am extremely sorry to hear what has happened to your wife. It is a terrible outrage."

"Thank you, sir," Logan said.

"I understand that you have been negotiating for financial backing in Tokyo." The Shah crossed one leg over the other. Kelly understood that the audience would be conducted between him and Logan from now on. The Shah did not deal with subordinates when the chairman was present. He accepted his relegation without resentment. The Shah had enjoyed talking to him; it might be true to say that he had liked James Kelly to the extent of which he was capable of liking any foreigner, but nobody as experienced as James would have presumed on the friendship. From now on, it was Logan Fields who had to answer all the questions.

"Yes, sir, I did. And I'm happy to say that my negotiations with the Japanese oil importers were followed by further negotiations with the Japanese government. I saw the Deputy Prime Minister on Thursday. I explained the full potential of the Imshan oil fields to him and also the terms put forward by Minister Khorvan. He appreciated our dilemma."

"I'm sure he also appreciated the strategic advantages," the Shah interposed. Logan nodded. He was not used to choosing his words with such care and he found it inhibiting.

"You will understand, sir, that I went to Tokyo without consulting my board in London. It seemed to me that if we were to meet the minister's requirements, we had to bring in financial support from a new source or a new refinery for Imshan would have been impossible. Our own cash flow could not support the refinery as well as the development of the field."

"I see that," the Shah said. "But since the advantages I mentioned are so enormous to your company personally, and to the Western world in general, I knew this difficulty would be overcome. I assured the minister on this point. I had no doubt, Mr. Fields, that an offer such as I made to you of a discount on your share of the oil would ensure that you would find a way to agree to my terms and build the refinery which Imshan needs."

"You were quite right, sir," Logan said. "After my discussion with the Japanese government I was able to conclude a provisional agreement with them and their oil importers for the full financing, in return for a guaranteed oil supply for the ten years after full production is achieved. That will build the refinery."

"Good," the Shah said. "That is the news I hoped to hear from you. When the minister was assassinated, there was some doubt about your sincerity in the matter. Understandable in view of the discoveries Colonel Ardalan made from the terrorist and from the Syrian. I am completely satisfied with your report, Mr. Fields."

"Thank you, sir," Logan said. He had thought the Shah relaxed; he saw now that it had been an attitude adopted for the interview. The man was coiled like a spring. He spoke faultless English, having learned it in his teens. Western languages do not come easily to the Iranian ear. Educated at Le Rosey in Switzerland, and widely traveled in his youth, there was a deceptive period in his life when he had seemed another Eastern playboy, until the English deposed his father in 1941, and placed him on the throne in expectation of a puppet who could be managed from Whitehall. Thirty-four years later, Logan Fields faced the product of that uneasy assumption of a throne. He had given him his refinery; produced by his own efforts the crucial agreement which permitted both Iran and Imperial Oil to get what they wanted. Mahommed Reza Pahlavi had loved his second wife, the Empress Soraya. For an Eastern king, with an unsecured succession, he had shown considerable sentiment toward his childless consort, even after he divorced her. Logan had never given anything in a business negotiation without trying, and usually succeeding, in getting something back. The idea came very suddenly to him, as he looked at the head of the Iranian state, a man like himself, and a man who had just been accorded everything he had demanded.

"Sir," he said slowly, "you were kind enough to express your sympathy over my wife." He could feel James going stiff on the sofa beside him. The Shah nodded.

"You know that the price of her release is our withdrawal from Imshan?"

"I believe that is what the Syrian admitted under questioning," the Shah said.

"I realize," Logan went on, "that I made a serious initial mistake.

When Homsi first approached me I should have come directly to you with the problem."

"It would have been wiser," was the answer. James watched him, desperately trying to see what lay behind the tinted glasses. He could distinguish nothing. "Although," the Shah continued in his quiet voice, "I don't see how I could have helped you, Mr. Fields. Your wife was not kidnapped in Iran. On the other hand, my Minister Khorvan might still be alive."

"I know that," Logan said. He sounded genuinely humble. "I regret it very much. But I was told that unless I kept the blackmail a secret my wife would be killed. I didn't think I had a choice."

"I appreciate that—it was a difficult decision."

"Sir"—Logan leaned forward toward the figure in the armchair—"it is possible to save my wife's life even now. If you will help me."

The Shah took a cigarette box, opened it, took one out, and offered it to Fields and James. It was a gesture that robbed Logan's last words of their dramatic effect.

"I would be glad to, if it were possible," he said calmly.

"It is possible," Logan said. "I will lodge my agreement with the Tokyo government with Minister Khorvan's successor. There can be no doubt about our sincerity in concluding this agreement with the National Oil Company here. We need Imshan desperately. You know this even better than I do, sir, because I'm just a businessman, not a politician. But if you will allow me to make a public statement withdrawing from Imshan, then my wife will be released."

"I don't understand your proposal, Mr. Fields."

"Let me appear to give in to their terms. Then, when my wife is safe, we resume the final negotiations and the deal goes through. It could be a question of a few days, no more."

"As I understand it," the Shah said, "you wish to publicly withdraw from Imshan and then resume when your domestic situation has been resolved?" He shook his head and removed his concealing glasses for a moment. The eyes were very dark and cold.

"I'm sorry, Mr. Fields. It's an impossible proposal. I cannot consider allowing any Western company to break off negotiations with us and then come back. It is not consistent with my policy to readmit anyone to Imshan if they have once withdrawn. I sympathize with your dilemma but I must advise you to divorce all personal considerations from your dealings with Iranian oil." He got up, quite casually, and held out his hand to Logan.

"I am very glad about your deal with the Japanese," he said. Then he turned to James. "It was nice to see you, Mr. Kelly." The audience was over. They went out and the chamberlain was at the door to see them through the hall. They walked down the steps side by side, and didn't speak. Outside the gates Logan saw the blue Rolls-Royce. There was a shadow in the back and it was Janet.

"I tried," he said suddenly to James. "There was just a chance he might have agreed to it."

"No chance at all," James said. "Why the hell should he bail you out? It's your choice. We're going round to Ardalan's office now. I told them to bring my own car. I'll follow behind you."

Janet put her arms around him and kissed him.

"Darling, thank God you're back! How did it go?"

"Fine," Logan said. He withdrew to his own side of the car.

"He's got what he wanted." He didn't want to talk about it. His choice: Kelly had kept on saying that from the beginning. Choose between the oil field and Eileen.

"Darling," Janet said gently. "I've got some bad news for you. Ardalan thinks Eileen may be dead."

"What?" He swung around on her. "What do you mean?"

"Homsi died under interrogation," Janet said. "Ardalan thinks they may have killed Eileen by now. If it is true, they did it because they knew Homsi would give everything away. So it's not your fault. You mustn't blame yourself." She took his hand and pressed it. He pulled it away and stared out of the window. "We're going to the office to listen to a tape. I'm afraid it's just a waste of time. Don't be upset. Please. It's not your fault if the worst has happened."

He didn't want to listen to Janet. He didn't want to hear that calm reasonable tone, telling him that his wife was very likely dead, and reminding him that his only link with the kidnappers had gone. He felt sick with shock. He remembered that chill injunction from the Shah.

He had to divorce himself from any personal considerations. So long as he held the power over the negotiations he could achieve that balance; he could do the thing at which he was an admitted master. Juggle a dozen possibilities in the air without letting one drop, bluff and promise and somehow come out with the advantage on his side.

But not now. The Syrian was dead, the secret was out. And if Janet was right and Ardalan's judgment not at fault, then Eileen was already lying dead in some cellar. He leaned his head against the window glass. It couldn't be over. It couldn't have happened so quickly before he had time to make a final decision. . . .

"Darling," Janet said, and reaching over, touched him.

"For Christ's sake," Logan said without turning around, "leave me alone!"

At one point on the journey James' car had overtaken them. When they went into the SAVAK headquarters and up to the colonel's office, he was already there. The colonel had given him a drink. He offered one to Logan and Janet. Both of them refused.

"Well," Logan said, "I've heard the news. You arrest the man who knows where my wife is being kept hidden and you bloody well kill him without finding out!"

The colonel waited a moment. He could appreciate the Englishman's distress. He was the type of man who would have to blame disaster on someone else. "Mr. Fields," he said patiently, "I'm afraid you cannot hold me responsible. You did not tell me the truth. You had every opportunity and instead you treated with terrorists who were acting against the interests of Iran, and you persisted in lying to me. So did Mr. Kelly, who I am sure was acting on your instructions. If you had dealt honestly with me, Mahmoud Khorvan would be alive today. And so might your wife. So don't try and lay the blame for this ugly mess onto me."

"You're talking as if it were certain Mrs. Fields was dead," Janet said. "Can't you see it's distressing Mr. Fields? There's no proof."

"Don't be a bloody fool," Logan said angrily. "He knows perfectly well that the minute his thugs arrested Homsi, the Syrians knew the whole plan was finished. I don't know what the hell you asked me to come here for. I can't do anything to save my wife, even if there was a hope of her still being alive!"

"The colonel asked you to listen to a tape," James Kelly said. "We asked Homsi where Eileen was hidden, just before he died. He said something but it doesn't make sense. Colonel Ardalan is doing his best to help us."

"I will play it for you," Ardalan said. "See if you can understand what it means. To me it is merely gibberish."

He switched on a portable tape recorder and reran to a certain point. James' voice came over clearly. "Ask him where Mrs. Fields is being held." Another voice repeated the question. A dreadful gurgling yell followed a few seconds later. Janet gasped. The same voice asked again. The words were a jumble when they came through; the voice was slurred and thick. There was a garbled plea for mercy, with English and Arabic intermingled, and then quite clearly the name Mrs. Fields, followed by a single Arabic word: *Kwayyis*. Then a groan that ended in a sigh.

"That was the last thing he said." Ardalan switched the machine off. " 'Mrs. Fields, *Kwayyis*.' "

"What does it mean?" Logan asked.

The colonel shrugged. "Pleasant, nice, sweet. It makes no sense."

"He was very confused," James said. "I'm afraid it's useless. It was some association of ideas between a woman and being sweet and nice."

Logan looked at the colonel. "What did you use on him?"

"Electrodes. Unfortunately, prolonged shocks over a period do disorient the mind. But he told us all about the plot to prevent Imshan being developed by a Western company; there was strong Soviet influence at work as well as Palestinian. A very serious threat to the independence of my country has been averted, Mr. Fields. His Imperial Majesty has been fully informed."

"Colonel," Janet said suddenly, "could you put that word *Kwayyis* into a sentence for me?"

"*Al hawa kwayyis ktir*. It is nice weather." He looked at her and shrugged. "The word doesn't mean anything, Mrs. Armstrong. It was just the wanderings of someone nearly dead."

"Of course it doesn't mean anything," Logan said bitterly. "You'd torn the bastard to pieces! If you'd gone a bit more slowly with him—"

"Please!" Ardalan held up a hand. "Don't try and tell me how to do my job—we got everything of importance out of him."

"Important to you—" Logan turned on him angrily.

"Wait a minute," Janet said. "For God's sake, I'm trying to think. . . . Sweet, Nice. Nice weather. . . . Colonel, you say he was very confused."

"More dead than alive," James broke in. "He didn't know what he was saying."

"Perhaps he didn't know how to say it," Janet said slowly. "Perhaps he couldn't think of the English word so he used the nearest Arabic equivalent. Supposing it wasn't an adjective. *Nice* . . . Oh, my God, wait a minute . . . N-i-c-e . . . Nice in the south of France!"

The colonel raised his eyebrows. "That is possible," he said. Then he shook his head. "But not very likely."

"Why not?" James demanded. "Janet could be right. He was trying to answer your question. Where are they holding Mrs. Fields? *Nice*. For Christ's sake it's worth a try!"

"It's too farfetched," Logan said angrily. "You're going into the realms of bloody fantasy. Nice, in the south of France—nobody would take her there!"

"On the other hand," Ardalan interrupted him, "it is not as fantastic as all that. There is a large Arab work force in that part of France. I think we should ask Interpol to investigate. They will know if there are any suspects in the area."

"She's dead," Logan burst out at them. "I know it." He glared at Janet. "I wish you'd mind your own bloody business!"

"I think the lady has been very helpful," the colonel protested. "I will send a Telex through immediately and see what the Interpol reaction is. If they consider it a possibility, Mr. Fields, I will arrange for you to be flown out. Whatever has happened, you will want to be there."

Logan didn't answer him. "We'll wait at your house," he said to James. He walked down ahead of them, leaving Janet to follow with James beside her. Outside the building he turned to them.

"You can both wait at Shemiran," he said. "I'm going to the office. I've got work to do." He got inside the Rolls and it drove off. James hesitated for a moment. Janet looked very pale and it was probably his imagination but he thought there were tears in her eyes.

He touched her on the arm. "Come on," he said. "We'll go home. To hell with Logan. I think you've got the answer."

"What happened with the Shah?" Janet asked him. As they got into James' car she kept her head turned away from him. Now he was certain about the tears.

He slipped the automatic gear into place and they moved off.

"I'll tell you when we get back," he said. "But I'm happy to say Logan met his match."

Eileen heard Madeleine shouting for the Frenchman. Peters lay like lead in her arms. She was overcome with sudden panic and began to shake him.

"Wake up! For God's sake, wake up, wake up. . . ." He groaned and she began to struggle to lift him into a sitting position. She was not nearly strong enough. The cellar door was open. Even if she shut it, they would be certain to look inside. The Lebanese girl had found the servant's body; they would know Peters was alive. There was no resignation left in her now, no sense of calm or fatalism. She pulled and shook at Peters, frantic with fear. "Darling! Wake up! Come on . . . please, please. . . ." He opened his eyes, trying to focus. Eileen began to heave at him, holding him under the arms.

"They're coming," she gasped, "we've got to hide. Get up—oh, try, for God's sake. . . ."

"All right," he mumbled, fighting the lethargy that didn't want to hear or know, but only to slide back into sleep. "All right. . . ." He could hear Resnais' voice. It came from the radio room. At any moment they would come to the cellar.

With Eileen's help he dragged himself to his feet. Hide, she had said. There was nowhere. He couldn't think clearly; all he knew was that she was still with him and in danger.

"Behind the door," Eileen whispered. "Hurry, get into the corner by the wine bin, hold onto it, but don't make a noise! I'll pull the door back." She heard footsteps running across the tiled floor of the kitchen above them. She pushed Peters into the corner, dragged the cellar door open, and slid behind it to hide with him. The bottles in the wooden wine rack rattled. She held herself rigid, praying wildly that he wouldn't move or lose consciousness. They were coming down the stairs.

"*Merde!*" Resnais' shout exploded a few feet away from them. "She's gone!"

They were standing at the open doorway. Eileen could see their shadows on the floor. Instinctively she closed her eyes and gripped Peters with all her strength.

Outside, Madeleine turned to the Frenchman.

"He wasn't killed," she snarled accusingly. "You fool—you should have made sure."

"They haven't gone far," Resnais said. "Ahmed's not even cold. And they can't have taken the car—you would have heard them! If they're on the road, we'll catch them. Come on!"

Peters was fully awake; the sound of Resnais' voice had driven away the urge to give in and drift off again. He was supporting himself fully, and Eileen felt his hand on her, telling her to stay absolutely still and quiet even when they heard Madeleine and Resnais going back up the stairs to the kitchen.

"I'm all right now," he whispered. They came out from behind the door.

"Jesus," Peters said. "They'll find the gate's still locked, and they'll think we're still in the grounds. When they don't find us there, they'll come back and search the house!"

"What are we going to do?"

"Fight it out," Peters said. "There's no other way. Can you shoot?"

"No," she said. "No, I've never touched a gun in my life."

"We'll get weapons. If my head would stop lifting off—we've got to get to the kitchen and quick. You'll have to help me."

Going up the stairs to the kitchen, he stumbled and fell on his knees. The pain in his head was so excruciating that he groaned out loud. Eileen helped him up, sobbing with the effort. He reached the kitchen and stopped, holding onto the door.

"Go to the cooker," he gasped. "Push button number four on the control panel. Hurry. . . ." She did as he said, and the cupboard fitment swung back from the wall. Peters went inside the little armory.

"Take this," he mumbled to her. He couldn't carry the weight of the Browning 308 and the box of ammunition. She took both. He pushed a grenade into his trouser pocket. They came back into the kitchen.

"Push button four twice," he said. The cupboard swung back into place. He leaned against the wall, exhausted.

"Why the hell didn't you go?"

"Because I'm not leaving you," Eileen answered. "So don't try to make me."

"Bullheaded Irish," Peters said. "We'll never make it walking. So I'll have to lay for them. I want you to do exactly as I say. No argument. We need to get to the garage. There's a way down through the outside door here. It's a covered way and there's only one exit. Let's go while they're out in the grounds."

It seemed to take them a long time; twice he had to stop and wait, attacked by dizziness. She watched him in agony, praying he wouldn't black out. But willpower kept him on his feet; he staggered like a drunken man as they reached the exit to the garage. They went in by a side door. Inside was the white Rolls-Royce laid up on chocks. The electrically operated garage doors were open. Resnais hadn't bothered to garage the Jaguar—it stood in the drive.

Peters leaned against the Rolls. He took the grenade out of his pocket and gave Eileen a ring with two keys on it.

"The big one opens the main gate," he said. "I want you to run and unlock it when I tell you. Okay?"

"While you stay here? What happens if you black out?" she said.

"I won't," Peters said. "I'm feeling better. I'm going to take cover here. They've got to pass the garage to get back in the house. That's when I pick them off. You go to the doors and look out. Be very careful—signal if you can see or hear anything."

Eileen kept in the shadow to the side of the garage entrance. She listened and at first heard nothing. Then there was a voice, calling something indistinct. It was the girl. The Frenchman answered.

"They've split up," she said to Peters. "I can hear them shouting to each other."

Peters swore. He had loaded the Browning, and the grenade was on the ground beside him. "Which direction?"

"To the right," Eileen said. "Not very close."

"Okay," Peters said. "If they're around there the driveway is screened by the oleander bushes. Run and get those gates open. And

stay put till I come out! Go on!" He watched her go. There wasn't a
hope in hell that he would join her. But the way was clear for her escape.

Eileen darted out of the entrance and ran as fast as she could down
the short drive to the main gates. She was gasping for breath; she
could hardly fit the key into the lock. She turned it and the gates
swung open easily. She leaned against the supporting pillars; she was
weakened physically from lack of exercise and her legs trembled. Outside was the road. She had only to walk through the gates and she was
free. That was what Peters intended when he sent her to open them.
He was going to stay behind and fight Resnais and Madeleine off while
she escaped. Telling her to wait there had been a ruse to make her
leave him. He knew when the firing started that she would be unable
to get back. She would have to save herself. She hesitated, but only
enough to scan the way back to the garage. She saw nobody and heard
nothing. He had called her bullheaded Irish—she remembered that as
she began to run toward the garage. As she reached it Madeleine
rounded the corner.

She and Resnais had split up to search; she was carrying her gun at
the ready, but her attention was not fully engaged. She had decided
that Peters and the woman were hiding in the house. She and Resnais
had searched every bush in the garden.

Resnais thought they might have climbed down the rocks and attempted to swim, but Madeleine disagreed with him. It was a long
swim against the tide, and she derided the idea that anyone as soft as
Eileen Fields could have attempted it.

She was completely unprepared to see Eileen running for her life
only a few yards away from her. So taken by surprise that she shouted
out after her, and loosed a couple of shots without taking proper aim.
Eileen vanished into the garage and Madeleine raced toward it. She
didn't get the chance to shoot again. A burst from Peters' Browning
caught her head-on. Three bullets hit her in the stomach, the impact
threw her violently backward, her pistol went spinning into the
oleander bushes. Madeleine gave a single scream, then lay still.

She felt a massive pain and the metallic taste of blood. She knew
that it was Peters who had shot her, and as she died she spoke his
name. Resnais, who was twenty yards behind her, came from the other
side of the house as the shooting began and saw her lying in the driveway. He didn't open fire; he froze while Madeleine died. Peters was in
the garage. There was no way to the front or back doors without crossing in view of the open garage doors. Unless he climbed to the first

floor. Once inside the house he could use the only method of attack which would turn Peters' strongpoint into a lethal trap. Inside the kitchen was the armory. He needed grenades.

The Interpol branch in Nice had recently been strengthened due to an influx of Algerian criminals into the area. There had been an outbreak of robberies and an attempted holdup of a German millionaire industrialist within the last nine months. The rich and influential raised an outcry, and the gendarmerie was also brought up above its normal strength. It was essential that the fashionable resorts along the strip of coast should remain peaceful for the rich inhabitants and for the tourists who were its livelihood. Ardalan's Telex caused a furor in the police headquarters. The suggestion that a Palestinian terrorist organization was at work in the region convulsed the prefect with alarm. The police were urged to act with all possible urgency to weed out and deport possible troublemakers. If the kidnapped woman were being held in the environs of Nice, then the French police would find her. There were large numbers of Algerians and other Arabs working locally, in restaurants and cafés, as hotel staff, and in the building and construction work along the coast. A list of them was already in the possession of the police, who kept records of all aliens with Arab connections, and the name of the Algerian millionaire was among them. While a squad of police set out on a dawn raid on the districts where the poorer suspects lived, a single squad car was dispatched to the villa, more as a gesture than for serious investigation, later that morning. In the meantime a Telexed reply informed the head of SAVAK that while no incidents of a suspicious nature had been reported, there was a strong nucleus of Arabs in the district, and it was not impossible for a European to be kept prisoner among them. On receipt of this news Logan Fields was notified in his office. He had been forced into hiring a private jet, and he had no excuse ready when Janet and James insisted on coming with him.

It was a bumpy, uncomfortable flight. James sat apart from Logan and Janet. He didn't want to talk to Logan, who seemed to have withdrawn into himself, shutting out Janet as well as James. Logan didn't believe they would find anything in Nice, and he seemed unaccountably irritated with Janet.

During the long journey, unable to read or to occupy his mind with anything but the imponderables waiting at the end of flight, James wondered whether it was dread of finding Eileen had been murdered that made Logan so resentful. The more he considered it, the more likely the explanation seemed. For the first time he understood the way Logan reacted without seeing it in callous terms of selfishness and greed.

Logan didn't think Eileen was alive and he didn't want to be there when he was proven right. Personally James had felt sorry for Janet Armstrong, and this surprised him. It had seemed impossible that she had feelings which could be hurt, but Logan proved him wrong again. She was miserable, and it was her flash of brilliant intuition which had broken the jumbled message of the dying Saiid Homsi. James had no doubt that she was right. Unlike Logan, he felt confident that Eileen would be rescued. She was being held somewhere in the French resort; a surprise raid by police didn't recommend itself to him, but Ardalan assured him that Interpol would handle the situation carefully. In the meantime, on the Shah's instructions, the Syrian government had been asked officially to help in contacting the terrorists holding Mrs. Fields and negotiating her release. No mention had been made by either government of Saiid Homsi. He had been buried along with SAVAK's other victims, in a lime pit outside Teheran.

Logan had hardly spoken since the plane took off. Janet didn't try to talk to him. He hadn't seen her the night before, and his attitude was cold and hostile. She had amazed herself by crying till she fell asleep.

He didn't thank her for finding out where Eileen might be hidden. He didn't want to know. Not because he was callous; Janet knew him too well to attribute it to that; not because he didn't care. But because he cared more than he had ever admitted to himself. He fastened his belt as the plane turned for the descent to the Nice airport.

They would find nothing. Everything in him, every intuitive sense told him Eileen would never be found alive. The night before, in the privacy of his room in James' house, Logan had broken down and wept. He hadn't wanted to come to Nice, but he had no excuse for staying in Teheran. It was Colonel Ardalan, cool and polite as usual, who offered to transport him by military jet if he was unable to charter a flight out at such short notice. They were all pressuring him to go and face the prospect of finding his wife dead in some empty house. Nobody would ever know the agony and horror which overcame him at the thought of it. He could hardly bear to feel Janet sitting beside him. If the nightmare became reality, he would hold her responsible, however unfairly. They landed smoothly, and an airport official met them at the plane and escorted them through customs. A captain of gendarmes and a young officer came forward and saluted them.

Logan broke out in a sweat even before the captain spoke.

"Monsieur Fields? I have a car outside. I'm afraid we have found your wife. Please come with me."

"Why did you come back?" Peters turned on her furiously. His head was pounding and sweat was running, stinging, into his eyes. Madeleine was dead; he could see her sprawled on her back on the drive. But the Frenchman was the real opponent. A professional killer, a trained expert. Peters felt so weak and nauseated that he could hardly see what he was doing. Yet here was Eileen kneeling beside him instead of having taken advantage of the opportunity he had given her to get safely away. He had a crazy desire to break into tears because nothing was solved. He loved her enough to have knocked her down for coming back.

"I told you, I'm not going without you," Eileen said fiercely. "I've opened the gates; come on, let me get you into the car and we'll run for it!" She was pulling at his arm; he shook her off.

"Resnais is out there," he said. "We'd be shot to pieces the moment the car came through the doorway. For Christ's sake, Eileen—*you* go in the car! I'll give you covering fire."

She shook her head. "We're going together. I'm not leaving you behind, so you can just forget it. Think of a way for us both to get out."

"There isn't one," Peters said wearily. "I'm as weak as hell. If I black out and Resnais rushes us, we're finished."

Eileen looked at him. "Show me how to fire that gun," she whispered. "Tell me what to do and I'll do it!"

"You wouldn't be quick enough," Peters said. "He'd blast you before you got to pull the trigger. He's a pro—I'd never get him like I did Madeleine." He closed his eyes for a moment, and panicked as the slide into unconsciousness began. His head felt heavy, his limbs numb. He fought against it with all his last reserves.

"I'm going to pass out," he mumbled to her. He saw the terror on her face, but he couldn't even hold onto the Browning—it slipped out of his hand onto the ground.

"Grenade," he said. "If he comes in firing stay down. Pull out the pin and count—count three—then throw it—on the floor. . . . Take it, darling. . . ." He slumped to the side, collapsed against the body of the white Rolls-Royce. Eileen bent over him. He was breathing hard, his face gray and filmed with sweat. There was no sound in the garage but the harsh labored breathing of someone who was deeply unconscious. Eileen moved the Browning to one side; the grenade lay on the ground. It was oval-shaped, corrugated. It looked evil, with the little pin on a ring sticking out of the side. You pulled out the pin, counted three, and threw. . . . The blast was what killed in a confined space. She remembered war films, with the inevitable pillbox or foxhole, exploding under a grenade attack.

She picked up the grenade and held it. It was cold and heavy. Her hands were shaking. If the Frenchman crept up on them, she had to remember the sequence and throw it at him. If she dropped it or miscounted. . . . She looked at Peters lying against the sumptuous car, and she was glad that she hadn't done what he wanted and run through the open gates. She was all the protection he had—the idea made her calm. She settled down to wait for the slightest sound that would warn of Resnais' approach.

Resnais swung himself up to the low balcony on the first floor; he had climbed by means of a drainpipe and a storeroom window, which was shuttered from the inside but had a substantial sill. He shouldered the window and it opened easily inward. He didn't waste time; he hurried down the stairs, and as he passed the study where Ahmed's body was lying, he heard the transmitter. He waited for a moment, then decided that he had better take the message. Peters wouldn't know he wasn't lying in wait for them in the gardens. He wasn't likely to make a run for it at that moment so soon after killing Madeleine. He picked up the earphones and took down the message. It was brief: "Confirm previous message. Operation canceled due to Homsi's arrest. Request confirmation of hostage execution. Repeat. Confirmation necessary and call sign for dispersal."

Homsi arrested. Resnais let them send the message a second time while he registered the shock of the information, and the fact that Damascus was repeating a message already received. Received by Peters. . . .

Eileen Fields was to be executed and the team was to disperse. It was all for nothing. Madeleine's death, his attempt on Peters, the highly organized exercise in top-level terrorism. He didn't answer the message. He left it clattering through a third time. Let Damascus think the villa was empty. The radio should have been destroyed if instructions had been properly carried out. But the hero he had personally reported killed in a car accident had come back from the dead and was holed up in the garage with the hostage. Resnais didn't know what final explanation would be offered, but he wouldn't be the one to make it. Not until he'd had time to get a story sorted out in Paris. He couldn't do that unless Peters and Eileen Fields were both dead. He ran on to the kitchen, opened up the armory, and stuffed two grenades into each of his trouser pockets. Then, moving at a light run and making no noise, he sped down the covered passageway that Peters had taken to the garage. As he approached the door, he crept like a stalking cat. He took one grenade out of his pocket, held it in his right hand, and with his left, he very gently depressed the handle of the door.

As it opened, he was standing at the back of the garage. He took a single step forward, well hidden by the angle of the door. He knew Peters and Eileen Fields were still there; he had an animal's sense for the presence of an enemy. Two grenades should do it; one after the other. He took the second out of his pocket and very slowly and carefully opened the door wide enough to lean forward and throw.

The patrol cars made their first raids on the houses occupied by Algerians and other Arabs soon after dawn that morning. Searches revealed nothing suspicious; several suspected sympathizers with the Palestinians were taken to Nice police headquarters and questioned.

A special squad, carrying a senior officer in the local gendarmerie and an Interpol liaison officer, accompanied by three armed gendarmes, arrived at the villa belonging to the millionaire Arab just after eight in the morning. The Algerian was a well-known member of the smart set in the resort. He was on excellent terms with the *maire* and the police; he owned a large yacht which was at that time on a cruise around the Greek islands. Apart from rumors of his political affiliations, he had done nothing to justify a raid on his house in his absence. Such nicety hadn't been evident in the case of the poor Algerian workers who had been dragged out of their beds and beaten up in the police station. It was unwise to upset the wealthy, and the police were reluctant to take any chance of doing so. At eight fifteen the captain of gendarmes who later met Logan at the airport was the first to jump out of the car as it came to a halt in front of the villa. His men sprang out after him, drawing their revolvers.

Tact was not needed. The scene in the garage on the left of the entrance was enough to tell them that they had come to the right place. The stink of death and explosions hung over the air. The captain was standing in a thin pool of blood that was making patterns on the gravel. He went to the garage, looked inside, and shouted to the Interpol official. He in turn shouted back.

The search was over. Within a few minutes, after a radio call from the car to headquarters, the villa was cordoned off and a team of police experts were going through the rooms and the grounds. The captain undertook the unpleasant duty of meeting Logan Fields and bringing him to the scene. He was a hard man, inured to violence, but the inside of the garage had upset him.

He wondered what effect it would have on the chairman of Imperial Oil.

It seemed to Eileen that she had been crouching beside Peters for hours. The sun was up and a cheerful bird twittered in the trees; it was a horrible contrast to the body of Madeleine, which lay in full view, arms at the sides. She looked as if she had been laid out after death. Blood had gathered in a pool on the ground. There was little shadow immediately in front of the garage; the oleander bushes and the pines were farther back. There it was dense and impossible to see if anyone were hidden. Eileen placed her hand on Peters' forehead; it was cold and clammy. His color was a frightening gray.

Somewhere out in the garden, Resnais must be waiting, preparing to rush them. Madeleine had been killed by a fluke—thrown off guard by the sight of Eileen running in the open. Now Resnais was alone, but as Peters said, he was the more deadly of the two. She listened, her nerves taut beyond endurance; the bird no longer sang, and the silence in the garden was horrible, unreal. Suddenly something snapped; the sound was like a pistol shot to her overstretched imagination. She grabbed the grenade and half rose, ready to pull the lever and throw it in the direction from which the noise had come. But there was no movement, no shape behind the shadows.

What she had heard was the shutter being forced open on the first-floor window. She held the grenade ready, but had no idea where to throw it. Resnais must know there was something wrong inside the garage. They would have tried to escape in one of the cars otherwise. If he rushed them from the front, the tremendous firepower from the Browning would cut her down before she could throw anything. But he wouldn't be expecting to face her; he might think one of them was hurt but he couldn't be certain it was Peters. And Peters had the same weapon. It would be crazy for Resnais to attack directly.

Then she remembered the door back into the house. The door through which she and Peters had come into the garage. That was where the Frenchman would come. She gave a cry of terror and tried to shake Peters, but it was useless. He was slumped against the Rolls. She almost panicked then; for a moment she felt paralyzed with terror, as if her body were frozen into immobility while at any moment that door might burst open. She ran to it, scrabbling desperately for a bolt, a key. There was no way of locking it from inside the garage. Naturally it would be fastened from inside the house. She crouched by it, listening, and heard nothing. No footsteps, no creak of boards, nothing. But she knew this was the way he would come.

She made her way back to the white Rolls. Peters hadn't moved. Eileen bent over him—tears fell on his face. Then she picked up the grenade. She sat on her heels and watched the door.

When it began to open she thought at first it was an optical illusion. It seemed there was a crack between it and the wall. For a second she closed her eyes tightly and as they opened, the crack was wider. She gave a gasp of terror and raised herself from behind the shelter of the Rolls-Royce. There was no possible doubt. The door was opening, very slowly and without making a sound. She pulled out the pin on the grenade and counted: *One. Two. Three.* Then she threw it with all her strength at the gap, which was widening; she had a glimpse of something like a hand coming around the edge of it, just before she threw herself on top of Peters.

The force of the explosion blasted her into unconsciousness, as the grenade in Resnais' hand blew up an instant after the one she had thrown. The wood of the door shattered into splinters as lethal as bullets, a rain of steel fragments bombarded the inside of the garage. Human remains splattered the walls and ceiling. Acrid fumes filled the area and hung over the wreck of the Jaguar, which had been in direct line with the explosion. The body of the Rolls-Royce was holed and pockmarked with splinters, its rear door buckled. Eileen and Peters lay under a coverlet of broken glass from the windows; her arm was flung across him as if she were trying to shield him. It was Peters who recovered first. He came back to consciousness confused and shocked; he could hear nothing, and his ears throbbed painfully from the force of the blast. He raised himself slowly and the broken glass slithered off him. He began brushing it frantically away from Eileen's body. He cut himself and at first he thought the blood was only his own. He lifted her, staggering and dizzy under the slight weight, and dragged her outside. The stench and fumes were choking in the garage; there was a loathsome charnel house smell.

"Eileen! Eileen! For Christ's sake—" He thought he was shouting but all sound was muffled. Her dress was soaked with blood; a long jagged splinter of wood had holed her in the side like a spear. She was just breathing.

Peters lifted her over his shoulder; he swayed on his feet and then began to walk down to the gate.

It didn't occur to him to go back into the house; he had to get help for her and all he could remember was abandoning the doctor's stolen car along the road. It hurt too much to think beyond the total necessity of saving her life.

He knew as soon as he saw the nature of the injury that unless she were attended to quickly she would die. He had to reach that car and drive to the hospital; his ears were buzzing and blocked. His blinding headache was in rhythm with every jarring step along the road. When he saw the blue sports car he broke into a stumbling run. Luck was with him—it hadn't been found. He lifted her into the passenger seat and bent over her, feeling the pulse in her slack wrist. Her eyes opened and she gave a groan of pain. She was losing a lot of blood; his shirt and hands were crimson with it.

"You'll be all right," he mumbled. "I'm taking you to the hospital. You'll be all right—Oh, Christ, don't fade out—hold on."

She was unconscious again, but for a moment she had known him. He got in beside her and started the car. His concentration was too erratic to risk driving fast; all he could hope was to stay conscious and reach the hospital. It took him half an hour, much less than the previous night's journey, when he was hopelessly confused, and then he pulled into the entrance to the hospital.

He went to the inquiry desk and saw the girl behind it open her mouth in horror at the sight of him.

"There's been an accident," Peters said. "There's a woman outside in a blue sports car. Her name is Mrs. Fields. Get someone quickly. . . . No—I'm all right—that's her blood—"

In the confusion, while two orderlies came running with a stretcher and a crowd of spectators surrounded the car, Eileen was lifted out and taken inside. The receptionist thought she was dead and turned to look for the man who had reported the accident. But he had disappeared.

They had covered the body with a rubber sheet. The policeman pulled it back and the captain stepped aside for Logan. Logan looked down at the face of Madeleine Labouchère. He turned to the captain.

"That's not my wife," he said. He walked a few paces back to James Kelly, who was waiting, sick and stricken, with Janet beside him.

"It's not Eileen," Logan said. He brushed one hand across his forehead. James saw it trembling. "It's another woman—shot in the chest."

The captain had joined them. "Monsieur Fields," he said, "we are certain that your wife has been held here. There is a dead Algerian in

the house and a radio transmitter. Grenades were used in a battle in
the garage. There are human remains. I think you had better go with
your friends and wait in our headquarters."

He hesitated. Logan's rejection of the woman's corpse had embarrassed him. From the way it was lying, it looked as if it had been arranged after death. The cruelty of death by having half the stomach
blown out had been dignified into an execution. This theory was disposed of when Madeleine's Walther P-38 automatic was found in the
oleander bushes. It did not occur to the captain, to Logan, or to
James, that Eileen was not among the victims whose mangled remains
were in the human debris in the garage. Janet had not gone near it.
She stayed apart, looking so pale that Logan heard James ask her if
she were feeling faint. He didn't bother to turn around. She shouldn't
have come on the trip and she certainly shouldn't have come out to the
villa. If she called attention to herself by fainting, it would be the final
error in a mounting total. He walked away to the car, leaving James to
bring her along, and they drove to police headquarters in silence. They
were shown into the captain's office, and a policeman brought them a
tray with brandy, Perrier, and ice. Janet poured them each a drink.
She handed one to Logan.

"I think she's alive," she said quietly.

Logan looked at her. "That's the most bloody stupid, insensitive
thing—"

"Monsieur Fields!" He swung away from her to the police lieu-
tenant who had accompanied him from the villa. He was in the doorway, and he shouted in excitement.

"Monsieur Fields—! The hospital has just phoned in a report that a
woman with that name was brought in twenty minutes ago! We must
go there immediately!"

Logan was pushing past him through the door, followed by James.
Janet didn't move.

James turned and called to her. "Come on—aren't you coming?"

She shook her head. "No. He'll be all right now. I'm going back to
England. If Logan wants me he knows where to call."

She shrugged and managed to smile. "You go along, James. And
good luck. Don't let Logan push you out."

"I won't," James promised. "I'm going to be right there."

The surgeon who operated on Eileen found a badly damaged rib
cage and a hole in the abdominal wall, with extensive internal hemor-
rhaging. He removed the part of the wooden splinter that had pene-

trated too far for Peters to see. It measured seven and a quarter inches. He came down after the operation and told Logan Fields that he could see his wife for a few minutes later that evening. In his opinion she would recover, but there was always the risk of postoperative shock. The hospital was under siege from the press and television. Logan was offered a room, and an appeal was put out over the television networks for the man who had brought Mrs. Fields to the hospital to come forward.

The gruesome scene at the villa was making world headlines. Logan saw the French papers. He and James were together in the little waiting room off the private ward where Eileen lay. He had taken James' presence for granted; he was his employee and liaison with the authorities. He spoke perfect French and he acted as a buffer between Logan and demands for an interview. He had gone outside the building and spoken briefly to the press on Logan's behalf. Until Mrs. Fields had recovered enough to tell them what had happened, Logan Fields could not issue a statement. He admitted that Eileen had been the victim of a kidnapping by an international terrorist group, but he refused to go into details at this stage.

James was adroit with the press where Logan couldn't have trusted himself to remain calm. He was the diplomat, expert at smoothing over difficulties, and it never occurred to Logan that his presence had any personal significance.

A nurse brought them coffee and asked if they wanted to eat something. Both refused.

"You haven't asked where Janet is," James said. Logan frowned.

"I'd forgotten about her. She can get herself into a hotel."

"She's gone back to England. I think you've been pretty rough on her, Logan. You ought to ring her up and let her know what's happened."

"I don't know myself, yet. I'll wait till tomorrow. I think you better fly back to Teheran after I've seen Eileen. Work out a statement for me, and it had better be very guarded. We don't want to start a political row and embarrass the Shah. I'll join you as soon as I know Eileen's out of danger."

James took out a cigarette and lit it. He looked at Logan. "I'm not going back to Teheran. I'm resigning. I'm staying here."

"Don't be a bloody fool," Logan said. "You're throwing everything away. Imshan goes ahead now, and you can reach the top in Imperial. All right, if you don't want to go to Teheran, stay on here for a few days. Think it over."

"I have thought it over," James said. "Whether you kick Janet out or not, Eileen will never go back to you. You think you've won, Logan. You risked her life for your bloody oil field and you come out with Imshan in the bag and think you can walk back to her as if nothing had happened. To hell with Janet, by the way. But it isn't going to work out like that. You're not going to have your cake and eat it this time."

There was a nurse sitting by Eileen's bed; the single light was shaded, and when Logan first came in he didn't see that her eyes were open. He came to the bed and bent over her. The nurse got up.

"Only a few minutes, Mr. Fields. She is still feeling the anesthetic. I'll wait outside."

Eileen saw Logan through a fog of analgesic. His face seemed to loom independently. For a moment she thought she was dreaming in the halfworld of returning consciousness. Then he spoke and the fog cleared a little.

"Darling," she heard him say. "You're going to be all right." Her lips were dry and she felt thirsty. The nurse had allowed her a sip of water at a time when she first came around. She opened her eyes fully and focused on Logan. He bent down closer to her.

"Where is he?"

"Who? Whom are you talking about?" Logan thought for a moment that she was wandering. But the expression in her eyes was clear. She raised her head from the pillow.

"Where is he? What happened to him?"

"I don't know what you mean."

"He brought me here," Eileen mumbled. "In the car—I remember seeing him, just for a second."

"Somebody got you to the hospital," Logan said. "But he disappeared afterwards. They're trying to find him now."

There was a very slight smile on her lips. It made Logan uncomfortable. He had never seen her look secretive before.

"He got away then. Thank God. . . ." She turned her head and closed her eyes. "I'm going back to sleep," she said. He stood watching her. The nurse came back into the room and touched him on the arm.

"You can see her in the morning," she whispered. "She'll be better then."

"Thank you," Logan said. He walked out of the room and asked to telephone the gendarmerie. He spoke to the captain.

"I've just seen my wife. You'd better get the man who brought her in; from what she said, I believe he was one of the kidnappers."

Roadblocks were set up, the strictest security was in operation at the airport, and no sailings were permitted from the harbor. An extensive search was carried out through the city of Nice itself. An Identikit picture of Peters was flashed on the television screens and put on the front page of the newspapers. There were stories in the world press that Eileen Fields was winning her fight for life, and pictures of Logan going in and out of the hospital.

Fifty miles outside Nice harbor, a motor yacht was on course for the Italian coast. The tiny yacht marina at Bocca di Magra had a berth reserved for it. Normally the boat remained at anchor there, going out for a day's excursion to Porto Venere or the Cinque Terra with tourists. Since Eileen Fields arrived at the villa, the yacht had been waiting in Nice, its two-man crew spending their time drinking in the bars and fishing.

It was a big, powerfully engined craft, capable of thirty knots, with a tiny cabin that slept three. Peters was lying on the bunk. The taxi driver who picked him up outside the hospital had thought that he was drunk and had been in a fight. He seemed unsteady and when they arrived at the quay, the driver had to help him out. He brought him to the boat, and hung around, beginning to fret about his fare, while one of the crew came and helped the American aboard. He was paid off, with a generous tip, and thought no more about it. He was used to Americans being drunk early in the morning on the coast.

The captain of the yacht was an Italian; his home was on the Magra, the river that runs into the sea hard by Lerici on one of the most beautiful curves of the Italian coast. He lived by hiring out his boat during the summer season, and he was an active member of the Marxist group who had settled in the little river port. He had been sent to Nice to take the commando group to safety if the operation failed. He knew nothing of their mission in France, and he didn't ask questions when only Peters appeared.

He brought him downstairs to the cabin, cast off, and started out of the harbor. He would take a full day to reach the Magra, as he had to go well out to sea to avoid searching aircraft. Once they were safe in the Magra, his own people would care for the terrorist. And it was obvious that he would need care, because he was confused and became unconscious while they steamed at a full thirty knots out into the Mediterranean. The second crew member, a young and dedicated activist, sat by his side and watched him. He didn't know how best to help his injured comrade. He could have coped very well with a physical wound, but brain damage frightened him. Twice during the day, Peters woke up and asked for something to drink. The boy left him and reported to his captain that there was some improvement. They heard the news of the hunt for Peters on the short-wave radio. Neither commented. They had a very long start and, in any case, the papers they had given to the port authorities were forged and gave the yacht's place of origin and registration as Marseilles. They wouldn't be traced. The American had got safely away.

It was early afternoon. In the hot, cramped little cabin, Peters lay propped up on the bunk, awake. The pain in his head was continuous and excruciating; the thud and rumble of the engines made his conscious periods unbearable. The heat and the smell of fuel were overpowering. He lay soaked in sweat, the lower half of his body covered by a sheet. A carafe of water was on the narrow ledge beside the bunk, and he drank continuously. They had given him aspirin to ease the pain, but the effect was negligible. It was a part of him, the pounding of a hammer, wielded with such force that it felt as if his head would split like an apple under the pressure. The movement of the boat was steady; the powerful engines were running at full throttle, her bows were out of the water and they were racing through a calm sea toward the haven of Italy.

He didn't think about his own safety; he seemed to have no control over his thoughts. His last memory was of seeing Eileen brought into the hospital on a stretcher; he couldn't remember taking the taxi and reaching the arranged escape point in the harbor. He kept seeing Eileen's face, smiling at him. It was the only pleasant part of being awake and he couldn't hold on to it for long. He saw other faces, floating like balloons in a void.

His mother, with her discontented expression and her whining voice in his head accusing him. "You talk about loving humanity—you're not capable of loving even one person." It made him very angry. He called her a liar and her face drifted away, as if someone had loosed the string on the balloon. His father—a high school teacher. . . . He didn't call them, but they came, without sequence or relevance to each other. Madeleine. Lying dead in the villa garden. He closed his eyes against her. He felt nothing. His mother said he had no feelings. . . . Incapable of love. . . . He tried to bring Eileen back, fighting the whispers and the faces, merging into a sad confusion.

The little doors to the cabin folded back and the young Italian came in. He had heard Peters call out and hurried down.

"Are you all right?" he asked in French. "Do you want anything?" Peters tried to lift himself. The Italian was very dark, with a drooping mustache and serious eyes. Peters wanted to say something but suddenly the pain in his head became a crescendo. The embolus lodged in the frontal lobe of his brain finally burst—a massive hemorrhage spread in seconds, and he fell back on the bunk. His eyes closed and he called out one word. The young man bent over him and then ran up on deck to call the captain. A few minutes later they stood beside the bunk; the yacht idled on the water, its engines shut off. The older of the two Italians shook his head.

"If you don't rest with a severe concussion, this can happen," he said. "Did he say anything?"

The boy looked distressed. "It sounded like a woman's name."

"He died for the Cause," the older man said. He raised his clenched fist in salute over Peters. "We can't take him into port. We'll bury him here."

In the early afternoon of that day, Eileen woke from a deep sleep. The room was full of flowers; a large vase of roses sent by James was the first thing she saw. She felt no pain, only a sense of profound disquiet, as if something were terribly wrong. The blinds were half drawn; the room was cool and shady, scented with the flowers. The nurse sat knitting in a chair near the bed. She heard a sound and saw Eileen with tears pouring down her face; she hurried to her.

"What is it? Are you in pain, dear? I'll get you something. . . ."

Eileen couldn't explain the indefinable, the sense of grief which had no explanation. She took the analgesics and held onto the nurse's hand; under their influence she fell asleep again. She didn't know, and never would, that it was the precise moment when she woke that Peters died a hundred miles away.

Chapter 11

In the autumn Logan gave a press conference in the VIP lounge at London airport. He had flown in from Teheran, and a crowd of press photographers, television cameras, and a special BBC reporter were waiting for him. He sat in the lounge with a glass of whiskey and soda, and read out a short statement. Drafting the statement was the last thing James Kelly did for him before he resigned. It was brief and anticipated most of the questions. Imperial Oil had signed an agreement with the National Iranian Oil Company to develop the massive field at Imshan. He had no comment to make on the reactions of the Egyptian government to the suggestion that the price formula would lead to lower oil prices.

"Did you see the Shah, Mr. Fields?"

Logan glanced toward the questioner.

"I saw his Imperial Majesty yesterday," he said. "I had a long audience with him."

"Would you describe him as a friend to the West, sir?"

Logan shook his head. "I would describe him as dedicated to the interests of his own people." James had told him to say something like that. He waited, enjoying himself. Publicity of this kind didn't frighten him; he looked fresh and good-humored, a man returning from a triumphant conclusion with just the right amount of modesty and authority. One of the reporters was writing that down.

Logan was concentrating on the television interviewer. He was a widely traveled man with experience in Middle Eastern affairs. Logan

explained the implications of Imshan, and touched on the attempt to
blackmail him into abandoning it some weeks earlier. He repeated his
answer to the question that had been asked both publicly and in private so many times.

"It was an impossible choice. I couldn't sacrifice my wife, but I
couldn't put personal feelings before my responsibility to the economic
survival of our Western society. Thank God the problem was solved
for me."

It was an answer that pleased everyone. The television interview
was concluded, and Logan stood up. He wanted to get to the City in
time for a meeting with his directors. It was a woman reporter who
edged up to him. He paused politely.

"Your wife is living in Ireland, Mr. Fields. Is it true that you have
separated?" He changed color—his face flushed red and he half turned
away from her.

"I have no comment to make on my private affairs."

The reporter raised her voice as he began to push his way to the
door. "Will you be seeing your wife, Mr. Fields?"

He didn't answer; he thrust his way through the exit door and hurried away to be taken through to where his company car was waiting.
The conference had ended on a painfully sour note.

The library at Meath House was a shabby room. Generations of
dogs had scuffed and worn the leather sofa; there were stains on the
chairs where Fitzgeralds had lounged in muddied hunting clothes, and
the big mahogany bracket clock was incapable of keeping accurate
time. It was walled with books, many of them unread and untouched
for years. It was supposed that there were valuable first editions
among them, but it didn't occur to anyone in the family to think of
selling them when money was short. It was a room that Eileen associated with big fires and smoke and the smell of leather and whiskey
—a place where her father loved to stand warming his back and talking
with a glass in his hand.

She had arranged flowers in two massive Waterford vases, just as
her mother used to do, and she had come there after playing with Lucy
in the garden. The child was very changed. She had lost her subdued
passivity. She laughed and shouted and her grandfather and Bridget
spoiled her; there were animals instead of fluffy toys: a spaniel puppy
which slept in her nursery, the same room Eileen had used until she
married Logan, and an ancient pony which she was learning to sit on
in a basket saddle. She was a free and happy child, overindulged per-

haps, but growing visibly. It made Eileen contented to watch her—their love for each other was very close. When she was still convalescing, and unable to do more than sit in the garden for a while if it was warm and the rain held off, she had found complete absorption in her child.

By the time Logan came over to see her, she was well enough not to be disturbed. She greeted him calmly and with courtesy as if he were a stranger calling on a visit. He had not suggested anything about Lucy's future, because he had hoped to persuade her to talk about their own. Eileen had told him quite without rancor that there was nothing to discuss. It was two months since he had arrived at Meath and gone away the next morning, sped on by her father, who hadn't attempted to be friendly. She had read about him in the newspapers and felt no personal interest. Her detachment from him and her past life was so complete that she felt no curiosity, resentment, or regret. It was all part of the life lived by another person. A person with her face and her name, but who had never really existed as she existed now. Now that she was strong, she spent a lot of time walking around the countryside. There was an air of expectancy about her which no one at Meath understood. It was Bridget, greeting James Kelly that autumn afternoon, who put it into words.

"How is Mrs. Fields?" He had written, asking to come and see her. To his surprise she telephoned inviting him to stay. They hadn't talked on the telephone. He had seen her twice in the hospital and found that she didn't want to talk about anything. There was a closed secrecy about her which disturbed him.

"She's fine now," Bridget said. "But she's not herself, Mr. Kelly. What she's been through left its mark on her. Everyone at Meath sees the change in her."

James paused. They were outside the library door.

"What kind of change?"

"She lives inside of herself," the Irish girl said. "It's as if she was waiting for something. Go in, sir. I'll bring the tea in a minute."

He thought she looked very beautiful; she was very thin, but there was brightness in her eyes and genuine pleasure in her smile as she came to meet him. He held both her hands for a moment and she didn't draw away.

"Dear James," Eileen said, "I'm so happy to see you. Come and sit down." They sat on the sofa side by side; she asked him questions about himself and he described his resignation from Imperial Oil. He had taken a job as a consultant to a firm of merchant bankers. His description of it made her laugh.

"You don't really fit into big business, do you? Why didn't you go back into the Foreign Office?"

"No future in it. I've decided to become a nine-to-five bore like everyone else. When are you coming back to England?"

"I don't know." She turned away from him, pouring tea which he didn't want. "I'm quite happy here. Lucy loves it."

"What about Logan?"

"He's busy with his oil field, I suppose. You know as much about him as I do."

James looked at her. "You're never going back to him?"

She smiled and shook her head. "No. That's all over and done with. I hope he marries Janet Armstrong. I told him I thought he'd treated her very badly."

"Funnily enough, I don't think she'd have him. She resigned too."

"He won't mind," Eileen said. "Logan isn't the kind of man to be lonely without people. He's never really needed anyone. I read about Imshan in the papers. They called him the tycoon who saved the West. It sounded like a title for a cowboy movie."

He put his hand out and touched hers. "You're looking very well," he said. "Bridget said you'd changed. I was worried about it. But she's right. You're a different woman."

"I feel different," Eileen said. "An awful lot happened to me in those three weeks. That's what Logan couldn't understand. He thought we could start all over again, living the same kind of life. Me playing hostess in that dreary house in Eaton Square, Lucy growing up in that artificial atmosphere—him living for his business and me living for him."

"And now you're living for yourself," James said quietly. "For the first time."

"Not altogether." The secret look was there again, lurking around her mouth. "I've found myself as a human being; that's part of it. And I've freed Lucy. She's having a wonderful life here. Father adores her and everyone spoils her to death."

"I suppose," James said, "you wouldn't tell me what really happened at the end?"

She said to him what she had said to the police and to Interpol. "I can't really remember. We were in the garage—there was an argument between the men and the woman. There was an explosion, and I woke up in the hospital."

"You said they were Arabs," James said. "The man who brought you to the hospital was an American."

"So I was told. Have some more tea."

F

"I wish you'd trust me," James said gently. "I wish you'd tell me the truth. They won't find him now. He's got clear away."

She didn't answer. She stopped putting the teacups in a pile on the tray and turned around to him. She sat very still and let him take her hand again.

"I love you very much," James said. "I came here to make sure you and Logan were finished and to remind you about what I said in Teheran. Tell me about him, darling. It may help us both."

"I can't," Eileen said. "I know you fought to get me freed while Logan was hanging on to the oil field and trusting to luck that they wouldn't murder me. While he was excusing himself he was telling me how much I owed to you. And I'll say this much, because I do trust you. There was a man, but I can't talk about it. All I can do now is sit here and wait."

James went on holding her hand. The room was quiet, peaceful. Outside, the pale Irish sunlight dappled the garden and made patterns on the faded carpet.

"He may never come," James said. "You realize that?"

There were tears in her eyes. "I know, but I have to hope. I have to give him time."

"All right." He gave her his handkerchief and slipped his arm around her.

"You wait for as long as you want to; and if you don't mind, I'll wait with you. If he doesn't come back, maybe you'll settle for second best."

He leaned over and kissed her lightly on the cheek. "Let's go and find your father. And I want to see Lucy."

THE

FUTURE

— OF —

ARCHITECTURE

— IN —

100

BUILDINGS

BY
MARC KUSHNER

EDITED BY JENNIFER KRICHELS

TED Books
Simon & Schuster

New York   London   Toronto   Sydney   New Delhi

TEDBooks

Simon & Schuster, Inc.
1230 Avenue of the Americas
New York, NY 1002
Copyright © 2015 by Marc Kushner

First TED Books hardcover edition March 2015

Cover and interior design by: MGMT. design
Series design by: Chip Kidd
Cover photo by David Frank

Manufactured in the United States of America

10   9   8   7   6   5   4   3

Library of Congress Cataloging-in-Publication Data is available.

ISBN 978-1-4767-8492-2
ISBN 978-1-4767-8493-9 (ebook)

EXTREME LOCATIONS

2   4   4   6   8

9   11   11   12   13

REINVENTION

16   17   18   18

21   23   23   24   24   27

GET BETTER

28   29   31   34   36   37

38   40   41   43   43

CONTENTS

POP-UP

45   46   46   47   48

SHAPE-SHIFTERS

52   54   55   56   58

58   60   62   63   64

66   67   69   69

70   71   72   74   75

DRIVE

77   77   78   80

80

81

82

NATURE BUILDING

87

87

89

90

91

92

94

SHELTER FROM THE STORM

94

97

97

100

102

103

104

106

109

109

SHRINK

110

112

114

114

115

SOCIAL CATALYSTS

116

117

120

121

123

123

CONTENTS

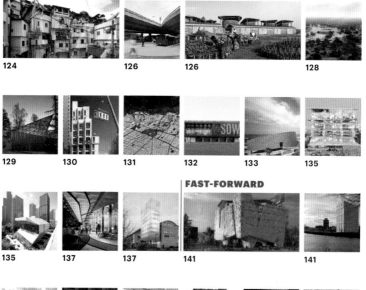

124 126 126 128

129 130 131 132 133 135

FAST-FORWARD

135 137 137 141 141

142 143 144 144 146 148

149 150 150 152 155

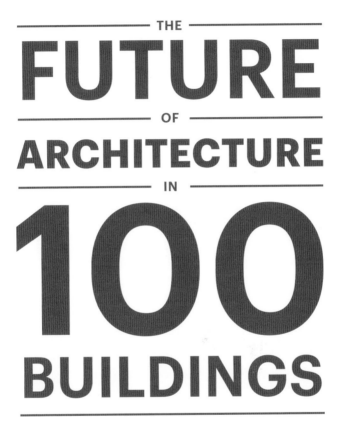

THE

FUTURE

OF

ARCHITECTURE

IN

100

BUILDINGS

Introduction

This book wants you to ask more from architecture.

You live in a house, you work in an office, you send your kids to a school. These places aren't just the backdrop to your life, they shape your life—they define who you see, what you see, and how you see it.

Architecture impacts how you feel every day, which isn't surprising considering how much time we all spend inside buildings. The average American, for example, spends 90 percent of their time indoors, yet so many of our buildings leave us without natural light, shelter us with low ceilings, and ignore our personal, social, and environmental needs.

It doesn't have to be like this. We can control this powerful force—we just have to start asking more from our buildings.

This architectural revolution is already upon us. The average person is more comfortable having an opinion about architecture today than ever before, mostly due to the dialogue enabled by social media. The world's 1.75 billion smartphones are fundamentally changing the way architecture is consumed, turning everyone into an architectural photographer. Photographs shared on social media liberate buildings from their geographic locations, enabling a new level of public engagement. We experience architecture today with an unprecedented immediacy, creating fodder for a global conversation about buildings and their impact.

This communications revolution is making us all comfortable critiquing the built environment around us, even if that criticism is just "OMG I luv this!" or "This place gives me the creeps." This feedback is removing architecture from the exclusive purview of experts and critics and putting power into the hands of the people who matter: everyday users. We have started "liking" and hating places out loud. Architects can hear us in real time, which has empowered (and sometimes even forced) them to pursue new ideas—to create solutions that respond to today's most pressing social and environmental issues.

In this new world, one in which people are asking more from their buildings, architects are no longer bound by any single style at any single time. People don't want their town library in Seattle to look the same as their grandmother's library in New Jersey. Even architectural historians don't know exactly what is going on right now because everything is changing so fast. In fact, they will never know what is going on again, because the future of architecture is a frenetic whirlwind of experimentation and a reevaluation of long-accepted habits.

This book considers the public to be a partner in architecture. The questions we can ask of buildings, and of architects, will create a new future—one that will look a lot different than the world we know today. Some of the questions this book poses may seem silly: What if a cow built your house? Can we swim in poop? Can we live on the moon? But two hundred years ago it was wild to ask, Will I live in the sky? Or, Will I need a sweater in the summer? Now that elevators and air conditioning enable us to live in the clouds and freeze in a heat wave, we must ask harder, more imaginative questions.

Architects have the know-how to design buildings that are greener, smarter, and friendlier—and now the public is a partner in this ambition. In one hundred examples, this book is a primer on how you and I and the entire world can ask for good architecture.

How we chose these buildings

The more than one hundred projects chosen for this book are a nonscientific and purely subjective collection of the most interesting and relevant work being done in the field of architecture. They represent every continent in the world and multiple building types. They are big and small, conceptual and concrete. They were initially culled from more than five thousand Architizer A+ Awards entries and supplemented by exhaustive research, conversations, and personal experience.

EXTREME LOCATIONS

Humankind's desire to explore and build in extreme locations raises a crucial question: How? How will scientists survive when they settle at the North Pole? How will naturalists take shelter when they observe reindeer in the Norwegian tundra? How will our children live when they land on Mars?

1 Can we live in the harshest place on Earth?

Forget outer space—scientists are still navigating uncharted territories here on Earth. This relocatable research facility sits on the Brunt Ice Shelf at the southernmost Antarctic station, operated by the British Antarctic Survey. Perched on giant ski-like foundations, hydraulic legs allow the station to "climb" out of the snow after heavy precipitation; when the ice shelf moves out to sea in warmer weather, modules can be lowered onto skis and towed to a new location. Setting a new bar for climate change research in the polar regions, its spaceship-like form draws much-deserved attention to this groundbreaking work.

Your survival depends on good design.

Halley VI Antarctic Research Station. Antarctica
HUGH BROUGHTON ARCHITECTS AND AECOM, CONSTRUCTED BY GALLIFORD TRY FOR THE BRITISH ANTARCTIC SURVEY

2 What does architecture look like above 10,000 feet?

Accessible only by gondola, this Austrian ski lodge sits 11,000 feet above sea level. It is designed to work with the natural landscape's sheer visual and physical power; the structure is perched on the mountain's summit to enable nature's unique "snow architecture" to accumulate and melt unimpeded. An abundance of glass windows allows for nearly 360-degree views, framed by a specially engineered floor and roof designed to withstand the elements and huge temperature swings of the setting.

Wildspitzbahn.
Tirol, Austria
BAUMSCHLAGER
HUTTER PARTNERS

Nature is the ultimate architect.

3 Can architecture be a path into the clouds?

These viewing platforms hover above the Trollstigen road, a mountainous tourist path that twists and turns up near-vertical slopes and perches on a dramatic pass between Norway's deep fjords. Humans may only visit—and build—there in the summer, when the weather is less harsh, but the platforms must withstand weather conditions year-round. Though the route delicately threads through the treacherous terrain, it relies on remarkable strength and careful engineering to stand the test of Norway's harsh elements.

Trollstigen National
Tourist Route.
Trollstigen, Norway
REIULF RAMSTAD
ARKITEKTER

The best architecture makes us forget how hard it works.

4 What do reindeer do all day?

A hiking trail leads to a spectacular site over-looking the Dovrefjell mountain range in central Norway, home to some of the last remaining wild reindeer herds in Europe. A sinewy pavilion invites visitors to warm themselves while observing the local reindeer population. The structure is an exercise in mate-rial contrast—a rigid outer shell of raw steel and glass houses a soft wooden core shaped like the nearby rocks, which have been eroded by winds and running water for centuries.

Architecture rewards the adventurous.

Tverrfjellhytta —
Norwegian Wild
Reindeer Pavilion.
Hjerkinn, Norway
SNØHETTA

Can modern architecture inspire pilgrimage?

The Ruta del Peregrino is a pilgrimage route that winds 72 miles through the Jalisco mountain range. Nearly two million people each year make the arduous walk to honor the Virgin of Talpa. This lookout point is one of nine pieces of architecture designed to provide landmarks and shelter for these travelers (and attract more casual visitors to the route as well). Balanced like a seesaw, it frames the view at one of the highest points on the trail and offers a moment of respite from the trail's harsh conditions.

Architecture can make the journey.

Ruta del Peregrino Crosses Lookout Point. Jalisco mountains, Mexico
ELEMENTAL

6 Can you dream beneath the Northern Lights?

This luxury hotel uses Iceland's otherworldly landscape to create a completely escapist experience for guests. The architects chose the location very carefully—local lore discourages disturbing cave-dwelling elves nearby. With the environment in mind, the architects made ample use of recycled materials; rubber tires were remade into bathroom basins and lava into lamps. A nearly infinite, yet sustainable, supply of hot water comes from a 190-degrees-Celsius hot spring heated by a nearby volcano. And when nighttime comes, the heavens above put on a show like none other.

Architecture reveals outer space on our own planet.

ION Luxury Adventure Hotel. Thingvellir National Park, Iceland
MINARC

7 Can a building stand on tiptoe?

At this desolate resort, the cabins are designed to encourage inhabitants to appreciate the isolation of the desert. Rather than planting each 20-square-meter EcoLoft hotel room on the ground like a traditional building, the architects designed them to hover over the land on thin steel supports. They are arranged like the boulders around the site, scattered in a picturesque composition.

Ecotourism needs ecoarchitecture.

Encuentro Guadalupe.
Baja California, Mexico
GRACIA STUDIO

8 Can an office float?

The Arctia Shipping Ltd. headquarters is a floating office building whose design references its neighbors: icebreaking barges docked on the Katajanokka shore, built to combat the region's extremely low temperatures. Its horizontal mass and customized black steel facades mimic the black hulls of the ships, while interior finishes of lacquered wood recall earlier shipbuilding traditions.

If buildings can float, whole cities could too.

Arctia Shipping
Headquarters.
Helsinki, Finland
K2S ARCHITECTS

9 Can a landscraper help us reach the stars?

In the Chilean Atacama Desert sits the Very Large Telescope, an instrument that's true to its name—it's one of the largest and most advanced pieces of optical equipment on Earth. At this flagship facility, operated by the European Southern Observatory, scientists working in severe climatic conditions (intense sun, extreme dryness, earthquakes) need lodging that will help them rest and recover between work shifts. This hotel is draped across the landscape, and has become a respite for those making extended visits to this beautiful, harsh environment.

Scientific progress requires healthy scientists.

European Southern Observatory (ESO) Hotel.
Cerro Paranal, Chile
AUER WEBER

10   Can we live on the moon?

When we all eventually live on the moon, we'll need to be protected from gamma radiation. This four-person dwelling will do just that, providing shelter from huge temperature swings and meteorites. Inflatable domes give the structure its unique shape. Robots powered by solar energy will 3-D print moon dust (regolith) onto its surface, creating a protective shell that is ultralightweight because it requires no glue or other fasteners—its particles bond together naturally. Architects have created a 1.5-ton mock-up and have tested small modules inside a vacuum chamber. Look for the first structure soon at the moon's south pole.

Architectural ingenuity isn't earthbound.

3-D printed lunar habitations. (Concept)
FOSTER + PARTNERS WITH THE EUROPEAN SPACE AGENCY

REINVENTION

It's bad enough to throw out a plastic bottle—imagine throwing out a whole building when you're done with it! New construction is wildly inefficient, which is why, for example, 90 percent of construction activity in the United States over the next ten years is expected to be on existing buildings. A grain silo becomes an art museum, and a water treatment plant becomes an icon. We can create a new future for our existing buildings by repurposing our past.

11 Can you shop in a cathedral?

As the number of brick-and-mortar bookstores in the world dwindles, the ones that remain have become sacred places to retreat. So what better place for a Dutch bookseller to reimagine itself than inside a thirteenth-century Dominican cathedral? The soaring nave allows ample space for a three-story-high bookshelf, which spans the length of the space and contrasts with the Gothic stone architecture around it.

Retail therapy can be a holy experience.

Selexyz Dominicanen.
Maastricht, Netherlands
EVELYNE MERKX,
MERKX + GIROD

12 Can rubble tell a new story?

Rubble from natural disasters is reborn, fittingly, as a history museum in China. Architects used the debris accumulated through earthquakes to build the facade of this building, commissioned by the city of Ningbo. Built in this way, the architects' vision becomes an icon of the past while advancing sustainable ideas of adapting existing materials to contemporary needs.

Bricks don't have an expiration date.

Ningbo Museum.
Ningbo, China
WANG SHU

13 Can ugly be pretty?

Newtown Creek is the largest of New York City's fourteen wastewater treatment plants. The city could have easily stuck with a utilitarian design, but instead it decided to put $4.5 billion into overhauling the outmoded and environmentally unsound wastewater treatment facility, following a design that is sensitive to the surrounding residential neighborhood. Working with a team that included lighting artists and an environmental sculptor, the architects created a complex that uses form, material, and color to create a striking visual composition.

Newtown Creek
Wastewater
Treatment Plant.
Brooklyn, New York,
United States
ENNEAD ARCHITECTS

Industrial architecture doesn't need to hide anymore.

14 Would you eat dinner in a sewer pipe?

Just try not to think about it—stacked precast concrete pipes traditionally used for wastewater become a dramatic, sculptural addition to an existing pub. Lined with wood, they create intimate dining nooks for those inside, and a sense of voyeurism for those who pass by.

Prahran Hotel.
Melbourne, Australia
TECHNÉ ARCHITECTS

Function follows form.

15 How much would you pay to sleep in a factory?

Repurposing factories into trendy hotels is happening around the globe—but this is a particularly striking instance of updated architecture bringing new life to a formerly industrial setting. On the East River in Brooklyn, the architects stripped and restored a brick, cast iron, and timber-frame building to create seventy-three guest rooms. A roof addition smartly uses contextual factory windows to create panoramic views of the Manhattan skyline while forming a visible icon on Brooklyn's own skyline.

Rest easy knowing you're cooler than everyone else.

Wythe Hotel.
Brooklyn, New York, United States
MORRIS ADJMI ARCHITECTS

16 How do you turn a grain silo into an art museum?

A historic grain silo composed of forty-two concrete tubes will become a museum on Cape Town's waterfront. The structure had no open space to begin with, so architects cut a cross section through eight of the central concrete silos (new concrete-cutting techniques will preserve their edges and add texture to the space). The effect is an oval atrium encircled by concrete shafts on every side. Artists will have the chance to create site-specific art in the silo's original underground tunnels.

Zeitz Museum of Contemporary Art Africa.
Cape Town, South Africa
HEATHERWICK STUDIO

A building can go from feeding mouths to feeding minds.

17 Can a bunker become a power plant?

In the landmark ruins of the World War Two-era Hamburg-Wilhelmsburg flak bunker, a drastic reimagining of the structure's purpose has taken place. It's now a green machine that converts heat to energy and almost wipes out its own carbon footprint. But its history hasn't been forgotten—located in the middle of a residential area, the bunker is also publically accessible as a memorial with a café.

Energy Bunker.
Hamburg, Germany
HHS PLANER
+ ARCHITEKTEN

Architecture reminds us that our memories are powerful.

18 Can superhighways make good houses?

We have all driven on highways without realizing their enormousness. This house awakens us to the scale of our transportation infrastructure. It's made using huge precast concrete beams that are traditionally fabricated for highway construction. A series of seemingly impossible cantilevers make us rethink our perceptions of gravity and scale. And check out that swimming pool!

Hemeroscopium House.
Madrid, Spain
ENSAMBLE STUDIO

Rethinking the obvious can create something entirely new.

19 Can a new skin save old bones?

When developers looked to transform a 1960s hotel into a high-end apartment building, their architects wanted to save as much of the building as possible while still upgrading its performance and overall image. They did this by creating a "second skin" for the building, which they installed onto the existing masonry facade. The new black aluminum panels host a vertical garden and drastically improve the thermal performance of the building (and look great doing it).

142 Park Street.
South Melbourne,
Australia
BRENCHLEY ARCHITECTS

Good for the environment can be good for the eyes.

20 Can historic cities have futuristic public spaces?

When Seville decided to replace the parking lot and bus station at its city center, officials were surprised to discover Roman ruins beneath the surface. What to do? Metropol Parasol was the winning scheme in an international competition that manages to protect the ruins, provide space for shopping and cafés, and create a grand new public square for the still-vibrant city. The six mushroomlike shading devices provide relief from the intense Andalusian sun, and visitors can climb to the top to take in a panoramic view of the walled city. Yet the craziest part of this swoopy landmark isn't its form: It is made mostly of wood and is the largest glued structure on Earth.

Cities are not time capsules.

Metropol Parasol.
Seville, Spain
J. MAYER H. ARCHITECTS

21 Can a subway station make you want to be underground?

This Budapest subway station extension was planned during the 1980s, but wasn't implemented until the new millennium. New construction techniques allowed the architects to excavate a giant box shape and use concrete beams to structure it. The haptic collection of columns, beams, and escalators is illuminated by the sun through a glass ceiling, making this subterranean space feel like a three-dimensional traffic intersection and transforming it into a valued public space.

Good architecture is worth the wait.

M4 Fővám tér and Szent Gellért tér stations. Budapest, Hungary
SPORAARCHITECTS

22 Can shipping containers be surprising?

Shipping containers—uniform in size, low in cost, available everywhere—offer an appealing building block for architects. Built to attract visitors to the Anyang waterfront's public art program, the APAP OpenSchool pushes the boundaries of what these modules can do. With one container skewed at a seemingly impossible 45-degree angle and another hovering 3 meters above the ground, the structure becomes a landmark within the city with the help of some bright yellow paint.

Architecture can invent extraordinary uses for ordinary materials.

APAP OpenSchool.
Anyang, Korea
LOT-EK

23 Can good architecture make 1+2=1?

The Museu de Arte do Rio and its adjacent school had an identity problem. The institutions are composed of three buildings: a 1910 palace, a midcentury bus station, and a former police hospital building. To create a single identity, the architects created a hovering concrete canopy to visually unite the disparate pieces. Thanks to barely-visible columns, the wave-like canopy seems to float over the museum campus, a bustling rooftop plaza, and the courtyard below.

With the right design, architecture can be more than the sum of its parts.

Museu de Arte do Rio.
Rio de Janeiro, Brazil
JACOBSEN ARQUITETURA

GET BETTER

Buildings impact our health and well-being. If you've ever felt depressed while sitting in a waiting room with low ceilings and harsh, flickering fluorescent lights, then you know the power of architecture over our psyches. The inverse is true too: buildings can have a hugely positive impact on the people who depend on them, from medical patients and doctors to students and the elderly.

24 Can a brick become a healing force?

In 2011, Butaro Hospital opened a 150-bed medical facility that serves nearly 350,000 people in this region of Rwanda. In spite of its impact, the hospital struggled to attract doctors to work there. The solution came in the form of these charming doctors' homes, which give foreign staff a permanent residence just five minutes from the hospital. In building the homes, architects took a truly holistic view of the community's needs and used the project as an opportunity to teach new skilled trades to the local community. On-site workshops taught local teams to make compressed stabilized earth blocks—bricks that are earthquake-safe and sustainable. These teams also learned to make the hospital's custom furniture and light fixtures, as well as the earth-stabilizing landscaping techniques crucial to bringing agriculture to the region. With a total of nine hundred skilled laborers trained during the construction process, the effort brought better building practices, not to mention better medicine, to Rwanda for generations to come.

Buildings build futures.

Butaro Doctors' Housing.
Butaro, Rwanda
MASS DESIGN GROUP

25 What can a spa teach us about light?

A distinctive hotel built in 1967 has become a mainstay on the island of Majorca. Its latest renovation includes a new spa—one that relies on an innovative natural lighting design to completely transform the interior spaces. In the pool area, the building can finally take advantage of its sunniest facades via a roof and walls punctuated by arrays of strategically placed windows. In the spa rooms and workout area, huge glass windows let guests see the landscape, whereas smaller openings create a dark, serene environment in quiet areas like the sauna.

Sunlight can be a transformative experience.

Hotel Castell dels Hams.
Majorca, Spain
A2ARQUITECTOS

26 Would you die here?

This unique housing complex for the elderly reflects Portugal's cultural emphasis on quality of life. The human component is crucial in each piece of the design, which is based on a Mediterranean town—streets, plazas, and gardens are an extension of each residence. Translucent roofs light up as the evening falls, to ensure that elderly residents can move freely at night. This lighting scheme also becomes crucial in an emergency: triggering an alarm inside the house changes the roof light from white to red, signaling the need for help.

Alcabideche Social Complex.
Alcabideche, Portugal
GUEDES CRUZ ARCHITECTS

Light sends a message.

27 Can architecture help fight cancer?

A cancer-counseling center creates a microcommunity for visitors, caregivers, and counselors. With a jagged roofline that clearly distinguishes it from other hospital buildings nearby, the center is made up of seven small houses encircling two grassy courtyards. Here, patients and their families can learn, eat, exercise, and rest close to the main cancer ward, fostering close collaboration between the hospital staff and the Danish Cancer Society. Functioning like a small community within the surrounding neighborhood, the center highlights the vital role that human contact can play in the treatment process.

Architecture can give a healing touch.

Livsrum.
Næstved, Denmark
EFFEKT

Reversible Destiny
Healing Fun House.
(Concept)
Palm Springs, California,
United States
ARAWAKA+GINS,
REVERSIBLE DESTINY
FOUNDATION

28 Can architecture give us superpowers?

The secret of longevity? Intergenerational contact, constant physical activity, social interaction, fun, and happiness. All of these attributes are embedded in the Fun House—the centerpiece of the progressive aging community in Palm Springs. Key to this building is Madeline Gins's trailblazing theory of "Reverse Destiny": using structures to challenge physical and mental capacities, and viewing architecture as a key ingredient to a longer and healthier life.

Architecture can keep us young.

29 Can this school help autistic children learn?

This school is designed for students with autism spectrum disorder—students whose elevated senses can trigger traumatic responses to sudden transitions between physical spaces, as well as to large, undefined spaces. Nine residences and three classroom buildings are arranged to foster a therapeutic environment by allowing students to move gradually through the campus. Change in direction is signaled by soft turns rather than abrupt angles, slowly leading students to the doorway of each building.

Architecture can create beautiful choreography.

Center for Discovery.
Harris, New York,
United States
TURNER BROOKS
ARCHITECT

30   Can mud keep us safe?

Mae Tao Clinic is a humanitarian organization that provides free medical treatment, shelter, and food for more than three thousand children. Located a few miles from the Burmese border, the clinic needed to expand to make room for its increasing numbers. Members of this growing community built a new facility with local wood and adobe (mud bricks), which have been used as a weather- and fireproof building material in Thailand for centuries. Now, the new center is host to a healthcare education program that will create an even stronger social fabric in this border region.

New training center
campus & temporary
dormitories.
Mae Mo, Thailand
A.GOR.A ARCHITECTS

Dirt can be the tie that binds.

31   Would your kids visit you here?

Getting old shouldn't mean living in isolation. This home for the elderly is a hybrid of a hotel and a forward-thinking hospital. Each white cube apartment on the facade has a projecting balcony designed to shade windows below from harsh sun. This privacy is offset by the great public space the building is arranged around: The long building is a meandering path (you can literally walk on the roof) that surrounds a public courtyard where patients can gather and make new friends.

House for elderly people.
Alcácer do Sal
Residences, Portugal
AIRES MATEUS

Buildings know there is strength in numbers.

POP-UP

Scientists have laboratories. Architects have pop-ups.
These temporary structures are tiny experiments in form and space.

Can architecture pop-up?

Off-the-shelf acrylic tubes are assembled to create a rigid pavilion whose shape is inspired by a rough gemstone.

Bulgari Art Pavilion.
Manarat Al Saadiyat, Abu Dhabi, United Arab Emirates
NOT A NUMBER ARCHITECTS

Designed with emerging chefs and food truck cuisine in mind, the lightweight, corrugated plastic shell can expand to accommodate dinners for two or fifty.

PDU (Portable Dining Unit).
San Francisco, California, United States
EDG

A temporary floating wedding pavilion barely touches the ground, thanks to a balloon canopy filled with helium and draped in diaphanous fabric.

Floatastic.
New Haven, Connecticut, United States
QASTIC LABS

A temporary social hub on Governors Island at the Figment arts festival is made of 53,780 recycled bottles—the amount thrown away in New York City every hour.

Head in the Clouds.
Governors Island, New York, United States
STUDIO KLIMOSKI CHANG ARCHITECTS

Entrance

Designers give a standard white party tent a makeover with a suspended landscape of white vinyl tubes.

Drift pavilion for Design Miami/2012,
Miami Beach, Florida, United States
SNARKITECTURE

SHAPE
SHIFTERS

Can walls be invisible? Can a concert hall be a balloon? Can a skyscraper bend over and touch the ground? New technology for drawing, digital modeling, and construction means that architects are no longer bound by the shapes of the past, and can create unique spaces that look unlike anything we've seen before.

32 Can a building zig?

A border crossing is the first thing you encounter in a country, and the last thing you see as you leave. Georgia has built what must be the most interesting border crossing in the world, which is no surprise—since it was reborn as an independent democratic country in 1991, Georgia has been using architecture to rebrand its image to the world. Cantilevered platforms allow for viewing of the rugged landscape, and a cafeteria, conference room, and staff facilities are arranged to create a composition that promises wonderful discoveries in the country beyond.

The gateway to a country should entice and inspire visitors.

Border checkpoint.
Sarpi, Georgia
J. MAYER H. ARCHITECTS

33 Can architecture swirl?

An inflatable and mobile concert hall made of a stretchy plastic membrane brings both art and hope to earthquake-devastated Japan. The five-hundred-seat venue can inflate in under two hours and, when deflated, can move to a new location on the back of a truck.

The line between art and architecture can be a curvy one.

Ark Nova.
Matsushima, Japan
ARATA ISOZAKI,
ANISH KAPOOR

34 Can architecture swoop?

The Soviet Union was well known for its imposing and rigidly monumental architecture. When Azerbaijanis looked to create a new cultural center in their capital, they made an extreme departure from precedent. The building rises out of the landscape in a series of undulating curves to enclose over 57,000 square meters of space. The design represents the fluid relationship between the city and what happens inside the cultural center.

Heydar Aliyev Center.
Baku, Azerbaijan
ZAHA HADID ARCHITECTS

Architecture can create new landscapes.

35 Can architecture drip?

An international airport is an opportunity for a city to showcase its identity to visitors. That's why the architects of Terminal 2 in Mumbai's airport chose to reference the patterns of local jali window screens along its 17-acre roof. (*Jali* is the term for a perforated stone or latticed screen, usually with an ornamental pattern, often found in Indian architecture.) The coffered ceiling's pattern that drips into columns lets in light from above with skylights, creating a strong visual gateway to the nation's capital.

Architecture lets you know you've arrived.

Chhatrapati Shivaji
International Airport
Terminal 2.
Mumbai, India
SKIDMORE, OWINGS & MERRILL

36 Do buildings wear stockings?

In historic neighborhoods, new buildings should strike a balance between past and present architecture. For a new gallery in the northern part of Seoul, the architects created a white box that was ideal for the art inside, but too rigid-looking within its historic surroundings. A little wardrobe change did the trick: Wrapped in a flexible chain mail veil, the white box changes as light plays across its surface, better blending in with neighboring buildings.

A well-dressed building is never out of place.

Kukje Gallery.
Seoul, South Korea
SOLID OBJECTIVES-
IDENBURG LIU

37 Can architecture be from outer space?

The quickly growing city of Dalian asked architects to create a functioning conference and opera center, but also a visual landmark for the city—something that could become an icon for the local community and excite an international audience. The result is almost entirely self-referential, as if an alien ship landed on the banks of Dalian's port. The building doesn't look to context for its reference, it looks to the future. It's a hopeful symbol of what the city will become: a place activated by visitors, commerce, and culture.

Architecture doesn't predict the future, it creates the future.

Dalian International
Conference Center.
Dalian, China
COOP HIMMELB(L)AU

38 What if an office building turned inside out?

Office design can be hard. Columns and pipes often get in the way of the much-vaunted "open-plan" design that, in turn, can get in the way of cubicles and conference rooms. Not so at O-14, an office tower that relies on a white concrete bearing wall three feet away from the windows to carry the building's load. That means there are no columns in the space. The structural wall creates a chimney effect that pulls hot air away from the building (good in the Dubai heat), and with 1,326 holes in five different shapes arranged artfully along the building's length, it makes an elegant statement about this new type of skyscraper design.

A hole new way of looking at structure.

O-14.
Dubai, United Arab Emirates
REISER + UMEMOTO

39 Can glitz be more than glam?

When this 40-year-old villa was transformed into apartments, it was at risk of losing its singular visual identity. To retain its identity and upgrade it for better environmental performance, architects installed a reflective outer wall in front of the existing building. This mirrored wall protects the building from the harsh sun, while unifying the apartments behind a single, continuous material—one that reflects the beautiful landscape.

Trevox Apartments.
Naucalpan, Mexico
CRAFT ARQUITECTOS

Mirror, mirror, be the wall.

40 Is pretty a public amenity?

In case you were wondering, this shape is called a rotated rhomboid. Clad in sixteen thousand hexagonal tiles, this Rodin sculpture museum's muscular structure is wrapped in a shimmering mirrored skin. The pattern references Mexico City's traditional colonial ceramic-tiled building facades and, like those buildings, changes in appearance with weather and the viewer's vantage point, becoming a sculpture itself.

A museum can be as important as the art within.

Museo Soumaya.
Mexico City, Mexico
FR-EE / FERNANDO
ROMERO ENTERPRISE

41 Can architecture be an Olympic sport?

Ski jumping is a death-defying sport; athletes risk life and limb to launch themselves impossibly high into the air. The village of Holmenkollen, in Norway, has been home to the most legendary jumps of the last century, and a recent international competition aimed to raise its reputation even higher with a new sports campus and jumping hill. Clad in stainless steel mesh and cantilevered 226 feet, the ski jump is the longest of its kind, making sure it is always the center of attention.

Architecture gives you wings.

Holmenkollen Ski Jump.
Oslo, Norway
JDS ARCHITECTS

42 Can architecture be pixelated?

A building that's a simple cube is complicated by a facade of square panels in ten colors—just like a pixelated image. The playful design breaks down the form of the office, but it also performs the serious task of concealing the proprietary research and development conducted by the technology company within.

Architecture can keep secrets.

Frog Queen.
Graz, Austria
SPLITTERWERK

43 Can stone flow like a river?

Inspired by the geomorphology of the Louisiana region's ancient riverbed, this museum's sculptural foyer uses 1,100 cast stone panels to form a pathway to the museum's interior galleries. The panels were designed and assembled using a custom automation process.

Technology is the new alchemy, turning rocks into water.

Louisiana State Museum and Sports Hall of Fame. Natchitoches, Louisiana, United States
TRAHAN ARCHITECTS

44 Have we been thinking about windows all wrong?

**The French call it a *brise soleil* ("sun breaker").
In Eastern architecture, it's a *muxarabi*.
Wooden screens have a universal appeal
for their dramatic appearance and serious
sun-shading ability in hot weather. At a residence in São Paulo, two huge wooden curtains
shelter the home of a young family, letting air
flow through and creating a private enclave
amid other houses. The best part is the mystery
of this seemingly "windowless" house.**

Every element of architecture is ripe
for innovation.

BT House.
São Paolo, Brazil
STUDIO GUILHERME
TORRES

45 Why can't walls be invisible?

**This is a museum for a glass collection, and
the architects decided that a building for
glass should be made of glass. The building is
composed of a solid floor and a solid ceiling
that appear to magically float on glass walls.**

The boldest architecture is sometimes
hard to see.

Glass Pavilion at the
Toledo Museum of Art.
Toledo, Ohio, United States
SANAA

46 Can a library be a mountain?

The illiteracy rate in the Netherlands town of Spijkenisse is a whopping 10 percent, so the city launched a type of architectural public relations campaign for books. Near the town square, community, educational, and commercial spaces were stacked into a pyramid, then wrapped with a 480-meter-long bookcase. Glass facades expose the library's collection, inviting everyone who passes to come inside.

Familiar buildings can still surprise us.

Stichting Openbare Bibliotheek.
Spijkenisse, Netherlands
MVRDV

47 Does a building need to be tall to change the skyline?

In Europe, residential buildings surround courtyards; in Manhattan, they reach for the sky. West 57th is the best of both worlds: its walls create a sheltered green space for occupants while maintaining the sweeping city vantage point offered by a skyscraper. Rising to a 450-foot peak, the building's shape lets sunlight deep into the block while keeping views of the Hudson River open for neighbors.

A condo tower doesn't need to be inward looking (and it doesn't need to be a tower).

West 57th.
New York, New York,
Unites States
ARCHITECT: BIG–BJARKE INGELS
GROUP

48 Can glass be a fortress?

This concert hall is a collection of delicate crystals perched on the punishing Reykjavik waterfront. A collaboration with artist Olafur Eliasson, the building's south face is made of 823 "quasi-bricks"—stackable twelve-sided modules fabricated from steel and ten different types of glass that shimmer like fish scales.

But they aren't just a pretty façade—the glass bricks block noise from disturbing the performances inside. The strength of the glass combined with its structure makes this concert hall nearly impenetrable by the roiling nature around it.

Some materials have hidden powers.

Harpa Concert Hall and Conference Center. Reykjavik, Iceland HENNING LARSEN ARCHITECTS WITH BATTERÍIÐ ARCHITECTS, RAMBØLL GROUP, AND ARTENGINEERING, AND OLAFUR ELIASSON

49 Can a light make a warehouse warm?

A warehouse is a warehouse is a warehouse, right? Well, not with a shape like this! The architects for KOP Warehouses replaced corrugated metal with corrugated transparent and translucent plastic sheets to let light in and out. The result is a simple twist on the traditional warehouse and proof that no building type is beyond innovation.

A smart architect can make a gem out of a lump of coal.

KOP Warehouses.
Puurs, Belgium
URA

50 Can a skyscraper bend over?

The new headquarters for China Central Television (CCTV) combines the entire process of TV-making—administration, production, broadcasting—into a single loop of connected activities. The building's form offers an alternative to the traditional skyscraper, encouraging collaborative activities inside, and offering an unprecedented amount of public access to China's media production system.

New public engagement creates new forms.

China Central Television headquarters. Beijing, China
OMA

51 Can balconies make waves?

Architectural innovation can take huge amounts of resources and time to bring to fruition. Sometimes though, the answer is in the smallest details. Underneath its exuberant form, this 82-story hotel and apartment building is really just a traditional rectangular skyscraper. When it came time to design the balconies, though, the architect became a sculptor and created curvy and changing platforms that jut out from the building up to 12 feet. From a distance, this minor alteration creates a huge spectacle— a sensual cloud floating on the Chicago skyline.

Opportunity is in the details.

Aqua Tower.
Chicago, Illinois,
United States
STUDIO GANG ARCHITECTS

52 How much does interesting cost?

A site at a busy São Paulo intersection offered architects an opportunity to create a new city landmark—all while using traditional building materials and techniques to keep costs down. Balconies arranged seemingly at random are actually a simple extension of each floor plate, granting the design complexity and character without blowing the budget.

Innovative architecture can add value to a city without adding cost.

Top Towers.
São Paulo, Brazil
KÖNIGSBERGER
VANNUCCHI ARQUITETOS

DRIVE

**There are over a billion cars on Earth.
They have to go somewhere.**

**Sometimes it's okay just to make
something beautiful.**

Gas station.
Matúškovo, Slovakia
ATELIER SAD

No disguises necessary here.
The garage is a shapely icon that
is proud of its function.

Parking structure for the Tyrolean Festival Erl.
Erl, Austria
KLEBOTH LINDINGER DOLLNIG

A collage of photos taken in Venice
was translated into a four-layered design
to create a modern-day baroque
facade for this garage.

Facade of multistory car park.
Skopje, Macedonia
PPGA ARCHITECTS

A recycled stainless-steel wrapper encloses
the first LEED-certified gas station in the US.

Helios House.
Los Angeles, California, Unites States.
OFFICE DA, JOHNSTON MARKLEE,
AND BIG

It's a gas station, a restaurant, a public park, and a reflecting pool. Because why shouldn't gas stations offer true amenities to travelers?

Fuel station and McDonald's.
Batumi, Georgia
GIORGI KHMALADZE ARCHITECTS

NATURE
BUILDING

Nature is an increasingly influential part of building design—we are being guided by trees, rather than overwhelming them. New architecture is finding innovative methods to incorporate natural landscapes into, onto, and around buildings.

53 Can you live in a rock?

With an entry and powder room fully carved from rock, The Pierre (French for stone) is a house that celebrates the rugged landscape of its site. Stone penetrates the structure—excavated rock was even crushed and mixed into concrete flooring—and construction involved dynamite, hydraulic chippers, wire saws, and hand tools. Rather than conceal this process, marks are left exposed to celebrate it.

The Pierre.
San Juan Islands,
Washington,
United States
OLSON KUNDIG
ARCHITECTS

Maybe cavemen were on to something.

54 Can you live on a rock?

A blackened-timber cabin built over the course of a few weekends gets a leg up from a boulder; inside, the incline turns into large steps that double as seating and sleeping areas, with storage underneath.

Tiny Timber
Forest Retreat.
Bohemia, Czech
Republic
UHLIK ARCHITEKTI

Bumps in the road can be a good thing.

55 Are treehouses just for kids?

A perfect 4-meter cube suspended midway up a tree trunk is a secluded living space large enough for two people. Its mirrored glass exterior lets it all but disappear into the wooded surroundings, but birds see and avoid colliding with it thanks to a transparent ultraviolet coating.

Architecture can wear camouflage.

Treehotel.
Harads, Sweden
THAM & VIDEGÅRD
ARKITEKTER

56 Can architecture hug a tree?

Architects have long considered the way different bodies move through spaces. Here, a woman who is confined to a wheelchair wants her home to revolve around the garden. This redesign of two 1830s brick cottages puts nature at the center of her family activities. Even from her wheelchair, she can enjoy views of mature trees from a home that is shaped to embrace them.

Design should work for all abilities.

Tree house.
London, United Kingdom
6A ARCHITECTS

57 Can a tree house become a house-tree?

Vietnam's tropical forests have given way to dense cities—less than .25 percent of Ho Chi Minh City is covered in trees. To help residents reconnect with nature, architects broke a house into five concrete boxes and turned the roof of each one into a giant planter. If this idea is applied to other houses in the future, the green spaces could collect and filter enough stormwater to reduce flooding citywide.

Architecture can have a green thumb.

House for Trees.
Ho Chi Minh City,
Vietnam
VO TRONG NGHIA
ARCHITECTS

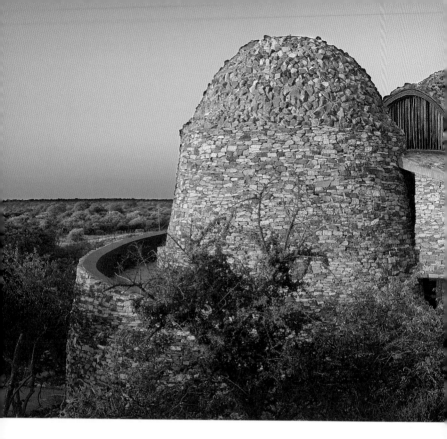

58 Can new buildings learn old tricks?

The plan for this visitor center began with a motif etched on stones uncovered at the former location of a South African trading civilization. Its free-form vaults were built with a 600-year-old construction technique that is both economically and environmentally responsible: Local laborers made the

200,000 pressed soil tiles as part of a poverty relief program. Though it's inspired by the past, the center's design is at home in the twenty-first century, with modern geometric forms that create a new topography in the ancient setting.

Modern construction can still learn from ancient techniques.

Mapungubwe Interpretation Centre. Mapungubwe National Park, Limpopo, South Africa
PETER RICH ARCHITECTS

59   Does balanced architecture need to touch the ground?

The shape of this house may be inspired by a traditional barn, but a dramatic 50-foot canti-lever that lets it hover over the ground makes it a thoroughly modern feat of architecture; exactly half of the building is floating in the air. A rigid structure that uses a heavy concrete core where the barn touches the ground makes this possible. Underneath the giant cantilever is an epic swing.

The Balancing Barn.
Suffolk, United Kingdom
MVRDV

Structural innovation, and a healthy budget, make the impossible possible.

60   Can a lawn be more than ornament?

This building is a gateway between the busy city and the silence of the botanical gardens in Brooklyn. That's why it's half building, half land-scape. And its roof is more than just a pretty feature—it's connected to a system that col-lects stormwater to facilitate natural filtration, and serves as an icon that attracts thousands of visitors to the garden.

Brooklyn Botanic Garden
Visitor Center.
Brooklyn, New York,
United States
WEISS/MANFREDI

Responsible architecture reconnects us with nature.

61 Can grass paint a city?

This five-story-high green wall incorporates 7,600 plants from 237 species to transform a historic corner in Paris into a piece of living architecture. Beginning with a plain concrete wall, the designer installed a metal, PVC, and nonbiodegradable-felt structure that prevents damage to the building while still allowing plants to grow without soil. A built-in watering system keeps the wall healthy, allowing it to mature and change the city landscape over the course of several years.

Le Oasis d'Aboukir green wall.
Paris, France
PATRICK BLANC

Plants help keep historic architecture alive.

62 Will the city of the future be a living organism?

In these fantastical renderings (produced for the History Channel's "City of the Future" Competition), plants become power producers that harness natural energy from the sun to power an entire city. As they grow, the plants take over the city and transform it into a hybrid place: part city, part forest. At the top, a canopy of biologically enhanced plants capture energy from the sun and water from the clouds. The canopy stays low in open, suburban areas and lifts off the ground in the dense remnants of urban downtowns.

MEtreePOLIS.
(Concept)
Atlanta, Georgia,
United States
HOLLWICH KUSHNER
(HWKN)

Urban planning meets the law of the jungle.

SHELTER
FROM THE STORM

Changing climates and weather mean danger—and opportunity—for our built environments. In the face of cataclysmic natural events, architecture is often the first line of defense. But architecture can also harness nature to empower inhabitants. With hundred-year storms now coming every ten years, and energy demands growing and changing exponentially, the world needs architecture that addresses nature in all its forms.

63 Can architecture retreat from a storm?

To avoid destruction during inevitable and intensifying storms, structures built within the coastal erosion zone of the Coromandel Peninsula must be removable. This house takes the requirement as a playful design challenge. The structure functions almost like a wooden tent—a two-story shutter winches open to form a sheltering awning, and closes to protect the house in inclement weather. Perched on two sleds, the home can move to the back of its site, or across the beach and onto a barge for a total relocation.

The Earth is changing, and so should our architecture.

Hut on Sleds.
Whangapoua, New Zealand
CROSSON CLARKE
CARNACHAN ARCHITECTS

64 Can we find salvation in paper tubes?

After an earthquake devastated the New Zealand town of Christchurch, citizens were left to grieve casualties as well as the loss of their central cathedral. One architect responded with a piece of "emergency architecture"—a rapidly built cathedral made of paper tubes, shipping containers, and a lightweight polycarbonate skin. The structure could not be more simple. The result is sublime.

Rebuilding after disaster is a moment for ingenuity.

Cardboard Cathedral.
Christchurch, New
Zealand
SHIGERU BAN

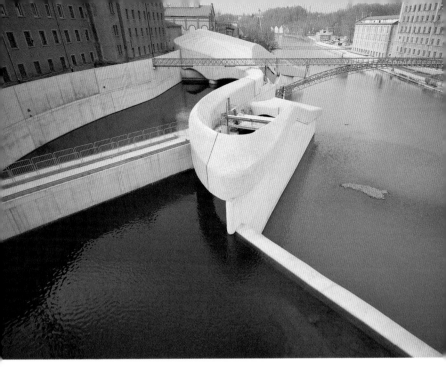

65 Can green infrastructure give us super powers?

This hydroelectric dam produces 10.5 million kilowatts of energy (enough to power three thousand homes), but that is not its most impressive feat! The amazing thing about this dam is the regard the architects showed for the project's surroundings. The architects considered noise, pedestrian paths, and even the water route that fish take. The sinewy shape makes it more than simply infrastructure—it is a working public sculpture that the city cherishes.

Protection can be more than security barriers.

Hydroelectric power station. Kempten, Germany
BECKER ARCHITEKTEN

Can playful be practical?

Our air quality is getting worse, especially in urban areas. Who can we look to for help? Meet Wendy. Wendy maximizes her surface area to expose as much titanium-nanoparticle-coated skin to the environment as possible. Every square foot of this surface sucks CO_2 out of the air—a total equivalent to taking 250 cars off of the road. The best part of Wendy is that she has a personality—she is big and blue and spiky, and she shoots out jets of water, and she has a name. The project was as much a social experiment as it was an ecological experiment.

Architecture can have personality *and* help the Earth.

Wendy: 2012 MoMA/PS1 Young Architects Program winner. Queens, New York, United States
HOLLWICH KUSHNER (HWKN)

67 Can we design for disaster?

In an area that was swampland two hundred years ago, the coastal playgrounds of Hunter's Point are prone to flooding in storms. The architects worked with the engineering team to anticipate this—the sunken oval playing field is designed to flood and act as a buffer for the rest of the park and the neighborhood beyond. It is a layered strategy that purposefully sacrifices playing fields in the event of a storm, rather than harder-to-replace infrastructure and houses.

Architecture helps us prioritize during a disaster.

Hunter's Point South Park.
Queens, New York, United States
THOMAS BALSLEY ASSOCIATES
AND WEISS/MANFREDI

68 Can architecture save us from the apocalypse?

Think of this as a safety deposit box for the world's seeds. Inside a mountain on a remote island halfway between Norway and the North Pole, this state-of-the-art storage facility provides what scientists believe is a failsafe way to protect food crops in the event of manmade or natural disaster. Built under thick rock and permafrost, the collection of millions of "backup" seed samples can remain frozen even in a power outage, securing the seed supply for centuries.

Svalbard Global
Seed Vault.
Longyearbyen, Norway
BARLINDHAUGKONSERNET

Give peas a chance.

69 Can architecture be a sponge?

New York has had some serious recovery work to do since Hurricane Sandy devastated its coastal neighborhoods in 2012. Six design teams have been chosen to develop innovative plans to protect the region from future storms. Plans range from huge berms that will protect the East River Park community from storm surges—while providing new recreational space—to green infrastructure that will store excess water and prevent flooding. Pictured here is the Big U, a series of green berms and landscapes to absorb storm surges.

The Big U:
Rebuild by Design
competition.
(Concept)
New York, New York,
United States
BIG TEAM, INTERBORO
TEAM, MIT CAU + ZUS
+ URBANISTEN, OMA,
PENNDESIGN/OLIN, AND
SCAPE / LANDSCAPE
ARCHITECTURE

Bad things can inspire us to do good.

70 How many ways can a roof serve a building?

With temperatures on the rise, roofs must be enlisted in the fight against climate change. In the spirit of technological advancement, this building will have what SHoP Architects calls an "Energy Blanket"—a roofscape designed to both collect and conserve energy using a range of innovative techniques, including solar panels, a water collection and recycling system, and huge overhangs to shade the building's interiors. The mission of this 270,000-square-foot research facility is to support innovation and entrepreneurship in Botswana. It includes a data center, engineering floors, and an HIV research lab run by an international consortium.

Even incubators need shade.

Botswana
Innovation Hub.
Gaborone, Botswana
SHOP ARCHITECTS

SHRINK

By 2050, more than 80 percent of the world's people will live in cities.
That means that every square foot counts.

How can we think smaller?

A polyester shell encloses an egglike multifunctional space. It includes a bathroom, kitchen, and niches for sleeping and storage. When the nose is opened, the whole structure becomes a porch.

Blob VB3
Mechelen, Belgium
DMVA ARCHITECTEN

This 914-square-foot transparent house is inspired by the concept of living in a tree, with twenty-one different floors at various heights to allow its owners never-ending variety.

House NA.
Tokyo, Japan
SOU FUJIMOTO ARCHITECTS

This 19-square-meter house has four rooms and was built for a quarter of the price of a similarly sized apartment in the same area.

Boxhome.
Oslo, Norway
RINTALA EGGERTSSON ARCHITECTS

A prefabricated, off-the-grid pod meets the
need for safe housing in South Africa's 2,700
informal settlements, which house millions of
inhabitants in substandard conditions.

Mamelodi POD housing unit.
Pretoria, South Africa
ARCHITECTURE FOR A CHANGE

Part art installation, part artist's residence, this house measures 28 inches at its narrowest and four feet at its widest point.

Keret House.
Warsaw, Poland
JAKUB SZCZĘSNY

A tiny office wedged like a barnacle between two larger buildings allows traffic to flow beneath.

Parasite Office.
Moscow, Russia
ZA BOR ARCHITECTS

SOCIAL CATALYSTS

Cities are living organisms—without the right cultivation, they wither and die. Architecture has the power to stitch individuals into a community and energize forgotten corners of our urban fabric. Communities use architecture to plant a flag and rally together. Catalysts can be youth centers, religious buildings, libraries, and even beehives, but regardless of its use, architecture is a potent tool for encouraging the act of community.

71 Would you let your kids play in a wasteland?

Postindustrial wastelands don't always spark enthusiasm from local communities, but this project transformed a defunct warehouse and brownfield (land previously used for industry) into a public park and performance space with an amphitheater that rises like a wave from a wooden boardwalk. Now, this economically strained Virginia rail town has a new sense of pride that is rooted in nature, rather than industrial decay.

Landscape architecture can transform brown to green.

Smith Creek Park.
Clifton Forge, Virginia,
United States
DESIGN/BUILDLAB
AT VIRGINIA TECH

72 Can you swim in poop?

New York City is surrounded by water, but you wouldn't want to swim there—the city drains effluent directly into its rivers every time it rains. That's all going to change thanks to a crowdfunded initiative to build the world's first water-filtering floating pool. This giant Brita-esque pool will filter up to a half million gallons of river water each day, making the rivers cleaner over time and creating a much-needed public amenity that will reconnect us to the urban waterfront.

It's your city. You should be able to use it.

Plus POOL initiative.
(Concept)
New York, New York,
United States
FAMILY AND PLAYLAB

73 Can honeybees fight blight?

A colony of honeybees that had taken up residence in an abandoned building needed to be relocated. So a group of local architecture students designed them a new home in a 22-foot-tall honeycomb-shaped tower with perforated steel panels made to protect the hive from wind and weather. Inside, a cypress wood box with a glass bottom lets visitors see the bees at work from below. The new habitat is an educational opportunity for children and adults alike, who get to see the economic and environmental regeneration happening throughout this Buffalo neighborhood.

Hive City: Elevator B. Buffalo, New York, United States
UNIVERSITY AT BUFFALO SCHOOL OF ARCHITECTURE AND PLANNING

Underused urban areas can become hives of activity.

74 Can architecture feed a community?

Sitting atop a former twentieth-century factory, a 40,000-square-foot field is the largest rooftop soil farm in the United States. Part of a local for-profit initiative that now spans two rooftops in New York City, the gardens produce more than 50,000 pounds of organic produce each year for residents. It's local, organic, and takes advantage of a structure that was sitting unused for decades.

Brooklyn Grange. Queens, New York, United States
BROMLEY CALDARI ARCHITECTS

Join the roof-to-table movement.

75 Can paint unite a city?

This public artwork project began in 2010 as a collaboration between Dutch artists Jeroen Koolhaas and Dre Urhahn and a local team in Rio de Janeiro's Santa Marta favela—favelas are Brazilian slums or shantytowns—turning it into a more vibrant, appealing place. Since then, they have spread their movement across the

world, transforming a dilapidated area in North
Philadelphia and working with communities
in Curaçao and elsewhere to alter depressed
public spaces in ways that will attract positive
attention and economic impulses.

Positive change can come in a few cans
of paint.

Favela Painting Project.
Rio de Janeiro, Brazil
HAAS&HAHN

76 Can color change your morning commute?

Just a few meters from one of Bratislava's historic squares, a dimly lit bus terminal sat neglected for years. To empower commuters, architects enlisted the local community to paint 1,000 square meters of pavement with green road paint. Two years later, they pushed the low-cost design intervention further with a crowdsourced lighting unit that was produced and installed with 4,000 meters of white packing tape. The resulting space is bright, cheery and a far cry from the drab station it once was.

An uplifting public space doesn't have to be expensive, but it does have to be smart.

Bus terminal under the bridge.
Bratislava, Slovakia
VALLO SADOVSKY
ARCHITECTS

77 Can design help women thrive?

The nonprofit organization Women for Women International teaches war survivors marketable skills, empowering them to remake their communities. A designer collaborated with the organization to create a community center with an inviting public plaza—a meeting place designed to bridge the gap between urban buyers and rural farmers. The facility's sustainable systems are maintained by the women who live nearby, ensuring a strong local network that can support the community for future generations.

Architecture helps rebuild lives.

Women's Opportunity Center.
Kayonza, Rwanda
SHARON DAVIS DESIGN

78 Can opera empower a village?

In 2009, Burkinabé architect Francis Kéré teamed up with the late German film and theater director Christoph Schlingensief to bring an opera house to the rural area of Laongo. The two embarked on an incredible journey to heighten the cultural identity of the region, which was already the center of African film and theater. Still in progress, this "opera house for Africa" and educational center is already bringing together local residents and local materials to create beautiful music on a 30-acre campus that includes a five-hundred-student school and a health center.

A creative community is its own oasis.

Opera Village.
Laongo, Burkina Faso
KÉRÉ ARCHITECTURE

79   Can a garden shed unite a community?

A humble garden shed takes on a fantastic form to avoid casting shadows on nearby garden plots. Made of chemical-free materials, the building creates a shaded meeting space, while the charred cedar siding doubles as a chalkboard wall for messages and tips. The herringbone pattern of the wooden slats filter light into the interior while creating a trellis for seasonal vines.

Architecture is like gardening: You reap what you sow.

Woodlands Community Garden shed.
Vancouver, Canada
BRENDAN CALLANDER,
JASON PIELAK, AND
STELLA CHEUNG-BOYLAND

80 Can small housing be great housing?

Demographers predict that New York will add at least 1 million more residents by 2040—and many of these are expected to be one- or two-person middle-income households that won't qualify for city subsidies or financing. Sponsored by the mayor's office, the adAPT NYC competition sought new housing options for this growing population. This winning plan uses a solution of modular housing units that can be stacked to create fifty-five new microunits sized to 250 square feet. The concept can be adapted to many different locations, allowing city developers to meet the changing needs of citizens as quickly as cities grow.

Cities need homes for teachers and nurses, too.

My Micro NY: adAPT NYC competition winner. (Concept) NARCHITECTS

81 Can architecture be crowdsourced and crowdfunded?

Mi Ciudad Ideal (My Ideal City) is an effort to crowdsource and document citizens' wishes for the future of their city and, eventually, to crowdfund them. Launched in Bogotá, Colombia, the program has already drawn participation from more than 130,000 residents. This new "bottom-up" approach to urban planning is well-suited to Latin American cities, where a huge boom in the number of middle-class citizens is requiring innovative solutions. The first example of this effort is BD Bacatá, a skyscraper created by Prodigy Network and sponsored by BD Promotores, that holds the world record in crowdfunding. It's a huge step in citizen participation and investment in a city's evolving needs.

130,000 heads are better than one.

Downtown Bogotá revitalization scenario from the My Ideal City initiative. (Concept)
Bogotá, Colombia

ARCHITECT: WINKA DUBBELDAM, ARCHI-TECHTONICS

CREATOR AND DIRECTOR: RODRIGO NIÑO

PRODIGY NETWORK SPONSOR: VENERANDO LAMELAS

82 What happens when architecture keeps score?

In less than six months, architects of this Nike-funded football training facility created a place where twenty thousand footballers of all ages can play throughout the year. The first of its kind in Africa, the facility is designed to have an open feeling, but crime is a daily reality in this Johannesburg township. The building's transparency welcomes the community with invisible security at all times. The center has limited access points, and its wooden louver facade creates a tight perimeter outside, while huge expanses of glass face inward, toward the protected playing field at the center of the complex. Architects even commissioned the local artist Kronk to turn the security fence into a site-specific artwork, masking its true purpose.

Football Training
Centre.
Soweto, South Africa
RURAL/URBAN/FANTASY
PROJECT

Architecture should protect and serve.

83

Can a library be a lighthouse?

The new library of Alexandria is built on roughly the same site as the library founded by Alexander the Great 2,300 years ago, but the similarities end there. The building is composed of a giant slanted circle 160 meters in diameter. The glazed roof lets sunlight in at optimum levels to protect the books and wash the space with natural illumination. Like many modern libraries, the institution has expanded its mission beyond just books (though it can house up to 8 million of those too, and claims to have the world's largest reading room). With a planetarium, four museums, an information science school, and conservation facilities, the library has a new, more important role in the community than ever before.

A new roof can give an ancient library new life.

Bibliotheca Alexandrina.
Alexandria, Egypt
SNØHETTA

84 Can you get married in a parking garage?

There are over 105 million commercial parking spaces in the United States, and they are not always full. This Miami Beach parking garage creates a civic amenity out of its three hundred parking spaces. They can be repurposed when empty, thanks to super-high ceilings and amazing views. When the cars are gone, the building is used for yoga in the morning and is rented out for events at night.

1111 Lincoln Road.
Miami Beach, Florida,
United States
HERZOG & DE MEURON

Inefficient parking can create great public infrastructure.

85 Can a library be relevant in the digital age?

At the Seattle public library, the architects considered the way we consume media in a digital age and turned the library into a relevant public amenity by redefining it as an institution dedicated to more than just books. All forms of media—new and old—are represented here. They even redesigned the Dewey decimal system to make the place more intuitive and welcoming. The building's shape is a direct result of this rearrangement.

Seattle Central Library.
Seattle, Washington,
United States
OMA/LMN, REM
KOOLHAAS AND JOSHUA
PRINCE-RAMUS

Libraries still have a lot to learn.

86 Can you sunbathe underground?

Manhattan's High Line proved that an elevated rail line could have a second life as a vibrant public space. Now, a project called The Lowline aims to convert an unused trolley terminal into a subterranean hub for year-round events and activities. The plan uses a cutting-edge solar technology called a "remote skylight" to collect sunlight and direct it underground, allowing plants, and people, to thrive in a previously uninhabitable space.

The Lowline.
(Concept)
New York, New York,
United States
RAAD STUDIO

As urban spaces become scarce, we appreciate them more.

87 Can flipping a switch enliven a neighborhood?

This light and slender building at Paris Diderot University neighbors a hulking academic building next door. The new building faces a public square and acts as a bright gravitational counterpoint to the existing building. The open first floor beckons visitors in, and at night the entire building becomes a place-making icon for the university.

M3A2 Cultural and
Community Tower.
Paris, France
ANTONINI DARMON
ARCHITECTES

Opposites attract.

FAST
FORWARD

We have been taught to expect the same thing from buildings over and over again: inert boxes made of concrete, steel, and glass. But in the near future, buildings will be wildly different than anything we experience today. This change begins with technology impacting our building materials, because the way we build impacts what we build. From 3-D printed houses to mushroom bricks, today's emerging technologies look beyond the hammer and nail to imagine a new way of constructing.

Can a building clean the air?

Welcome to the age of smog-eating architecture. Slated to make its debut at the 2015 Milan Expo, a 13,000-square-meter building will become an air purifier for the city, with a concrete facade that absorbs airborne pollutants and converts them into harmless salts that are then washed away by the rain.

Italian Pavilion.
Milan, Italy
NEMESI & PARTNERS

Architecture helps us breathe easy.

Can we print a house?

The 3D Print Canal House is an exhibition and experimentation site that remakes the typical Dutch canal house into a 3-D-printed home for the twenty-first century. The process of making turns digital files into physical building blocks using a KamerMaker, a large-scale version of a desktop printer. This makes it possible for the designers to create detailed components in a local style. The house is produced on-site, so there are no material transportation costs, and the potential for local manufacturing is high—meaning cities may no longer have to seek cheap building materials from far away as 3-D printing technology takes hold at the local level.

3D Print Canal House.
(Concept)
Amsterdam, Netherlands
DUS ARCHITECTS

Knowledge comes from making.

90 Can mushrooms replace stone?

These bricks are made of mushrooms. Mushrooms! The "bio-bricks" were grown inside of reflective trays made out of a mirrored film. These reflective containers were later used at the top of the tower to bounce daylight into the structure and the space around it. The tower's shape is designed to be efficient, too, cooling itself by pushing hot air out at the top. In contrast to the energy-gobbling skyscrapers on New York City's skyline, Hy-Fi offers a thought-provoking glimpse of the future. Hope you like mushrooms.

We can grow the future.

Hy-Fi: 2014 MoMA/
PS1 Young Architects
Program winner.
Queens, New York,
United States
THE LIVING

91 Can worms replace workers?

Silk doesn't seem like the sturdiest building material, but a group at **MIT** turned to 6,500 live silkworms to build a structure that connects nature with technology in a whole new way. They programmed a robotic arm to create a framework across a metal scaffold that gave the silkworms a roadmap to follow. When the worms were let loose on the structure, they responded to light, heat, and geometry, producing patterns that were a reflection of their environment. The resulting dome could inspire researchers to design and make man-made fiber structures never before imagined.

Architecture can imitate the beautiful efficiency of nature.

Silk Pavilion.
Cambridge, Massachusetts,
United States
MIT MEDIA LAB MEDIATED
MATTER GROUP

92 Can metal breathe?

The outside of a building, its skin, should be more similar to human skin—dynamic and responsive to the environment. That's the idea behind smart thermo-bimetal. Because it is made of two strips of different metals that respond differently to heat, this experimental building material requires no controls or energy to react to changes in temperature. When installed, its reactive property allows the system to ventilate on hot days, while shading it at the same time.

Humans breathe—so should our buildings.

Bloom.
(Concept)
DORIS KIM SUNG

93 What if houses were made of meat?

In the future you will be able to live inside a pig—sort of. No animals are harmed in the creation of Meat Habitat, a to-scale model of a house made with meat cells grown in a lab. The concept is a glimpse at replacing traditional building materials with pig cells that are 3-D-printed to create full-size architecture. And don't worry about preservatives. The skin is grown with sodium benzoate to kill yeasts, bacteria, and fungi—it will last longer than a Twinkie in its cellophane wrapper.

In Vitro Meat Habitat.
(Concept)
MITCHELL JOACHIM OF
TERREFORM ONE

We could grow our houses by rethinking material structures.

94 Can bacteria be your architect?

A 6,000-kilometer-long inhabitable wall in the Sahara Desert isn't built—it is grown, with the help of a bacteria that turns sand into sandstone. This is the concept behind Dune, a naturally generated sand structure that relies on a biological reaction: The sandstone is grown with the help of *Bacillus pasteurii*, a bacterial microorganism found in marshes and wetlands. Once introduced, the bacteria might be able to create a structurally sound and livable structure in less than a week, opening new possibilities for rapidly deployable refugee housing in the desert.

The desert is a living place.

Dune.
(Concept)
Sahara Desert, North Africa
MAGNUS LARSSON

95 Can architecture go wiki?

WikiHouse is a small experiment with a big idea: That regular people (read: not architects) can build a house anywhere with minimal tools and training. The open source construction system makes it possible for anyone to design, share, download, and "print" (with a CNC mill) quickly buildable houses from sheet materials like plywood that are low-cost but also suited to local needs. Continuously under development, solutions in the works include post-earthquake housing and a factory in one of Rio's favelas.

WikiHouse.
(Concept)
ALASTAIR PARVIN

Design for the 100 percent.

96 Can a building have reflexes?

The attention-grabbing Media-ITC building was designed as a collaborative space for the advancement of new technology. Its outer walls reflect this mission, with a translucent skin of temperature-regulating inflatable bubbles. Sensors automatically inflate the shading cushions to block light and reduce cooling costs on hot days, or deflate to let in more light on cloudy days.

Architecture made of air can help keep us cool.

Media-ITC.
Barcelona, Spain
ENRIC RUIZ-GELI/CLOUD 9

97 What if drones carried bricks, not missiles?

Flight Assembled Architecture is an installation built by flying robots. To build the 6-meter-high structure, a group of four-bladed helicopters carried fifteen hundred foam bricks and placed them based on digital design data that dynamically controls their behavior. This visionary approach to building is the result of a collaboration between architects Gramazio & Kohler and inventor Raffaello D'Andrea, who belong to a new generation of architects seeking to push the limits of digital design and fabrication.

Flight Assembled
Architecture.
(Concept)
Orléans, France
GRAMAZIO & KOHLER AND
RAFFAELLO D'ANDREA

No cranes. No ladders. No limits.

98 Can a skyscraper be built in a day?

Building a skyscraper used to take years. But a group in China is changing everything we know about construction, building a fifteen-story hotel in six days, then a thirty-story hotel in just over two weeks. The secret is prefabrication: Large sections of the building were assembled in a factory, eliminating waste and delays at the building site. According to the China Academy of Building Research, the tower is five times more earthquake-resistant than a similar one built with traditional methods.

T30 Hotel.
Hunan Province, China
BROAD GROUP

Even if buildings can happen in the blink of an eye, they should still stand the test of time.

99 Can skyscrapers be made of wood?

The idea of a wooden skyscraper raises eyebrows—and a lot of questions: Can it stand up in an earthquake? What if it catches fire? But this design competition winner proposes a thirty-four-story wooden skyscraper that would have the safety attributes of steel or concrete, with less construction waste and better acoustics than traditional high rises. The idea is more than speculation; Sweden's largest housing association plans to complete the tower by 2023.

New ideas can grow on trees.

HSB Stockholm competition winner. (Concept)
Stockholm, Sweden
BERG | C.F. MØLLER AND DINELLJOHANSSON

100 What if a cow built your house?

To create this experimental structure, cleverly named The Truffle, a group of architects dug a hole, packed it with hay, and then poured concrete around it. After the concrete dried, a calf named Paulina moved in, eating the hay for a year and hollowing out a small cave in the process—all that was left in the end was the scratches and imprints of how the place was made. It is a fantastically hideous little building that became the most sublime place to watch a Spanish sunset. It's also a true melding of the most important tenets of future building: reliance on known techniques, forward-thinking environmentalism, whimsy, and brilliant simplicity. Moo.

The future of architecture will surprise you.

The Truffle.
Laxe, Spain
ENSAMBLE STUDIO

After journeying through these one hundred buildings, hopefully it's clear that there is no perfect, universal solution for the future of architecture. All across the globe, architects are eagerly working with clients and skilled builders to design unique buildings, tailored to changing environmental and social needs. They are pushing the envelope, barreling towards the unknowable future. And they need your help.

Don't be a bystander and let architecture simply *happen* to you. Find an architect. Study up on the latest ideas in architecture. Talk with the people designing the places where you spend your time. Talk with your neighbors, coworkers, friends, and family, and together, insist on good architecture.

Remember: Architecture doesn't just represent your community— it shapes your society. If you ask architecture to work for you, and to reflect the priorities of your community and the Earth, you will be amazed by the possibilities architecture can bring to every aspect of your life.

Happy building!

PHOTO CREDITS

1   Anthony Dubber and James Morris

2   Marc Lins Photography

3   diephotodesigner, Reiulf Ramstad Arkitekter

4   diephotodesigner, courtesy of Snøhetta

5   Iwan Baan

6   Minarc (Tryggvi Thorsteinsson, Erla Dögg Ingjaldsdóttir)

7   Luis García

8   Mika Huisman

9   Roland Halbe

10   © Foster + Partners / ESA

11   Roos Aldershoff Fotografie

12   Lv Hengzhong

13   Jeff Goldberg / Esto

14   Peter Clarke

15   Morris Adjmi Architects

16   Heatherwick Studio

17   Johannes Arlt, laif / Redux

18   Roland Halbe

19   Brenchley Architects / Elizabeth Allnut Photography

20   Fernando Alda David Franck

21   Tamás Bujnovszky

22   LOT-EK

23   Bernardes + Jacobsen

24   Iwan Baan

25   A2arquitectos

26   Ricardo Oliveira Alves

27   Thomas Ibsen

28   Reversible Destiny Foundation

29   Turner Brooks Architect

30   Jan Glasmeier

31   Fernando Guerra FG+SG

POP-UP

BULGARI Abu Dhabi Art Pavilion
NANA

PDU (Portable Dining Unit)
Cesar Rubio, courtesy of EDG Interior Architecture + Design

Floatastic
Net Martin Studio, B. Lapolla & Mahdi Alibakhshian

Head in the Clouds
Chuck Choi

Drift Pavilion for Design Miami/2012
Markus Haugg

32   Marcus Buck

33   Lucerne Festival Ark Nova 2013

34   Hufton + Crow

35   Robert Polidori

36   Iwan Baan

37   Duccio Malagamba

38   left image: Imre Solt, right image: Torsten Seidel

39   Craft Arquitectos

40   Rafael Gamo

41   Marco Boella, courtesy of JDS Architects

42   Nikolaos Zachariadis and SPLITTERWERK

43   Timothy Hursley

44   Studio Guilherme Torres

45   Iwan Baan

46   Scagliola Brakkee

47   BIG - Bjarke Ingels Group

48 Nic Lehoux and Gunnar V. Andresson / Fréttablaðið

49 Filip Dujardin

50 CC-BY Verd gris

51 Steve Hall, Hedrich Blessing

52 Leonardo Finotti

DRIVE

GAS - gas station chain
Tomas Soucek

Parking structure for the Tyrolean Festival Erl
Günter Richard Wett

Facade of multistory car park
Darko Hristov, courtesy of PPAG architects

Helios House
Eric Staudenmaier

Fuel station + McDonald's
Giorgi Khmaladze

53 Benjamin Benschneider

54 Jan Kudej

55 Åke E:son Lindman

56 Johan Dehlin / 6A Architects

57 Vo Trong Nghia Architects

58 Obie Oberholzer

59 MVRDV and Living Architecture

60 Albert Večerka / Esto

61 Patrick Blanc

62 HWKN

63 Simon Devitt

64 Shigeru Ban

65 Brigida González

66 Michael Moran / OTTO

67 Albert Večerka / Esto

68 Crop Trust / Mari Tefre

69 The BIG Team

70 SHoP Architects

SHRINK

blob VB3
Frederik Vercruysse

House NA
Iwan Baan, courtesy of Sou Fujimoto

Boxhome
Sami Rintala

Mamelodi POD housing unit
Architecture for a Change

Keret House
Polish Modern Art Foundation

Parasite Office
Za Bor Architects

71 Jeff Goldberg / Esto

72 Plus POOL

73 Hive City

74 Alex MacLean

75 Haas&Hahn

76 Pato Safko

77 Elizabeth Felicella, courtesy of Sharon Davis Design

78 Kéré Architecture

79 Dave Delnea Images

80 MIR

81 Archi-Tectonics

82 Wieland Gleich

83 Snøhetta

84 Iwan Baan

85 Ramon Prat

86 Rendering by Kibum Park. Photograph by Cameron Neilson.

87 Luc Boegly

88 Nemesi & Partners

89 DUS Architects

90 Barkow Photo

91 MIT Media Lab
    Mediated Matter
    Group

92 Brandon Shigeta

93 Mitchell Joachim,
    Eric Tan, Oliver
    Medvedik, Maria
    Aiolova

94 Ordinary Ltd
    (Magnus Larsson &
    Alex Kaiser)

95 CC By Lynton Pepper

96 Luis Ros

97 Gramazio & Kohler
    and Raffaello
    D`Andrea in
    cooperation with
    ETH Zurich

98 BROAD Group

99 C.F. Møller Architects
    & Dinell Johansson

100 Roland Halbe

AUTHOR THANKS

This book would not have been possible without the amazing work
of Jennifer Krichels, who smiled all the way from Building 1 to
Building 100. Special thanks to Matthias Hollwich, and to the teams at
TED and at Architizer, especially Catherine Finsness, Siddharth Saxena
and Luna Bernfest. To Chris Barley, the most patient speaking coach in
the world—none of this would have been possible without your support.
Thanks to the photographers for capturing all of this amazing work.
Finally, thanks to the architects and their clients for designing and
building such a magnificent group of buildings.

ABOUT THE AUTHOR

MARC KUSHNER is a practicing architect who splits his time between
designing buildings at HWKN, the architecture firm he cofounded, and
amassing the world's architecture on the website he runs, Architizer.com.
Both have the same mission: to reconnect the public with architecture.

Kushner's core belief is that architecture touches everyone—and everyone
is a fan of architecture—even if they don't know it yet. New forms of media
empower people to shape the built environment, and that means better
buildings that make better cities that make a better world.

Marc Kushner spoke at the TED Conference in 2014. His TED Talk, available for free at TED.com, was the inspiration for *The Future of Architecture in 100 Buildings*.

PHOTO: JAMES DUNCAN DAVIDSON / TED

RELATED TALKS ON TED.COM

Michael Green: *Why We Should Build Wooden Skyscrapers*
go.ted.com/Green

Building a skyscraper? Forget about steel and concrete, says architect Michael Green, and build it out of wood. Green explains that it's not only possible to build safe wooden structures up to thirty stories tall (and, he hopes, higher), it's also necessary.

Alastair Parvin: *Architecture for the People by the People*
go.ted.com/Parvin

What if regular citizens could design and build their own houses? The concept is at the heart of WikiHouse, an open source construction kit that means just about anyone can build a house, anywhere.

Thomas Heatherwick: *Building the Seed Cathedral*
go.ted.com/Heatherwick

A showcase of five recent projects featuring ingenious bio-inspired designs. Some are remakes of the ordinary—a bus, a bridge, a power station—and one is an extraordinary pavilion, the Seed Cathedral, a celebration of growth and light

Bjarke Ingels: *Building With Nature*
go.ted.com/Ingels

Danish architect Bjarke Ingels rockets through photo/video-mingled stories of his eco-flashy designs. His buildings not only look like nature—they act like nature: blocking the wind, collecting solar energy—and creating stunning views.

ABOUT TED BOOKS

TED Books are small books about big ideas. They're short enough to read in a single sitting, but long enough to delve deep into a topic. The wide-ranging series covers everything from architecture to business, space travel to love, and is perfect for anyone with a curious mind and an expansive love of learning.

Each TED Book is paired with a related TED Talk, available online at TED.com. The books pick up where the talks leave off. An eighteen-minute speech can plant a seed or spark the imagination, but many talks create a need to go deeper, to learn more, to tell a longer story. TED Books fills this need.

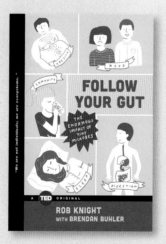

COMING SOON

Follow Your Gut: The Enormous Impact of Tiny Microbes by Rob Knight with Brendan Buhler

In this groundbreaking book, scientist Rob Knight reveals how the microscopic life within our bodies—particularly within our intestines—has an astonishing impact on our lives. Your health, mood, sleep patterns, eating preferences, and more can all be traced in part to the tiny creatures that live on and inside of us.